DRUID

TAM DERUDDER JACKSON

DRUID

THE TALISMAN SERIES

Talisman

Warrior

Prophetess (a Talisman Series novella)

Bard

Druid

For Grady
With all my heart.
Never stop adventuring, babe.

PROLOGUE

RIPPLE IN THE cosmos jolted Davy Sutherland. Actually, the cosmos grabbed him by the scruff of the neck, shook him like a rag doll, and shot a bolt of electricity straight through him. The surge of sexual heat staggered him. Fearing the worst, he looked around for the goddess. Sensing himself alone, he drew in a deep breath. *Maeve prefers warriors, old son. Ye're safe enough from the likes of her.* Still, he thought it best to return to the safety of Conlan Manor.

Powering up the motor, he turned his skiff toward shore. He'd been feeling restless lately. Something was off, but damned if he knew what. An early morning outing on Loch Broom had seemed a fine idea. The beauty of high summer reflecting in the smooth surface of the loch seized him by his guts and dragged him out onto it. As he absently wove stories in his mind, he'd drifted much farther from shore than he'd intended. The simultaneous jolts, like a punch to his solar plexus coupled with his sudden erection, woke him out of his reverie in a rush. The sixth sense he'd honed over years of druidic training made his exceptional communion with the natural world second nature. He knew better than to ignore a warning.

As the skiff skimmed across the loch, he kept a wary eye out for signs of the triple goddess. The Morrigan, Morgan as she preferred to be called these days, and Maeve, two powerful entities of the goddess of war, had taken a series of beatings at the hands of the Sheridan and Conlan clans and their friends recently. The third member of the terrible trio, Macha, usually confined her activities to warriors in Ireland, but Davy understood that even though he was a druid rather than a warrior, he still had to be careful. His connection as a resident druid to the powerful Conlan and Sheridan clans could—and probably would—make him a target of the deities sooner or later. Better not to be caught out alone on open water with his guts roiling like they were.

As he neared the tiny village of Ullapool on the shores of Loch Broom, he thought he saw his friend Hamish Buchanan dancing a little jig on the pier. Steering his boat closer to shore, Davy noted Hamish indeed jumped up and down in a manner clearly indicating he wanted Davy's attention. Looking around to see if there was something dangerous in the water, he spotted what had Hamish in such a state. Directly behind him, something huge and fast, something creating a wake sending waves crashing ahead of it bore down on him.

Davy ramped up the skiff's motor and tore across the loch. When he reached the pier, he wrenched the rudder, sending the boat into a precarious slide that nearly capsized it. Simultaneously, he cut the engine and bumped the small craft roughly against the wood planking. Hamish wasted no time reaching into the skiff to link his arm around Davy's bicep and yank him from the boat. For a man of indeterminate age, Hamish demonstrated incredible strength and power as he jerked Davy to safety.

Right as the two men jumped back onto the dock, a kelpie leapt from the water. Its flashing hooves crashed down in the middle of the skiff, smashing it to splinters with a ferocious crack. From somewhere above them, Davy heard the otherworldly cackling of a vengeful goddess, the first salvo in yet another battle in the ongoing struggle between the goddesses of war and the warrior class they never left in peace.

CHAPTER ONE

Six weeks later: Conlan Manor, Ullapool, Scotland

DAVY TRIED TO sleep, but the swirling tattoo on his right bicep was giving him fits again. No doubt the design he'd felt weirdly compelled to have inked on himself on a trip to Glasgow right after *Lughnasadh* had some sort of supernatural power. He couldn't decide if the omens were benign or not, but the intense sexual heat and the erection accompanying the throbbing in his tattoo definitely meant something. He knew about the war goddesses' lust for warriors. Some legends said Maeve could only be satisfied if she had thirty warriors a day. Warriors. Surely as a druid, he was safe, right? Maeve—and her sisters—had to have little interest in him.

Or maybe Maeve wasn't behind the omens at all. Perhaps the signs meant something else. Though the heir to Conlan Manor, the beautiful Ceri Sheridan had rebuffed his advances—rightfully too as it turned out—perhaps there was another woman nearby who would succumb to the power of his stories and welcome spending the rest of her life listening to them. He sighed. Not for the first time did he wish he'd been born a warrior whose mate the gods preordained for him. Taking himself in hand, he eased the throbbing both in his arm and in his groin. A sense of peace washed over him as he indulged his favorite fantasy—being a warrior worthy of his fated talisman. Afterward, for another blessed hour or two, he slept with a smile on his face.

"The bard this clan produced will wed her warrior here in a fortnight on the autumnal equinox. That means we need tae prepare fer a whoppin' big *ceilidh* tae honor her and her warrior," Hamish said, his face alight with glee. Seated around the scarred kitchen table for breakfast were Hamish's cousin Ceri Ross Sheridan, her warrior husband Rio Sheridan, and Davy, who tried to hold back a grin as he watched the usual byplay between Rio and Hamish.

Rio glared at the old druid. "I suppose there are some especially nasty members of the Celtic pantheon we need to invite along with the assorted neighboring civilians you just can't leave out," he grumbled.

Everyone at the table knew exactly what Rio referred to. Rio and Ceri's bonding as a warrior pair included the rather harrowing experience of hosting a large ceilidh on the previous *Samhain*. A ceilidh for Celtic New Year at Conlan Manor necessitated extending an invitation to Taranis, the thunder god who tried to steal Ceri and her best friend Alyssa Sheridan. With some coaxing, he'd contented himself with two unsuspecting civilians who washed up on the shores of Loch Broom the following morning after a squall the god had visited on the loch. Usually, Hamish also invited Morgan, but since she'd especially targeted Rio and had an eye toward killing Ceri as well, Hamish didn't invite her to the last Samhain ceilidh. She had attended anyway with an army of rogue warriors and zombie champions who nearly succeeded in sending Rio over the ford and into the mists forever.

"Och, lad, dae ye still take it as a personal affront that we follow the auld ways in the auld country?" Hamish teased.

Rio remained silent.

Preferring some peace, Davy inserted himself into the conversation. "Since the autumnal equinox is a low feast day, we have nae obligation tae invite any deities tae the party."

Rio sat back and crossed his massive arms over his equally massive chest.

Undeterred, Davy continued. "However, as I understand it from yer Aunt Shanley, Fallon Graham's patron goddess Brighid was pretty handy in rescuing her from Maeve's nasty prison on summer solstice. Perhaps it would be wise tae invite her tae the party and ask her blessing on this pair."

"Good idea, lad, especially since Brighid is our patroness tae. I knew I trained ye well. Invitin' the mistress o' stories would be a mighty fine gesture." Hamish saluted him with his mug of tea before taking a sip.

"And Scathach. We must invite her. Since Seamus is so close to Rio's family, she's trained him almost as much as she's trained the Sheridan warriors," Ceri reminded them.

Rio smiled at his wife's suggestion. "Scathach and Brighid will be welcome additions to the guest list," he said before he added with a pout, "Wish they were the only two we had to invite on Samhain this year."

Hamish chuckled. "Samhain belongs tae Morgan and Taranis. I'll be sure tae be the one serving 'em their drams o' my finest whisky and a draught o' my special mead this year. They expect it."

"Uh-huh. Last year, I believe Taranis demanded a slice of Alyssa's birthday cake served by my wife and Alyssa herself." Rio's raised brow mirrored the skepticism in his voice.

"That was a test, and our Ceri and Alyssa passed with flyin' colors. This year will be different," Hamish insisted. "But first, we need tae take care o' the party celebratin' yer friends' weddin' and the autumnal equinox. How many are comin' over from America did ye say?"

Ceri named off their guests. "All the Sheridans, Seamus and Fallon of course, Aunt Shanley and Alaisdair who suggested having the wedding here, Fallon's aunt and uncle, and Fallon's friend Sloane." She blew out a breath. "I think that's it."

Rio slipped his arm around her, a reassuring gesture.

Ignoring the wave of longing that came with watching them together, Davy said, "Maybe we should make a point o' invitin' Druantia, our druid patroness tae this shindig as well."

"Another good idea, lad. Ye dae an old man proud, ye dae." Hamish beamed. "That's settled. We'll invite some o' our particular favorite deities along with some other folks"—he grinned mischievously at Rio—"and enjoy a lovely party. O' course, we'll have tae dae some extra chantin' around this auld pile before the big day."

"I suppose that means you'll be wearing out my wife again, old man." Had Rio been a druid, he might have turned Hamish to dust with his suggestion.

"Och, lad, right when I think ye're makin' progress, ye get all ornery on me." Hamish sounded innocent, but Davy didn't miss the glint in his eyes. "Ceri understands the requirements her role as mistress o' Conlan Manor demands. Ye could make it easier on her by participatin' yerself. If Davy and ye took the upstairs and Ceri and I took the downstairs, we could enchant this place in half the time with half the strain on yer lovely talisman."

"If I didn't know better, Hamish, I'd think you led me deliberately to this point where if I refuse your suggestion, I'm a hypocrite and a terrible husband, but if I accept it, I'm a willing participant in your druid activities against my principles. Caught between a rock and a hard place." Rio scowled.

"Admit it, Rio. Ye have a soft spot for the auld man. Or he's been working especially hard on yer dinner," Davy said with a smirk. "Either way, ye know ye're going tae help me with my part of enchanting this place against the very deities ye despise the most."

Ceri leaned into her husband. "Hey, warrior," she said softly, "you've come a long way in overcoming your prejudices against the druids in our community. Besides, helping these two with the enchantments over our home adds layers of protections to *you*, and after what happened to Seamus's friends, I want you to have all the additional protections you can get." She punctuated her words with a soft kiss on Rio's mouth, and when she pulled away, he sighed.

Inwardly, Davy sighed too. Watching the two of them often left him wishing he could compose a story wherein he could be a warrior with the privilege of experiencing bonding with a talisman.

"Fine. I'll help but only because you asked me so nicely," Rio said with a smile for his wife before he sent a scowl Hamish's way.

Hamish and Davy burst out laughing while Ceri secretly winked at them.

As Sloane MacIntosh packed her bags for the trip to her best friend Fallon Graham's wedding in Scotland, she tried to think happy thoughts about what an adventure it was going to be to see a new country with the opportunity to meet new people and try new things. At their insistence, she'd stayed with Fallon and her fiancé Seamus Lochlann for a week following her warrior's death. But watching them fall in love with each other more and more every day only increased her sadness and sense of loss for what she would never have herself.

As she'd grown up, she'd understood there was always the possibility her warrior would never find her at all, and she would live alone as she awaited him. However, having found and lost him in the space of an evening created a whole new dimension to being alone, a dimension centered on grief. Her friends were great, but they couldn't keep their eyes—and usually their hands—off each other. Then they'd apologize and try not to show how much they meant to each other whenever she was around. At last, she knew she needed to give them the freedom to have what the gods had fated for them without the audience of a talisman who'd been widowed before she'd ever had the chance to become a bride. Before she'd even had the chance to bond with her fated mate.

Fallon's powerful druid friends Siobhan MacManus and Griffin Walsh added enchantments to Sloane's home, and she'd felt relatively safe there in the month since she'd returned to it. The murder of crows taking up residence in the trees in her neighbor's yard across the street the last couple of days worried her though. Leaving town seemed a good idea both for boosting her mood and for giving her some peace from Macha's dark reminders of her loss.

The night before she'd met Gavin, she'd witnessed a blood moon and had been so excited to see such an event. The pulsing of a russet shadow across the face of the moon and the illusion of the full moon shrinking in size as the earth eclipsed it intrigued her. The silver sliver of light emerging on the edge of the moon before it widened across the face, restoring it to a bright silver-white disk in the western sky, awed, enchanted, and, oddly, frightened her. The ancients saw a full lunar eclipse as a portentous moment, an occurrence provoking fear and wonder. In the weeks following the events of Lughnasadh, Sloane mirrored their atavistic response. She'd forever associate the coming of death with a blood moon.

When Fallon and Seamus arrived to pick her up for the trip to the airport, they discovered her on her front step with her packed bags beside her, deep in her musings as she contemplated the squawking cacophony deliberately irritating the neighborhood and her. As a goddess, Macha could be anywhere at any time. Sloane knew this. However, she thought Macha sent the crows to torture her rather than to impart evil intent. In any case, she was glad to be leaving home for a few weeks.

"Should you be taking a chance sitting out on your porch with that bunch watching you from across the street?" Seamus asked as he bounded up the sidewalk toward her.

"I don't believe they signal any harm to me other than emotional. I think Macha wants me to remember what she took from me. What bothers me is why she won't let up. Honestly, it'll be good to have something much more hopeful to think about," she said as she followed Seamus, who carried her two small suitcases, to his truck.

"For a two-week stay in Scotland, you packed light. You sure you have everything you'll need?" Fallon asked as she stepped out of Seamus's truck.

"Apparently, some women don't think they need to pack every outfit they own," he said in a long-suffering tone as he slid Sloane's bags into the bed of his truck beside the myriad pieces of luggage already riding there.

"I did have to bring along a wedding dress, you know," Fallon said with a huff.

"Not on my account. My favorite outfit of yours is the one you came with." A wicked grin spread over his features.

"You want me to marry you naked?" Fallon asked, her eyes dancing.

"Hey, hey Fireworks. I didn't say that—"

"Oh, I guess I misunderstood. So, there's actually no problem with my luggage then?" she asked sweetly.

"None whatsoever," Seamus said with an eye roll he ruined with a smirk as he hauled himself into the driver's seat of his truck.

Sloane sighed wistfully as she watched their exchange before

Fallon caught her eye, the little smile on her friend's lips turning upside down.

"For the last time, Fallon, don't apologize in any way for finding and falling for your warrior. You didn't steal mine and leave me alone," Sloane said as she buckled herself into the back seat. "We're off to celebrate the joyous occasion of your wedding, and we're all going to have a great time. Agreed?"

Fallon leaned over the front seat and grabbed Sloane's wrist. "Agreed."

"Let's get this show on the road, ladies. The sooner we arrive in Scotland, the sooner you become Mrs. Seamus Lochlann"—he squeezed Fallon's knee—"and I've waited long enough for that," Seamus declared as he put the truck in gear and sped toward the airport.

CHAPTER TWO

HE NARROW RIBBON of road coupled with navigating traffic from the left side of it forced Rowan Sheridan to take his time as he drove the lead van from Inverness to Conlan Manor outside Ullapool, Scotland. It stood to reason that as maid of honor, Sloane would ride with Fallon and her family. Yet, she deliberately chose to ride with Rowan and Alyssa Sheridan and Rowan's parents Owen and Sian, and his brother Riley and his wife Lynnette, giving Fallon and Seamus the opportunity to enjoy their first taste of Scotland without feeling like they had to tone it down for her. Since Brighid, Fallon's patron goddess, decreed that Fallon's parents couldn't be present at her wedding as penance for their prejudices against the druid race, her druid uncle Griffin Walsh would walk her down the aisle. Siobhan MacManus and Shanley Graham, who was married to one of Fallon's distant relatives Alaisdair Graham, were serving as bridesmaids, so that particular company rode with Seamus and Fallon.

When the group touched down in Inverness, Sloane had noted Fallon's melancholy. The idea she wouldn't be sharing one of the greatest moments of her life with her parents had finally hit her, and Sloane decided some concentrated family time with those who *could* be with her might help her friend. Riding in a car with established warrior pairs also meant she could ignore her jealousy of her best friend as Fallon snuggled close to her warrior fiancé while they enjoyed discovering a new country together.

"You're quiet, Sloane," Rowan observed as he caught her eye in the rearview mirror.

"Taking in the view. How many times have you been over here?"

"Three times so far. Samhain, Christmas, and *Beltane*," Rowan replied.

Sian added, "I have to say that without the prospect of losing one of my sons hanging over us this time, I'm finally enjoying the scenery. It's stunning, isn't it?"

"Absolutely beautiful. Especially with the trees turning color. The thick forest along this road is going to be amazing in another couple weeks," Sloane said as she drank in the passing countryside.

From the front seat, Alyssa exclaimed, "Look! There's the turnoff to Corrieshalloch Gorge. I wanted to see this when we were here at Beltane, but *someone*"—she glared at Rowan—"said we didn't have time to stop. We've been cramped on a plane and now in a car. Let's stop for twenty minutes and stretch our legs."

"You're not going to give me any peace whenever we visit Scotland if I don't give in on this, are you, Pixie-girl?" Rowan asked playfully.

"You're quick, warrior," Alyssa replied in the same tone.

"This little detour is going to throw off our friends, but Alaisdair can explain if he decides to follow us." Rowan signaled a left turn onto the dirt road leading to the car park for the gorge.

As the party exited the van and stretched their legs, the other van with the rest of the crew pulled up beside them. From the passenger window, Seamus called out, "Hey Rowan. What gives?"

"Alyssa's been bugging me about stopping here each time we've come over, so today we're taking a look."

"On the way to my wedding?" Seamus sputtered.

"Relax, buddy. You're not getting married for two weeks, and after you've been married for a while, you'll figure out why you take some detours when your wife wants to take them," Rowan said with a laugh his father and his brother echoed as they stretched their bodies beside him.

"'Tis a beautiful sight, this gorge. Worth the stop, Seamus," Alaisdair said as he exited the van he'd been driving.

"Hmmph!" Seamus grunted, but he climbed out and stretched.

The group set off together along the graveled path leading down to the gorge, the women walking ahead of the men as they marveled at the gaudy display of russet and apricot, chartreuse and deep maroon dressing the foliage of the trees and shrubs along the trail.

When they came to the tiny footbridge spanning the gorge, Rowan laughed at the sign cautioning only six people on the bridge at one time. "Looks like this might take a bit longer than twenty minutes, Pixie-girl."

Alyssa batted her eyes saucily at her warrior. "I promise, you'll be glad you stopped to let me see this," she said as she sashayed ahead of him onto the bridge.

Obviously ogling her backside, Rowan followed her. "I have no doubt about that, Pixie-girl."

Watching their exchange, Owen and Sian Sheridan exchanged a conspiratorial grin before joining their son and daughter-in-law on the metal suspension bridge spanning the gorge.

Sloane stood to the side and took in all the love and shared experience in her friends' words and the family patriarch and matriarch's charged exchange and sighed quietly in her mind. Sucking in a fortifying breath, she followed the others onto the bridge.

From the car park side, a wide graveled path lined with gorse and broom zigzagged its way down to the bridge. The muted sound of water sluicing through the gorge intensified as they neared the bridge, so the narrowness of the chasm surprised Sloane when, from a vantage point mid-way across the suspension bridge, she finally laid eyes on the water carving through dark charcoal-colored basalt walls. The walls looked solid, but they tended to slip like tectonic plates, thus the warning sign on the bridge. Trees as tall as skyscrapers rose from the creek bed at the bottom of the gorge. Even though the forest was dense, looking through it down to the bottom of the ravine gave Sloane a rush, making her want to explore more of the place. She stepped around her friends and continued across to the footpath on the other side of the bridge.

By the time the rest of the party caught up to her, she'd made it to the observation deck about a quarter mile downstream. Again, a sign warned to limit visitors to six on the deck, so only Sian and Owen along with Riley and Lynnette joined Sloane for the first look back at the suspension bridge and the water tumbling behind it.

"This is absolutely gorgeous," Sian enthused as she leaned on the railing of the deck. "It looks like the water drops for half a mile in a straight line before it reaches the bottom."

"I'm glad Alyssa suggested this detour. I bet Rowan is too," said Lynnette as she joined her mother-in-law.

"You know, if Alyssa hadn't noticed this, we would have driven right by and not even known it was here," Owen added. "The cars traveling along the road seem to be on a level with the tops of the trees along the path. As dense as this forest is, it's easy not to see what's down here from the road."

"With Alyssa's observational skills, we shouldn't be surprised she saw this," Riley said as he walked over to them. "You're awfully quiet, Sloane. What do you think of this place?"

"It's lovely. Truly lovely. Did you notice the unusual color of the water as it gushes over the rocks?"

"As a matter of fact, I did." Owen grinned. "Reminds me of a thick Guinness, which I hope Rio stocked at the manor to indulge his old man."

"I think you're right, Dad. The water kind of foams like a good dark beer too. Makes me thirsty just watching it." Riley smacked his lips.

"If you all stop hogging the view, the rest of us might get to see what we stopped to see and then hit the road for that beer you're suddenly thirsty for," Seamus called as he and Fallon joined the others searching for footing on the uneven ground among the exposed tree roots and large rocks at the narrow entrance to the observation deck.

"You know, old son, I don't think I've ever seen you this impatient for anything." Rowan laughed.

"Well, if certain people hadn't preempted my wedding plans"—Seamus glared first at his sister then at Griffin Walsh—"I'd already be married, which would make me infinitely more comfortable on a whole host of levels." The comical pout he didn't even try to hide made Sloane smile.

"The autumnal equinox will be here soon enough, and you'll have your golden wedding exactly like you planned, Seamus. Have a little patience. After all, your talisman is worth the wait," Griff said with a conspiratorial wink at Siobhan.

Siobhan nodded at Griff in understanding. As the odd woman out, Sloane listened to all the banter, detached from the rest of the players in the wedding party, which only reminded her of her single status in the group. She related to the dense forest clinging to the edges of the gorge, a lone talisman clinging to the edges of a bonded group of warriors and druids. The thought left her melancholy. Rather than letting anyone see, she edged around the platform and returned to the muddy track where the others awaited their turns to take in the view.

As she stepped lightly around Rowan, she smiled at Alyssa, both to hide her feelings and to boost her mood. "You were so right to insist on stopping here. Thank you."

Alyssa batted her eyes at her warrior. "Told you so."

"Yes, you did, Pixie-girl," Rowan said as he pulled her into a one-armed hug.

While the rest of the party enjoyed the view from the observation platform, Sloane hiked back to the bridge alone. The occasional hum of cars traveling over the ribbon of road above the path interrupted the steady roar of water crashing down over the rocks as the water lost its never-ending battle with gravity. The sounds soothed her. By the time she reached the other side of the suspension bridge, she found herself in a much better frame of mind.

The others were laughing and joking as they joined her, crossing the suspension bridge in small groups before reuniting for the mile-long trek back to the car park. The stop at the gorge left the entire party in high spirits, even Seamus who only pretended to grump about the delay as he held Fallon's hand and led her all the way out of the gorge and into the van to continue on to Conlan Manor.

As the party topped the hill leading down to Conlan Manor, Alyssa sighed contentedly before glancing over her shoulder at Sloane. "This place is gorgeous in every season but most especially in fall. Fianna Conlan, the matriarch who built the manor, knew what she was doing. A golden home in the golden time of year must appeal to both of the deities the druids hold dear—Brighid and Druantia."

"That's another reason Siobhan and Griff insisted on moving

the wedding to Conlan Manor, I presume," Sian said. "Stop the van for a second, Rowan, so Sloane can see what we're talking about."

Obediently, Rowan pulled to the side of the paved track leading down the hill to the manor and put the van in park. Sloane stepped out onto the gravel roadside to see Conlan Manor for the first time.

As she gazed in awe at the beautiful square building constructed in golden sandstone with its wide veranda and verdant gardens in Celtic knotwork patterns, Fallon and Seamus joined her. She let out a breath. "It's magnificent, isn't it?"

Fallon sighed. "I've never seen a more beautiful place. Like something on a postcard."

"I give in completely. Siobhan, Griff, thanks for putting off my wedding day so I could marry Fallon in this unbelievable place," Seamus said as he stood behind Fallon with his hands resting on her shoulders.

"I had no idea my family's ancestral home would be so amazing," Griff's wife Keela said as she scanned as much of the estate as she could see from their vantage point on the hill.

"I see my suggestion meets with yer approval." Alaisdair beamed as he joined the others staring down at Conlan Manor.

"It's perfect, Alaisdair. Thank you so much," Fallon said.

Coming to stand beside her husband, Shanley said, "The inside is equally amazing. Wait'll you see it." Smiling up at him, she added, "Right, Alaisdair? I can tell by the look on your face you're overjoyed at being home again."

"That I am, lass. That I am."

The group soaked in the view for a few more minutes before Rowan suggested they'd kept the rest of the family waiting long enough for their arrival, and maybe they should finish the trip to the manor. Conversing happily among themselves, the group loaded up the vans and made the short drive down the hill to the house.

❧

Holding hands, Ceri and Rio Sheridan awaited their guests at the car park behind the manor. When the vans pulled in and spilled their occupants, the Sheridan and Graham families rushed to greet the Scotland branch, while the rest of the group hung back to allow for the family reunion.

Fallon extended her hand and said, "Ceri, thank you so much for opening your home to us for our big event. It's so gracious of you."

Ceri gave Fallon's hand a funny look before using it to pull the other woman in to her, wrapping her arms around Fallon. "We're so honored to have you here. You're a gift not only to this family, but to the warrior community as a whole. Our druid, Hamish Buchanan, is especially eager to meet you, but he insists we follow all the rituals, so—" Ceri turned to the rest of the group. "If you'll follow us, we'll invite you into our home properly. However, after today, please do as we do and use the back door whenever you wish. It's much more convenient."

She grinned at her husband, who arched a brow before he smiled back at her.

"Ceri's been working on her shield, which is tae bad, 'cause I would have liked tae have heard what ye said tae her, Rio, tae give her such a rosy glow," Alaisdair said with a chuckle before turning to the others. "However, if I know my friend Hamish, he has a wee dram o' his best whisky awaitin' us in the front parlor."

Taking Alaisdair's rather broad hint, Ceri turned away from her husband and said brightly, "Follow me. It's important for new visitors to Conlan Manor to enter through the front door. Plus, it's really pretty, so we want to show it off. Come on."

Rio brushed a kiss over Ceri's cheek before taking her hand and walking beside her as they led the rest of the group around the side of the manor, through the arch of the garden gate covered with ivy in its rich autumnal scarlet, up the walk, and around to the front of the house. Once they reached the wide front steps leading up to the veranda, the women in the party couldn't stop remarking on the pink and peach beauty of the begonias cascading from huge pots set along the wide stone wall, which served as a railing.

"This porch looks exactly as I pictured it should when I first saw it last fall," Alyssa exclaimed as she admired the foliage.

"These flowers are beautiful, Ceri. Filling these huge pots must have taken some work, but it was worth it. No wonder you wanted to show this off," Shanley remarked to her niece.

While the family raved about the front of the house and the view of the gardens from the long porch, Sloane held back and watched the family dynamics. Ceri Sheridan was a born hostess and the life of the party, making sure to engage the Walshes and Fallon in her conversation as the newcomers to her home. Her willowy blond beauty complemented the tall, dark handsomeness of her husband Rio who kept her close to him and seemed a tiny bit tense for some curious reason.

Seamus stood somewhat aloof from Rio as well, and Sloane wondered at the relationship between the men since she knew Rowan and Seamus were close. If she hadn't already known about Seamus and Rowan's tight friendship from her experiences with the two men during the battle at summer solstice, she'd certainly seen it in the weeks following Lughnasadh when she'd spent so much more time with Seamus and Fallon.

The close family relationships, which were the heart of the reason her friends chose Conlan Manor as their wedding venue, left Sloane feeling like a third or fifth or seventh wheel. Standing apart from the others, she wondered how long it would take for her to adjust to her permanently single status. Then Ceri turned to her, and in what Sloane would come to discover as typical straightforward Ceri fashion, she said, "Sloane, I'm so sorry for your loss."

"Thank you."

"I hope you can enjoy your stay with us."

Rio said, "Our family experienced the loss of an incredible warrior as well. Morgan stole my uncle when my brothers and I were still kids. It probably doesn't feel like it now, but the pain will fade to a dull ache you can deal with. In the meanwhile, between my wife and her pain-in-my-ass cousin who happens to be the resident druid of Conlan Manor, you're going to be kept very busy. Maybe that will help."

"Thank you."

Oddly, Ceri and Rio acknowledging Gavin's death so directly eased the ache in her chest that watching the happy couples together always caused.

The two led the way into their house, followed by the guests of honor—Seamus and Fallon. Next came the Walshes and the MacManuses. When Sloane held back, Alyssa assured her that she must be among those entering closest to the owner of the manor since she was entering the house for the first time. Finally, all the Sheridans, followed by the Grahams who were tied to the house by blood, walked through the front door, sealing the manor as the family refuge it was.

Before the Sheridan horde descended on Conlan Manor late in the afternoon, Davy attended Hamish in the grand salon pouring drams of Hamish's special whisky. The magic Hamish employed to brew his dark drink was yet another thing on Davy's list of essential knowledge his old teacher needed to share. Not that Hamish seemed in any hurry to do so, much to Davy's disgust. Chanting over rowan branches, while no doubt necessary, didn't inspire Davy's imagination like a dram of Hamish's whisky.

"All in good time, lad. All in good time."

"*Again*, Hamish?" He didn't bother to hide his exasperation.

"I wasnae muckin' about in yer thoughts, lad. The scowl on yer face as ye poured those last drams gave ye away."

Davy blew out a long-suffering sigh. "If ye would let me see yer recipe and assist ye *just once* when ye're brewin' yer *uisge-beatha*, I'd leave ye alone about it."

With a chuckle, Hamish said, "Patience, Davy. Patience. Nae doubt ye'll pick it up on yer first go, but this water o' life is powerful fer a number o' reasons, and ye're goin' tae need some backup when ye learn tae distill it."

Hamish finished arranging the tea things on the sideboard to the right of the doors of the grand salon as Davy capped the bottle of whisky and returned it to the cabinet next to the sideboard. Without missing a beat, Hamish produced a key from his pocket and locked the cabinet. Davy rolled his eyes and walked over to stand near the settee facing the front veranda.

Crossing his arms over his chest, he stared out of the long windows, his gaze landing on the front gardens of the manor. How many hours he'd spent over the years tending the plants flourishing there—healing plants, poisonous plants, enchantment plants, spell-casting plants—but never once did he tend the grains needed for Hamish's famous whisky. No druid or warrior who'd ever tasted it forgot it. Fiery and peaty on the front of the tongue before moving on to notes of oranges, chocolate, and hazelnut in the middle of the palate and finally finishing on a delicious caramel on the back of the tongue, Hamish's whisky tasted like nectar of the gods. The glow it gave a man's chest left him feeling powerful—a singular sensation of strength Davy adored. Probably a good thing Hamish limited imbibing his uisge-beatha to one dram.

Davy sighed. Admittedly, he hadn't attained the requisite wisdom to learn this particular druidic secret. He hated it when

Hamish was right. Laughter and loud conversation interrupted his morose thoughts. The Sheridans had arrived.

Ceri walked through the doors to the salon first, followed by several people Davy recognized from the festivities at the manor during the previous year's Samhain celebration. Alyssa Sheridan chattered in Ceri's ear while Lynnette Sheridan laughed at something her mother-in-law Sian said, their warriors close behind them. Two women Davy didn't recognize trailed the Sheridan women into the room. The auburn-haired one looked back at the raven-haired woman, and Davy forgot to breathe.

Eyes the color of violets glanced away from the auburn-haired woman's face and locked with his for an eternity—or maybe half a minute. Long enough for Davy to know he definitely wanted to come back as a warrior in his next life. The raven-haired goddess in the company of so many talismans could only be a talisman herself, a woman Davy could never have. Didn't stop his cock from suddenly straining at the fly of his jeans. Didn't stop his palms from itching to cup the silky skin of her cheeks. Didn't stop his fingers flexing with the need to slide through the sleek mass of all that black hair.

The tattoo high on his right bicep flared to life. Stuffing his hands in his pockets, he willed himself under control. If the stories of the ancients warning against the poaching of talismans weren't enough, his recent training sessions with Rio reminded him quite effectively that a druid had no business lusting after a talisman.

"Hamish, you remember this lot," Ceri said, laughter bubbling in her voice as usual.

"Och, lass. How could I ferget the bonny ladies o' yer family? Welcome back Alyssa. Lynnette. Sian," he said as he embraced each woman in turn.

Ceri beamed as she presented the auburn-haired woman. "This is the guest of the year. Fallon Graham meet Hamish Buchanan, my cousin and very special friend."

The woman called Fallon offered her hand. "Pleased to meet you."

Davy had to smile at the stern look Hamish gave her outstretched hand before he took it to pull her into his arms.

"Ye're related tae the Conlans on the warrior side o' the family, lass. Family doesnae shake hands."

Davy wondered at the tears shining in Fallon Graham's eyes after Hamish let her go. Oblivious to the little drama happening in front of her, Ceri drew Hamish's attention to the goddess among them—for that's the only way Davy could understand the tall, willowy perfection of the raven-haired woman.

"This is Fallon's best friend, Sloane MacIntosh."

Sloane nodded at Hamish, gifting him with a closed-mouth smile.

Quiet? Shy? Wonder how this gorgeous lass fits in with this bunch?

Ceri interrupted his thoughts. "This is Davy Sutherland, Hamish's protégé and Rio's new favorite sparring partner." She gave him an impish shoulder bump, the tinkling bells of her laughter echoing in his ears.

He rolled his eyes. "Ceri, lass, don't sell me short like that. You know I'm Rio's very best friend."

From her spot on the settee in front of the fireplace, Sian gasped. "Is my son still giving you a hard time, Davy? Sounds like he needs some reminders about manners."

Rio shrugged, but from previous experience, Davy knew Sian wouldn't let it go.

Davy thought she looked kind of adorable in her indignation as she marched over to stand in front of her son with her hands on her hips. But he didn't fancy appearing weak in front of Sloane even if she did belong to a warrior somewhere.

"'Tis fine, Sian. Rio and I get on well enough." Turning his attention to the newcomers, he turned up his grin in the way he knew most women couldn't resist. "Welcome tae Scotland,

Fallon"—he nodded at her—"and Sloane. His eyes lingered on the beauty standing across from him. "It must be a requirement in America that all talismans are gorgeous."

Fallon smiled at him. "It must be a requirement in Scotland that all druids are charmers."

A smile ghosted Sloane's lips, but she said nothing.

"Our druidesses are gorgeous too," Ceri said with a wink as another blond beauty entered the salon with Shanley Graham. "This stunning creature accompanying my aunt is Seamus's sister Siobhan MacManus, Fallon's future sister-in-law."

Davy shot Hamish a look. "Well, auld man. That settles it. Since ye willnae teach me how tae make yer fine whisky, ye leave me nae choice but tae follow this lot over tae America after the wedding."

Hamish raised his brows, his eyes twinkling. "How is that, lad?"

"Seems America might be the next closest thing tae paradise fer a single man."

Shanley laughed. "Still as charming as ever, Davy."

Surprising him, she crossed the room and pulled him into a hug before she walked over to Hamish for a long warm embrace.

"When are ye goin' tae make up yer mind tae come home, lass?"

"Hamish—" Ceri warned.

Hamish didn't look the least chastised. With Shanley's hand in his, he glanced around at the assembled company. "Seems tae me that fer the next fortnight at least, the bonniest lassies on the planet are gathered right here under this roof. We're lucky indeed, Davy."

As if he'd conjured them, the rest of the Sheridan men filed into the salon. A stocky blond warrior who looked like most of the warriors Davy would see on any given evening down at the pub strolled in with another warrior and another man who must be Fallon's druid uncle. Before he could introduce himself to the man he assumed to be Fallon's warrior, Alaisdair Graham blocked his view, pulling him into a one-armed hug while he took Davy's arm in the traditional warrior way, hands clasping elbows.

"Davy! Good tae see ye, man."

"Ye tae, Alaisdair. Glad tae have ye back, even if only fer a visit."

Alaisdair's eyes danced. "Ye've been entertainin' the lassies have ye?"

"Hamish bribed me with the promise o' an extra dram o' his uisge-beatha," Davy shot back.

Alaisdair barked out a laugh. "The auld man is a wily one."

While Alaisdair turned to the man in question, Ceri pulled the blond warrior over to Davy. "This is Seamus Lochlann, Fallon's fiancé and Siobhan's brother. As you'll no doubt discover, Seamus is really good people." She beamed at him. "Seamus, this is Davy Sutherland, Hamish's student."

As Ceri performed the introductions, Davy glanced over Seamus's shoulder to see Rio glaring at them. Judging from the dark looks Rio kept shooting at Seamus's back, there was some history between the two men, something Davy determined to discover before he stepped into the training room with Rio again.

Keeping his expression neutral, he extended his hand. "Welcome tae Scotland, Seamus. Ceri's been in an uproar preparing everything fer yer wedding."

Seamus pumped Davy's hand and grinned. "Been keeping you guys busy, has she? After the job she did for Rowan and Alyssa when they married, I bet Fallon's and my big day will be quite the show." He bumped Ceri's shoulder with playful affection, and Davy decided he liked the man despite Rio's continued glowering from across the room.

Indicating the spread laid out on the sideboard, Hamish said, "We have some wee refreshments fer ye. Please, help yerselves."

The women arranged themselves on the sofas facing each other in front of the central fireplace. Each balanced a plate holding their selections from the cakes, scones and jams Hamish had had catered from the village bakery in Ullapool. Cups of steaming tea rested on the low coffee table between them. With one arm casually resting on the mantle, Davy stood before the fireplace and sipped tea from his favorite mug and let feminine conversation wash over him while he watched the other men familiarize themselves with the room. Yet he couldn't stop his eyes from repeatedly straying in Sloane's direction.

As if aware of his attention, she trained her focus on Shanley Graham who was describing to Fallon and Sloane the wedding held for Alaisdair and her at the manor the previous Christmas. Idly, Davy wondered about Sloane's warrior. The thought had him choking on his tea. The ladies' conversation stopped mid-sentence, and he cleared his throat to cover his gaffe. "Tea went down the wrong way."

He sought out Hamish who was adding more scones to the dwindling pile on the sideboard. "How long until we check on dinner and carry luggage upstairs?"

"Tired o' listenin' tae weddin' plannin' already, lad? 'Tis only the first day o' their visit," Hamish said with a chuckle. "Ye'll have plenty o' time tae show Griffin around the gardens and maybe even learn somethin' new from the man before the weddin'." Hamish hummed beneath his breath. "And maybe learn about that bonny lass who has yer attention."

Davy knew better than to rise to the bait. Instead, he ambled over to where Rio and his brothers stood in front of the windows facing the garden.

"We're all paired up now, Rio. You can stop looking over your shoulder. Besides, if I were going to poach your talisman, I could have done it a long time ago when I met her and Alyssa at a bar one stormy night," Seamus said. "Turns out, tall blondes are your type. My tastes run to an auburn-haired beauty whose eyes are never the same color when I look into them."

"He's got a point, little brother," Rowan said.

"If you keep scowling like you have been, your face will freeze like that, and I'll remain the better-looking twin." Riley smirked over the rim of his mug of tea. "Since it's a given I already corner that market."

Even with his attention on the drama brewing in front of him, a part of Davy remained tuned into Sloane MacIntosh. Though she sat in the middle of the women, thus keeping herself aloof from him, he couldn't help but be aware of her. Absently, he rubbed at the tattoo tingling on his shoulder like it had right after he'd had it inked onto his skin. His skin seemed to tighten every few minutes, and he didn't need to glance in her direction to know she stole covert peeks at him. Of course, being himself, he couldn't—didn't want to stop stealing looks at her. A woman that beautiful demanded a man's attention.

His neck prickled again. This time he deliberately caught her eyes. She blinked, and then as though taking him up on his challenge, she returned his stare. In the violet depths of her eyes, he detected a combination of interest and defiance. Huh. Did she challenge him or the warrior community in general? Over the course of the afternoon, she'd been quiet, but perhaps if he was lucky, she was a risk taker or a rule breaker. Either way, he wanted to know her. He wanted her. Even though he knew he couldn't have her.

Shifting his stance, he covered his mouth with one hand, clearing his throat while he discreetly adjusted himself with his other hand. "What was that, Rowan?"

At last he tore his eyes from Sloane's gaze and tuned back in to the conversation.

"I said, now you can have a break from Rio in the training room."

"Why would ye think I wanted one?" he asked perplexed before he grinned conspiratorially at Seamus. "I got a couple o' good shots on him the other day."

As the men in the party rejoined their wives, Sloane surreptitiously watched the druid called Davy Sutherland. He wasn't as tall as the Sheridans. Rather, he stood closer to Seamus's six feet. He combed his rich dark chocolate hair back from his face, but it was long enough for her to notice its natural waves. The charcoal-colored fisherman's sweater he wore fit his broad shoulders and deep chest perfectly. His jeans weren't nearly tight enough for Sloane's taste though, making her wonder about the contours of his legs and if they were as muscular as his torso. He stood with his big arms crossed in front of his chest, his stance strong and watchful. As Sloane stared at him, she thought the man looked like he could rival Atlas holding up the world.

His unusual amber-colored eyes arrested her attention until he released her long enough to take her in as well, thoroughly looking her up and down. A slow lazy smile, wicked in its heat, spread over his features, and a squadron of butterflies took flight in her belly. Curiously, she felt a pleasurable throbbing on the tattoo on her thigh. The sensation on her skin startled her, and she gazed back at him with wide eyes. No one knew about that tat, not even Fallon, yet this man's stare had her thinking—feeling—things she thought had been reserved for her warrior alone.

CHAPTER THREE

"AFTER YE MOVED over tae the States, Davy moved intae the cottage, Alaisdair, and now he trains with Rio at *An Teallach*," Hamish said.

"You train with Rio?" Seamus asked, looking more closely at the druid.

"I'm more like a practice dummy," Davy said with a laugh. "Have ye seen the way the man moves?"

The rich timbre of Davy Sutherland's voice washed over Sloane, ratcheting up her already heightened awareness of the man.

"A druid who trains with a warrior? Why?" Seamus asked. Then he turned to Rio, "You *willingly* train with him? What the hell?"

"Considering Rio's history of attitude toward druids, I can see why you'd wonder, Seamus," Ceri said. "But he's come a long way in the last year." She wrapped her arm around her warrior's waist and looked at him with so much love it made Sloane's heart hurt.

"This house has a way o' workin' on people, lad," Hamish said, addressing Seamus.

"That and possibly Hamish's cooking." Davy grinned.

"Do you still make the world's most unpalatable coffee, Hamish?" Owen asked with a smirk that left Sloane wondering what he was talking about.

"Of course, he does, Dad. Sometimes if he can beat Hamish to the kitchen, Davy rescues us with a pot of decent coffee," Rio said and turned to the newcomers. "Hamish's coffee is legendarily terrible. So of course, my entire family tries to drink it. Secretly, we all think Hamish, being such an accomplished druid and all"—he smirked at the man in question—"can make a decent pot, but he chooses not to 'cause he's trying to convert us all into tea drinkers." Rio rolled his eyes at the old druid, leaving no doubt about what he thought of Hamish's machinations.

Hamish shrugged unapologetically, a tiny smirk playing over his mouth.

"I'm still trying to wrap my head around the fact that Rio trains with a druid. And lets him live nearby." The bewildered look on Seamus's face made Sloane look more closely at her host.

"Why, Seamus? Back in the day, druids regularly trained with warriors. They could never be sure if they'd be called upon to join a battle or find themselves in a position in which they needed to defend themselves as they wove battle stories," Griff said, turning away from studying the painting of a mountain hanging on the wall beside the double doors to the salon.

"Yeah, I know that. My sister is a druid after all and in damn fine shape." Seamus gifted Siobhan with a warm smile before he sobered again. "That isn't the issue. What I'm having trouble with is Rio."

"Seamus, Siobhan, I'm sorry," Rio said with a sigh. "When Dad's brother Conor died, it kind of messed me up. I was young and didn't understand things very well, but that imperfect understanding colored all my attitudes from then on. When I married Ceri, that all changed. She's tied to this place and its matriarch, who, by all accounts, was an incredibly powerful druid. I've been having my attitude adjusted ever since." With one arm he hugged his wife to him while extending his right hand to Seamus. "I'm not sure how I'll make it all up to you, but maybe hosting your wedding is a start?"

Ceri beamed at her warrior, and Rio rested his cheek on her hair.

"Be damned. Will wonders never cease?" Seamus asked in a bemused tone as he shook Rio's hand.

"So ye've cleared the air then?" Hamish asked. "Siobhan?" he added, looking pointedly at her.

"Thank you, Rio," Siobhan said quietly. Duncan, who was standing behind her, wrapped his arms around his wife, silently supporting her as she leaned into him.

So that's the story behind the tension I sensed when we arrived. Sloane noticed a pair of amber-colored eyes were now focused on her again, and she stared boldly back at the druid whose unusual relationship with the host had paved the way toward reconciliation of old hurts within the family.

"It appears it's time tae celebrate fer all sorts o' reasons. We poured each o' ye a dram o' my finest whisky, and it's been neglected long enough, what with yer detour"—Hamish gazed at Alyssa—"and yer introductions and whatnot. Please." He indicated the tray on which rested two neat rows of dram glasses filled with amber liquid.

Sloane and Davy reached for their drams simultaneously, and he brushed her wrist with the back of his hand. A sizzle of awareness shot up her arm at the contact, and she blinked in surprise. He nodded his head at her. Did she see a hint of a smile in his eyes? Had he touched her on purpose?

Before she could figure it out, Hamish commandeered everyone's attention again, calling for a toast. "Here's tae a long and happy marriage fer ye, Seamus Lochlann and Fallon Graham.

May yer union be a blessin' tae ye and tae the entire warrior community."

As the rest of the party congratulated the lucky couple, memories of Lughnasadh and the cheers following a toast to her that
day stabbed at Sloane's heart. Hope had existed then. Now she
closed her eyes to try to shut out that night and drained her glass
in a breath. When she blinked her eyes open, she caught Davy
Sutherland looking at her quizzically, and she averted her gaze.

"Well, then. It's time to get everyone settled. You lot"—Ceri
indicated the Sheridans in attendance and Shanley and Alaisdair Graham—"know where your rooms are. The rest of you can
follow me, and I'll show you where you're sleeping. Davy, could
you help with the luggage, please?"

"Oh yeah, that would be appreciated. Right Fallon?" Seamus
said, all innocence.

"The offer for the other mode of dress still stands, warrior."
There was a warning in Fallon's voice.

"Save that til the honeymoon, Fireworks." Seamus turned to
Davy. "I'll take care of Fallon's luggage." He glanced back at her.
"As penance."

"Bet I can guess what that's about," Rowan said with a smirk.

"Bet we all can." Rio laughed.

As Owen was about to join in the fun, Sian preempted him.
"Before you start in on Seamus, perhaps we should settle into the
manor. It's been a full day, and I for one need some rest."

"I'll just bet you do, darlin'." Owen winked at her.

As the party topped the stairs to the third floor, Fallon said,
"This place is enormous. How in the world do you take care
of it?"

"Since the manor belongs to the entire clan, a trust oversees
it. Luckily, part of the management includes maid service," Ceri
replied as she walked down the hall past the ballroom taking

up one side of the third floor. "The wedding reception will be in here."

"This place is cavernous for the size of our wedding," Fallon said, skeptically eyeing the huge room. "The room we were in downstairs will be more than adequate for our small party."

"Um, the thing is, since you're related to the matriarch of Conlan Manor and you're a bard, you're kind of a big deal here, Fallon, whether you know it or not. Hamish has organized quite a ceilidh in honor of your wedding. We can have the actual ceremony in the grand salon if you like, but there *will* be a party in this room. Believe me, this 'cavernous' space"—Ceri air-quoted Fallon's word—"will be overflowing with people on the autumnal equinox."

Fallon turned an accusatory glare on her fiancé. "Did you know about this party, Seamus?"

Raising his hands in defense, he said, "First I've heard of it, I swear."

"It has to do with creating layers of protections for both of you," Griff said.

Fallon turned on him. "*You* knew about this?"

"As a bard and a member of the clan associated with this house, you will have certain obligations. You know that, Fallon. You and Seamus are also going to be targets for the more vicious deities in the pantheon for the rest of your lives. Creating relationships with the people connected to this house is one way we can add to the layers of protections we weave over you," her uncle explained.

"Look at it this way, Fallon. It's another adventure. Besides, a genuine Scots shindig will be fun," Sloane said from her place at the back of the group.

Fallon blew all the air out of her burgeoning rant. "You're right, Sloane. If we decide it's going to be fun, it will be." She sighed. "I know you're right too, Uncle Griff. I have a gift, and

I need to pay attention to how it affects more than only me and those I love." Turning to Ceri, she apologized. "Excuse my rudeness, Ceri. I'll be sure to thank Hamish as well."

Seamus took her in his arms. "Don't worry, Fireworks. The honeymoon will be very, very private. I've taken care of that." He punctuated his words with a kiss behind her ear, and Fallon melted into him.

Watching and listening to them, Sloane suppressed a sigh of grief. Psyching herself up, she said, "Since we have that taken care of, I'd love to see where you've put me so I can grab a shower before dinner."

"I can help ye with those, lass," Davy said when Sloane topped the stairs from the kitchen to the foyer with her luggage in hand.

"I can manage. I didn't bring much," she said, trying to put the handsome druid off.

"'Tis nae trouble. Here," Davy insisted as he snagged Sloane's suitcases from her hands. "I'll leave that little one tae ye. Where did Ceri put ye?" he asked as he headed up the wide staircase connecting the foyer to the upper stories of the house and leaving Sloane no choice but to follow him.

Trailing him up the stairs, she said, "Third floor in the small room at the end of the hall to the left of the stairs."

From this angle, she could appreciate Davy's tight ass as he took the stairs two at a time in front of her. *Yep, those jeans are hiding too much.* She hauled herself up short. *What am I thinking?*

When they reached the third floor, Sloane noticed Davy wasn't the least winded by his quick trip up two flights while carrying both of her suitcases. Admittedly, the cases were small, but still, the man was in ridiculously good shape. What was it Hamish had said? Davy trained with warriors? *That explains his fitness—and his impressive physique.*

Breaking into Sloane's reverie, he asked, "Is this yer first trip tae Scotland, lass?"

"It's my first trip to anywhere out of the States," she said with a little laugh.

"Beautiful country is our homeland, isn't it?"

"Scotland is enchanting. The stark beauty of the rolling hills and rugged mountains leading into Ullapool have quite a bit in common with the part of Montana where I'm from."

"Ye feel at home here, dae ye?"

Sloane thought Davy asked the question with more intensity than it warranted and wondered why, but she didn't ask. Instead, she said, "Conlan Manor and its owners are very welcoming."

A scowl flitted briefly across his face before he turned toward the door to her assigned room. "Here ye are. Did Ceri have a chance tae show ye all the amenities o' yer room?"

"Yes, thanks."

"Including the intercom system?"

"Intercom?"

"Ah. She must have left out that part. May I?" Before she could form a reply, Davy set down one of her cases and opened the door to her room. He grabbed the case and preceded her into the space.

For reasons she couldn't or wouldn't articulate to herself, Sloane didn't want Davy in her room, something she suspected he had all figured out. Yet here he was standing in the middle of it. And damn, if seeing the hot druid standing in front of the comfy-looking bed with its vast array of fluffy pillows atop a puffy down comforter didn't make her skin warm and her belly flutter.

When he opened his mouth and addressed her in that rich voice his rolling Scots burr only enhanced, a curious sensation rippled over her tattoo again. It wasn't as pronounced as before when he checked her out so thoroughly upon their first encounter, but the sensation stirred her up all the same.

"Where did ye say ye wanted yer cases?"

His question implied that while she busily tried to rein in her responses to the man, he'd been talking to her. The smile on his face only confirmed it.

Blowing out a breath at being caught with her mind somewhere it didn't belong, Sloane said, "Drop them anywhere. I'll figure out where I want them later."

Trying to appear nonchalant, she turned away from him and walked over to the tall dresser near the door and deposited her purse. In the mirror above the dresser, she caught him checking out her ass, and she couldn't hold back a tiny smile.

"You mentioned something about an intercom?"

Davy cleared his throat before answering, "Yeah. Here beside the door is the intercom system. It's linked tae the kitchen so ye don't miss a meal while ye're here. But I have tae warn ye. Hamish likes tae use the system fer his personal entertainment. Don't be surprised tae have the man wake ye at some ungodly hour with a boomin' 'good mornin'!' even on yer first day here." Thinking it over for a second, he added, "Especially on yer first day here."

"Is there some way I can turn the thing off?"

"Sure. I'll show you," he said, but he was standing in front of the unit, and she couldn't see around him, necessitating her to move closer to him.

She had the idea he blocked her view on purpose to force her to stand closer, but since she didn't want her sleep interrupted on her first full day at the manor, she stepped beside him for a better view of the device on the wall.

"Ye move this little lever here tae the off position, and then ye can wake when ye want tae. Hamish serves breakfast at seven on the dot though, and with that pack o' warriors ye came with, ye probably better be in the dinin' room close tae that time if ye want anythin' tae eat," he added with a grin.

The infuriatingly intriguing man just had to have dimples,

didn't he? She had to check herself from reaching up to test their depths with her fingers. Then there was his smell. Standing this close to him, she breathed in deep woods and citrus and something uniquely him. It occurred to her she'd like to breathe him in for a long time.

"Ye see it?" he asked.

Only when he spoke to her again did she realize she'd leaned in close to him, and she took a step back.

"Yes. Thanks very much for the help—and the warning," Sloane said, locking her fingers together behind her back.

"Any time, lass. Ye're the maid o' honor?"

"How did you know that?"

"Hamish has been talkin' nonstop about this weddin' ever since Alaisdair proposed hostin' it back in June. Hamish is a druid of uncanny skill, is that one. Don't know if someone told him about ye or if he divined it, but he was very keen tae have a seer in this house fer the weddin'. Yer friend isnae the only talisman here with an important gift." A haunted look crossed his face as he absently rubbed his right shoulder.

Davy's revelations staggered her.

Sloane's tattoo tingled at his words and his unconscious action, and she had to tighten her hands together behind her back to keep herself from rubbing her thigh. "Since Fallon and Seamus found each other, I'm discovering how fast news travels within the warrior community. You're pretty up-to-date on us, aren't you?" she asked, curiosity and indignation warring inside her.

"I'm a druid, Sloane MacIntosh. It's my job tae know about the warriors and talismans I may be called upon tae aid or protect," Davy replied, his tone serious.

The sound of her name on his tongue sent little shivers through her, shivers she didn't know what to do with, so she took another step back from him and held the bedroom door open.

"Thanks very much for your help with my luggage and the intercom. I'm sure we'll run into each other during the preparations for the wedding."

"I have nae doubt o' that, lass," he said with a wicked grin as he gracefully took the hint and walked out of her bedroom.

Chapter Four

S SHE HELPED Ceri and Fallon set one end of the massive table in the dining room, Sloane managed a private moment with her best friend. Arranging silverware as Fallon set napkins, she casually commented, "That druid doesn't look like any druid I've ever met."

Fallon blinked at her. "Hamish? He looks exactly like what I pictured every druid looks like. Except for Uncle Griff who's a stud." She ducked her head impishly.

Sloane snorted. "You know who I mean. Davy Sutherland. He's as fit and buff as any of the men in your wedding party."

"You noticed that too, huh?"

Sloane banged a fork down onto the table and immediately regretted it when Fallon added, "You think he's hot."

She shrugged. "He doesn't look like any other druid I've ever met. That's all."

"You're talking about Davy?" Ceri asked as she added wineglasses to the place settings. "He trains with Rio at least once a week. Sometimes more." She cocked her head. "Honestly, I was grateful for Davy's martial training when I foolishly placed myself and others…" She blew out a breath.

"When I screwed up and got Finn killed." She set the remaining wineglasses in her hands down on the table, wrapped her arms around herself, and stared into the middle distance. "If not for Davy, I'm not sure Lynnette and I would still be here."

"What do you mean?" Sloane asked.

"During the battle Morgan initiated here last Samhain, Davy saved us from a rogue warrior." Ceri turned to her with a meaningful glance. "With his claymore, not a spell."

Shanley set the stack of plates in her hands onto the table behind them and wrapped her arms around Ceri. "You have to stop blaming yourself, Ceri. No one else blames you." She squeezed Ceri close. "Finn didn't blame you. Rio was in danger and you wanted to help him." Turning to Sloane and Fallon, she continued. "In Scotland and Ireland especially, but all over Europe, actually, the druids train with warriors. As Hamish says, sometimes you need a sword faster than you need a spell or a story."

"That explains it," Sloane said, motioning to Fallon to continue laying out the rest of the napkins.

Her interest in Davy Sutherland was purely academic. It had nothing whatsoever to do with the breadth of his shoulders, the depth of his chest, his wavy, dark chocolate-colored hair, or his dimples. Definitely not his eyes. The deep brown rings intensifying those amber depths certainly didn't mesmerize her when he'd stared at her so blatantly in the salon earlier or in her room when he'd helped her with her luggage. Nothing good could come from involving herself with a man, especially a hot druid. If nothing else, the events of last summer had taught her that lesson.

Deliberately, she changed the subject. "Tell me about this room. Do you always eat in here?"

Ceri snorted, breaking the tension of their previous conversation. "We only use the dining room when the Sheridans come to visit since there are too many of us to fit around the table in the kitchen where we usually take our meals."

"Bummer. Here I was envisioning you hoarding the salt on one end of the table, forcing Rio to use a bullhorn to ask for it from his end."

Ceri grinned. "Now there's a visual."

"Still, this table must seat at least forty or fifty people, what with the benches along it. Do you use that fireplace to heat the place in the winter?"

As Ceri resumed setting out the wineglasses, she said, "Back in Fianna Conlan's day"—she nodded in the direction of the portrait above the massive stone fireplace at the opposite end of the double doors that led into the room—"the clan would meet here to plan strategies, celebrate victories, and generally hang out together. Nowadays with the clan literally scattered all over the world, it's only those of us who are directly related to Shanley and me who visit the manor for the most part."

"So, the people at the top of the table roasted during a meal while those at the foot relied on the shared body heat of those seated near them not to freeze before dessert was served?" Sloane laid the last of the silverware in her hand at the final place setting at the foot of the table.

"I guess I never thought of that. These days, the radiators along the walls keep the room relatively pleasant in the winter. And we never sit at the head of the table."

Sloane raised a brow.

"Since there aren't any servants to serve dinner, we bring the food up the front stairs and through the double doors rather than up the back way through the servants' stairs behind the fireplace. It would be silly to walk the meal all the way to the head of the table from that direction. I suppose we could use the dumb-waiter—" She lowered her voice and added with a conspiratorial whisper, "But I think Hamish likes to stare down Fianna while we eat. So we only use this end of the table."

The rest of the Sheridan women interrupted their conversation when they walked through the double doors carrying covered platters of food and setting them on the table between the rows of table settings.

"Dinner is served," Alyssa said as she set the platter she carried onto the table with a flourish.

Smiling at her, Ceri said, "I think the guys are checking out the new security features Rio added to the manor since you were here last spring. Maybe one of you could search them out and let them know dinner is ready?" She glanced at her in-laws.

"Did someone say dinner?" Seamus asked as he led the other warriors through the doors behind Alyssa, Lynnette, and Sian.

"Comin' through," Hamish said from somewhere behind him.

The Sheridan men stepped smartly into the room, followed closely by Hamish carrying a large tureen in his hands. Davy trailed him, carrying another large tureen.

"Whatever is on the menu smells delicious," Seamus said.

"So it begins." Clapping Seamus on the shoulder, Alaisdair ushered him toward the long table.

Sloane glanced away from the beautiful play of muscles over Davy's forearms as he set the tureen on the table to catch the confusion on Seamus's face and the grin on Alaisdair's.

Fallon caught her eye and shrugged, as confused as Sloane and, apparently, Seamus.

"Did ye help the auld man with preparin' that stew?" Alaisdair asked.

Davy lifted the lid from the tureen, and Sloane covered her growling belly with her hand when the scent of savory meat and spices wafted over her.

"Made yer favorite, Alaisdair. Cut the herbs myself, as a

matter of fact." Davy winked and headed over to the sideboard to retrieve ladles from a drawer.

"Ye're in fer a treat, Seamus. Something tae tickle yer taste buds and empower yer spirit." Alaisdair snagged Shanley by the waist as he guided her to sit beside him on the bench to the left of the end of the table. "Join me, lass. Food always tastes better when we're sharin' it."

Shanley's expression of pure love remained on Alaisdair as she seated herself beside him. As Sloane watched them, a shaft of longing shot through her, leaving her breathless. Never would she know such love and adoration from her warrior. The loss of Gavin, always a dull ache inside her, morphed into a searing pain. She closed her eyes against it, only to blink them open seconds later as a warm hand settled low on her back, tingling her blood.

"Ye all right there, lass?" Davy whispered beside her. "Ye look like ye saw a ghost."

Sloane shook her head and stepped away from the large hand radiating sparks over her skin from the spot where Davy rested it above her hip. Nothing could happen between her and a man, not even one as hot as Davy Sutherland. Macha had made herself clear when she attacked and stole her warrior from Sloane within hours of the two of them discovering each other. The goddess was never going to allow Sloane to come into her full powers, not after the way the Sheridans outplayed Morgan and the way Seamus and Fallon thwarted Maeve. The triple goddess would have her sacrifices. Mortals should count on that.

"Fine, thank you. Dinner smells delicious. We should join the others."

Deliberately, she chose a seat between Fallon and Keela. It might be bad manners to split up niece and aunt that way, but she needed to preclude Davy from choosing to sit next to her—if that was his intention. Her skin still tingled from where he'd touched her.

She pretended not to notice the cloud passing over Davy's face as she sat. Then the man did something truly alarming—he chose to sit directly across from her. All through dinner, he watched her. Her usual self-confidence, still smarting after the battering she'd sustained at Macha's hands at Lughnasadh, tried to exert itself in the face of Davy's unwavering interest as she joined the conversation. Or maybe joining the conversation was an avoidance tactic. If she focused on the others, she could pretend not to notice his steadfast attempts to see inside her.

Then there was the food. A rich, hearty fish stew disappeared alarmingly quickly from the two tureens on the table as well as the loaves of crusty bread and the platters of vegetables and roast beef. It had been a while since Sloane had enjoyed a meal with the Sheridan clan, but like the two previous times she'd dined with them, she marveled at the way the warriors could put away food. From the corner of her eye, she noticed Davy matched them without even trying, it seemed. For a druid, the man sure acted—and ate—like a warrior.

At last, Owen stood and reached for his place setting. "As patriarch of this family, I declare bedtime."

"Showing your age, are you, Dad?" Rio teased.

"Easy for you to say. You slept in your own bed last night while the rest of us rode in coach for seven hours," Owen said, a sour expression distorting his face.

"Donnae worry about the washin' up. We've got it, right Davy?" Hamish said, rising from his chair at the foot of the table.

"Absolutely." Davy stood and collected his place setting as well as Siobhan's; she'd sat to his left during the meal. "Go settle yerselves in yer rooms. We've got this."

❧

"I donnae think I would have noticed except the Sheridans are so affectionate. Their friends tae, if ye paid attention tae the MacManuses and the bride and groom." Davy poured himself a mug of coffee and sat the scarred table in the kitchen to savor it.

He enjoyed making good coffee for no other reason than to needle his old druid teacher who insisted on brewing tar whenever someone asked for a hot beverage other than tea.

"Is no' touchin' anyone the real problem, or is it that ye've taken an interest in the lass?" Hamish didn't look up from stirring a generous dollop of cream into his coffee.

No matter how much he complained, Hamish never passed up an opportunity to drink his coffee, Davy noticed. He chuckled as Hamish sipped and closed his eyes to savor the smooth brew. Then he flashed his eyes open, their dark brown irises seeming to see straight into Davy's soul, and he sobered on a breath.

"She's a talisman, Hamish. She belongs tae a warrior somewhere out there."

Hamish said nothing, the silence stretching like a rubber band.

"I donnae poach," Davy snapped. "Ye o' all people should know that."

"She's a bonny lass. I'd wonder about ye if ye dinnae take an interest in her." Hamish grinned broadly, and Davy slumped in his chair.

The debacle with Ceri Sheridan a year ago had taught him well. Or rather, Rio's regular reminders every time he bested Davy in the training room taught him. Aye, Sloane MacIntosh was quite possibly the most beautiful woman he'd ever laid his eyes on, and yeah, the mystery of her intrigued the hell out of him. But the Graham-Lochlann wedding was scheduled for the autumnal equinox less than a fortnight away. Afterward, Sloane would board a plane and return to America. He'd never see her again. Best to put his curiosity—all right, fine—his intense interest in the woman aside and concentrate on something else.

"What potions dae ye need help with taemorrow, auld man?"

he asked, deliberately changing the subject he never should have brought up in the first place.

"Nae potions, lad."

Davy's brows shot to his hairline. *No potions for an important family wedding?*

"I need ye tae spend some time with our new druid friends. Since Griff is fillin' in fer Fallon's father tae give her away tae her groom, and Siobhan is one o' the bridesmaids, it falls tae one o' us tae tell the story o' this pairin' durin' the ceremony." He sipped leisurely from his mug, swallowed, and continued. "Ye're the best storyteller in this whole shire, so the job falls tae ye. Taemorrow, I want ye tae learn the details o' the events that brought Fallon and Seamus taegether at summer solstice."

Having spent the last sixteen years of his life training with Hamish, Davy knew better than to question his mentor. That amiable note in his voice was nothing more than window dressing. He'd given a direct order rather than answer Davy's question, which meant Davy would be pondering Hamish's decision about the potions all night.

Chapter Five

NUGGLING INTO THE most comfortable bed she'd ever experienced, Sloane expected to fall asleep immediately—or maybe even sooner. After all, it neared four in the morning back home, so she'd been awake for nearly twenty-four hours. Twenty-four hours in which she'd flown, driven, hiked, wandered, and finally eaten a full druidic meal. By all accounts, she should be exhausted. Yet her mind refused to quiet.

Chalk that circumstance up to one annoyingly handsome druid. What was it about the man anyway? Several times throughout the late afternoon and evening, he'd gone out of his way to touch her. A brush of the wrist, a soft bump of a shoulder, his hand at her waist. Every single time, the swirl tattoo on her thigh tingled and throbbed, butterflies careened into each other in her belly, and her core heated and tightened in anticipation of his next touch. He had to know she was a talisman, didn't he?

She sat up as a terrible thought invaded her brain. He knew she'd lost her warrior and pitied her. He was being especially nice because she was such a pathetic creature.

Throwing herself back into her pillows, she groaned. "Let him think that."

Once Fallon trained into her full powers, perhaps Sloane would ask her to weave a story about her that allowed her to enjoy a man from their community. A widowed warrior. Or maybe a druid. But that time was somewhere in the distant future. Not now. Which meant she couldn't take a chance and expose a man to Macha's version of delight. Sloane hadn't had the chance to fall in love with her warrior, but she had no doubt love would have blossomed between them as the gods designed. Resigning herself to a life without the love of a man left her desolate. But the alternative—being responsible for the death of a man at the hands of the goddess because she selfishly wanted to be loved—made her physically ill. Sacrificing her happiness seemed a small price to pay for the life of another person.

Someone as fine as Davy Sutherland deserved for her to keep her distance. If she could only convince her body not to react to him. At last, she fell into a fitful sleep, memories crowding into her dreams.

As she filled her plate from the bounty on the table, Sloane heard a soft baritone voice behind her say, "I take it you know the host and hostess well."

She flicked a glance over her shoulder to see the owner of the smooth voice and did a double-take at the boyish grin on the handsome man's face.

"I might." Returning her attention to her plate, she willed her heart to slow down. She watched herself place kiwi slices on her plate before she pulled herself up short. She hated kiwi. But the hot man standing behind her made her forget.

Concentrating on finishing filling her plate with food she actually would eat, she reached the end of the table and looked around for a place to sit with her meal. She drifted over to two empty chairs near Fallon and Seamus. After seating herself, she glanced up to see the man from the buffet standing beside her. He raised a golden blond eyebrow as he nodded toward the empty chair beside her, a clear request to join her.

"Please," she said.

He smiled that devastatingly boyish smile at her again and sat down. After settling his plate and utensils on the table, he turned to her. "Gavin Scanlan."

She took in the way the university logo distorted slightly over his pecs while the sleeves of his T-shirt strained to contain his biceps. She wasn't sure if he bought his jeans distressed or if they were merely well worn. Either way, they molded enticingly to his long legs. The chocolate brown of his eyes contrasted startlingly with the golden honey of his hair, but it was that dimpled smile that sent her heart on a tear.

"How do you know Fallon and Seamus?" Sloane asked, trying to distract herself from drooling over Gavin's sculpted perfection.

"I came with Griff."

"Grad student?"

"Yeah. How 'bout you?"

"Graduated. Managed to finish as my soccer scholarship timed out."

"Soccer, huh? I played baseball. The coach liked my bat speed," Gavin said before forking a bite of steak. "I majored in chemistry as an undergrad. Now I'm studying the ancient Celts while I wait to get into med school." He chewed and swallowed. "Professor Walsh helps a lot of people get into med school."

"You're taking summer classes?"

"Just finished. Now I don't have to juggle work and school for a month. Gotta say, I'm looking forward to a break."

"Where do you work?"

"Outside."

She quirked a brow.

"I'm a landscaper."

"That explains your impressive—" She stopped herself. "Tan."

Gavin smirked while she tried to cover her slip with a bite of salad.

He prolonged her embarrassment by watching her over the top of his beer, mischief dancing in his eyes, before he took a pull. As heat crescendoed to fire on her cheeks, he swallowed and let her up. "What do you do?"

"I work for an investment firm."

"You like numbers?"

"They're a means to an end," she said with a shrug. "What I like is playing the odds, taking a risk."

"What are you doing in this town? Why aren't you in Vegas?"

She grinned. "Because the kind of gambling I do is considered respectable. Besides, the games in Vegas are predictable. Playing the market is more nuanced. You don't always know all the players in a deal, which cloaks their intentions. It makes the game more fun."

He sat back in his chair and eyed her speculatively. "With the way you're built and the way you move, I would have guessed a dancer or a yoga instructor. High finance, making deals with other people's money, that's a surprise."

She tasted her potato salad, swallowed, and gestured to him with her fork. "As is your wanting to be a doctor. I would have thought you might have tried to pursue a professional baseball career, what with your bat speed and all." She batted her eyelashes and he grinned.

"Touché." He saluted her with his beer. "Guess looks are deceiving." He didn't sound apologetic.

"Guess so." A smile played over her mouth. "If you're going back for seconds, would you mind bringing me back a brownie?"

She indicated Gavin's plate, which had been laden with some of everything on offer when he brought it to the table and was now empty with the exception of the bare bones of his T-bone steak.

"Sure, beautiful. Would you like a beer to go with your dessert?"

"Eww! Brownies and beer? I'll pass."

"Don't knock it till you've tried it." He waggled his brows as he stood to retrieve dessert for the two of them.

When he returned to the table, he pulled his chair closer to her and set a plate with several brownies on the table between them. "I didn't know how much dessert you like, so I came prepared," he deadpanned as he grabbed a brownie and ate half of it in one bite.

Though he devoured the first bite quickly, with the second one he closed his eyes and tipped back his head to savor. She had to work exceptionally hard to put the brakes on as she watched his Adam's apple work to swallow. It was all she could do to stop herself from leaning over to taste his neck with her tongue. Sitting so close to him, she could smell the light wood notes of the cologne he used and the faint tang of his sweat, a powerful combination that had her lady parts perking up and taking notice.

Then he opened his eyes and trained their chocolaty beauty on her as he grabbed another brownie and offered it to her. "You really should try one rather than drool over mine," he said, teasing her.

As she leaned forward to take a bite of the brownie Gavin offered, she felt a peculiar sting followed by a hot swirl on the top of her thigh, and she stopped midbite to blink up at him, her entire body tensing.

Her mouth suddenly dry, she didn't taste the bite of brownie she hastily swallowed before choking out, "Did you just brand the top of my thigh?"

His eyes widened before settling into a predatory gleam. "I don't know. What did it feel like?"

"Like you stung me followed by a hot swirl radiating out from the site of the sting."

"Hmm. Other women thought I'd tickled them," he said neutrally while he retraced his sign on her.

She hissed in a breath. "Can't think how anyone would consider what you're doing tickling, but it is having a desired effect."

Placing one hand on the table and one on the back of her chair, Gavin boxed her in. "You know, I had a long day at work today and *thought about skipping this little gathering even though it is Lughna-sadh. Now I'm glad I let the professor badger me into coming over,"* *he said. "Otherwise, who knows how long it might have taken me to* *find you." He grinned.*

"I had a feeling when I watched you walk into the party that you *were a talisman." He glanced around at some of the men standing* *near the buffet. "So did a couple of other unattached warriors Profes-* *sor Walsh invited. We sort of drew straws to see who would be the first* *one to try his sign on you. Lucky me—in every way," Gavin said as* *he scooted his chair closer to hers and slid his arm around her back.*

She raised her brows. "You were hinting rather broadly about *being a warrior, at least to someone who would know. I have to be* *honest though. I was hoping you were just another grad student since* *if you weren't my warrior, I was going to have a hard time not think-* *ing about you after tonight," she admitted. "Now what?"*

"You know what." His eyes danced. "But I think it would be *rather rude of us to walk out of the party right now."*

As usual, Sloane awoke in a rush, her core aching for a touch she would never know. She traced the tattoo on her thigh, the one thing she'd discovered gave her some respite from the longing her dream memories always wrung out of her. During the weeks after she'd returned to her own home, she hadn't dreamed of Gavin. She thought about him at odd times during her days, but her nights had remained blessedly silent. Until tonight.

As she lay quietly in her cozy bed, she listened to the sounds of the manor. Though the place had been built of solid stone, it was old. Like most old houses, it voiced itself continuously. During the day, people moving around inside it muffled its vocal-izations. But in the deep silence of the night, it made itself heard in the groaning of wooden beams settling against their stone sup-ports and the rattle of a window in the breeze. From somewhere nearby—the roof perhaps?—an owl hoo-hooted a deep-throated note at once melancholy and comforting.

After she counted one hundred sheep jumping over a stone fence, she gave up trying to return to sleep. Tossing the blanket and quilt off herself, she slid out of bed and pulled on a pair of leggings before layering a sweatshirt over her sleep shirt. She hoped Ceri and Rio didn't mind guests raiding the fridge in the middle of the night because she needed a mug of warm milk. Coupled with a walk down three flights of stairs and back, a warm drink might be enough to nudge her jet lag into kicking in and letting her sleep. Of course, the universe might have other ideas.

CHAPTER SIX

SHARP PAIN STABBING the spiral tattoo high up on his left bicep jolted Davy awake. The pain eventually toned down to a dull ache, but it kept him from returning to sleep and the beautiful dream he'd been having of a raven-haired beauty with eyes the color of violets. Throwing on a pair of sweats and his favorite ratty old fisherman's sweater, he shoved his feet into his trainers and made the quarter kilometer trek through the underground tunnel from his cottage to the manor.

He didn't worry overmuch about waking Hamish as he entered the old druid's apartment via the special door in the basement of the manor. After the year Davy had spent living in the cottage and using the passageway between it and the manor, he knew Hamish was used to him. After all, tonight wasn't the first time his tattoo had rocked him out of a deep slumber and sent him to the big house for something to calm it down—or to distract him from it.

No doubt Hamish could have helped him with his little problem. But he hadn't told Hamish about the tat—his involuntarily desperate need to acquire it or the frequent sensations often radiating from it. He couldn't explain even to himself the importance of keeping his body art private. Instead, he accepted his weird desire and took care of the pain or pleasure it forced on him as best he could.

Blowing out a frustrated breath, he wondered again why tonight's wake-up couldn't have been pleasurable. He'd been dreaming of Sloane, for crying-in-his-beer. As he crossed Hamish's living room, he stopped midstride. Of course he'd experience pain. He'd been dreaming of Sloane. He had no business dreaming of Sloane. Hadn't he been having this same conversation with Hamish in the kitchen after dinner?

Frowning, he snicked the door to Hamish's apartment closed and wandered down the short hallway to the kitchen. With one hand on the open door of the fridge and the other wrapped around a bowl of leftover berry compote, he stilled. From the corner of his eye, he caught a glow of light as it descended the stairs from the foyer. Straightening himself to his full six feet, he stood beside the open refrigerator and awaited his midnight snacking partner in crime.

When she stared at him from the bottom of the stairs, she could have knocked Davy flat on his ass. Like he'd conjured her from his dreams, Sloane stood before him, her hair an inky cloud descending over her shoulders, her lithe figure partially hidden beneath her voluminous oversized sweatshirt. The glow of the flashlight on her phone gave her an otherworldly pallor. Or maybe her face paled in surprise at finding someone else raiding the fridge ahead of her.

They spoke simultaneously.

"I couldn't sleep—"

"Join me?"

He gave her his most disarming grin, and she tentatively smiled back at him. In the back of his mind, he wondered what her smile looked like at full wattage and wanted to be the recipient of that expression. Then he rolled his eyes at himself and his ridiculous thoughts.

Though he could find his way around in the dark kitchen fine, he flipped on the light above the sink so as to orient Sloane. Her glance at the bowl in his hand had him grinning as he set the dessert on the counter while he retrieved plates from the cupboard. Silently, Sloane took the plates from him and walked them over to the table.

"After the day ye've had, I'm surprised ye can't sleep," Davy said as he ladled a generous helping of compote onto a plate and handed it to Sloane who'd seated herself across the table from him—again.

"Too keyed up, I guess. What's your excuse?"

As she lifted a bite of berries and cream to her mouth, Davy lost the thread of the conversation. *That mouth is a berry I'd love to taste.*

"Davy?"

He blinked away his wayward notions and concentrated on scooping compote onto his own plate. "There are some nights when the gods decide tae invade my sleep. Taenight's one o' those nights."

"Something wrong?"

"What?"

She nodded at his hand where he absently rubbed his aching shoulder.

Jerking his hand down to the table, he said, "Nae, o' course no'."

She took another bite and gestured with her spoon. "Your Scots is more pronounced when you're not being honest."

He stared at her.

She shrugged. "An observation. That's all."

"Is that one of yer talisman traits? Observation?" he asked. No way was he telling her about his ongoing problem with the tattoo he'd felt compelled to acquire last summer. She'd probably think he was looney.

Changing the subject, he asked, "What did ye think o' yer first day in Scotland?"

He watched in fascination as her pink tongue slid along the outside of her spoon to lick blackberries and cream off it. A tiny half smile played at the corner of her mouth when she caught him staring, forcing him to execute a discreet adjustment in his lap.

"I loved the little hike Alyssa insisted we take down to a waterfall alongside the road. Wandering down the path among the trees beside the stream was like losing myself in a fairyland."

"Ye like tae take a wander every now and then, dae ye? Enjoy an adventure?"

"When the easiest way is the best way, I've been known to take the road less traveled just to do it," she said with a self-deprecating laugh. "Fallon can tell you all sorts of stories about my *adventures*."

"I'll be sure tae ask her." He smirked at her. "Of course, if it's adventure ye like, I'd be happy tae take ye adventuring during yer stay with us."

A cloud passed over her lovely features. "I'll have so much to do with the wedding and everything. I doubt there will be time for adventures." She laser-focused on her dessert like it might contain the secrets of the universe.

Huh. Appeared the lady had secrets.

When the silent tension threatened to steal the sweet from his midnight snack, Davy said, "It's rather lucky fer the clan and those of us associated with it tae have a bard among us. Yer friend is a precious rarity."

Sloane blinked up at him, her eyes haunted, and he gripped the underside of the table to stop from rubbing the searing pain assaulting his tat at the expression on her beautiful face.

"We are lucky." Her scratchy voice warred with her words.

"Did something happen, lass?"

She cleared her throat, tried again, and said, "We nearly lost her. We nearly lost both Fallon and Seamus. If not for Scathach and Brighid, none of us would be in Scotland now to celebrate their wedding."

"Yeah? Then why are ye so sad?"

Sloane stood from the table. "I'm not the only one who may be too observant. Good night, Davy. Thanks for sharing your snack."

Turning her back, she dismissed him and walked her plate and fork to the sink.

Standing so fast he almost knocked over his chair, Davy grabbed his own plate and in two strides joined her where she rinsed her dish. "I didn't mean tae offend ye, Sloane. Please." He placed his hand on her forearm and froze.

Lightning shot through him, electrifying his blood and ricocheting pleasure from his tattoo to his throbbing cock.

Sloane gasped, her violet eyes seeking his, and the heat he watched darken them only intensified his already out-of-control reaction to her.

Backing away from him, she stammered, "I-I better go. There's so much to do. I—"

Without finishing her sentence, she turned and fled up the stairs like the devil himself gave chase while Davy stared after her. A long while later, he registered a splashing noise and saw they'd left the faucet running. Determinedly shutting down his libido, he finished the washing up and wandered back to the cottage, playing the entirety of his unexpected encounter with Sloane over and over again in his head. It was near dawn when at last he found sleep.

❧

Sloane slammed her bedroom door behind her and muttered a quiet apology to the house for the way she'd interrupted the stillness of the night. Slumping against the door, she smashed her hand against her chest and willed her heart to slow down. Racing up three flights of stairs hadn't been the best idea for a sleep aid. Well, hell. Neither had sharing a middle-of-the-night snack with Davy Sutherland.

What was it about that man? From the first moment she'd laid eyes on him, he'd riveted her attention. All afternoon, she hadn't been able to stop herself from sneaking peeks at him, which, to her utter embarrassment, he'd caught her doing more than once. Finding him in the kitchen raiding the fridge in the middle of the night had been a surprise, one she liked at first if she were being honest.

Then he'd made his offer of adventure and his too-close-for-comfort observations, and the tattoo high on her thigh prickled. Not knowing what to make of her reaction, she'd decided it was time to put some distance between them. But he didn't allow her to do that. Instead, he touched her arm, and sexual heat fizzed her blood. Pleasure bounced between her tattoo and her core, plea-sure she'd experienced only once before on a hot summer night with the man the gods had fated for her—the man a vengeful goddess had stolen from her almost as soon as she'd enjoyed those few precious seconds of joy she now knew would have to sustain her for the rest of her life.

What did it mean that Davy's hand placed innocuously on her forearm could elicit such a response from her? Was this another of Macha's sick games to remind her of what she'd lost?

She jerked her sweatshirt over her head and flung it onto the chair beside the bed. A second later, her leggings joined it before she climbed between the rumpled sheets and desperately tried to settle her churning thoughts. It was a lost cause as she proceeded to toss and turn for the remainder of the night in a fitful doze filled with images of playful brown eyes fading into the heated gaze of amber-colored irises and sounds of an American accent morphing into a Scottish burr that had her motor running for the rest of the night.

∾

The crackle of the intercom followed by Hamish's voice booming a greeting startled Sloane out of the only sleep she'd managed all night. An anemic light hovered at the edges of the thick drapes covering her windows, telling her morning arrived early in the Highlands of Scotland. At least when Hamish Buchanan was cooking breakfast.

Yawning, she snuggled back under the covers and contemplated skipping breakfast for another blessed hour of rest. The loud rumbling of her stomach put paid to that idea. Flopping back against the pillows, she contemplated the ornate molding where the walls of her room met the ceiling while she talked herself into getting out of bed.

At last, she stumbled to the bathroom. With the distraction of Davy Sutherland helping her with her luggage the previous day, she hadn't taken the time to appreciate her accommodations. Staying in Conlan Manor, even in a "small" bedroom on the third floor, beat any four-star hotel she'd ever had the good fortune to enjoy, if for no other reason than its gorgeous bathroom. The floor, walls, and walk-in shower were constructed of light gray marble shot through with charcoal-colored veins. The gilded frame of the mirror over the marble sink and the brass sconces bracketing it warmed the stone in the room. A pretty landscape painted in golden autumn hung above the toilet, adding color to the space. Fluffy black towels draped over a warming rack on the wall at right angles to the shower. When she turned the knob for the shower, she smiled at the showerhead raining—she jerked her hand from the spray—freezing cold water onto the marble.

Leaving the water to warm, she returned to the bedroom to strip off her sleep shirt and retrieve her toiletries bag from her suitcase. When she returned, she scrolled the dial on the towel rack to hot, stepped under the now warm rain of the shower, and closed her eyes in bliss. If not for her growling belly, Sloane thought she could quite easily spend an entire morning in her perfectly appointed bathroom.

Half an hour later as she pulled a spring-green sweater over her head, her intercom once again crackled to life. "Breakfast is waitin' in the dinin' room, but no' fer long," Hamish warned.

The old druid's voice twinkled, and she laughed to herself. Then she sobered. Hadn't Davy shut off the intercom for her when he dropped her suitcases in her room last night?

"Probably just as well," she told herself. "Otherwise, I might have slept through breakfast and ended up alone in the kitchen with Davy again sharing a mid-morning snack."

The idea of another intimate téte-a-téte with Davy gave her a warm glowing feeling in her chest. Her smile dropped as she impatiently reminded herself she had no business experiencing warm glowing feelings. They only led to heartache, and she'd endured enough of that to last for the rest of her life.

Animated conversations wafted into the foyer as she descended the stairs. She found the others gathered around the massive dining room table when she stepped through the double doors into the room. As she glanced around, she zeroed in on the fact that Davy was missing. Distracting herself against her weird disappointment at not seeing the man, especially after she'd spent nearly every minute since she'd awakened instructing herself to give him plenty of distance, she walked over to the sideboard and helped herself to the overwhelming buffet laid out there.

On the drive to the manor, Rowan had regaled her with descriptions of the full Scots breakfast Hamish was fond of serving, descriptions she knew had to be exaggerated. Her eyes saucered at the reality. If she listened closely, she could swear she heard the sideboard groaning under the weight of all the food sitting on it. Fried ham, platters of sunny-side up eggs, roasted halves of tomatoes, toasted and fried bread, pretty little hot potatoes, a tureen giving off some sort of delicious, oaty aroma, bowls of fruit and berries—she struggled to take it all in.

"'Tis quite a spread, eh, lass?"

She jumped at the sound of Davy's voice directly behind her.

"Didn't mean tae startle ye, Sloane." His laughter said otherwise. "Guess ye were tryin' tae decide where tae start?"

Her tingling response to the man left her dizzy, but somehow, she managed to keep her voice steady. "I thought Rowan was making this up when he told me about breakfast on the drive in yesterday."

An involuntary shiver rippled over her skin as she sensed Davy's heat on her back. Common sense said she shouldn't want him standing so close to her. Common sense said she should move away from him. Common sense was overrated. She sighed inside herself and stepped closer to the sideboard—away from Davy Sutherland. Her parents had spent most of her growing-up years trying to drill common sense into her, but she only learned it when her warrior made a fatal decision not to use it. She needed to rein in her responses to the handsome druid.

Davy's cheerful voice interrupted her morose thoughts. "Hamish is famous fer his breakfast spread. Yer friends"—he indicated the Sheridan women seated at the long table—"enjoy the porridge. 'Tis Ceri's favorite. Ye might try it first." He reached past her shoulder and lifted the lid on the tureen, and Sloane's stomach rumbled—loudly. Davy chuckled. "It's every bit as good as it smells."

Ignoring the way her skin tightened when Davy brushed her arm, she grabbed a bowl from those stacked beside the tureen.

"We Scots like tae eat our porridge seasoned with a little salt and a dollop o' cream, but yer friends prefer it with berries, cream, and sugar."

She slanted him a look. "Well then, when in Rome…" Sloane

spooned warm cream over the ladleful of porridge in her bowl before lightly sprinkling salt over it. After snagging a napkin and a spoon off the sideboard, she carried her breakfast over to join the others at the long table.

Unlike at dinner, she didn't have the option of wedging herself between any of her friends to avoid sitting beside Davy, a circumstance he took full advantage of when he seated himself on the bench next to her a few minutes later.

Sloane willed herself not to engage with the man who kept setting her senses on fire without seeming to try. Then she horrified herself when words slipped out of her mouth. "I take it you enjoy Hamish's breakfasts."

The mound of food on Davy's plate begged for comment, she consoled herself when he grinned at her like he knew exactly what she was thinking. And that was despite having her shield firmly in place.

"Since I spent the better part of the morning helping him cook for you lot, I think I deserve tae enjoy the fruits of my labors." With his fork, he motioned toward her bowl of porridge. "What dae ye think?"

Sloane tasted another bite and nodded. "I like it. I've never been a big cooked cereal fan, but I could get used to this."

"Glad tae hear it. Ceri won't give the Scots way a try." He winked at the woman seated across the table from them.

Ceri wrinkled her nose. "It *needs* sugar, Davy. And berries. Lots of berries stirred through it. Then it's divine." Punctuating her words, she shoved a huge spoonful of porridge into her mouth and dared him with her eyes to say something.

Davy laughed and shook his head before returning his attention to his own breakfast. Sloane spooned another bite into her mouth and tried to understand why she felt bereft at Davy and Ceri's easy banter. After all, they were friends. He was nothing to her. Nothing at all.

With a low murmur, Davy interrupted her thoughts. "Did ye sleep well, Sloane?"

She blinked up at him. The laugh lines bracketing his arresting eyes deepened as he watched her try and fail to stifle a yawn.

"Guess that answers my question."

"As a matter of fact, I was sleeping quite well when Hamish interrupted me. I thought you turned off my intercom last night."

He shrugged. "I showed ye how tae dae it, lass. But I left it up tae ye if ye wanted it on or off."

"Hmmph."

She returned her attention to her porridge but not before she caught a smirk curling Davy's lips.

"Ye up fer a little adventure later this afternoon?"

"I doubt there will be time. What with the wedding preparations and all."

From across the table, Ceri interrupted what Sloane had thought was a private conversation. "We have nearly everything in place for the wedding. Mainly, the family wanted to come over early to enjoy a little vacation—and to be certain Seamus didn't try something foolish like eloping."

The stern expression she sent down the bench in Seamus's direction told Sloane that Ceri had heard all about his original plans for marrying Fallon.

"You mean like you did with Rio?" Alyssa asked with a saccharine tone from her seat beside Ceri.

"Hey, no fair. You know I had no idea we were eloping until we stood in front of Hamish and the vicar at the altar in Gretna Green," Ceri responded with a put-upon air.

Alyssa rolled her eyes before she wrapped her arm around Ceri's shoulders and hugged her. Watching the two women, Sloane saw they enjoyed a friendship much like the one she was lucky enough to have with Fallon. "You know I'm teasing. Honestly, none of us would have wanted to be around Rio if he'd had to wait to marry you." She gifted Seamus with a beaming smile. "Seamus is much more patient than my brother-in-law. For which we're all eternally grateful."

"Whatever," Rio growled from where he seemingly materialized behind his wife.

After meeting him yesterday, Sloane had the impression Rio lived his life with a focused intensity she was sure would wear her out if she had to spend much time around him. She stared as he leaned down and nuzzled Ceri's neck before kissing her behind the ear, visibly melting the woman. Seeing the two of them share such an intimate moment stabbed Sloane with longing. Absently, she rubbed her thigh over the sudden ache centering on her tattoo and wondered again what she'd done to attract the vicious attentions of the war goddess.

"Ye all right there, lass?" Davy asked in a low tone beside her.

With a mental shake, she jerked herself out of her melancholy thoughts. "Fine. I'm fine."

The way he quirked his brow told her he didn't believe her.

So she did what she'd been doing ever since Lughnasadh—she deflected. "You were right about the porridge. But I think I need some fruit. Excuse me."

She stood from the bench and made her way back to the sideboard for a helping of fruit she didn't actually want. What she wanted was some time to herself away from happy warrior-and-talisman pairs who didn't mean to keep reminding her of what she'd lost and would never have. Choosing an array of blackberries, raspberries, and sliced bananas, Sloane filled a small plate. Having no choice that didn't leave her looking like a total jerk, she returned to her place on the bench beside Davy.

"Since we don't have much work to do around here for the wedding, how 'bout we drive over to Ullapool and poke around in the village shops?" Ceri suggested as she leaned back to gaze up at her husband. "The Walshes, MacManuses, and the bride and groom haven't seen our little town. And Alaisdair might like to reacquaint himself with his old haunts. What do you think?"

"I think that's a great plan. Far less taxing on you than a few others I could name."

Sloane wondered at the blazing glare Rio shot Hamish who met it with a twinkle in his eyes.

"Great!" Ceri clapped her hands and nudged her husband to step back so she could stand. "We'll clean up breakfast and head to the village."

At Ceri's pronouncement, the remainders of everyone's breakfasts disappeared in a blink. Before Sloane knew it, they'd cleaned up their meal and gathered everyone together in the foyer. A minute later, she was whisked out of the manor on a whirlwind of happy, chatty Sheridans headed out on a lark.

CHAPTER SEVEN

S EVERYONE CROWDED into the array of vehicles parked on the tarmac behind the manor, Davy somehow managed to sit right beside Sloane in the van carrying Fallon and Seamus, Alaisdair and Shanley Graham, and Griff and Keela Walsh. Though two layers of denim impeded skin-on-skin contact, Davy's heat seeped into Sloane's skin as though the two of them were naked. His scent washed over her, and she couldn't help but breathe in the smell of coffee under which she detected his unique scent of citrus and the sea and something unavoidably *him*.

She gripped her hands together in her lap to stop herself from rubbing the top of her thigh and clamped her legs together against the intense pleasure centered on her core that his nearness always seemed to provoke. Then Alaisdair said something to make Davy smile, and when his dimples came out to play, she gasped as her body surrendered to the mini-orgasm that had been building inside her almost from the first words he'd spoken to her at breakfast.

"Ye all right there, lass?" he asked in an undertone.

"Y-yes. Of course. Everything's great."

She smiled to cover the breathlessness of her voice. "Um, so tell me about—Ullapool, is it? Did I pronounce it correctly?"

"With a short 'u' like a true Scot. Well done."

There were those dimples again. Kryptonite. Pure, unadulterated kryptonite. Sloane couldn't stop the tiny smile quirking the corner of her mouth, which only encouraged him.

"The pub's my favorite place." He winked at her. "But I imagine ye'll want tae visit the shops. They sell some pretty sweaters and such, eh Shanley?" he asked without looking away from her.

Shanley glanced back from her seat beside Alaisdair who was driving the van. "The woolens store is my favorite." She slanted Davy a look. "There's also a great little book store."

"Having access tae the incredible library in the manor, I often forget about the bookshop. O' course, I can tell ye some stories if ye like."

The intense way Davy looked at her made her think that more than anything, he wanted story time with her—something she instinctively knew she'd enjoy, which was dangerous.

Tearing her eyes from his, she answered Shanley. "The sweater store sounds great."

Throughout the morning, the group explored the tiny village on the shores of Loch Broom. The high street, the name the locals gave what Sloane would have considered the main street, was a charming one-sided affair facing the water. Constructed of narrow, two-story buildings abutting each other wall-to-wall, most of them sported brightly whitewashed facades with the occasional building erected using the same golden stone as Conlan Manor. Some of the buildings differentiated themselves with doors painted intense red or spring green or black.

As advertised, the touristy shops and the stores selling locally knitted clothing were a big hit with the newcomers and the

Conlan clan alike. Sloane bought a pretty muffler knitted of variegated colors she knew she could wear with any of her jackets in the coming winter. A deep violet sweater with a Celtic knotwork design caught her attention as well. The way Davy's eyes darkened when she stepped out of the changing room to show Fallon might have had something to do with that purchase too. But a team of wild horses would never drag that admission from her.

No matter which shops they visited or how the women gathered themselves around some display or other, the gorgeous druid managed to stay close to her during the morning shopping excursion. When the group crowded into the Seaforth Restaurant for lunch, Davy pulled out a chair for her and proceeded to seat himself beside her. It made a kind of sense with the two of them being the odd ones out among the throng of warrior-and-talisman pairs, but something about the proprietary way Davy seemed to want to take care of her left her feeling simultaneously warm and worried.

Davy's closeness during the ride into the village had sent hot desire throbbing through and from her tattoo, a throbbing that only settled down to a tingle as the morning wore on. She didn't know what to make of it, but something about Davy Sutherland literally resonated through her.

When the waitress dropped off their menus, Davy drew Sloane's attention to a dish described in the middle of her open menu, deliberately brushing her forearm with his, she thought. A tiny puff of air escaped her as gooseflesh pebbled over her skin beneath her sweater.

She thought she detected a smile ghosting over Davy's mouth before he said, "This dish is my favorite."

"Salmon tart?"

"Can't beat it. Or the fish soup. Delicious."

Sloane did her best not to squirm at the way Davy's Scots burr dragged out the word delicious. Of course, he meant the food.

But his amber eyes were on her.

A ruckus brewing across the table at last drew her attention away from the too-handsome-for-her-own-good druid.

"Come on, Seamus. We're in Scotland. You have to try the local food," Fallon insisted. "You can eat a hamburger anytime, anywhere back home."

"Alaisdair, am I correct about black Angus beef originating in Scotland?" Seamus asked.

"Ye're right," Alaisdair began before Seamus cut him off.

"See, Fallon. Eating a burger is definitely trying the local food." He crossed his arms over his massive chest and smirked at his fiancée.

"But this afternoon, ye're havin' lunch a stone's throw from the ocean. The *local* food is fish." Alaisdair winked conspiratorially at Fallon and sat back in his chair.

Seamus rolled his eyes and groaned.

"Ye could compromise," Davy suggested.

Seamus cocked a brow and waited.

"The most important animal totem in Scots lore is the boar. It represents the ferocity of the hunt and the pleasures of feasting, companionship, and hospitality," Davy said. "The boar tenderloins on the menu are very tasty."

Was there a dare behind the benign way he gazed at Seamus?

Sloane watched in fascination as Seamus studied Davy, turned his attention to his menu, and then looked up at the druid again.

"Why do I get the distinct impression I've just been had?"

Beside Sloane, Siobhan and Duncan burst into gales of laughter.

When at last he calmed himself down, Duncan said, "How long have you been Siobhan's brother? And you still haven't figured out how powerful a druid's suggestions can be?"

Seamus scowled, but when the waitress took their orders, Sloane heard him ask for the tenderloins while she followed

Davy's lead with the salmon tart. Guess they were both susceptible to a druid. And what did that mean with Davy deliberately sticking so close to her?

❧

He didn't need Rio's constant glares to remind him his attraction to Sloane MacIntosh was pure madness. Yet he couldn't help himself. The woman drew him like a moth to a flame, and even knowing he could—probably would—burn, he couldn't manage to tear himself away from her.

Though he deliberately crowded her, she didn't try very hard to avoid him, he noticed. He also noted the way her breath hitched whenever he touched her, no matter if he brushed her arm or lightly placed his hand at the small of her back or grazed her thigh with his own as he settled next to her first in the van and then at the table at lunch. Sloane's subtle tells goaded him to try for bigger responses, no matter how dangerous for his relationship with the Sheridans, especially Rio. His own reactions to the woman might have played a part in his campaign for her attention as well. All morning long, his tattoo had throbbed pleasantly, sending electric pulses along his body that left him perpetually half-hard.

Discovering that Seamus's sister, a druid, was married to a warrior whose talisman still lived gave him hope for a chance to pursue Sloane. Then there was Fallon's aunt, another talisman who had lost her warrior and married a druid. He knew the druid matriarch of the Conlan clan, Fianna Conlan, had first married a warrior who hadn't found his talisman in time. Clearly, intermarriage among the ethnicities of their culture was nothing new to these people, a situation he thought might play in his favor…if he could interest the lady in question.

He jerked himself up short at the direction of this thoughts. Of course, he couldn't pursue Sloane. She belonged to a warrior out there somewhere, a warrior who'd been given an extra fourteen years to find her, thanks to the efforts of the Sheridan clan. This intense attraction he felt for the woman had to be the machinations of a trio of vengeful goddesses who'd been bested soundly and often the last few years. Perhaps the attack of the kelpie he'd narrowly escaped on the loch earlier this summer had been a warning, coming as soon as it did after the intense sexual awakening he'd experienced that day.

He slid a sideways look in Sloane's direction as she smiled at something Fallon was saying. Damn, the woman was a walking, talking temptation. The husky rasp of her voice was pure sex. All that black hair tumbling in waves over her shoulders, the inviting swells of her breasts the cut of her sweater hinted at, the perfect roundness of her ass, and those long, long legs enhanced by her choice of skinny jeans begged him to touch her. To have her. Yet he knew he had to stop. Even without Rio's censorious looks, his own innate sense of justice told him he had no business pursuing another man's fated mate. If the gods saw fit to give him Sloane MacIntosh, it would be through a twist of fate they controlled, and he had no business trying to influence the outcome.

When the group left the restaurant to wander the shores of Loch Broom, Davy tore himself away from Sloane. For the rest of the afternoon, he swapped stories with Griffin Walsh, learning as much as he could about the events at the time of Seamus and Fallon's bonding the previous summer. As one of the resident druids at the manor, he had the role of chief storyteller during the rituals on the autumnal equinox. When the time came, he would serve the bride and groom properly and well during their wedding ceremony, no matter how much he would rather be serving the maid of honor instead.

Sloane didn't seem to notice his absence from her side as she walked along in front of him with Fallon and Seamus. When the time came to return to the manor, he commandeered the front seat of the van beside Alaisdair with the excuse the two of them needed to catch up after Alaisdair's long absence from home. Again, the lady didn't seem to take notice of his absence at her side, which stung, if he was being honest. Even though he knew it was for the best.

Still, his tattoo hadn't let up all day. As long as Sloane remained in his vicinity, his shoulder pulsed, his blood fizzed through his body, and his cock reminded him how much he wanted her. Even as he concentrated on Griff's stories of Morgan releasing a Formorian against Seamus and the Sheridans, and Maeve erecting an ethereal palace floating in the air above a mountain lake somewhere in America, his subconscious persisted in following Sloane's every move as they walked along the loch. And again as the group chatted in the van. He zeroed in on her husky laughter, sensed her heat, and finally caught her staring at him.

Ah. The lady wasn't immune to him after all. The knowledge pleased him. Too much, as Alaisdair cleared his throat, drawing Davy's attention back to his old friend.

"Ye enjoying yer stay in the cottage, Davy?"

"Ye did a mighty fine job of fixin' the place up. Not sure Rio likes me living so close, but after ye moved out, it seemed a shame tae let the place sit empty. Wouldn't want it tae fall tae ruin again." Davy chuckled at his own joke.

Alaisdair laughed too. "Uh-huh. Ye're lookin' out fer me, are ye? Couldn't be that Hamish and ye are gangin' up on our boy, could it?"

"Och, Alaisdair. Ye're no' accusing us of anything nefarious, are ye?" Davy feigned innocence.

Alaisdair shook his head. "Ye know ye're askin' fer trouble with that one."

"Sparring with the likes of ye was a walk in the sunshine compared tae what I endure with Rio in the trainin' room these days." Davy watched the road through the windscreen, deliberately avoiding Alaisdair's quizzical glance. "But Hamish insists it's necessary fer both of us."

"So that's the way of it. The auld man does want his layers. Should have known."

Davy nodded as the van topped the hill above the manor.

"Does anyone want tae stop fer a photo op?" Alaisdair asked with a twinkle in his voice.

"Great idea, love," Shanley said from the back of the van.

They pulled over to the side of the road, and the van and the Land Rovers following them stopped behind them.

"We need to look at the manor again?" Rowan asked, his tone perplexed when he strolled over to stand beside Alaisdair.

"We're taking a family photo with the manor as the backdrop," Shanley explained as she slid her arm around her warrior, and Alaisdair hugged her close.

Davy didn't envy his old friend's new happiness. More than anyone Davy knew, Alaisdair Graham deserved the second chance at love—and life—the Sheridans' defeat of Morgan's ancient curse on warriors had given him. Still, Davy couldn't help wishing he too could bond with a mate the way warriors and talismans bonded. Druids' relationships were more like those of civilians, usually a slow and steady development from friendship to love rather than the swift hot fire that ignited when a warrior successfully tried his sign on a talisman and discovered her to belong to him. He understood the necessity of the intense mating warriors and talismans experienced in order to bond them together as a unit. After all, their complementary skills were necessary for success in the never-ending battles the goddesses insisted on waging against their community and civilians alike. Being fated to love each other only strengthened their bond.

From a purely intellectual viewpoint, the whole system made perfect sense. But that clinical knowledge didn't stop Davy from wishing for the thousandth time in his life that he'd been born a warrior. If anything, watching Alaisdair and Shanley together—seeing all the bonded pairs together—left him yearning for another kind of experience.

He gave himself a mental shake. Being a druid gave him powers equal to—and sometimes superior to—those of his warrior friends. Perhaps someday when he met the right druid and fell in love, he'd experience the kind of mating for which he envied his warrior brothers.

"If ye want tae gather taegether tae the right of the tarmac, I can fit the lot of ye in my viewfinder with a perfect view of the manor behind ye," he said, gesturing to the group to move to the side of the road.

"But you should be in the photo too, Davy," Ceri insisted.

"Nae. I'm the auld sorcerer's apprentice, no' a member of the family. 'Tis fittin' fer me tae take the photo." He slanted her a look, and she stuck her tongue out at him as she melded herself into Rio's side. Laughing, he said, "Would serve ye right tae have me take the shot with that expression on yer face, lass."

She stuck her tongue out again, and he pushed the button on his phone, capturing her silliness in the moment.

"Make sure to send a copy of that one to me," Rio said with a grin while Ceri poked him in the side. "Careful, woman. Or maybe you want to pay for that later."

Satisfied at last that everyone was arranged so each person's face at least was visible in the photo, Davy sucked in a breath to take the perfect picture when he noticed Sloane stood aloof from the others. Though still in the frame, she'd put enough distance between herself and Fallon to make her look out of place. Davy walked over and put his hand on her waist, silently insisting she take one more step into the picture. Yet when he touched her, she gasped and twisted away from him as though he'd singed or poked her or something equally painful.

The easy laughter and teasing going on among the Sheridan

and Conlan families stopped midsentence when they noted the miniature drama playing out between Davy and Sloane. Standing nearest them, Seamus broke the silence. "If I didn't know better, I'd swear you just tried your sign on her, Davy, and made a sweet discovery."

Sloane's eyes widened as Fallon turned on her fiancé. "That was mean, Seamus. I can't believe you said that."

"Hey, hey, no. I didn't mean anything by that. Geez, I'm sorry Sloane. I wasn't thinking," Seamus said, a stricken expression twisting his features.

"It's fine, Seamus." Sloane cleared her throat. "I overreacted. I'm sorry Davy." She blew out a breath. "Really, since I'm not family, I should step over here out of the shot."

Fallon reached for Sloane's arm, hauling her in close to Fallon's side. "You're the sister of my heart, and you know it. Now snuggle in and smile for the camera."

Davy watched in fascination as Sloane squeezed her eyes shut, appearing to count to ten before she opened them again and nodded at Fallon.

He stepped back and held up his phone. "Say ceilidh."

The group smiled, and he held the button down, taking several photos in a row. Now was not the time to try to figure out what exactly had happened between Sloane and him when he put his hand on her and felt fire rip through his arm, flaming his tattoo into red-hot life at the same time she desperately attempted to escape his touch.

CHAPTER EIGHT

"GIRLS AGAINST THE boys?" Ceri asked. "Seriously? You're on. You are so on—for getting your very fine asses handed to you," she taunted Rio whose bland expression did nothing to hide the fire in his eyes.

"Hope you ladies packed a lunch, 'cause you're going to need it to back up that threat."

Unless Sloane missed her guess, no matter the outcome of the croquet match they were set to play, Ceri would be one very happy talisman before the day ended. Inside herself, she sighed. She didn't resent these people. Truly, she didn't. After all, several of them had tried to help her save her warrior when Macha attacked at Lughnasadh. But from the moment Seamus and Fallon had picked her up at her house to give her a ride to the airport with them, she'd experienced a bone-deep sense of loss for what she'd never known and would never know, thanks to a vengeful goddess's ability to trick her warrior into walking straight into his death.

Fallon bumped her hand with the business end of a mallet,

breaking her out of her melancholy reverie. "Here you go, Sloane. We're all playing yellow while the guys are playing red."

"What? How can we do that when croquet sets come in six colors?"

"While you disappeared into your own head, Ceri explained they have multiple sets, so they cherry-picked colors in order to play as teams. You're our secret weapon, Ace, so try not to disappear on us during the game," she said jokingly, but she studied Sloane as if she were a code Fallon needed to crack.

"Secret weapon, huh? You haven't told anyone about our epic games during freshman year in the dorms?"

"It never came up." Fallon grinned conspiratorially. "By the time the guys figure it out, we should all be well on our way back to base from the second peg while they're still trying to knock their balls back onto the pitch from wherever you've sent them."

Fallon waggled her brows and walked over to join Siobhan MacManus and the Sheridan women.

With a flourish, Rio magnanimously invited Ceri to start the game. Sloane appreciated Ceri's croquet prowess as she sent her ball through the first wicket and used her bonus stroke to land it very near the second one. Rio followed her, aiming to send her ball off course rather than put his own ball through the wicket. When he missed Ceri completely, the men groaned while the women high-fived each other with glee.

Lynnette took the next turn. Although she didn't have the same skill as Ceri, barely hitting her ball in the same direction as the first wicket, it seemed Riley had the same ideas as his twin. When he followed his wife, rather than aim at the wicket, he aimed for Lynnette's ball, managing to bump it and earn himself a chance to send hers off course. Which meant the men were high-fiving each other to hoots of laughter and some good-natured taunting of their wives.

When Shanley stepped up for her turn, her reaction when

she bumped Riley's ball told everyone that little bump had been a happy accident. Her reluctance to risk smacking her foot rather than her ball with the mallet meant that Riley's ball barely moved when she had the chance to send it off course. The ladies groaned while the men laughed. Until Alaisdair completely missed Shanley's ball and bumped Riley's, compelling him to send his teammate off course.

Alyssa smiled sweetly at Rowan and proceeded to miss the course completely. She sighed and trudged over to stand near her ball where it landed in the tall grass, easily at least two turns away from a shot at the first wicket. Rowan grinned at her and slipped his ball through the first wicket and sent it within inches of the second one, seemingly deliberately avoiding all the other players' balls on purpose.

Fallon winked at Sloane as she took her place at the opening wicket. Deliberately, she aimed to miss the traffic jam near the first wicket and neatly set herself up to move through it.

"Impressive," Seamus said as he watched his fiancée. "But you're not going to get off that easy."

He lined up his shot to make sure he'd send Fallon's ball on a ride, took a mighty swing—and topped his ball, moving it inches instead of feet. Even his teammates couldn't help but tease him about his opening play.

By some silent agreement she didn't know she'd made, Sloane and Davy as the odd pair out were the last to play. She gave Fallon a tiny nod with her chin and commenced sending the other team off the course, beginning with Seamus who was such an easy mark. Next came Riley, then Alaisdair. When she cleared the first wicket and came after Rowan, the guys were starting to figure out they might be in trouble.

"No fair!" Riley cried. "You brought in a ringer."

Rowan leaned on the head of his mallet, his legs nonchalantly crossed. "Should have seen this coming after the way you were able to give us so much help at summer solstice even though you were far from the action."

Sloane shrugged and waited for Davy to play his turn. With a precision that both impressed and worried her, Davy neatly jumped Shanley's and Lynnette's balls as he cleared the first wicket. He didn't even glance at Fallon's or Ceri's as he zeroed in on Sloane's.

"Looks like you boys brought your own ringer," Alyssa said as they watched Davy land his red ball on top of Sloane's yellow one before it toppled directly into the grass.

Davy grinned wickedly at Sloane, positioned his ball and mallet, and let fly with a mighty stroke that sent her ball on a high trajectory before it crash-landed loudly in the woods abutting the croquet pitch.

A chorus of "Yeah!" and "Way to go, Davy!" and "Did ye see that, ladies?" and "Oh, hell yes!" erupted from the assembled men, accompanied by fist bumps and high fives like they'd all done the work of Davy's aim. Lynnette tossed her mallet to the ground in disgust, Ceri tried not to laugh, and Fallon stared first at Davy then at Sloane with an incredulous look on her face.

"Was it something I said?" Sloane asked. She cocked a brow at Davy and waited.

"Nae, lass. Just evening the playing field a mite. Ye know, after ye sent so many of my mates off course." The smirk on his face told her how much he'd enjoyed his little display of mad croquet skills.

Not yet willing to admit the man could be in her league, she said, "Using druid magic in lawn games hardly seems sporting."

"Though I hate to say this after what he did to you, Sloane, there is no druid magic he can apply to this game," Siobhan said.

"True that," Duncan added. "'Cause if there were, no doubt Siobhan would have used it to keep me from going after her."

"Exactly," she said, batting her lashes at her husband.

Sloane sighed. There was some double entendre there she didn't understand. "Whatever. Guess I'm headed to the woods on a snipe hunt."

Davy fell in step beside her as she walked off the pitch. "A snipe hunt?"

"It's a Montana saying. Listen, I'm perfectly capable of finding my ball myself."

"Where would be the fun in that?" Playfully, he bumped her shoulder. "You were saying?"

She gave him the stink-eye, and he made the universal gesture for "go on."

"When someone is headed off on some foolhardy adventure—usually involving a trek through a forest or a cornfield or some other wild, rugged place—we call it going snipe hunting."

"But there is such a thing as a snipe?"

"Not in Montana. They don't live that far north. Sometimes boys will convince girls to go snipe hunting, and when the girls come up empty, the boys suggest perhaps there are other things they could be doing together in the woods."

"I think I like this 'snipe hunting.'"

Davy's dimples appeared, and Sloane suddenly realized they were far enough into the woods so as not to be seen by the others.

Alone together in the woods. Probably not one of her smartest moments. Not that her body was having a problem with it. Her tattoo pulsated from the inside of the spiral out to the end, like LED lights chasing each other on a sign advertising the party starts here on her thigh. If she didn't know any better, she could swear her tat was glowing beneath the denim of her jeans, a signal calling out to Davy like the Batman beacon over Gotham.

His nearness got to her. Her senses tracked his citrusy ocean scent over the earthy aroma of fallen leaves and forest detritus. His rumbly Scots burr resonated through her every time he spoke. Though she tried to keep her attention on finding her errant croquet ball, her eyes kept straying to the broad expanse of his chest and shoulders. Because, shoulders. She was such a sucker for a man who looked like he could wield a claymore for hours.

She rolled her eyes at herself.

"Since this is the first you've ever heard of it, I know you didn't send my ball out here for the purpose of snipe hunting." To her own ears, her words didn't sound convincing.

Davy shrugged. "Of course no'."

Something in his tone dragged her gaze to his face. The twinkle dancing in his amber eyes told her he may not have heard the term, but he was quite familiar with the concept. Damn. The last thing she needed was more alone time with Davy Sutherland. She was more than aware of him when they were in a crowd.

Still, a smile at his maneuver tried to tug at her lips when a pain searing through the tattoo on the top of her thigh took her mind off Davy and his machinations. Without meaning to, she cried out and doubled over to try to manage a sensation like a hot poker piercing her skin. Yet even through her agony, she heard Davy hiss in a breath. Turning her head to look at him, she saw he held his right bicep with his left hand, massaging it like he'd been punched there or something.

As the stinging ache subsided, she could resume breathing—until another form of torment assailed her ears. She stilled and glanced up into the trees where a murder of crows descended, momentarily blacking out the feeble light filtering through the autumn-colored branches as the birds landed in a cawing cacophony above them.

Why is she here? What more does she want to take from me?

Immediately, Sloane's thoughts turned to Fallon and Seamus, and she knew she had to warn her friends. Whatever Macha was planning, it would happen here in Scotland. No doubt she intended to stop the wedding, which could only mean one thing—Sloane was going to lose someone else she loved.

Watching Sloane play croquet had been a revelation. The woman was beautiful, intelligent, and athletic. The more time he spent around her, the more she attracted him. He knew better than to give in to that attraction, but he couldn't seem to help himself. Sending her ball into the woods had been an obvious ploy, something she let him know she saw right through when she described her "snipe hunt."

He'd located her ball rather easily, landing as it had on a pile of twigs, a bright yellow orb in its newfound nest. Instead of pointing it out when he realized she hadn't seen it, he followed as she led him deeper into the stand of beeches and elms bordering the croquet pitch. The husky timbre of her voice was an aphrodisiac to his already heightened awareness of her, and he wanted to let her keep talking because, aye, that voice. After the way she deliberately distanced herself from him after lunch, he wanted a chance to spend a few precious moments alone with her.

The ever-present pleasant throbbing in his right bicep whenever she was near morphed into a bone-numbing ache with the arrival of a murder of crows. The way Sloane cried out in pain and doubled over told him she was well aware of the omen the goddess sent. The mystery he needed to solve was their connection, for he had no doubt they shared one. It was the only explanation for the two of them experiencing similar physical reactions to the arrival of the scores of birds sagging the branches above them.

Sloane interrupted his thoughts. "I have to go. I have to warn the others, especially Fallon and Seamus." She sounded out of breath, like she'd been running for miles through the woods rather than strolling a hundred meters.

"Warn them about what?" he asked the air as she raced away from him.

Trailing after her, he snagged her croquet ball on his way out of the woods and joined her on the pitch a few minutes later.

The laughter and good-natured teasing he'd heard coming from the others stopped like hitting a pause button when Sloane cleared the trees.

"She's here." Sloane panted. "We have to return to the shelter of the manor *now*."

Seamus's eyes shot fire. "Who's here?"

"Macha," Davy said as he walked over to stand near Sloane. Though the goddess made him nervous too, Sloane's reaction had his heart pounding. Something had happened. Something terrible judging from the fear pulsing off her like a concussion from a dropped bomb.

Fallon moved closer to her warrior. "How do you know?"

"Listen," Sloane said.

The cacophony of ill-mannered cawing emanating from hundreds of black crows assailed their ears, a terrifying sound that reminded Davy of the old Hitchcock horror flick. Because he knew who was behind this particular avian infestation, the sound was infinitely more terrifying than psycho birds flying amok in some small town.

"Ye must have some ability that scares the auld girl, Sloane."

Sloane lifted a brow as she gazed at Alaisdair.

"How else dae ye account fer the way she willnae leave ye alone?"

This visitation from the goddess is about Sloane? *How does that square with the kelpie Macha sent at Lughnasadh? Or the ache beneath this tattoo when the crows appeared just now?*

"She took that away when she—" Sloane swallowed, and Davy noticed the way she rubbed the heel of her hand into her leg high on her left thigh. "Fallon is precious. No doubt the goddesses want to prevent her from coming into her full power, which as we all know will happen when she and Seamus consummate their marriage. I think this omen is telling us Macha has decided to join forces with Morgan and Maeve to prevent such a powerful union."

"Sloane has a point," Griff said as he flanked Fallon. "Have you enchanted these grounds, Davy?"

"'Tis tae big a tract of land tae enchant properly. We chant the ritual around it every year on Samhain. But as ye all are aware after the events of last Celtic New Year, those enchantments are no' enough." He shoved his hands into the front pockets of his jeans to avoid rubbing his shoulder in front of this audience. "I did chant over this area as Rio and I set up the course. It didn't occur tae me tae enchant the woods as well."

Ceri huffed out a sigh. "Well, that infernal noise has definitely dampened my enthusiasm for playing outside today. Even though there's no doubt the girls were going to win." She smirked at her husband.

"Perhaps we can take up the game tomorrow, after Griff, Davy, and I reinforce the enchantments Davy placed on this area," Siobhan suggested.

"Great idea, babe." Duncan brushed a kiss over Siobhan's cheek, and it struck Davy anew how he and Sloane were the odd ones out at this bonded family gathering. And not only because they had no blood relationships among the guests.

He curled his fingers in his pockets and gritted his teeth against the pain intensifying in his shoulder.

"I agree with Alaisdair. I'm not convinced that racket in the woods is about us," Seamus said as he hugged Fallon closer to his side. The intensity of the expression on his face when he stared at Sloane told Davy something else was at play here, something everyone else knew about. Turning his attention back to his sister, Seamus added, "But it probably won't hurt anything if we add protections to our play area."

Siobhan nodded at him, some telepathic agreement passing between the siblings.

"I vote for leaving the game as it is." Seamus looked around at the balls scattered over and near the pitch. With a smirk in her direction, he said, "But Sloane has to wait two rounds before she can come back in owing to the fact that Davy rescued her ball from the woods."

Davy flicked him a look, and Seamus gestured to the ground at Davy's feet where Sloane's ball rested. In all the speculation about Macha's latest omen, he'd completely forgotten he'd dropped it there.

"It won't matter in the end, warrior." Fallon gave Seamus an impish hip check. "We're still going to win. The question is what will be our prize? We didn't discuss that before we began the game, but now we have all night to think about it, right girls?"

The expression on her face was pure mischief as she scanned her teammates.

"I wouldn't get too cocky if I were you, Fireworks. We're going to be through the wickets before your ringer can get back in the game."

"Oh, Seamus, my sweet man. You have so much to learn."

The charged look the two exchanged left Davy wishing for the thousandth time that he'd been born a warrior. Or that he could compose a story wherein he somehow became a warrior. Never had he seen his parents look at each other the way the pairs in this lot did. Had to be their warrior blood. Then he glanced over at Sloane, and the naked longing he saw on her lovely face nearly brought him to his knees.

There was no doubt in his mind the two of them shared a connection. After today's events, punctuated by the infernal noise still disturbing the woods, he was determined to discover what it was before she had a chance to leave him in a fortnight.

CHAPTER NINE

LOANE STARED INTO the flames dancing in the fireplace in the salon as the memories washed over her.

"It seems several people have picked up on what just happened between us." She glanced over at the nearby table where Fallon and Seamus, Alyssa, and Rowan watched with undisguised interest.

Gavin nodded toward the others before he whispered in Sloane's ear, "Yeah. A little decorum is a good thing."

"Oh warrior, you have so much to learn about me," she challenged as she lifted her hand to his face and brought his mouth to hers for a kiss. When her lips touched the heated firmness of his, she thought, Decorum is for people who never have any fun.

"I heard that—"

She'd been dying to taste Gavin almost from the moment she looked over her shoulder at the buffet and lost herself in his smile. Sipping at his lips, she tasted chocolate from the brownies and a faint hoppiness from the beer he'd drunk, and she smiled against his mouth, learning she rather liked the combination—as long as she tasted it on him. Then he took over the kiss, tracing the seam of her lips with his tongue, seeking entrance into her wet heat. Willingly, she let him in and met him eagerly as they plundered each other's mouths, their tongues gliding and dancing over each other, the kiss deepening with each stroke.

She plunged her hands into Gavin's thick mane of blond hair and anchored him to her as he kissed the breath out of her, showing her with his mouth what she could expect from their bonding. Each of them was so lost in the other that neither remembered where they were or that they had an audience.

From somewhere very far away, she thought she heard thunder. As she slowly, slowly backed out of Gavin's kiss, the thunderous sound intensified until she recognized it as applause and laughter. Pulling away from Gavin's mouth, she sucked in a deep breath and turned to find Seamus with a huge grin on his face leading the rest of the company in a standing ovation. It seemed her disdain for decorum met with approval.

"Most of us bond privately, but I've noticed you're not too concerned with how other people do things, Sloane," Seamus teased.

"Sorry, Seamus. Guess we got carried away," Gavin began before he gazed meaningfully at her. "So, about decorum?"

"Maybe it's not so overrated," she admitted as she slid gracefully from her perch on Gavin's lap and back into her chair. Somehow, she'd missed when she'd climbed on top of him or he'd hauled her onto his lap. Either way, it was clear to her the teasing she'd started with a soft kiss had morphed into something else entirely. Apparently, everything she'd been taught in her talisman training had been true—making love with a warrior far exceeded any other kind of sex one could experience.

"I guess we're learning some things about each other already, warrior," she said, her cheeks hot.

"Guess so." Gavin's eyes danced.

"Public displays of affection aside, congratulations you two," Seamus said, stepping over to shake Gavin's hand. "Do you mind?" he asked Gavin with a grin as he leaned down to kiss Sloane's cheek.

"I think it was probably fate that kept today from being my

wedding day," Fallon said as she hugged Sloane, adding her congratulations to her fiancé's.

"What do you mean?"

Fallon raised a brow and replied, "Well, if today had been my wedding day, as my maid of honor you would have been too busy to sit down long enough for Gavin to have a conversation with you let alone to have the chance to try his sign on you."

"Oh." She peeked at her warrior from beneath her lashes.

"Now that what went on here over dinner is common knowledge, you all won't mind if I spirit off my beautiful talisman so we can begin getting to know each other a whole lot better." Gavin stood up in one athletic motion and reached a hand down to her. His words implied asking permission, but his actions made it clear he had plans for them, plans that didn't need to wait any longer and certainly didn't require an audience. Setting her hand on his forearm sent a wave of heat through her that made her gasp, and again, several members of the party smiled.

Seamus laughed out loud. "Darlin' it's like that for all of us. Your physical response to your warrior bodes well for your bonding. When the time comes for you to use your skill to help him, the necessity of that connection becomes abundantly clear. You'll see." He brushed a kiss over his fiancée's knuckles and waggled his brows at her before turning back to Sloane. "Now run along, kids, and enjoy yourselves," he finished with a smirk.

"Seamus Lochlann, you are a menace," Fallon exclaimed.

"Yeah, and you love me that way, so much that you wouldn't change a thing about me even though you can."

Seamus's reference to Fallon's special skill as a bard, a storyteller with highly advanced abilities for changing events and people, elicited a mischievous smile from her. "Don't tempt me, warrior."

"Or what, Fireworks? You'll tell a story that makes me even more heroic than I already am?" He tugged on her hand, pulling her toward him.

"Maybe I'll tell a story that has you racing at my beck and call for every little thing I want, followed by a 'yes, your perfect loveliness, and what else can I do for you?'"

"Tell me again how that story is different from the way things are right now? I think I missed that part," Seamus said as he pulled Fallon into his embrace.

The rest of the guests laughed at Seamus and Fallon's antics, while arm in arm, Gavin and Sloane slipped quietly from the party.

Walking along the front walk of Seamus and Fallon's house, Gavin casually asked, "Did you drive over here, I hope? I rode with some of the other unattached warriors."

"Yes." She smiled. "I take it we'll start bonding at my place since I assume at least one of those other warriors is your roommate?"

"See, we're already on the same page, and we've known each other less than an hour."

"I know what I learned in my training, but I didn't believe things with my warrior would move so fast once I met him."

She remembered feeling wary as she and Gavin had left Fallon's house, though she didn't understand why—then. As she continued to stare into the fire crackling in the fireplace in the grand salon, a tear slipped down her face. Still, she couldn't stop thinking about that night.

"It's the way Danu and the Dagda intended it to be. We never know when the more vicious deities in the pantheon are going to go on a tear that requires our intervention, so we have to bond quickly."

Oh, Gavin. He couldn't know how true his words were.

He lifted her hand to his mouth and kissed the back of it. "Fortunately, there's a lot of fun involved in the experience if those kisses we were sharing back there are any indicator." His eyes danced, and she laughed.

"There is that."

"I'd say our chemistry is flaming hot and sustainable."

"You think so, do you?"

"You doubt me, woman? You did catch that I majored in chemistry, right?"

They grinned at each other, and Gavin couldn't seem to resist a quick taste of her lips as they neared the sidewalk running in front of their friends' home.

As they stepped off the property that Siobhan MacManus and Griffin Walsh had enchanted when Seamus and Fallon moved in, a murder of crows flew overhead, their raucous cawing jarring the couple from the promise of their kiss. Immediately, night eclipsed the long summer twilight, and a chill wind blew over them.

Sloane shivered and Gavin tightened his arm around her waist. "Is your place enchanted, by chance?" he asked hopefully.

"Yes, but not like the fortress we're leaving."

"I think we've just been warned not to waste any time discovering your special skill." The intensity of Gavin's tone chilled Sloane even more.

"Alyssa said something about hoping we had an easier time of it than the couples we left at the party. I'm not sure she's going to get her wish," Sloane said as she snuggled closer into his side.

"If that's going to be the case, we need to be at your place at least five minutes ago. Where's your car?"

She pointed across the street.

"Sweet ride, Sloane. Why am I not surprised this is what you drive?" He appreciatively eyed her bright red Mustang convertible.

"If you're really good, someday I might even let you drive it," she said with a wink.

Their reprieve lasted a few seconds before another murder of crows flew overhead, their cawing loud and ominous even as they disappeared into the night.

"Crows flying at night. The deities who love to give the most trouble are nearby, and we need to be somewhere much safer than a ragtop car, no matter how sweet it is," she said as another chill shivered through her.

They slid into her car simultaneously, and Gavin reached across the console to trace his fingertip over the slope of her cheek, leaving a trail of heat in the wake of his caress. "We're going to be fine, Sloane."

"Maybe we should go back inside and ask the MacManuses or the Walshes to follow us or maybe chant over us before we head out."

"Sloane, we don't need—or want—chaperones tonight." He patted the dash. "Besides, I bet this baby has some serious horses under the hood." His confidence and eagerness to get her alone allayed the darkness she'd experienced from an imperfect understanding of the goddess's intentions.

Sloane eased out of her parking space before shifting into sport and racing up the street toward the east side of town and the one-bedroom cottage she rented there.

Nearing a stoplight, they heard sirens tearing up the street running perpendicular to the one on which they were driving. As they reached the intersection, a black SUV screamed through a red light followed closely by three police cars, blue lights flashing in the night, sirens piercing the soft summer air. Sloane slammed on the brakes while Gavin covered her hand over the gearshift.

Sloane sucked in air. "It's a trap, Gavin! Macha is nearby, and she intends to take you before we have a chance to bond. Whatever you think you're being told to do, don't do it," she pleaded.

"The guys in that SUV are rogue warriors who robbed a convenience store. Scathach demands I do something to help the civilian they kidnapped in the robbery," Gavin said. "You know as well as I do that when our patron goddess demands our presence in battle, we have no choice but to obey her." He squeezed her hand. "I'm twenty-four, and like every other warrior I know, I've been fighting rogues since I turned twenty-one. And I'm still here. Have some faith, talisman."

The gentle tone of his voice softened his words, but it wasn't enough. Sloane knew what was coming. "I'm your talisman, and my job is to direct you in battle. If you leave me now and visualize yourself into the battle Macha's devised purely for you, you will die. Please, Gavin, let me take you to my home where I can show you my skill."

"Scathach is growing impatient. You have to let me go, Sloane. You know that," Gavin said softly, but steel girded his tone.

He slipped his hand over her nape and pulled her toward him. Looking deep into her eyes he said, "Wow, your eyes are the color of the most beautiful spring violets. Looking into them every day from now until forever will be a highlight of my life." He smiled. "Go back to Seamus and Fallon's and wait for me. I'll visualize myself there after I've taken care of business."

After he gave her a searingly hot kiss, he stepped from her car. In sorrow, she watched as he summoned his claymore to himself and then he was gone, having visualized himself into the fray and out of her life.

Silent tears flowed freely down her face as she gradually became aware of the blaring of a car horn behind her. Slowly, she pulled through the intersection and turned onto the next block. In a daze of pain and sorrow, she drove herself back to Fallon's house and parked her car across the street.

She had no idea how long she sat alone in her car until familiar voices called out as the party broke up and merry guests chatted amiably as they walked to their vehicles.

Alyssa Sheridan noticed her first. "Sloane, what are you doing here alone? Why aren't you off somewhere bonding with Gavin? Where is Gavin?"

Alyssa's questions washed over her like a breath-stealing flood.

Several of the others congregated beside Sloane's car. Before she could gather herself enough to answer even one question, a loud whoosh filled the air, and the great goddess herself appeared, decked out in her inky black cloak of raven's feathers.

"You are very powerful, Sloane MacIntosh," Macha began. "The warrior race contains many who are very powerful—your friend

Fallon Graham comes to mind." She nodded at Fallon who remained safe inside the druidic enchantments at the edge of her yard. "But you are all still mortal. Being mortal, you are prone to certain character flaws such as susceptibility to deception—and perhaps hubris." An evil smile stretched her lips.

"You heeded my warnings, but your warrior did not understand you already knew your skill before the two of you met this evening. Of course, you could not tell him until you had properly bonded, but it is my feast day, and I demanded a sacrifice."

Macha's words lanced through Sloane like knives.

But Macha wasn't finished. "My sister, the Morrigan, guided Gavin Scanlan across the ford into the mists at the same time you arrived back here—but you knew that. It was my intention to take a warrior from this particular party of warriors on this day in retaliation for the recent beatings the Sheridans and their friends have given my sisters." She shook out her raven-feathered cloak, inviting the circling crows to land. "As you likely have guessed, I usually confine my activities to the Gaelic lands of Ireland and Scotland, but I am honor bound to do something for my sisters here."

She petted a crow that landed on her shoulder, seeming to give it her undivided attention as she uttered the words that shattered Sloane's whole world. "You should not grieve overmuch. After all, you were not yet bonded to your warrior."

"You are a goddess. You have no human feelings, Macha. I will grieve for my warrior for the rest of my life," she said through her tears.

"Even better, for then Gavin Scanlan truly was a sacrifice. Though men have named this day for Lugh, *god of the sun, it is my day also. Like men of old, you have given back to the gods something of great value to you. Perhaps you will earn something in return."* *With that parting shot, Macha disappeared into the night, a lone black raven feather floating silently to the ground where she'd stood.*

The sofa cushion beside her sagged, but Sloane didn't turn away from the flames crackling in front of her.

Fallon slid an arm across her shoulders, and she leaned back into her friend. For several long minutes, they sat silently. At last, Fallon said, "I'm so sorry, Sloane. I thought making this trip would be an adventure for you, a way to take your mind off things."

Sloane patted her friend's knee. "I'm glad I'm here." She swiped at the tears wetting her face with her other hand. "Truly, I am."

"Which explains why you're sitting in here by yourself while everyone else is in the sitting room watching a silly British comedy on TV."

"I was fine, excited to be here even, until—"

"Until Macha sent her minions to haunt you this afternoon."

Sloane sagged into the cushions of the sofa, not even trying to hide her feelings from her best friend. Which would have been pointless anyway.

"She stole my whole world from me before I even had a chance to experience it." She sucked in a breath then let it out slowly. "You're all I have left. If I lose you too—" She swallowed. "Or if you lose Seamus, and I have to watch you go through this, it'll break me."

"Sloane, you're so much stronger than you think, than you give yourself credit for." Fallon played with her hair the way Sloane thought a mom might do for a child she wanted to soothe—not that Sloane would know firsthand. Her parents had spent her life admonishing her for being too adventurous, too quick to have fun, too willing to take a risk. The only respite she could remember from their incessant scolding came when she spent time with her best friend. Fallon's parents had been equally hard on her, but the two of them found solace in each other, a friend who could empathize.

But Sloane never wanted Fallon to be able to empathize with this kind of loss.

CHAPTER TEN

HE NEXT AFTERNOON after Davy returned to the manor following a trip into Ullapool for Hamish, he sought out Sloane. Finding her seated on a stone bench reading a book in the knot garden in front of the manor, he stopped to gaze at her. Damn, the woman was beautiful. Long curls spiraled her inky hair, their waves catching the sunlight as they fell down her back. She held her lithe form in perfect posture, only her head inclined toward the book she held in her lap. He wouldn't be surprised to discover she was a dancer or perhaps a yoga instructor.

It pleased him to see she wore the violet sweater she'd purchased on their excursion into Ullapool the previous day. Black leggings hugged her legs and disappeared into tall brown boots. Sitting there in the garden, she looked like a painting, a picture he wanted to imprint on his memory and hold onto forever.

He sighed. He needed to stop dreaming. He knew that. But every time he looked at her, the feeling they were connected intensified.

A puff of wind blew strands of hair across her face, interrupting her concentration enough to sense his presence. Those violet eyes blinked up and captured his. For several long seconds, he stared into their depths, unable to look away. Another tiny gust of air blew her beautiful black hair across her face, and she pushed it away, momentarily breaking the spell she cast over him.

"Hello, bonny lass."

"Hello, Davy."

Gesturing to the seat beside her, he asked, "May I join ye?"

For a second, she hesitated. "Sure."

He suppressed a grin as he watched her close her book and set it on the bench beside her, a flimsy barrier between them.

"'Tis quiet taeday. Nae omens from the goddess."

Shooting him a side-eye, she said, "Hamish suggested she wouldn't bother me out here among all your special herbs and plants."

"It's no' the plants that hold the power by themselves. 'Tis all the chantin' Hamish insists on from every druid who enters this sacred space." He leaned back on his hands and curled his fingers over the edge of the bench.

Flashing him a perplexed look, she said, "I didn't hear you chanting when you entered the garden."

"I'm no' surprised. Ye seemed engrossed in yer book." He nodded at the tome she'd laid facedown between them. "What are ye reading?"

"Sir Walter Scott's *Lady of the Lake*." She shrugged. "Ceri said I could help myself to the library, and I found this. Reading a book written by one of Scotland's great heroes seemed appropriate while I'm here." A tiny grin tugged the corner of her mouth.

What he wouldn't give to see a full-on smile. Preferably directed at him.

"Reading a story about a heroic woman seems appropriate fer ye, Sloane MacIntosh."

She flinched. "What do you mean by that?"

More than anything, he wanted her to stay for a wee while—with him. He looked around the garden with a nonchalance he was far from feeling. "Ye experienced a pain that doubled ye over in the woods yesterday." She hissed in a breath, but he plowed on. "Yet when ye recovered, ye didn't think twice about yerself." He let his eyes return to her. "The first thing ye did was race out tae warn yer friends." His eyes strayed to the book laying on the bench between them. "Ye're like the lady in yer book who dedicated herself tae looking out fer King Arthur."

A snort met his words. "There's absolutely nothing heroic about me, believe me."

"Yesterday as we played croquet, Rowan mentioned something about yer ability tae help Fallon and Seamus from a remote location. What did he mean by that?"

She shrugged. "When we were kids, I suspected Fallon's skill when she started changing the old stories. Like this one." She patted the cover of the book resting between them. "I mentioned my suspicions to Griffin and Siobhan, and they took things from there, guiding Fallon as she and Seamus battled Maeve during last summer's solstice."

His eyes tracked her hands as she rubbed them down her thighs to her knees and back up and tried not to stare as her left hand palmed her upper thigh.

"What happened, if ye donnae mind my asking."

Sloane stared into the middle distance, her voice sounding hollow. "The goddesses were determined to take Seamus. Fallon too, if they could manage it, but Maeve was obsessed with Seamus. When everyone else showed up to rescue them, Morgan unleashed a Fomorian."

"Seriously?" Davy's voice traveled up an octave as he dragged out the syllables of that one word. *How could the goddess be so foolhardy? What is it about this clan that's riled her up so?*

"Yeah, Balor of the One Eye, but with Siobhan's help, Alyssa was able to recreate the circumstances that killed the giant long ago so she could kill him again." A melancholy-sounding sigh puffed out of her. "Siobhan is very devoted to her brother. It would take more than a Fomorian to take him away from her."

Davy whistled. "Ye run with a powerful crowd, Sloane MacIntosh."

Chuffing out a laugh, she said, "That's an understatement. You do know the Sheridans are responsible for eradicating the ancient curse against warriors, the one the goddesses invoked to steal fourteen years of a warrior's time for finding his mate?"

Davy's right bicep started throbbing at the mention of warriors finding their mates. Absently, he rubbed it.

"They're responsible fer adding protections tae the Conlan clan that stretch tae ten generations as well. Like I said, the lot ye run with is quite powerful."

Turning a little on the bench to face him, Sloane said, "Does it hurt?"

"What?"

Pointing at his left hand where he rubbed his upper right arm, she said, "Your arm. Does it hurt? I noticed you massage it often."

"'Tis nothing." He dropped his hand to his knee and curled his toes in his boots. He needed an outlet she wouldn't notice. "So the auld girl unleashed Fomorians. Did ye know that Beira made all the hells of Ross Shire, the very county we're sitting in at the moment."

Sloane's raised brow assured him he'd piqued her curiosity and diverted her attention from his arm.

"Beira, the Queen of Winter, is the mother of the Scots Fomorians. Like most Scots, that lot liked tae fight amongst themselves rather than take on warriors like their Irish and Cornish brethren." With a tiny grin, he peeked at her from beneath his brows. "If ye had an interest, I could take ye on a wee tour of the places where the likes of Ben Ledi won a stone-putting contest with other giants or where Torvean, Dunain, and Phadrick enjoy tossin' a hammer between 'em in the mornings outside Inverness."

"That would be an adventure." A tiny smile curved her lips. "Except I won't be here long enough for adventures. We're all flying home the Monday after the wedding."

"'Tis no' far from here. We could dae a day trip. Take a picnic," he coaxed, turning on the charm with a smile he knew showed off the dimples the lasses at the pub told him could get him anything.

"I don't know," Sloane began.

Without thinking, he put his hand on her knee, and a jolt of sexual heat shot through him from his hand to the spiral high on his arm, down through his solar plexus, and straight to his cock.

In fascination, he watched her eyes darken from violet to midnight. Then he noticed her hand squeezing the top of her thigh.

"Ye know ye want tae, Sloane."

He wasn't referring to a day trip to check out the sights anymore. When she remained quiet, he gave in. Lifting his hand from her knee, he cupped her cheek and let his fingertips slide over the shell of her ear to skim the silk of her hair. Still, she stared at him with those eyes.

"Ye're the most beautiful woman I've ever seen," he whispered. He raised his other hand to her neck, caressing her skin with his thumb, delighting in the way her pulse raced at his touch. When she didn't move away, he leaned in and brushed the soft rose petals of her lips with his own. A tiny sigh parted her lips, and he took advantage, slipping his tongue inside her mouth.

She fisted the front of his shirt in her hands and leaned in, silently inviting him to deepen the kiss. He didn't need to be asked twice. Never in his life had he felt lips as soft as hers. Never in his life had the stroke of a woman's tongue along his set his body aflame like this. Never in his life had he flashed from zero to out of control in a heartbeat.

Sloane tasted of mint and something dark and erotic. Changing the angle of his lips on hers, he deepened the kiss even more, devouring all the sweetness she offered him. She was every story he'd ever told, every delight he'd ever experienced, every dream he'd ever wished would come true. When she chased his tongue with her own, he sucked hers hard, pulling her even closer to him like he could compose a new story using nothing but sensation and desire.

Minutes, hours, weeks later, he discovered he needed air. Yet he couldn't stop kissing her. With closed-mouth touches between breaths, he took a tour of her jaw with his lips and tested the plumpness of her earlobe with his teeth. Her gasp of pleasure was all the encouragement he needed. But when he tried to pull her closer, the corner of her book poked his thigh. Letting her go long enough to move it, the distant cawing of a crow detonated the pretty bubble of the moment with a bang.

Sloane jumped up away from him, panic wilding her eyes. "That was—"

Fucking hot. The best kiss o' my life.

"—ill-advised, Davy."

"Lass?" He was still dazed from the fireworks shooting through him from that kiss.

Sloane turned in a frantic circle, scanning the area around them. "She's targeting me. I have no idea why, but she insists I lose everything I care about." She stared at him, fear and desire at war in the depths of her mesmerizing violet eyes. "Everything I want," she whispered.

"Who? What are you talking about?"

"Macha."

When he stood and reached for her, she flinched and backed away from him.

"Whoa, lass." Like talking down a frightened horse, he put up his hands and gentled his voice. "Why dae ye think the auld girl is after ye?"

"*Lughnasadh.*" She said the word like it should mean something to him.

Before he could stop her, she turned on her heel and fled the garden like a pack of wild dogs snapped at her feet. Fisting his hands on his hips, he blew a frustrated sigh toward the heavens. In the distance, the crow cawed again, and he shot it a filthy gesture. Whatever Sloane had experienced involved Macha. Macha, the goddess who'd been subtly harassing him since the previous summer.

A thought struck him. The old witch started her annoyances at about the time he acquired his tat. But that had been on the summer solstice, not Lughnasadh. Still, it had to mean something that Macha had decided to target both Sloane and him. The overwhelming attraction he felt for the lass was definitely not one-sided. Not after the way she'd responded to him. His body still tingled, especially the swirls of ink high on his arm.

When he glanced back at the bench where he'd experienced the hottest kiss of his life, he saw Sloane's book lying there. Its bright red cover sharply contrasted with the gray stone of the bench. Scooping it up, he flipped it over, studying the art on the front. A beautiful woman, waves of onyx hair cascading down her back, stood inside a tiny boat as she used a single oar to navigate the roiling waters beneath her. He traced the title with his fingertips: *The Lady of the Lake.*

Staring at the waves the artist had so skillfully drawn along the bottom half of the book cover took him back. It had been a gorgeous high summer afternoon when he'd set out on Loch Broom the day the goddess sent the kelpie after him. At the time, he'd thought he'd somehow found his way into the Morrigan's sights for some inexplicable reason. Subsequent visitations by murders of crows cawing through the night when they should have been roosting, the sense of something watching him whenever he stepped foot away from the enchanted safety of Conlan

Manor, and the near-constant sensations fluctuating between pain and orgasmic pleasure emanating from his tattoo told him he had the attention of some deity. With the arrival of Sloane MacIntosh and the avian visitations plaguing her, he started to catch a clue about the connections between the beautiful talisman, Macha, and himself. Macha cultivating an interest in a talisman he understood. What made no sense at all was that the third deity in the unholy triumvirate of war goddesses had interested herself so thoroughly in a druid.

Lughnasadh, Sloane had said with such vehemence. Lughnasadh, the high summer feast day, celebration of the early harvest and dedicated to Lugh, god of the sun. As he tried to work it out, the crow cawed again and flew off in the direction of Loch Broom. Like someone out of an old Monty Python movie, he smacked Sir Walter Scott's bestseller against his forehead. Lughnasadh didn't only belong to Lugh. Lughnasadh was also a feast day for Macha. Like her sisters, she loved battle with a ravenousness bordering on obscene, giving her one of her sobriquets as the great slaughterer of men. Represented by crows and horses, she controlled the vicious water horses called kelpies. She'd been sending him signs for months, but what did they mean?

As he strolled through the garden, he chanted protection spells along the Celtic-knot-patterned hedges with only half his attention. Turning toward the manor with Sloane's book in his hand, he knew one thing for certain. He needed to find out what Lughnasadh meant to her and why she feared the goddess like facing a fate worse than death.

CHAPTER ELEVEN

WHEN HE RETURNED to the house, Davy sought out Ceri. It took him about twenty minutes to wander the rooms of the manor before he finally found her bossing Rio around in the ballroom on the third floor.

"Fallon's a *bard*, Rio. Of course every warrior, talisman, and druid in this part of Scotland is going to want to witness her marriage. Which means we need more tables and chairs."

Leaning against the doorframe, Davy crossed his arms and settled in to watch the show. Rio gifted his talisman with a long-suffering look before sighing—loudly—and returning to the storeroom behind the dais to retrieve more furniture. After the regular beatings Rio gave him during their sparring matches in the training room, he rather enjoyed watching the man scramble to do his wife's bidding.

As Rio rolled yet another table into the room, he caught sight of Davy. "Were you here to watch, or do you think you could lend a hand?"

"I could lend a hand, I suppose," he offered, "but where would be the fun in that?" He smirked. "I much prefer tae enjoy the show when Ceri puts ye through yer paces."

"Uh-huh." Rio glanced at Ceri who didn't try to hide her amusement as she pointed to where she wanted the table. "Guess I'll be remembering that on our next trip to *An Teallach*."

At the mention of the mountain harboring the training room in its core, Davy straightened and sauntered into the room. "How can I help, Ceri?"

From the corner of his eye, he caught Rio's smirk, and he couldn't help but grin. They both knew the threat wasn't necessary, but they'd long ago fallen into the habit of baiting each other to save face in front of the lady each man had courted until Rio finally tried his sign on her and discovered her to be his fated mate.

As Davy carried two heavy high-backed oak chairs over to the table Rio had set up, he casually asked, "What dae ye know about Fallon's friend Sloane?"

"Why are you asking about a talisman, druid?" Rio's tone told him they weren't playing their game anymore.

Ignoring him, Davy turned to Ceri. "We were chatting in the garden a while ago, when a rather annoying messenger interrupted us. Before Sloane ran away, she said Lughnasadh like I should know what she meant." He pushed a chair in under a table and leaned against it. "Apparently, I'm out of the loop, so I thought ye might be able tae enlighten me."

Ceri furrowed her brow. "Messenger?"

"Aye. There we were having a pleasant conversation," *or something,* "when a loud obnoxious crow landed outside the enchanted boundary of the garden and started making an unholy racket."

Rio walked over to stand beside Ceri, their attention dialed in on Davy.

He crossed his arms again and stared back at them. "Sloane jumped up like an asp bit her, said "Lughnasadh" like I should know what she meant, and ran off like she had Cerberus on her tail, all three of his heads snappin' at her."

Ceri exchanged a look with Rio who stared her down for several long seconds before nodding to her. From the looks of it, they'd enjoyed a private telepathic argument, one Ceri had won.

"From what I've gathered from Alyssa, Sloane's warrior discovered her at a party at Seamus and Fallon's house on Lughnasadh."

Davy nodded once in what he hoped his friends interpreted as mild interest rather than the sucker punch Ceri's words delivered to his solar plexus.

"It was a rather public discovery," she continued.

Davy fisted the hand beneath his crossed arm and tried hard not to react more than that. *What the hell was Sloane, a bonded talisman, doing kissing me back like that in the garden, rocking my world in a way I've never experienced before?*

"Then Macha staged a battle with some rogue warriors, and Sloane lost her warrior within an hour of discovering him."

All the air whooshed out of Davy. Good thing he still leaned against that heavy chair, or he might have found himself on his arse on the floor. Relief and sorrow warred within him. Sloane wasn't betraying a warrior with him in the garden, but she'd suffered a terrible loss. Even as his heart broke a little for the beautiful talisman, he couldn't help wanting her to take a chance with him—something he had to admit to himself he'd wanted even when he thought she belonged to another man who was fated to have her.

"Sloane lost her warrior?" he managed to say, his voice sounding harsh in his ears.

"Rowan told me about it. Macha has it in for Sloane," Rio added.

"What dae ye mean?"

"According to Rowan, she's had a murder of crows cawing in the trees across the street from her house since her warrior's death, like the old girl is gloating over taking her warrior."

"Jesus. Nae wonder the woman has a healthy fear of those

birds." Davy ran a hand over his face. "Guess that answers my question. Mostly."

Rio hiked a brow. "Mostly?"

"Aye." He arranged another chair. "Can't imagine what Macha was doing in America. She usually leaves that part of the world tae her sisters and confines her mischief tae those of us living on the islands on this side of the Atlantic."

Ceri pointed at some chairs that needed moving before adding, "Alyssa said right after Gavin died, Macha visited Sloane to taunt her."

Davy joined Rio as he carried another pair of chairs over to a table near the high windows facing the gardens. "With the crows?"

"No. Macha made a point of telling Sloane in front of Alyssa and Rowan and Seamus and Fallon that she required a sacrifice on her feast day, and the Sheridans"—she gave her husband a pointed look—"had been successful enough against her sisters recently. Guess she thought she needed to even the score."

A terrifying thought occurred to him. "Is Sloane related tae ye lot?"

"No. But she is Fallon's best friend, and she helped Fallon rescue Seamus from Maeve," Rio said over his shoulder as he headed back to the storeroom. As he wheeled out another table, he continued. "It's my guess that since Macha is as sexually voracious as Maeve, she probably has some sympathy for Maeve not being able to steal Seamus from Fallon." He looked to Ceri for where she wanted him to place the table.

"In the corner please." Turning to Davy, she picked up where her warrior left off. "Because Sloane and Gavin had yet to bond, they were easy targets."

"Can't say Macha's tactics surprise me."

He hoped he sounded dispassionate. It wouldn't do for a bonded warrior-talisman pair to know what was running through his head. Hearing the name of Sloane's warrior grated at Davy's conscience. It was one thing to think of a nameless, faceless warrior claiming Sloane for his mate. Naming the man was something else. Naming him made him real, someone Sloane cared about because the fates had decreed it. Someone with whom he was competing for Sloane's heart if her response to the crow in the garden was any indication.

Wait. What? Sloane's heart? Holy Saint Brighid, I only met the woman two days ago.

Yet as he continued to help Ceri and Rio set up the ballroom, the idea grabbed hold of him and wouldn't let go.

❧

"What else can she take from me but you?" Sloane asked.

Davy's wickedly handsome features flashed behind her eyes, the crow cawing from somewhere behind his broad shoulders. Fear gave her the shakes, and she set her cup of tea on the table beside where she sat with Fallon in the library.

"She's not after me. At least not at the moment." Fallon reclined in the chair opposite her in front of the fireplace, her feet tucked beneath her as she sipped her tea. "You were in the garden reading a book, you said. What were you reading?"

"Does it matter?"

Fallon rolled her eyes.

"Sorry." Sloane sighed. "I know stories matter."

"Stories are everything." The blue, green, and gold in Fallon's hazel eyes seemed to swirl and intensify as she emphasized her point.

Sloane had seen that look more times than she could count in the sixteen years the two had been friends. Owing to the way Fallon liked to tell stories during those years, Sloane had suspected Fallon's skills as a bard, a powerful talisman possessing both talisman and druidic traits that allowed her to change a person's story.

But it wasn't until Seamus, Fallon's warrior, discovered her that Sloane's suspicions became realities. Of course, if Fallon's parents hadn't harbored such deep and dangerous prejudices against the druidic race, perhaps Fallon and Seamus wouldn't have been in so much danger last summer.

A picture of Gavin Scanlan's laughing face flashed in Sloane's head closely followed by another picture—Davy Sutherland's dimpled smile before he lowered his lips to hers.

Heat suffused her body, the swirl tattoo on her left thigh pulsing in a way that tightened her core with pleasure. On the heels of her body's response to her thoughts, guilt reared its shaming head as Sloane's mind strayed to Davy's kiss. How could she have forgotten Gavin so completely for the space of an afternoon with the too-handsome-for-her-own-good druid?

Yet her traitorous body refused to give her peace. Gavin's kisses had caused her to lose control enough to give her a rare moment of embarrassment in front of her friends. Now she couldn't remember those kisses at all. Instead, her head filled with pictures of Davy Sutherland's smile, those dimples deepening as he'd looked into her eyes. No doubt he saw desire there, something she had no business feeling for the druid. Something she had no business feeling for any man after the way Macha stole Gavin from her. She could still hear the cawing of the crow, the sound assaulting her ears even in her memories.

Shuddering, she returned to the moment to find Fallon studying her closely. She picked up her mug of tea and sipped, stalling, but her friend knew her too well.

Finally, she said, "I was reading Sir Walter Scott's epic poem about the Lady of the Lake."

"I haven't read that version of King Arthur's story in ages. Did you borrow it from here?"

Sloane glanced around the room that had reminded her of

the library scene in the live-action version of *Beauty and the Beast* when Ceri toured them through the house the first day. "Yes."

"May I see it?"

Sloane frowned. "Why?"

"Perhaps there's something about the volume that drew the goddess's attention to you as you read in the garden. After all, the Lady of the Lake's story is one of loss too," Fallon said, her tone gentle like she was trying not to upset Sloane.

When the crow interrupted the most erotic kiss she'd ever experienced in her life, she jumped away from Davy and ran inside the safe confines of the manor. Her idea had been to close herself inside her third-story guest room and stay there until her crazy attraction to the hot druid subsided—or until after the wedding, whichever. But Fallon, who had been walking up the stairs with a mug of tea in her hand, took one look at her and told her to wait right there in the foyer. Now she sat in the library— without the book in question.

Her expression must have given her away because Fallon said, "You weren't alone in the garden, were you?"

"Why would you say that?"

"Because when you rushed into the foyer, you weren't carry-ing a book."

Damn. That was easy.

Sipping her tea wouldn't give her enough time. Not that she didn't try that tactic. Fallon raised a brow and waited. Sloane glanced around the room again, caught her best friend's expres-sion, closed her eyes, and sighed.

Leaning her head back against the pillowy cushion of the tall wing-backed chair in which she sat, she blurted, "Davy."

"Why am I not surprised?" A smile colored Fallon's voice.

She sat up so fast she nearly sloshed out the tea left in the bottom of her mug. "What?"

"The man hasn't been able to take his eyes off you since we

arrived." With a smirk, she added, "And you've been having trouble keeping yours from straying to him anytime he's around."

Sloane looked away. "Whatever."

Fallon cracked up. "This is great, Sloane."

"How do you figure?"

"For the past two months, you've been grieving for a man you knew for an hour. But now you're opening yourself up to possibilities."

"How can you be so callous? That man I only 'knew for an hour' was my fated mate." She stood abruptly and walked over to the windows overlooking the car park and the grounds beyond it. In the distance, a tiny stone cottage caught her eye. As she stared at it, her back to her friend, a shiver of awareness raised goose bumps on her skin.

Fallon joined her, rubbing her hand lightly along Sloane's upper arm. "You're right. That was a terrible thing to say. I'm so sorry, doll."

Sloane nodded.

"It's only that I know you."

"I will never have what you have with Seamus, what every Sheridan in this house has with each other. Macha took that away from me." She swallowed over the lump in her throat. "I will never experience bonding with my warrior. I will never be able to help him," she whispered.

For several minutes they stared silently out the window. Instead of the cottage, she saw visions of laughter and shared purpose with a man whose face even now was fading from her memory. Yet her sorrow for a warrior she'd barely met told her their bond would have been strong.

"Perhaps that's what you're grieving, Sloane."

"*What?*"

" You dropped your shield, doll. And I'm standing right here.

And I'm your best friend." Fallon continued to rub Sloane's back, comforting her outside while eviscerating her inside.

Stepping away from her friend, she wandered the library, fingering the leather-bound spines of old books lined up on the shelves by the hundreds.

"You can't let this loss change you. Break you."

Sloane halted for a beat before continuing her aimless movement framed by shelves upon shelves of books. Books containing stories of love and loss. Stories told in ink and held captive on paper. Like hers, stories that would never change.

"Tell me. What was going through your mind while Maeve confined you to your floating prison while she tortured Seamus last summer?"

Fallon remained silent. When Sloane thought her friend wouldn't answer, she said, "You're right."

Something in Fallon's tone stopped her in her tracks.

"But you're still here. You did everything you could to save your warrior. You know that." Fallon stood before her, her hands on her hips, Sloane's diminutive auburn-haired stalwart taking up her battle stance. "Did it ever occur to you the Fates have a different plan for you?"

Sloane frowned.

"Think about it. You've never been conventional—in our world or in the civilian one. You've always opened yourself to adventure and risk-taking. You always want to try something new."

She closed her eyes, her friend's words stabbing her.

But Fallon either didn't notice or didn't care. "Seamus and I have been worried about you."

She blinked her eyes open. "A permanent choir of Macha's minions hanging around me worries me too."

"That isn't it." Fallon huffed out a breath. "You haven't even tried to be yourself. You've stayed close to home, fallen into a boring routine. You don't go to the rock gym anymore, and I know how much you love the sport."

Her face went blank as she stared at the floor.

"It was all we could do to convince you to fly to Scotland to attend our wedding." Fallon stepped into Sloane's space and glared up at her. "An event you and I have been dreaming about since we were little girls."

Sloane shrugged and returned to her chair. Taking a sip of her now cold tea, she held the mug in her hands between her knees, swirling the dregs and trying not to feel anything.

Fallon kneeled in front of her. "If you stop taking chances, stop going on adventures—stop being you—Macha wins. Can't you see that?"

Squeezing her eyes tight, she sucked in a long breath through her nose and opened her eyes to stare at where her friend's hands covered her wrists. "By definition, a risk means possible loss. I know that loss because I didn't tell Gavin about my skill before he visualized himself from my"—she cleared her throat. "Before he visualized himself from my life. Nothing about that was an adventure."

"I know. But you've been beating yourself up because you didn't tell Gavin something about your bond that could have weakened it to the point of being useless. You were bound to take a risk either way." Fallon squeezed her wrists and stood up. "Like you do every day in your finance job, you calculated the risk and understood that if you saved him that day, you could lose him forever with your weakened bond. If you let him go, there was a slim chance your Sight was imperfect, and he'd return to you."

The stern expression on her friend's face sent Sloane's heart into her stomach.

"You know I'm right, doll." She resumed her seat in the chair opposite Sloane's. "That hot druid piques your interest."

Though she said nothing, her face heated.

Fallon's expression softened. "There's no reason to feel guilty about that." She sipped her tea. "You know, Ceri says our mutual ancestor Fianna Conlan, the founder of this house, was married first to a warrior who didn't find his talisman on time—apparently I descend from that side of the family—and then she married a druid. Siobhan and Duncan have a wonderful relationship, as do my aunt and uncle. A druid and a warrior. A druid and a talisman. Both work."

"What does that have to do with me?"

It was a stupid question, and she knew it. Fallon's coy smile only reiterated that fact. Hot thoughts of Davy conjured by her friend's words caused the tattoo on her thigh to pulse pleasantly again. What was up with that?

CHAPTER TWELVE

"ARE YE CONSPIRING against the newlyweds, Hamish?" Davy asked with a laugh as he walked in on the conversation taking place around the battered kitchen table.

"Och, lad. There's nae conspiracy here. We're lookin' out fer the pair o' them." His old mentor's eyes twinkled as he saluted the other druids seated with him enjoying a mug of tea.

Davy pulled his mug from the cupboard and walked over to pour himself some steaming brew from the pot resting on a trivet in the middle of the table. "The lot of ye look a bit like a cabal. Or I know at least one warrior residing in this house who might think so."

At his oblique reference to Rio Sheridan, Davy noticed Siobhan MacManus's shoulders hunch, her fingers tightening around the mug she held in her hands. *There's a story there.* But he didn't have the chance to pursue it.

"Siobhan and I were telling Hamish about the methods Maeve employed to imprison Fallon and Seamus," Griffin Walsh explained. "Though we don't think she'll try anything during the wedding, you never know with such a mercurial and vengeful goddess as Maeve."

Davy nodded.

"We thought it best to prepare for anything rather than to react. She came far too close to taking my brother during summer solstice." Siobhan shuddered at the memory. "Join us?" She indicated the open seat beside her, and Davy sat.

"Sloane mentioned something about Maeve convincing the Morrigan tae unleash a Fomorian, one ye took on yerself, Siobhan." He raised a brow, savored a sip of Hamish's unnaturally strong tea, and waited.

"A Fomorian! The auld girl has more than a passin' interest in yer brother." Hamish's tone when he addressed Siobhan was decidedly less jovial than it had been when Davy walked into the room.

"You see now why we feel we need more protections around the manor," Griff added. "Fallon in her own right is quite a prize."

Davy rested his forearms on the battered oak table. "A bard is a once-in-a-century talisman. We certainly need tae protect her."

"And she's a package deal with a warrior coveted by a sexually voracious goddess who will obviously stop at little to possess him." Fear warred with determination in Siobhan's voice.

Across the expanse of the table, a charged look passed between the two American druids.

"Are we missin' somethin' here?" Hamish asked from his chair at the head of the table.

"Like all warrior-and-talisman pairs, Seamus and Fallon need each other to take on the more virulent deities in our pantheon," Griff began.

Siobhan continued. "Without Seamus, Fallon has only half her strength. She's unable to change the story for anyone other than Seamus right now. The stronger their bond, the stronger her storytelling skills become."

"Neither of them is home safe until the marriage rite is complete," Griff said. "Even then, they'll always be targets."

"But as long as we keep Fallon safe, she can change the story." Siobhan sighed. "Something she was unable to do for her friend at Lughnasadh."

The speculative expression on Hamish's face had Davy sitting up straight. "The twa o' them aren't the only ones sharin' somethin' special between 'em."

Another glance passed across the table before Griff spoke. "Siobhan and I were at cross-purposes, each of us putting our family member before the other's as we tried to help Seamus and Fallon."

"Brighid used a natural event to intervene," Siobhan said.

"And the twa o' ye now share common druidic traits, common knowledge, somethin' akin tae a warrior-and-talisman pair." Hamish sat back in his chair, steepling his fingers beneath his chin as he contemplated the druids in front of him.

The richness of Griff's baritone laugh resonated around the stone walls of the kitchen. "Can't imagine what gave us away."

"Certainly not our habit of finishing each other's thoughts whenever we're together." Siobhan smirked.

"The pair o' ye dae have a rather uncanny way about ye when ye're taegether." Hamish nodded then changed the subject. "At Davy's suggestion, we've already invited Brighid and Druantia tae the weddin'. O' course, with the interest I hear Scathach has in yer brother, nae doubt she'll be on hand as well."

Siobhan turned on the bench, half-facing him. "Thank you, Davy." The sincerity in her voice warmed him. "Are you still Hamish's student?"

"Aye. Though since I moved intae the cottage after Alaisdair followed his talisman tae the States, I think I'm more of his acolyte." He gave Hamish a cheeky grin.

Siobhan cocked her head.

"Or his legs when he doesnae feel like doing something strenuous, like gathering herbs from the garden."

"Doin' ye favors, lad."

Pretending to ignore the look Davy threw his way, Hamish topped off his tea, leaned back in his chair, took a sip, and closed his eyes. Davy wasn't fooled. He'd seen the old man's lips twitch before he'd hidden his mirth behind his elaborate tea-taking.

"Layers," he and Hamish said simultaneously. Then both burst into gales of laughter.

Griff and Siobhan joined them. At last when everyone managed to regain control, Griff said, "It appears we aren't the only druids with a strong attachment to each other. I think that bodes well for the rituals we need to practice in the coming days."

"Aye, Griff, it will." His eyes dancing, Hamish addressed Davy. "Ye willnae mind takin' our guests out tae the woods tae gather rowan branches this afternoon, will ye lad?"

Davy grinned before giving Griff and Siobhan a conspiratorial glance. "See what I mean? Now the auld man's made the two of ye his legs tae."

⁓

As the three of them finished gathering rowan branches from the woods on the manor grounds, Davy debated with himself. At last he gave in and asked the question that had bothered him since Sloane brought it up in the garden the previous afternoon.

"Ceri told me a little about Sloane losing her warrior at Lughnasadh. Taeday as we planned our ritual strategy fer the wedding, ye mentioned something about how Fallon could have changed events of that day if she'd been in full control of her powers." His wicker basket nearly full of rowan branches, he rested it on his hip and addressed Griff. "What did ye mean?"

"Macha reminded all of us that Lughnasadh doesn't belong exclusively to Lugh. It's one of her feast days too, and she demanded a sacrifice." Griff cut another branch and added it to his basket. "Demanding that sacrifice of Sloane was calculated and cruel."

Davy worked at finding his customary patience as Griff silently continued his task. It wouldn't do to let on how desperately he wanted—needed—to know more about Sloane. Somehow, the woman had sneaked under his skin. Judging from her response to his kisses when they'd been alone together, he'd found a way under hers too. Then she'd run from him like the devil himself gave chase, and he hadn't seen her since—a situation needing a remedy sooner rather than later.

Griff interrupted his thoughts. "Sloane has known her skill for years."

"*What?*" Davy cried. "How can that be? Discovering a talisman's skill is part of bonding with her warrior. From what Ceri said, Macha denied Sloane and her warrior the experience."

"Think about the specialties of the deities in the pantheon. For example, Macha is not only a goddess of war."

He couldn't help it. His mouth turned down as he said, "She's also a fertility goddess who can be vengeful with whom she gives fertility—and from whom she takes it away."

Griff pulled a bandana from his pocket and wiped sweat from his brow. Davy, being used to gathering rowan branches, hadn't broken a sweat at all from the exertion. Thoughts of Sloane MacIntosh were what had him hot and bothered.

Griff folded the cloth and returned it to his pocket. "Macha is also the goddess of seers."

"Which means she might have a clue about who in the warrior population possesses that particular skill." Siobhan finished Griff's explanation as she joined them. She rubbed the sleeve of her sweatshirt over her brow and sighed. "Collecting rowan branches is hard work. I think I like it better that we can order them delivered for when we need them back home."

Davy nearly dropped his basket of branches. "Ye're saying Sloane is a seer?"

"Yes," Griff and Siobhan said together.

Davy grinned. "You two really are connected." Then he sobered. "She saw the fate of her warrior, didn't she? Macha exacted that cruelty on the lass."

"Having a bard and a seer who are such close friends concentrates a great deal of power among our kind. If the two of them are bonded to their warriors, their individual and collective power increases exponentially," Griff explained.

Davy nodded.

"When Macha stole Sloane's warrior before the two of them had a chance to bond, she insured the loss of some of that power," Siobhan said. "And she was callous and vicious about it." The tone of her voice tugged at Davy's heart.

"What dae ye mean?" He girded himself for her answer, knowing instinctively it would gut him.

"She set Gavin up. Sloane knew it and tried to warn him, but like every warrior I know, he couldn't resist the chance to battle the bad guys, best the rogues harming civilians." Siobhan blew out an exasperated breath. "The odds were three to one, which normally, Gavin could have probably handled, considering he had access to training the rogues didn't. But they weren't alone."

She looked to Griff who continued the story. "Gavin was one of my university students. I'd brought him and a couple of other unattached warriors to Fallon and Seamus's Lughnasadh celebration on the off-chance there might be an unattached talisman or two there."

Siobhan rolled her eyes, and Griff shrugged, a tiny smirk tugging at his mouth. "Everyone at the party caught on when Gavin discovered his connection to Sloane."

Inside himself, Davy had to stomp down his jealousy of a

dead man as he watched Siobhan and Griff smile at each other at the memory.

A shadow passed over Griff's face. "They left the party to do what warriors and talismans are expected to do. The rest of us stayed behind, enjoying the beautiful evening, the warriors teasingly speculating about Gavin's first night with Sloane."

"You mean lewdly speculating," Siobhan broke in.

"As you said, Siobhan, they're warriors." Griff cleared his throat to finish the story. "About an hour later, the party ended. When we walked out of Fallon and Seamus's backyard, we discovered Sloane slumped in her car parked across the street from their house. Macha arrived to taunt Sloane with Gavin's death. Macha was the rogue warriors' secret weapon." He stared unseeing into the distance. "Gavin didn't stand a chance."

Davy's heart broke for the beautiful talisman. *Sloane knew what was going to happen but remained powerless to stop it. Macha made her watch. Jesus. No wonder the lass turned skittish when crows clamored near her.*

"Bloody hell." He didn't even try to hide his disgust for so vindictive a deity as Macha. "Nae wonder she freaked out in the woods the other day. A murder of crows descending out of nowhere is an omen that strikes fear intae anyone possessin' half a brain." Glancing from one nodding druid to the other, he added, "But Sloane knows firsthand the loss such a visitation can mean, poor lass."

"It's good you can sympathize with her, Davy," Griff said offhandedly.

Davy blinked at him. "What the hell dae ye mean by that?"

"Understanding where she's coming from will make things easier for you." Siobhan didn't look directly at him, but he heard the smile in her voice all the same.

"I donnae know what the two o' ye think ye're on about, but—"

Siobhan sidled up beside Griff and nudged him. "Have you noticed how Davy's Scots is more pronounced when he's riled up?"

Griff winked at her.

Davy threw his hands up. "Are we done here?" He hitched his basket of rowan branches up to his shoulder and headed back towards the manor, his thoughts tumbling and swirling around in his head.

Siobhan and Griff's laughter followed him as he marched smartly ahead of them out of the woods. Apparently, he hadn't been as smooth as he thought he'd been, dammit. But as he strode through the clearing abutting the manor gardens, one thought rose above all the others crashing through his mind: his American counterparts approved of his interest in Sloane MacIntosh. Of course, both of them being married to members of the warrior race might have colored their opinions, not that he was asking for permission to pursue the woman or anything.

She was only going to be in his life for a fortnight. Something that would have been easier to deal with if he didn't know how good—how perfect—she felt in his arms. If he didn't know how his body reacted to her kiss. If he didn't know his interest in her was reciprocated no matter how well the lady in question had avoided him for the last day and a half.

As he let himself into the back door of the manor, he decided Sloane had been without his company for long enough.

CHAPTER THIRTEEN

HOLIDAY ATTITUDE INFUSED the trip to the training room. After several days of sightseeing around Ullapool and some additional wedding preparations in the form of decorating and performing rituals, it seemed the warriors needed to let off steam. What better way to do that than to beat each other up in the guise of sparring?

On the drive to the docks in Ullapool, Sloane heard more than one hissed admonishment from a talisman to her warrior to see to it he kept his face pretty for the wedding photos. She smiled in spite of herself. Although she would never share this experience firsthand, she could admit she liked being around her friends and sharing in their happiness. Perhaps she'd started to relax into her vacation. Perhaps it was the way everyone included her as though she were an unattached talisman rather than a widowed one. Perhaps it was the way a certain druid looked at her—and he had no shame about it either.

Said druid had gone ahead of the group to ready the small boats that would motor the party across the lake. Their destination, the trailhead, would be the starting point for their hike to the training room. As Hamish had explained to those who had never been there before, ancient Celts had carved the training room into the bowels of *An Teallach*, the towering *ben* across Loch Broom from Ullapool. Sloane rather liked the Scots way of delineating a mountain in a chain as opposed to a *munro*, which was a mountain that stood aloof from others. Or maybe she just liked the way the words sounded with a Scottish burr.

The vans were considerably less crowded than any other time so far when the group had traveled together. Several members of the clan had chosen to visualize themselves to the training room rather than make the trip the civilian way. Since Seamus and Fallon, Griff and Keela, Siobhan and Duncan, and Sloane herself had never seen this particular training room, they required the longer trip. The hosts of their party, Ceri and Rio, accompanied them as did Hamish who said he preferred to travel the civilian way when the weather was as fine as this sunny late-summer afternoon. As they all knew from their training growing up, some dicey—or downright terrifying—things could happen if one attempted to visualize herself to a place she'd never seen before. From Ceri's descriptions of the place, Sloane couldn't wait to see where the local warriors and talismans practiced for the battles they hoped to avoid but always knew would come.

When she stepped out of the van, she caught sight of Davy waiting for them on the docks. She knew when he saw her because he turned up his smile to a thousand watts, deepening those maddeningly gorgeous dimples from hot to panty-melting. Oh, yeah, the man was aware of how his smiles affected her. The-too-sexy-for-her-own-good jerk. Still, she pretended not to notice him as she deliberately walked toward the boat, which Hamish had nimbly dropped himself into.

Before she could make a move to join him, Hamish addressed Seamus. "Hand me that polystyrene box if ye would please, lad." He glanced at the large cooler in Seamus's hands. "If it's all the same tae ye, I'd like the Walshes and the Lochlanns tae join me in this boat."

Sloane had just lifted her foot to step into the boat when Hamish spoke. Windmilling her arms in a desperate attempt to keep her balance, she surely would have landed in the drink if a pair of strong arms hadn't wrapped around her.

"Whoa, lass. I've got ye." Laughter edged Davy's voice as he spoke into her ear.

Air backed up in her throat as sensations flooded her body, tiny electric shocks everywhere her back touched Davy's front. Through layers of clothes no less. *Dammit.* Why did she have to be so aware of this man?

Realizing he still held her, and she'd not done one thing about it, she pushed at his hands. "You can let me go. I'm fine."

Davy chuckled. "Ye're welcome."

She gifted him with an eye roll and walked over to the other boat. From her seated position beside her husband on the bench in the boat, Siobhan grinned up at Sloane, an expression of pure mischief. Blessedly, she didn't say anything as Sloane clambered aboard and took the seat on the other side of Duncan Mac-Manus in the middle of the boat. From the corner of her eye, she caught the conspiratorial wink he gave his wife and sighed. The afternoon looked to be shaping itself into an exercise of her patience—and her sanity.

Davy took his place on the bench in front of the motor. The boats were open-seated skiffs, perfect for a quick sightseeing trip on the loch or for a day of fishing it. Or in today's case, quick transportation over the water to the base of the mountain and their destination.

Before he fired up the motor, Davy said, "Ye better hold on."

Something in his voice turned Sloane's head, and then she wished she'd kept her eyes trained forward. Davy gifted her with another of his heart-racing grins and a mischievous waggle of his brows before he flipped a switch, and the boat's motor roared to life. Expertly, he angled the boat to launch them straight out into the loch before he throttled up the motor and raced them across the water. Sloane white-knuckled the gunwale with her right hand and the seat between Duncan and her with her left hand. All the while, she heard Davy's joyous laughter as they raced Hamish's boat across the smooth surface of the loch.

His laughter made a home for itself in her chest. It seemed Davy Sutherland was a man after her own heart in the sense of loving an adventure, though he wasn't actually after her heart, was he? Of course not.

After Macha's obnoxious reminder in the garden the other day, Sloane had managed to avoid Davy Sutherland for an entire day and a half. Not that he'd ever strayed from her thoughts. Dammit. His kisses really should have come with a warning label: caution, will render a woman a quivering puddle of need with one touch. More than one will cause power outages in her brain.

She couldn't develop feelings for this man—or for any man. Doing so put the man in question in danger of losing his life to a vengeful goddess bent on destroying Sloane's happiness. She still couldn't understand why she'd become the goddess's target. After all, she wasn't remotely related to either the Sheridans or the Conlans. The sobering thought almost stole the fun from the boat race in which she played an unwitting participant.

Appearing out of nowhere, a pod of porpoises joined the party, racing beside and ahead of the skiff and jolting her out of her morose thoughts. Sloane laughed and leaned closer to the gunwale to watch the animals cavort with the boats. Everywhere, it seemed, porpoises skimmed the water right below the surface or cleared it entirely, giving them an advantage in the race.

The wind whipped her hair back and plastered her jacket to her chest. Salt spray drenched her hand where she grasped the side of the boat. Beside her, Duncan and Siobhan smiled and laughed, sharing her delight in their outing and the unexpected mammalian armada guiding them across the loch. Looking over her shoulder at Hamish's boat running slightly behind them, she saw Fallon waving toward her and gesturing at the porpoises playing beside them. She shot her friend a thumbs-up and grinned before returning her attention to the show going on in the water.

When they'd eyed the mountain from the car park at the dock, Sloane had thought the trip across the loch would take at least half an hour. But between racing Hamish's skiff and enjoying the antics of their sleek aquatic companions, it seemed they'd barely boarded before Davy was powering down the motor and guiding them into the docks at the base of *An Teallach*. Like one long-practiced at mooring a boat, Davy hopped out, tied off the skiff, and reached down to help her out. Knowing what she did about herself and her special skill, she eyed his outstretched hand with trepidation.

Behind her, Duncan whispered, "Arm clasp."

Nodding at him in acknowledgment and gratitude, she reached up and clasped Davy's elbow, giving him no choice but to clasp hers to haul her up out of the boat. He furrowed his brow at her for a second before something like understanding flashed in his amber eyes, and then it was gone. Did he feel the same electric zing she did where her forearm pressed against his?

"Did ye enjoy the ride, lass?"

"Yeah, it was fun. Do you always have such an exuberant group to play with when you make the trip?"

He grinned. "Nae doubt that lot was hoping fer us tae toss some bait overboard."

Fallon ran up to her, wrapping her in a hug from behind. "What a rush! Wasn't that great, Sloane?"

"Loved it," she said, turning to her friend.

Seamus strolled up behind his fiancée. "Your boat cheated," he grumped as he joined them.

"How do you figure?" Duncan asked, his arm slung over his wife's shoulders as he smirked at his brother-in-law.

"Your boat wasn't as full."

"Maybe you should have hopped out and caught a ride on one of those porpoises, lightened the load," Duncan deadpanned.

"That's a rodeo I'd pay good money to watch," Rio said with a chuckle as he and Ceri joined them.

Seamus snorted, but Sloane thought she saw the shadow of a grin playing over his mouth.

Dragging the cooler on its little wheels behind him, Hamish stopped beside them. "I trust one or twa o' ye strong lads will be happy tae carry the polystyrene box o' snacks up the mountain."

"Got it," Rio said, hefting the loaded cooler onto his shoulder like it weighed nothing.

Sloane lifted a brow in Fallon's direction.

"Ceri is a lucky woman to have a warrior that strong," she communicated to her friend.

"From what I hear, Rio's the lucky one." Fallon gave her an impish grin and grabbed Seamus's hand.

When Hamish saw that Griff and Keela had finished taking photos of the loch on their phones, he said, "Looks like we're ready tae go. Davy, would ye take the lead?"

Davy nodded at Hamish and turned to Sloane. "Looks like we're setting the pace, lass."

"Wait, what?"

He didn't give her any chance to protest as he linked arms with her and started walking down the dock toward a trail that rose vertically up the mountain from the edge of the water. For some reason, he was determined to spend time with her. Fearing the goddess's determination to harm those Sloane cared about, she glanced around. But there wasn't a bird in sight. The bright sunny day demanded she enjoy it. So with a tiny grin tugging the corner of her mouth, she nodded and fell into step with a dangerous man.

Chapter Fourteen

THE TRAINING ROOM was less elaborate than Sloane had expected. Considering its age and the hundreds—or more like thousands—of warriors who'd used it over the centuries, she'd thought they would have embellished it more. The paintings of ancient heroes adorning the rough-hewn stone walls had been rendered with great skill and artistry, no doubt. But there wasn't much in the way of amenities. A tiny bathroom with a sink and toilet had been added near the entrance during the previous century, and track lights tripped by motion sensors lit the long hallway and the training room itself. Otherwise, the space was empty. Vast and empty. It seemed to be the hollow center of the mountain itself.

Granted, she hadn't had much experience with using training rooms. When she was growing up, all of her talisman training had taken place in a fortified bunker dug into the hill behind her parents' house. The only other training room she'd ever seen had been constructed by the Sheridan clan inside a mountain bordering Flathead Lake back home in Montana. The elaborate Celtic knotwork tiled into the floor and painted on the walls and ceiling of that room had given her the impression all training rooms were highly decorated. Guess she needed to adjust her expectations.

Exchanging a glance with Fallon, she communicated, *"Not exactly what I thought it'd be."*

"I know. Impressive though, considering the ancients hollowed it out with pickaxes and shovels."

Sloane nodded and wandered around to admire the paintings of King Arthur taking on a mountain dragon in France, Tristan besting the *Morhaus*, and Cuchulain defeating *Ysbaddaden* among the heroic events depicted on the walls. Meanwhile, all the warriors, and, interestingly, Davy Sutherland limbered up like a team of athletes readying themselves for a big game. From the corner of her eye, she saw the other talismans stretching as well. She hugged her arms around herself as a wave of sadness washed over her. Her skills wouldn't be put to the test today.

Being without a warrior meant she wouldn't be participating in the training. Deciding she had no business wallowing in self-pity in this place, she walked over to where Hamish busied himself setting out drinks and snacks on a table tucked up against the wall a few meters from the entrance tunnel.

"What can I do to help?"

"Ah, lassie. Ye can arrange the snacks on the table. Thank ye kindly."

She appreciated how Hamish didn't treat her as a casualty. Though she knew her friends were well-meaning, sometimes, she wanted to try to remember who she'd been before she'd lost her chance at happiness, something days like today made especially trying.

Then there was Davy. The man had kept up a steady banter the entire climb to the halfway point on the mountain where the hidden door leading to the entrance to the training room was located. He'd told her about the sorcerer Mathgen who helped the *Tuatha dè Danaan* against the Fomorians by shaking the mountain summits so hard it seemed even the mountains were at war with the Fomorians. Apparently, her revelation about Morgan calling up a Fomorian against Seamus and Fallon still weighed on his mind.

The climb left her winded, but he hadn't been fazed at all. He'd talked nearly every step of the way. As she thought about it, she could only marvel at Davy's fitness. Which was another reason to keep her distance. Though his clothes hid his physique, she'd had her hands on his arms and shoulders and chest and had an idea he'd steal her breath if she ever saw him naked.

Where the hell did that come from?

The clanging of claymores jolted her from her wayward thoughts. Her heart hammering in her chest, she spun around to see all the warriors paired off and sparring with their swords. Not one of them wore his protective leathers, which she still found strange. When she'd actually trained with these people back home, Sian Sheridan explained that the idea was to perfect moves, not draw blood. Practicing without their leathers kept the warriors honest and forced them to concentrate on their moves rather than rely on brute strength and the opponent's reaction to injury.

Her head tilted to one side, she crossed her arms and leaned against the wall beside the table to study the men as they practiced. The intricate dance of battle mesmerized her. The athletic footwork, the leaping and hurdling of opponents to land behind them to deal a deadly blow, the pirouetting and rolling and somersaulting to avoid such a blow, the thrusting and parrying of the impossibly long blades of the claymores riveted her. The grunts and shouts, trash-talking and congratulations left her by turns covering her eyes with her hands or chuckling or cheering the men on.

As the training progressed, despite how hard she tried to pry them away, her eyes wouldn't stray from Davy. No matter which warrior he took on, be it Alaisdair, Seamus, or Duncan, the Sheridan patriarch Owen, his eldest son Rowan, or the other twin Riley, he held his own and often bested his opponent. He'd long since shed his sweater, and the dark green T-shirt he wore beneath it clung to his sweaty torso, showing off the sculpted muscles of his shoulders, pecs, biceps, and abs. It was all she could do to keep herself from drooling over the man.

It seemed some sort of tournament had taken place with sparring with Rio as the prize. To Sloane's utter shock, Davy was the last man standing. A druid. *How could that be?* Then the two of them began to battle, and Rio's superior skills shone in the velocity of his flashing blade and the grace of his body as he bent time and space to move at ludicrous speed around Davy. Yet Davy showed no sign of fear or intimidation. Instead, a single-minded determination fiercened his features, rendering him even more handsome in Sloane's eyes.

Davy moved with an elegant, muscle-defining economy that made Sloane's heart race. Using the heel of her hand, she tried to calm the throbbing of the tattoo on her upper thigh, a throbbing her core echoed and reechoed. As the bout gained momentum, she feared she might orgasm in front of everyone as she watched Davy's incredible display of skill, strength, and strategy. The man called to her on every level. The more she watched him move, countering Rio's assaults, tactically initiating his own, recovering at lightspeed when he erred or when Rio's superior skill bested him for a second, the more she wanted him.

No doubt Rio was a warrior master, living up to his reputation as the best warrior of the age. Yet Davy never once wavered, never weakened. His courage reached inside Sloane's chest and squeezed her heart.

As the two continued to spar, it seemed Rio toyed with his opponent. Right when it looked like Davy might land a devastating blow, Rio executed a move Sloane would never have believed humanly possible—even after seeing it, she still wasn't sure Rio had achieved it—and Davy lay in the middle of the floor on his back.

Without thinking, Sloane raced to him, dropping to her knees on the floor by his side.

"Davy, are you all right?" Tentatively, she placed her hand on his bicep and gave him a tiny shake.

In a rush, he came to and boiled up off the floor, immediately balanced in his battle stance, his two-handed hold on his claymore in front of him. Then the wild look in his eyes cleared, and he focused on her where she sat sprawled on her ass on the floor.

"Sloane?"

Gracelessly, she dragged herself to her feet. "Sorry. I thought you were hurt."

He pulled his sword down and rested his head on the tops of his hands clasped over the hilt. His labored breathing alarmed her, but a slow clap from the warriors encircling them crescendoed into enthusiastic applause, drowning out the sound of Davy's labored breath. Like a swimmer slowly surfacing from a deep dive, Sloane came out of the trance into which she'd fallen as she'd witnessed Davy preparing for battle like a warrior. Embarrassed, she tried to step out of the center of attention, but Davy's hand shot out, snaring her. His calloused fingers lightly circled her wrist with enough pressure to stop her in her tracks. "Lass."

She sensed more than heard him rumble out the word. Butterflies started practicing gymnastics in her belly while goose bumps pebbled her skin from her hairline to the soles of her feet. And that tat she'd just had to have inked on her skin last summer? That was doing some sort of electric slide that shot sparks straight through her clit and deep into her core. Involuntarily, she gasped, and Davy's head shot up, his amber eyes blazing into hers like he knew exactly what was happening inside her.

Before she could make sense of anything going on around

her and through her, Hamish came to the rescue. Stepping out of the circle, he said, "That was some show the twa o' ye put on, lads. If the nasty auld girls want tae bother our festivities in a few days, they might be surprised at how much force this small band o' brothers presents."

Hamish's chortle broke the spell Davy's battle prowess, his touch, and his voice wove over her, and Sloane gently extracted herself from his hold. He signaled his reluctance to let her go in the way his eyes never left hers. Sparks of awareness tightened her skin, and she gritted her teeth to stop herself from moaning at the loss of his touch. At last, she looked away, avoiding the risk of letting him see something she herself had yet to process.

Stepping between Fallon and Seamus, she made her way to the table where she and Hamish had set out the food and drink warriors and talismans needed in order to refuel following such an intense training session. Though talismans practiced their skills telepathically, their expended energy rivaled the warriors' exacting physical training. Sloane needed a different kind of breather, one that allowed her to figure out exactly what had happened to her as she'd watched Davy train with—and best—warriors of superior strength and skill. Obviously, the man was no ordinary druid.

"The lad surprised the hell out of me tae, Sloane," Alaisdair said as he walked up behind her.

Lost in her thoughts, she jumped and tried to cover her reaction. "I'm sorry. Were you speaking to me?"

Her cheeks heated as she caught the teasing grin on Alaisdair's face. Clenching her jaw to keep from saying anything even more inane, she looked back at the table. Sucking a breath in through her nose, she counted to ten in her head and let the air out. "When Hamish and I started unloading the cooler," she said, "I had no idea the kind of goodies he'd packed in there. Beef sandwiches, little cakes, smoked salmon…"

Alaisdair cleared his throat, interrupting her. "It's all right, lass. I've seen the way he looks at ye, tae." He reached around her to grab a bottled water and downed it in one long drink. Swiping the back of his hand across his beard, he dried himself and grinned at her again. "Davy started trainin' with me when he was a lad of fourteen. But training with Rio over this last year has certainly accelerated his skills. If one dinnae know better, he'd think the lad was a warrior rather than a druid." He tilted his head. "Which he is."

"I'm sure I have no idea why you're telling me this."

"Of course, ye dinnae." Alaisdair shrugged nonchalantly, his tone mocking her. "Ye're young and beautiful and—through no fault o' yer own"—he stared her down—"ye're free tae pursue happiness wherever ye find it. Ye could dae worse than my friend Davy Sutherland."

On that note, he walked away from her to rejoin his wife Shanley, who, judging from her hand gestures, was in serious conversation with Ceri Sheridan. Once again, Sloane's eyes wandered in the direction of a certain druid who fielded congratulations and admiration from the other warriors for his battle readiness. He nodded politely, grinned at something Riley said, and glanced up to lock eyes with her. The intensity of his stare demanded she open her shield to him, hear what he wanted to communicate to her.

But she couldn't. Not here. Not with an audience.

Fortunately, Fallon chose that moment to step between them, breaking the hold Davy had on her.

"Seamus says Siobhan often works out with a claymore, even sparring with her husband occasionally." She glanced over her shoulder toward where Davy stood among the warriors. "But I don't think she can battle like that. I don't think Uncle Griff can battle like that. Seamus even resorted to telling me off when he sparred with Davy because I lost my concentration on Seamus's story." The expression of admiration on her face echoed her words. "I liked him from the moment we met him, but after seeing that…" She reached out and rubbed Sloane's arm. "Don't walk away from that man's interest in you," she whispered. "It would be a mistake."

Sloane blinked at her friend's cryptic words, but before she could ask what Fallon was on about, the warriors descended on them en masse. Their congratulations to each other out of the way, they needed sustenance. Mere seconds later, nothing remained of any of the food and drink she and Hamish had spent at least fifteen minutes retrieving from the cooler.

Their training for the day complete, the warriors and talismans disbanded. Ceri and Rio decided to visualize themselves back to the manor to prepare the evening meal while Rowan and Alyssa elected to take the physical journey on the return trip. Having lost the final battle with Rio, Davy was relegated to carrying the now empty cooler back down the mountain, for which he received plenty of good-natured ribbing. After making a big show of hoisting the thing onto his shoulder, much to everyone's delight, he led them out of the training room and back down the mountain.

Deliberately, Sloane held back. Somehow, she'd developed feelings for this man…after she'd sworn off feelings for any man. Yet as she watched his easy athletic gait descending the trail and heard his laughter carried back to her on the breeze, she couldn't help herself. Davy Sutherland made her feel all the feels. The revelation gave her no comfort.

Chapter Fifteen

STANDING IN THE shower stall that accommodated the breadth of his shoulders by a mere inch on either side, Davy let the hot water splash over his neck and back, easing the stiffness of muscles that had endured the mother of all workouts. He'd known, of course, the American warriors would test him, Rio Sheridan most of all. As usual. What he hadn't counted on was how much he'd wanted to impress a certain unattached talisman whose violet eyes darkened to midnight blue as she'd watched him spar.

The entire afternoon, he'd remained hyperaware of the beautiful Sloane MacIntosh. He'd heard every gasp as he sustained a blow, every sigh as he'd landed one, or even better—when he'd perfectly executed one of the moves Alaisdair had taught him over the course of half his life. Whenever he chanced a glance in her direction, he discovered to his great satisfaction that her eyes never left him. Those gasps and sighs had been all for him.

As steam rose around him, his smile sagged into a scowl. Of course, just when Davy had been about to outmaneuver him, Rio performed his signature move, the one Scathach, his patron goddess, had demanded he perfect.

The one that landed Davy on his arse—again. In front of all the other warriors and talismans. In front of Sloane.

Like always, the hard landing made him see stars. But he must have been out for longer than usual because while he lay inert in the middle of the floor in the training room, Macha visited him in a dream. At least he hoped it was a dream and not an omen. Baring her teeth, she showed him scenes of battle, scenes of death. But she withheld the faces of the dead. Then a searing pain shot through the tattoo on his bicep, and he came awake in a rush. When his vision cleared, Sloane sat on the floor at his feet, her legs sprawled out in front of her as she shook her head and tried to apologize to him. Which made no sense. Neither did the fact that he gripped his claymore in his hands, ready to take on the goddess or whatever minion she'd sent against him.

Afterward, Sloane had avoided him. She'd been smooth about it, conversing with Alaisdair and Fallon after the team called it a day, holding back to walk with Alyssa as the group hiked down the mountain to the skiffs waiting for them on the loch. Seeming so engrossed in the conversation that she bypassed him to ride with Alyssa and Rowan Sheridan and Keela and Griffin Walsh in Hamish's boat. Not once had she glanced his way on the return trip to Ullapool. Then she slipped into a seat in the back of Hamish's van for the ride to the manor where she disappeared inside before he could scramble out of the van he'd driven.

In the training room, he'd seen the admiration—and desire— in the depths of her arresting eyes as she watched him spar with the warriors. He'd also seen fear when the warriors encircled them, applauding his prowess in taking on Rio. Had she somehow breached his shield while he'd been out cold? Seen the dream Macha sent? Or did she fear *him*? He rolled his shoulders and tried not to think that way. Yet she'd gone out of her way to avoid him after he lost his match with Rio.

"Shite!" he growled as he whacked his elbow on the side of

the shower stall when he raised his arm to shampoo the sweat from his hair. While he appreciated the incredible amount of work it had taken Alaisdair to build the indoor facilities in the cottage, for the hundredth time, he wished the man had chosen to use the large pantry in the kitchen rather than the hall closet. It'd be nice for once to shower in a space where he didn't have to fear an injury every time he slightly shifted his position to wash. Then again, it certainly beat a bucket bath in the old outdoor privy.

The savory smells of beef stew greeted his nostrils when he entered the manor kitchen twenty minutes later. Rio and Ceri stood in front of the AGA laughing while they worked together to season the dinner cooking in a huge stockpot on top of it. Beneath the aroma of meat, onions, and celery, he could detect the yeasty yumminess of baking bread, and his stomach rumbled, loudly.

"Sorry, Davy. Dinner won't be ready for at least an hour," Ceri said. "But if you hurry, there may be sliced sausages, cheese, and crackers left in the salon."

"Thanks, Ceri."

He nodded at Rio who stared blandly back at him.

As he headed up the stairs to the ground floor, he nearly missed a step when Rio's hand landed heavily on his shoulder. *How does the man move so damn fast?* Even for a warrior, Rio's speed was impressive.

"You deserved all the accolades you got in the training room today."

Davy blinked. In the year since he'd met Rio Sheridan, not once had the man given him anything but grief.

"No doubt you were trying to impress a certain talisman," he said with an edge to his voice. "But your battle skills today would probably even grab Scathach's attention. Nice job." He stuck out his hand, and Davy shook it.

"Are we friends, then?"

"Depends. What are your intentions with her?"

Davy quirked a brow. "She has nae warrior."

"So?"

"Makes her fair game. Fer a widowed warrior—or an unattached druid."

He didn't wait for Rio's response. Taking the stairs two at a time, he made his way to the salon where he found Hamish and Alaisdair standing in front of the fireplace and enjoying a dram of whisky, while on the sofa facing the windows overlooking the gardens, Shanley and Keela visited over cups of tea. Griffin busied himself loading a small plate with food at the sideboard while Duncan and Siobhan waited their turn behind him. Davy sighed. Sloane was nowhere in sight.

"That was some clinic you put on this afternoon," Duncan said as Davy stepped into line behind him.

"I gather druids donnae train the same way in America as we dae over here."

"We train with weapons. I often train with Duncan," Siobhan said. "But I've never seen a druid who can fight like a warrior. Not the way you can."

The admiration in her voice warmed a smile from him. "I was fourteen when I apprenticed tae Hamish. He thought I had a bit tae much energy and set Alaisdair the task of containing it. We spent a deal of time taegether in the training room."

"It appears you've surpassed your teacher." Duncan smirked. "And maybe one or two others of us as well."

Davy shrugged. "Rio needs a sparring partner. I happen tae be available."

His plate full of snacks, Griff stopped in front of them. "From what I saw today, there's more to you than sparring with Rio can explain."

Davy said nothing.

A smile ghosted Griff's mouth, but he walked away to join his wife and Shanley.

When it was his turn, he piled his plate with white cheddar cheese, venison sausages, and some of the homemade crackers Hamish purchased from a baker in town. Dinner might be soon, but he was starving. This little snack would take the edge off for the next five minutes—maybe. As he walked over to join Hamish and Alaisdair, he built a little sandwich and popped the whole thing into his mouth.

The air in the room shifted. He didn't have to turn around to know Sloane had found her way into the salon. It was all he could do to stop himself from executing a one-eighty, marching right up to her, and demanding an answer for why she'd withdrawn from him so completely at the end of the afternoon. Hamish must have understood his thoughts. His eyes twinkled even as he gave a subtle shake of his snowy-white head.

After chewing and swallowing the bite of cheese, meat, and crackers, he cleared his throat and addressed the old druid. "I dinnae notice a tray of drams on the sideboard. Wonder where the two of ye found yers."

Hamish chuckled. "Ye're not yer usual observant self taeday, son." He nodded in the direction of the coffee table flanked by the two sofas near the front of the fireplace. "O' course, that's tae be expected under the circumstances."

Davy followed Hamish's gesture to discover a tray of poured drams of whisky, the flames of the fire winking off the cut glass of an opened bottle resting on the low table.

Deciding the best course of action was not to take Hamish's bait, he stuffed another cracker sandwich into his mouth.

Hamish and Alaisdair burst into gales of laughter, while Davy tried not to choke on his own stupidity. He should have known there was no way the two of them were going to leave him in peace with Sloane in the room. Still, he would have appreciated a little loyalty for all those years they'd shared as three bachelors rattling around together in this old pile of rocks.

Hamish slapped him on the back while Alaisdair stepped over to the table and poured himself another dram before grabbing one for Davy. Without waiting for whatever asinine toast Alaisdair planned, Davy downed his dram in a breath, the fiery liquid momentarily smoothing away both his snack and his annoyance with his friends. Then he glanced up and locked eyes with the woman who became more beautiful each time he saw her.

"Can't blame ye fer havin' an interest in that one." Alaisdair sipped his whisky. "But after watching his little demonstration this afternoon, it's clear Rio isnae completely on board with the intermingling of the races in our community."

"The lad will come around. Dinnae ye worry," Hamish said.

"Ye've been workin' on his dinner fer nearly a year, Hamish," Alaisdair began.

"Davy's been sparrin' with him fer most o' that time tae. And Ceri's been educatin' him from the histories o' this clan as the twa o' them have made themselves at home in the manor's library." Hamish helped himself to another dram. "He's stubborn in his prejudices, I'll grant him that. But he'll come around fully. After the baby comes."

"*What?*" Alaisdair's shout silenced the other conversations going on in the room.

Hamish placidly sipped his dram. "They'll announce it when the time is right," he said in an undertone. "Sloane, lass. Thank ye fer yer help taeday."

Like the rest of the guests following Alaisdair's outburst, Sloane stared in their direction. Though he hadn't overtly been watching her, Davy kept her in his peripheral vision as she'd talked quietly with Fallon near the sideboard. Hamish, may the goddess bless him, gave him a reason to stare back at her.

"You're welcome."

A tiny smile played over her lips, drawing Davy's eyes from the mesmerizing violet depths of hers. Vividly, he remembered exactly the softness of those lips beneath his own. More than anything, he wanted to touch her lips with his again. Like a dream, the rest of the room and everyone in it soft-focused, dropping away at the edge of his vision. Sloane stood out in sharp relief. Her raven-colored hair fell in shiny waves over her shoulders and curled over her round breasts. A bright green turtleneck sweater hugged her body, molding over her perfect chest and clinging to her taut belly before disappearing beneath the waistband of her black skinny jeans. He couldn't help but appreciate the flare of her hips and the wonder of her long, long legs. Truly, the gods had created a work of art when they made Sloane MacIntosh.

From some great distance, or right at his shoulder, the sound of a throat clearing jolted him from his blatant perusal of the beautiful talisman. Hamish thought Davy's attention needed to be elsewhere.

"That was a quite a session today," Griffin was saying. "Next time, Keela can work with you, Sloane, on ways you can aid warriors in battle."

Someone not watching her as closely as he might have missed the shiver that stole over her at Griff's words. Fear flashed in her eyes before she composed herself. Her entire reaction lasted a nanosecond, yet Davy saw it all. For some reason, Sloane's skill scared the hell out of her. Someone so beautiful and intelligent, someone whose friends loved her as much as this lot obviously loved her, should never live in fear. Seeing that fear made him want to wrap her tight in his arms, reassure her, hold her safe.

"If you ask them, my parents will tell you that I was a bit of a handful when I was growing up." She side-eyed Fallon who gave a snort at her words before continuing. "Recent events have left me more"—she searched for the word—"circumspect. For now, it might be wise to confine my training to maintaining a strong shield and mastering visualization."

"Perhaps."

Davy homed in on Griff's voice. Something in the tone told him he should find an opportunity to get the American druid alone, discover what he knew or suspected about Sloane's background.

Ceri's tinkling laughter preceded her into the room, interrupting the tension Griffin's suggestion had engendered. "If you all haven't imbibed too much of Hamish's 'water of life'"—she hooked her fingers in the air—"Rio could use some help setting the table and bringing dinner up from the kitchen." She glanced around at the assembly. "Translation—the girls and I will enjoy another few minutes visiting here in the salon while you guys help Rio serve us dinner."

Rowan, who had been lounging a hip against the back of the sofa after he'd entered the room a few minutes before Ceri, nearly choked on his dram of whisky. After clearing his throat, he said, "Why, exactly, are the men serving the women dinner?"

Ceri gifted her brother-in-law with a coy grin. "You'll have to ask Rio about the bet he lost."

"But we weren't involved in any bet," Duncan protested.

"You know that Rio rarely loses at anything." Ceri's eyes danced. "But when he goes down, he goes down hard." She broke up into fits of giggles.

Davy's curiosity propelled him toward the doors to the salon. "Come on, lads. Let's go rescue the greatest warrior any of us have ever battled from his domestic responsibilities." He shot Ceri a look. "And maybe discover what he did tae land the rest of us on chore duty."

The men silently fell in behind him as he led them into the foyer. In their wake, uproarious female laughter carried through the doors of the salon.

CHAPTER SIXTEEN

"THEY'VE BEEN KEEPING ye busy with wedding preparations, yeah?"

At the sound of Davy's voice, Sloane nearly jumped a mile out of the depths of the sofa onto which she'd gratefully sunk in the corner of the salon. "*What?*" Covering her chest with her hand, she willed her heart to slow down to a gallop from the flat-out run it had taken when he spoke to her. "What are you doing here?"

Chuckling softly, he walked toward her. "Looking fer ye, lass."

Sinking back into the cushions, she raised her eyes to heaven and blew out a breath. "I've missed something, I take it." She pushed herself out of her comfy spot and stood. "Where's Fallon, and do you have any idea what she needs?"

"Last I saw Fallon, she was giggling at Seamus as he hustled her up the stairs." Davy's eyes danced and a grin tugged the corner of his mouth.

The hint of a dimple there was enough to race Sloane's heart again. Dammit. This man was so dangerous. He was the reason she'd chosen the sofa in the corner of the salon farthest from the double doors when she'd finished making mints with Fallon earlier. Mints were their only wedding task for the day, she'd thought. But even as she'd laughed with her friend and enjoyed squishing butter-mint batter into molds, visions of a certain hot druid kept sneaking into her head. Seated in the corner of the salon and looking out the windows at the gardens on the side of the manor, she'd been completely lost in thoughts—of Davy Sutherland. As though she'd conjured him, he now stood in front of her.

"Oh." She crossed her arms over her chest. "Why were you looking for me?" Her voice sounded harsh in her ears, but she couldn't regret it. Every time Davy was near her, the tattoo on her thigh went a little haywire. She didn't want to investigate what that might mean, especially after Macha sent her the warning the other afternoon in the garden.

Davy stood at the edge of invading her space. "Ye've been avoiding me lass. Which is a bit puzzling considering the fireworks of that kiss we shared in the garden the other afternoon."

"Yes, well. That was a lapse in judgment."

He stepped all the way into her space, his chest brushing her crossed arms. "I don't agree."

The low timbre of his voice resonated through her, tingling her already hyperaware senses and flooding her core with heat. She took a step back and lost her balance at the edge of the sofa, causing her to fall into the cushions. With predatory intent, Davy leaned over her, bracing his hands on the back of the sofa on either side of her head.

"We have a connection, Sloane. I know ye feel it tae."

"You don't understand, Davy. I lost my warrior. I was there when Macha took him." Pain ripped through her hands, and she sucked in a breath to relax enough to stop herself from wringing them. "Don't you see? I can't risk getting involved with anyone else."

"Again, I don't agree."

His arresting amber eyes stared into hers as he lowered his head and brushed his lips over her mouth. Something bigger, stronger than desire flickered there, drawing her in like a magnet to true North. Unable to stop herself, she closed her eyes and lifted her chin, adding pressure to the kiss. Davy took over then. Cupping her face in his calloused hands, he held her steady as he slid his tongue over the seam of her mouth, demanding entrance. She gripped his wrists like a lifeline and opened for him. When he swept his tongue into her, she met him with an eagerness that terrified and thrilled her in equal measures. Like stepping off the four-story-tall platform the first time she zip-lined, she feared the harness might not hold her, yet she couldn't wait to take the ride.

Without breaking the kiss, Davy dropped to his knees on the sofa, straddling her. The proximity of his body to the swirl of ink on her thigh had her clamping her legs together as pleasure pulsed through her core. She slid her hands up the hard muscles of his forearms and held on tight to his biceps. His body tightened, hardened beneath her touch. His kiss intensified into fire, a wild heat ravaging her, consuming her. Of their own volition, her hands found their way to his shoulders and the back of his neck, her fingers tangling in his hair, pulling him closer, holding him to her.

A tiny voice in the back of her mind told her to stop, to throw a bucket of cold water over the raging firestorm ignited by his kiss. Then he changed the angle of his mouth, deepening his penetration, his tongue doing such erotic things to hers she forgot where she ended and he began. The whole world fell away as Davy kissed his way into her soul. She squirmed beneath him, trying to move even closer to him as he ground his mouth down on hers and devoured her even as she met him with a desperation she didn't understand.

The need to breathe at last became urgent, and she tore her

mouth away from his. He rested his forehead on hers, each of them gulping air. At last, he pulled away enough to gaze into her face.

"Always, ye're so beautiful, it's impossible no' tae stare. But right this minute, with yer cheeks flushed rosy and yer lips kissed red, ye're the most incredible woman I've ever seen." He traced his fingertip across her hairline, down the contours of her cheek, along her jaw, and over the whorls of her ear before he tangled his fingers in her hair.

He followed the progress of his finger with his eyes, giving her a moment to study his features. A strong forehead and dark brows drew attention to his eyes, their gorgeous amber color accentuated by thick black lashes women went to salons to obtain. The perfect straightness of his nose and the sculpted perfection of his cheekbones gave his face a classic handsomeness on their own. But combined with the strength of his square jaw and the fullness of his lips, the man looked like he could grace the cover of *GQ* every other month.

He smiled, his dimples on full display, and Sloane was lost. "Ye like what ye see tae, don't ye, lass?"

"Too much," she admitted.

Davy blinked, and his is expression turned serious. With an agility and grace that stole her breath, he popped up from the sofa and reached his hand down for her. "Come, Sloane. There's something I want tae show ye."

She stared at his hand for a beat before remembering what Duncan had reminded her about at the lake. Bypassing Davy's hand, she clasped his elbow, and he automatically clasped hers, pulling her up in one smooth motion. After seeing the way the man fought in the training room, his power and strength shouldn't have surprised her. But it did. With a gasp, she wrapped her free hand around his neck in order to steady herself, bringing her lips close to his.

His hand came around her waist, and he stared at her mouth

for an eternal beat. Then he raised his eyes to hers and winked. "I like how ye think, lass. But ye're going tae have tae control yerself fer a bit."

"You have nerve, Davy Sutherland," she said with a huff, but neither of them moved.

"Nae, but ye're certainly testin' my discipline."

He let her go long enough to reach for her hand. At the last second, she stuffed her hands in the pockets of the red puffy vest she wore over her matching red-and-white striped long-sleeved Henley. The question in his lifted brow demanded an answer she couldn't give. Not without telling him more about herself than it was safe for him to know. With a tilt of her head, she told him as much as she was willing, and with a nod, he accepted it.

Yet he insisted on touching her, on making sure she stayed with him. His arm fell heavily across her shoulders, his hand cupping her upper arm as he tucked her into his body and began walking them out of the salon. Before she could react, he jumped right into his patter. "Did ye know in addition tae the gardens and the croquet pitch, the manor has an ancient maze?"

After the warnings Macha had sent on each of their previous outings, Sloane knew better than to follow Davy into a maze. Yet she heard herself saying, "Do you mean a hedge maze? I've always wanted to walk one of those." Ever since she could remember, she'd loved puzzles. No doubt, it had been that love that had drawn her into her profession, puzzling out the markets, trying to outsmart the next person deciphering where the next lucky strike would hit. So of course, when Davy mentioned a maze, her curiosity overtook her reason.

"We have a tricky one constructed of blackthorn. This time of year, the sloes are ripening, so ye may even enjoy a treat or two." He glanced at her from the corner of his eye. "Or ye might wait a bit until we gather 'em up and let 'em ferment intae a tasty beverage."

"The sloes?"

"The blue-black berries that grow on blackthorn hedges are called sloes. Perhaps ye've enjoyed a sloe gin sometime?"

"I had no idea it came from berries."

Davy laughed. "It's one drink I'm allowed tae make. Perhaps later this evening, ye'd like tae try some of my brew."

"What do you mean, it's one drink you're *allowed* to make?"

As they exited the salon, Davy glanced over his shoulder like he didn't want to be overheard. "Hamish keeps his whisky recipe tae himself. He says I'm no' ready fer it yet. Which might be a bone of contention between us," he whispered.

The edge of Sloane's mouth curved up. "Ahh, he's hiding the keys to the kingdom from you."

"Ye have nae idea, lass."

As they stepped through the front door of the manor, Davy chanted something in a low tone. She couldn't make out the words, so she assumed he spoke in Gaelic.

"Do you always do that?"

He urged her down the stairs of the veranda and tugged her to the left toward the gardens she'd been admiring from the salon.

"What? Chant?"

She nodded.

"'Tis ingrained in me. Every time I use the front doors tae the manor, I chant. Hamish insists the chanting protects us. After some of the things I've seen happen in and around the manor, I know he's right."

They walked along a stone path past rose gardens that even in late September bloomed with a dizzying array of colors. Peach, apricot, orange, red, and mauve caught her eye, the beds resembling an autumn sunset captured in fragrant petal cups.

"I agree, lass. 'Tis the most beautiful garden on the manor grounds."

Sloane gasped. "Did you breech my shield?"

Davy chuckled. "Dinnae have tae try, even."

She almost tripped when she stopped midstride.

Davy didn't stumble. Instead, He tightened his arm over her shoulders, turned her toward him, and trailed the pad of his forefinger along the contours of her cheek. "Yer face said it all." With a tiny squeeze of his hand on her upper arm, he urged her to continue walking. "Besides, if I breech yer shield, what chance dae I have at winnin' ye?"

"Davy—"

"Don't try tae protest what's happening between us," he warned. "We were both there in the salon a few minutes ago. And in the garden the other afternoon."

"But—"

He changed the subject. "Our maze was designed and built by Fianna Conlan, the matriarch of the Conlan and Graham clans and founder of this house. The rose gardens in front of it and the hawthorn hedges surrounding the other three sides protect the sacred space of the maze."

She followed his eyes when he gazed ahead at what she assumed was the entrance to the maze. Neatly trimmed bushes formed impenetrable walls on either side of an opening in them. The path they walked changed from gray stone to fine, tan-colored gravel that crunched under her boots with a kind of comforting sound. No doubt she'd be able to hear if others were in the maze with them.

Davy let her go and gestured for her to lead the way. As they continued along the intricately laid out path, she scanned her surroundings, noting the dense hedges edging their way were at least ten feet high. The tiny serrated leaves of the plants were in various stages of changing color from green to deep purple to red to orange. Among them, dark blue, nearly black almond-shaped berries clung to black branches made sinister by the thorns sticking out from them. One truly didn't need an imagination to understand why the bushes were called blackthorns. Still, she stopped and ran her hand over them, wincing when a thorn pricked her finger.

Davy's eyes darkened as he grabbed her wrist, drawing her hand to his mouth where he kissed her hurt away.

At his touch, Sloane's heart attempted to gallop out of her chest, taking her air with it. With a jerk, she reclaimed her hand from him. Unfortunately, she couldn't control the breathy quality of her voice. "This maze is two hundred years old?"

The flare of desire flickered in his eyes, yet he merely nodded. "Thereabouts," he said, but his eyes told her he knew exactly what his touch did to her. "Dae ye know the story of the maze?"

"This one?"

"Any one."

"Um, the Minotaur lived in the center of one and demanded a sacrifice of the Greeks until Theseus, with the help of Ariadne, took him on and defeated him, allowing those who entered the labyrinth to return from it safely."

They reached the first crossroads, and Sloane turned to Davy for guidance. His raised brows told her the choice was hers alone. When she took a step to her right, she glanced back at him, but his expression remained impassive, giving her no clue as to whether or not she'd made a good decision. Squaring her shoulders, she continued down the path she'd chosen, determined to be her normal, decisive self rather than the fearful woman who'd been second-guessing herself since Lughnasadh.

Behind her, Davy said, "Western symbolism of the hero going into the labyrinth to rescue the maiden is a rebirth process."

She stopped and turned back to him. "What do you mean?"

"It's symbolic of the hero recapturing the feminine, intuitive part of his nature. The heroes who embraced the feminine followed the old ways of the Celts." He smiled at her. "The trip into the maze symbolizes a descent into death and a reemergence into life."

She shivered. "No pressure, then."

With a chuckle, he gestured for her to keep moving. When she came to another crossing, she didn't bother to ask for help, knowing he wanted her to find her own way. Instinctively, she chose the right-hand path again. "Is it just me, or is it getting darker in here?"

"'Tis a trick of the light tae make ye question yerself."

"So you're saying I'm on the right path?"

"All of the choices seem tae darken in this part of the maze."

Sloane huffed out a breath and headed in her chosen direction. "You're no help at all."

Like a sixth sense, she could feel Davy's dimples deepening at her expense, and she willed herself not to look back at him. It was enough that his smiles had distracted her into this escapade. She didn't need more trouble.

As they continued deeper into the maze, Davy explained how mazes and labyrinths had worked their way into the collective unconscious of cultures beyond the Celts. The girls in northern folktales being abandoned in the woods or "given" to trolls were sacrifices to the beast. The old legends were reimagined as Little Red Riding Hood heading off into the forest to be given to the Minotaur in the guise of the Big Bad Wolf. Snow White is sent into the forest where the hunter is instructed to kill her, but she's rescued by the prince. The miller's daughter is locked in a tower and told to spin straw into gold in order to save her life and become the prince's wife. In each story, the heroine is transformed, rescued by a hunter or a prince or a nasty old gnome.

But, Davy explained, the Celts knew the truth. The women in the stories rescue themselves, reclaiming the masculine side of their nature. The journey into the woods or the completion of a seemingly impossible task was actually the woman wandering through the maze, finding the center, and learning the secrets of the Underworld or finding the Cauldron of Regeneration or the Cauldron of Plenty. Such a circumstance meant that a goddess like Hecate was not the witch Shakespeare portrayed her to be, but rather the mother part of the triple goddess—maiden, mother, and crone. A woman making her way through a maze is always transformed.

As Davy spoke, Sloane wandered deeper into the warren of turns and dead ends. His voice became her lodestone, his stories the only reality she could understand as she became increasingly turned around in the endless sameness of uniform hedgerows and even pathway. Davy's explanations of the maze echoed in her head as she turned a corner and found herself at yet another dead end.

"Huh. Well, this"—she waved her hand at the wall of foliage in front of her—"does not bode well for any sort of transformation for me." She stared at him for a long beat as she tried to decide if she was going to ask him for advice. His stories of women finding their own way, rescuing themselves, resonated with her. Staring past his shoulder at the most recent wrong turn she'd made, she sucked in a breath and made up her mind.

As she brushed past him on her way to another option, she could have sworn she'd heard him whisper, "Well done, lass," under his breath.

CHAPTER SEVENTEEN

FTER TRACING AND retracing her steps, finding one or two additional dead ends, and feeling thoroughly turned around, Sloane rounded a corner and stumbled into the center of the maze. If not for Davy's quick reflexes, she might have landed flat on her face when she came upon the three steps leading down to the square at the end of her journey. Recovering her usual grace, she shook her hair back and walked down the stone steps onto the grassy expanse of the square, her eyes drinking in the beautiful tableau laid out before her.

Lush grass so green it nearly hurt to look at it carpeted the ground. In the center of the square, a perfectly sculpted apple tree grew in the middle of a heart-shaped garden of roses whose blood-red blooms appeared to be made of velvet. A tiny path through the point of the heart led to a mahogany bench, the slats on the backrest catching the dappled light while the cushions on the seat matched the color of the roses blooming around it.

As though guided by forces beyond her will, Sloane walked steadily into the core of the maze until she stood in front of the bench beneath the tree. Breathing deeply, she embraced the rich perfume of roses as it filled her head.

When she turned around, she discovered Davy standing directly behind her, a smile playing over his lips.

"Worth it, yeah?"

"So worth it," she breathed. "Thank you for bringing me here."

"I believe ye found yer own way, Sloane."

Something in his tone alerted her, but before she could figure it out, he gestured for her to sit. When she did, he reached up and picked two gorgeous reddish-orange apples from the tree, handing her one before he took a huge bite out of the other. Seating himself beside her, he swallowed and said, "'Tis delicious. Try it."

A drop of apple juice slipped down the side of his face when he took another bite, and it was all Sloane could do not to lean forward and lick it off for him. His eyes glittered as if he knew exactly what she was thinking, and she hastily checked to be sure her shield was in place. With the hand holding his apple, he gestured at hers, silently urging her to take a bite as he chewed, swallowed, and lifted his fruit to his mouth for another bite. She watched in fascination as he nearly devoured his whole apple in three bites.

"Ye don't like apples, lass?"

Her face heated as she realized how rude she must look sitting mutely with her apple in her hand as she watched the man eat. Hastily, she lifted her apple to her mouth. The crunch of her first bite echoed in the quiet space at the epicenter of the maze. Sweet and tart exploded over her tongue, and she squinted her eyes against sudden wateriness and sucked in her cheeks as the juices filled her mouth.

Davy laughed. "Tasty, yeah? A little tart, a little sweet. Sort of like ye, Sloane MacIntosh."

Not knowing how to respond to that, she took another healthy bite. Since she knew what to expect this time, her second bite came with less fanfare than the first, but it gave her time to think. She swallowed and said, "Of all the things I thought I might see in the middle of this maze, an apple tree in full fruit wasn't anywhere on my list."

"Like the maze itself, apples symbolize life and rebirth." He contemplated what was left of his treat before continuing. "The Christians believe the apple symbolizes life and death in the Garden of Eden. The Norse believe a man could be preserved in death by the apples given tae him from his wife. They're associated with the Morrigan in her form as a crone."

Sloane snorted. "Is Morgan anything other than a crone?"

"Careful, lass. Ye know how powerful a goddess the Morrigan is."

She shot him the side-eye and took a defiant bite of her apple.

He chuckled at her insolence as he glanced around the garden. "The apple, the rose, and the hawthorn are all members of the same family, and all are sacred tae us. The hawthorn especially has protective powers, which is why Fianna Conlan planted it around her maze. Did ye know it can have blossoms, ripe fruit, and ripening fruit on it at all times? Maid, mother, and crone simultaneously."

"Wow." Sloane blinked at him. "I had no idea any plant could do that."

Sliding his arm across her shoulders, Davy closed the small gap between them on the bench and gazed hungrily at her mouth as she took another bite of fruit. "In some legends, children are conceived after one eats a magical apple."

The low timbre of his voice mesmerized her until his words sank in. "I don't think so," she warned as she tried to reassert some space between them.

"Nae, no' taeday, I expect," he said matter-of-factly, but he held them close together, Sloane's arm tucked along his side, their thighs touching from hips to knees, his fingers tracing patterns over the top of her shoulder and down her arm.

He took the core of her apple from her and dropped it on the ground beside his. Then he reached up and thumbed her cheek. "Better."

She tilted her head in question.

He licked the pad of his thumb. "Ye had a drop of juice just there near the corner of yer mouth."

A picture flashed of the apple juice sliding down his cheek and how she'd wished to lick it off him. A sigh escaped her, one Davy didn't misinterpret. Cupping her cheek in his hand, he held her and stared deeply into her eyes, letting her see the desire in the amber depths of his. Giving her a chance to say no.

Unable to stop herself, she leaned toward him, which was all the encouragement he needed. He brushed his lips over hers once, twice, before he fused his mouth to hers. She clung to his shoulders as she opened herself, inviting him in. Something seemed to ignite inside him, turning his kiss into molten lava, and Sloane melted into him. A groan escaped him as he wrapped her in his arms and hauled her onto his lap. His tongue twirled and twined with hers, no longer exploration and discovery, but desire and need. Even as he claimed her, she molded herself to him, giving and taking in equal measure.

She tightened her arms around his neck, flattening her breasts to his chest, which only slightly eased the ache in her taut nipples. Davy cupped her ass and pulled her center closer to his before his hands took a tour of her body, smoothing up and down her back and the sides of her torso then sliding over her thighs. When his palm contacted the swirls of ink beneath the denim of her jeans, she gasped as excruciating pleasure pulsed over and through her. Showing himself to be a sensitive lover, Davy returned to the spot, and Sloane couldn't help but clamp her legs to him.

Tearing his mouth from hers, Davy trailed kisses along her jaw to the delicate spot behind her ear where he teased her with his tongue, her gasps of delight goading him on. Throwing her head back, she gave him more access while mindlessly, she writhed against him. Reveling in the lovely sensations he gave her with his lips and tongue, for a second she stopped paying attention to his hands until cool air rushed over her skin. He pulled away from her enough to tug her sweater and vest over her head. Willingly, she allowed it, raising her hands above her head to help him reach his goal.

With a light brush of his fingertips over her collarbones, he moved her hair before he slid his hands down her arms. All the while, he seemed to drink her in with his eyes. She followed his glance, relieved she'd worn her lacy red bra today rather than the utilitarian beige one she'd grabbed first when she'd dressed before breakfast. His forefingers traced the edges of the lace before moving to the swells of her breasts above it. A tiny frown creased his brow before he reached up to slide his fingers beneath the straps to pull them off her shoulders until they were even with the cups of her bra. With speed and deftness that surprised her, he unclasped her bra with one hand while he dragged it down the front of her and off her body with the other.

"Holy Saint Brighid," he said, the awe in his tone thrilling her. "Ye're the most perfect woman I've ever laid eyes on."

Her breasts seemed to spill from his big hands as he palmed them, his thumbs teasing her dusky nipples. His single-minded focus on her breasts was an unexpected erotic delight. The ache that had started when she'd pushed herself against his chest intensified as the tips of her breasts tightened in pleasure in his expert hands. When he leaned forward and pulled one hard nub into his mouth and sucked, she cried out and arched into him, begging for everything he wanted to give. He swirled his tongue over her before biting her exactly the way she needed before drawing her in again and sucking her hard.

Mindless with desire, she rocked into him as he transferred his attentions to her other breast. Time stood still as Davy loved on her body before it registered that the moaning and whimpering she heard emanated from her, and time started again. Reaching between them, she palmed him through the fly of his jeans, delighting in the hard thickness she discovered there.

Now it was his turn to groan. "Och, lass. Ye have nae idea how much I need ye."

With her eyes locked on his, she slid backward off his lap and stood to undo the fly of her jeans. The shade beneath the apple tree seemed to darken as she pushed her fingertips beneath the waistbands of her panties and jeans, shoving them all at once down to her ankles. Not bothering to undress fully, she toed off her right boot then stepped on her jeans and pulled her foot from them.

Right with her, Davy pulled a foil packet from the pocket of his jeans before he unzipped his fly and pushed his jeans and boxers down his thighs, releasing his very impressive cock for her viewing enjoyment. When he opened the packet and moved to sheathe himself, Sloane stayed him with her hand on his wrist.

"Let me. Please."

A slow smile deepened his dimples and had her clenching her inner walls in pulsing counterpoint to the heavy beat of her heart. Still, she willed herself to take her time, to savor this man in this suspended moment of her life. Deliberately, she smoothed the condom over him, delighted in the hiss of air he sucked in through his teeth at her touch. Delighted in the way desire blazed in the amber of his eyes as she jacked him. Delighted in the way he clenched his fists at his sides as he let her have her way.

When at last she straddled him again, he gripped her hips and positioned her over him. Yet he didn't let her join them. Instead, he stared into her eyes like he tried to see into her soul and said, "If ye're sure about this, Sloane, truly sure about this, open yer shield tae me."

Understanding of what he asked slowly penetrated the lust hammering through her veins. Before she could follow her instincts and refuse what he offered, the tip of his little finger edged the outer swirl of the tattoo on her thigh, sending a jolt of awareness through her. Involuntarily, she arched her back, her hands grabbing his biceps to stabilize herself. They cried out as one as an arc of electricity passed diagonally between them. Simultaneously, they opened their shields to each other, each letting the other hear their thoughts.

"Sloane, lass. Ye're mine. Ye've always been mine."

"Davy! I need you so much. Please."

With one smooth stroke, he entered her. Pleasure beyond her imagination overwhelmed her as they moved together. Simultaneously, they found each other's lips, their mouths imitating their bodies. Though they'd allowed each other in, neither could form coherent thought as their bodies took care of their communication for them. She clenched her inner walls around him, meeting his deep thrusts in a perfect rhythm. The tattoo on her thigh throbbed in harmony with their movements, and she ground down on him, demanding an even deeper connection as he thrust inside her.

Digging his fingers into her flesh, he tore his mouth from hers. "Now, Sloane. Ye need tae come *now*."

As though she no longer controlled her will, she dropped over the edge of ecstasy, screaming Davy's name. With another deep thrust and a shout, he leaped off the cliff and joined her.

An eternity later, she slumped against his body, her face resting in the crook of his neck. For long minutes—hours, maybe?—they remained silent, even in the recesses of their thoughts. When she could finally breathe somewhat evenly, she sat up and stared into his face.

"What just happened here?"

"Destiny."

"I never had the chance to bond with my warrior before Macha took him," she began out loud and sensed him tense. "But

I think if I had, it would have felt like what happened between us just now."

Beneath her, Davy's body relaxed. "We have a connection, we two. Ye knew that before taeday every bit as much as I did."

Sloane nodded, at last admitting what she had known almost from the first moment she gazed into Davy's amber eyes the day they met. Fear shivered over her, and she glanced frantically around, haunted.

"She cannae touch us here, lass. 'Tis beyond her power tae touch ye here in this protected space. Especially with the way the two of us are joined."

He flicked his eyes to where her inner muscles continued to pulse around him. When she tried to move away from him, he pulled her close, smoothing his hands up and down her back. "I understand yer fears, Sloane. But what happened between us was meant tae be. I know it deep in my bones. Ye're a part o' me." He leaned back enough to push her hair from her face. His eyes bored into hers. "What we did here in the sacred center o' the maze was always going tae happen. If no' taeday, if no' here, then another day in the near future in an equally sacred place." He cupped her face in his hands. "We belong tae each other Sloane."

The conviction in his words, in his voice, reverberated through her, echoes of the feelings she'd had for another man for a short hour during one summer night a lifetime ago. She closed her eyes as a faint sensation of pain rippled over her right thigh, closely followed by a soothing warmth. When she opened her eyes again, she watched as the frown furrowing Davy's brow smoothed out, replaced by a gentle smile. Dusk had fallen, shadowing the depths of his eyes, forcing her to trust her body's response to the man who had flown her among the stars and insisted he was her destiny.

"You said something about the journey to the center of the

maze was a transformation, masculine to feminine, feminine to masculine. But it's more than that, isn't it?"

In answer, Davy kissed her, a tender sweet promise.

Silently, they dressed and walked to the stairs leading back into the maze.

"Follow me, lass. I can find my way even in the dark."

Somehow, she knew he spoke of more than navigating the return trip to Conlan Manor. Trusting him would be easy if only she could shed the cloak of foreboding that seemed to drop onto her shoulders the farther they moved away from the enchanted garden.

High above them, a lone crow winged across the sky, silent and invisible in the coming night.

CHAPTER EIGHTEEN

S DAVY WAS about to touch his knuckles to the heavy oak door, it opened, revealing the gorgeous talisman who had starred in his dreams all through the night.

"Couldn't wait tae see me, eh lass?" he asked with a grin.

Even though she rolled her eyes, he didn't miss the tiny smile tugging one side of her mouth—a mouth he desperately wanted to kiss, but that would have to wait.

"Ready tae go?"

"Sure. Let me grab my jacket."

She stepped back into the room, and through the open door, he noted the disheveled state of her sheets and blankets. Perhaps Sloane had had as much trouble sleeping without him as he'd had spending the night without her in his bed. The thought cheered him.

"Where are we going again?" she asked as she pulled the door closed behind her, the two of them falling into step together as they walked past the third-floor ballroom to the stairs.

"Hamish wants me tae harvest the last melilot flowers of the season. Most of them stopped bloomin' a couple weeks ago, but I noticed a stand of them as we climbed *An Teallach* on our way tae the training room."

Unable to help himself, he kept a hand on the small of Sloane's back as they descended the stairs to the foyer. The fact she didn't flinch away from his touch gave him hope. Perhaps the tension he'd sensed in her in the heart of the maze when he'd mentioned their entwined destiny had to do with something else entirely.

"Why is this melilot so important?"

"'Tis a protection plant. Hamish wants tae wrap it around the rowan branches Griff, Siobhan, and I harvested the other day. We'll hang it over the front door of the manor and in strategic places in the ballroom fer the wedding."

As they reached the foyer, Sloane stopped, her tone wary. "Who are you trying to keep away from the ceremony?"

The way her body vibrated beneath his hand told him all about how much fear she harbored even without the wariness he heard in her voice.

"The Morrigan of course. That sort of goes without saying. Maeve since she seems tae have it in fer Seamus." Tilting his head, he gazed deeply into her eyes. "And Macha because she threatens ye," he added softly.

She puffed out a breath. "I don't think I'm the one she threatens." Pinching the bridge of her nose, she remained quiet for several long seconds. "For reasons only the goddess knows, Macha requires me to sacrifice to her." Pain flashed in her eyes before she glanced up at the ceiling then squeezed them shut. "She made that clear the night she gave Gavin to Morgan to escort across her wicked river of blood," she whispered.

Cupping her face in his hands, he waited for her to look at him. "Bothering the Irish and the Scots is Macha's favorite pastime. We're used tae dealing with her over here." Dropping his hands to her shoulders, he gave her a little squeeze. "Trust me.

She isn't going tae get away with her mischief in this enchanted house."

The violet depths of Sloane's eyes held a sorrow that tore at Davy's heart. He probed her shield even as he opened his thoughts to her.

"I can't do this again. Because it will be so much worse this time."

"Lass."

Her eyes widened as she realized what she'd revealed.

"We share a destiny. I know it. Ye must believe me."

With a glare, she said, "I don't know how you did that because I've worked hard on my shield. If you're not aware, Rowan Sheridan is *the* master of shielding, and I've worked with him several times since we met last summer. Is there some special druidic magic you'd like to share with the class?"

Her annoyance would have made him chuckle if he hadn't sensed they were at a crossroads. Instead, he gestured toward the stairs, and as they descended into the kitchen, he said, "The special 'magic' is the connection the two of us share. I thought you figured that out in the maze yesterday."

As he ushered her through the room, Hamish rounded the corner from his apartments.

"There ye are, lad." Hamish's tone stopped Davy in his tracks. "Hello, Sloane. 'Tis good ye're accompanyin' Davy on his task."

One inky brow lifted in question, but she said nothing.

"Layers, lass. Layers. As Fallon's maid o' honor, ye're daein' her a service by gatherin' protection plants fer her weddin'."

Turning to Davy, she said, "So that's why you invited me on this outing."

"Among other reasons." He smirked and tried not to laugh out loud at the huffy way she crossed her arms over her beautiful breasts.

Interrupting, Hamish said, "While ye're gatherin' the melilot, could ye see if ye can find any ripe juniper berries?"

"Plannin' a little something special fer the groom, auld man?"

"It worked fer Rio."

Hamish's chortle put Davy on alert. "You know something the rest of us should know?"

"All in good time, lad."

A frown passed over Sloane's features. "What is he talking about, Davy?"

He glared at Hamish who unabashedly grinned back at him as he felt the flush creep up his neck to heat his face. "Juniper berries are used as a sort of male enhancement. Tae improve potency." He forced the words out through gritted teeth.

Sloane's brows shot to her hairline. "Seriously?" With a tilt of her head, she addressed Hamish. "You think Seamus needs that? Wait. You thought *Rio* needed that?"

Hamish's grin grew even broader. "Those berries are also known tae improve psychic ability and tae attract love. Perhaps I should add them tae Davy's dinner as well."

"Stop meddlin', auld man. 'Tisn't necessary."

"Have I taught ye naethin', lad?" Hamish began.

Feeling like Hamish's apprentice all over again, Davy answered his rhetorical question simultaneously with him. "It never hurts tae add layers."

"So ye dae listen once in a while."

Pointedly pretending not to notice the daggers Davy glared at him, Hamish turned to Sloane who'd been watching their exchange like a spectator at a dodgeball match. "Ye'll need this. With any luck, ye'll gather more plants than ye can stuff in yer pockets." Laughing at his own joke, he handed Sloane a canvas satchel, one Davy had used often as he'd gathered plants with Hamish over the years. Like a magician pulling rabbits from a hat, he produced another satchel, which he handed to Davy. "I took the liberty o' packin' the twa o' ye a snack and some water. No tellin' how long yer task might take, even on as pretty a day as taeday."

Davy glanced out the window set in the back door to the kitchen at a shaft of sunlight illuminating the tarmac and the grassy field beyond it. As usual, the old man had taken the mickey out of him and smoothed it over with a gift. Just like Davy's da liked to do whenever he visited his parents. With a sigh, he let it go.

"We should take advantage of the sunshine, lass." He walked to the door and held it open for her. "Thanks fer the snack, auld man, but could ye make sure the horde leaves a little something behind fer lunch?"

Hamish dismissed him with a wave of his hand as Davy pulled the door closed and followed Sloane to the van.

Motoring the skiff over the loch, Davy managed to learn more about Sloane. Specifically, what Fallon had meant when she'd made the comment about Sloane's wildness the other evening when they were all gathered in the salon. He'd loved hearing about the two of them defying their parents to practice fighting like warriors rather than practicing directing battle like generals the way talismans usually trained. He'd admired the photo she shared of her Mustang but kept to himself how much he wanted to ride in it with her someday. He'd adored how her eyes sparkled when she talked about the risks associated with handling vast sums of money as she traded on the stock market. It stunned him how Sloane's parents could want to hold back so passionate a woman as Davy's firsthand experiences had shown her to be. Especially because he intuited her innate passion had made her strong enough to withstand Macha's attack that resulted in her great loss.

Though knowledgeable about plants and their medicinal and magical properties, Davy's true druidic talent lay in his ability to tell a tale. That ability included a finely tuned sensitivity to his audience. Ever since those first kisses he'd shared with Sloane in the garden, he'd picked up on her dwindling sadness at the loss of her warrior. Yet her fear of the goddess never wavered. Where her parents had failed in harnessing her spirit, the goddess had managed to steal a part of her fire. Under the piercing blue skies of a rare and perfect late-summer day, she never quite relaxed. As they hiked the path up the side of the mountain, he'd caught her scanning those skies over and over, almost like expecting the goddess's appearance had become a habit.

"Ye're a quick study, Sloane MacIntosh. In no time, it seems, ye've mastered the recognition of the melilot plant, whether it's flowering or no'."

For a moment, he saw the mischievous and carefree woman who had existed before Lughnasadh when she turned a full-on grin at him. "Had to. As a favor to you."

Reeling from the wondrous beauty of her smile, he cleared his throat. "What dae ye mean?"

"If I'm busy gathering melilot, then you have the task of picking juniper berries."

He furrowed his brow, waiting.

"Because I imagine some of their 'potency' rubs off on the person gathering them."

He snorted. "Ye're a funny girl, Sloane." A wicked grin spread over his face. "I noticed ye were quite satisfied with my 'potency' during our trip intae the maze."

The heat that flared in her eyes suddenly made the front of his trousers uncomfortably tight. If they hadn't been standing on the exposed side of a mountain in full view of the skiffs and pleasure boats cruising the loch, he would have taken her up on her challenge. As it was, all he had was a promise. "Donnae worry, lass. That was definitely not a one-off."

Tilting her head and quirking a brow, she left her challenge hanging.

He hiked his satchel higher on his shoulder and deliberately brushed her body when he stepped around her to start picking berries from a nearby juniper bush. It took him a minute to recover from the hammering desire that ripped through him at the touch of their bodies even through layers of clothes. His lesson to her on goading him backfired on him in spectacular fashion. Gritting his teeth against his need for her, he willed himself back under control. Still, the sound of his voice in his own ears was harsh when he said, "The civilians enjoying their day on the loch today have forgotten about the giants who once roamed these coastal areas of Scotland."

"Giants still roam here?" she asked. The breeze sent her laughter back to him.

"No' so much anymore," he deadpanned. "But there was a time when a nasty fellow called Benandonner roamed the inlets and islands of Scotland. He was a creature possessed of ferocious manners and resembled no animal anyone had ever seen. Folks around here were terrified of him."

"Bet when their kids acted up, they warned them against having the manners of Benandonner," she said.

When he looked up at her, he saw the smirk on her mouth and grinned back at her. "I might have been told that a time or tae."

"Who else were you warned against?"

"We were always instructed tae watch out fer Cubbie Roo." He tossed a handful of berries into his canvas bag before moving on to a nearby bush.

He barely managed to talk himself down when Sloane straightened and arched her back in a stretch from bending over to pick another bouquet of melilot flowers. "Cubbie Roo? Sounds like a big teddy bear."

Clearing his throat, he said, "Nae, lass. Cubbie Roo was a fearsome giant who lived on the isle of Wyre in the Orkneys. It's said 'twas he who built the stacks and islets of the North Sea for stepping stones so he could travel back and forth tae terrorize the mainland."

"I've seen pictures of those stacks. They're quite impressive. Would it be possible to visit them?" She seated herself on a moss-covered rock and watched him as he gathered more berries.

Keeping his eyes on his task, he casually asked, "Are ye plannin' tae stay past the wedding, then, lass?"

"No, why?"

"I'd love tae take ye out tae explore Cubbie Roo's home territory." A thought occurred to him. "Wonder why that old titan chose tae bother the Scots when there were such easy pickings in Norway?"

"Didn't you say he's a Scots giant?"

"Though the Orkneys belong tae Scotland, they're located closer tae Norway than tae our mainland." He slid her a sly glance. "If ye had a mind tae extend yer stay, perhaps we could go exploring, try tae solve the mystery."

She wrapped her hands around her knees and stared down at the lake. "It's beautiful here." Her words sounded wistful.

"But—"

"But I have a job at home. Family. Friends." Though her eyes were on the loch, he caught the wistfulness in her tone.

He left off gathering berries to squat down in front of her. "People have those things here tae." The storm swirling in her violet eyes warned him not to press, at least not at the present moment. He stood, but his eyes held hers. "Something tae think about."

The storm settled into something that looked a lot like longing, which Davy interpreted as encouraging. Sloane wouldn't—or couldn't—yet believe they were destined to be together, but there was no other explanation for the speed and power of his feelings for her. Nor for the omen. When they'd made love in the maze, the tattoo on his shoulder beat in rhythm with their movements, intensifying his pleasure beyond anything he'd ever imagined and goading him on to give her that same overwhelming sensation of being utterly and completely one.

Giving her a brilliant smile, he changed the subject. "Looks like we're finished here. How 'bout we head back tae the skiff and I show ye around the loch fer a bit. Ye up fer that, yeah?"

Blowing out a breath, she stood and scanned the skies again. "Sounds like a plan."

Davy led the way back down the trail and stowed their satchels in the skiff before helping her into it. As he turned the boat toward the Summer Isles at the mouth of the loch, he powered it up to put it on plane and raced across the water. Sloane's laughter rang above the noise of the motor, encouraging him to speed even faster through the still morning's gentle waves. In no time, it seemed, they approached Tanera Mòr, the largest of the Summer Isles.

He throttled back the motor, and they idled along the shoreline. In the quiet, he launched into a story. "The Sheridan clan tends tae produce warriors. This was true even before they immigrated tae the States."

Sloane turned around on her bench to face him.

"The Sutherlands, on the other hand, tend tae produce druids. Family lore has it we descend from the Feans, offspring of ancient deities in Scotland."

"Not grand at all, are you?"

Her gentle sarcasm put a smile on his face. "No' a bit, lass."

She grinned back at him, and he continued. "The Feans produced three powerful druids—Ossian, the bard o' the Feans, his son Oscar who slew the Dark Prince's horse, and Jeermit, son o' Aengus the Ever Young, who had the healing power of touch that prolongs an ill person's life until a cure can be found."

Her eyes saucered. "Wow. That would be some skill."

He nodded. "'Tis rumored that Fianna Conlan, the matriarch of the manor, had the skill tae."

"Seriously?"

Her elbows on her knees, her chin resting on her closed fists, she gazed at him in fascination, making him feel ten feet tall.

"So Hamish tells me. Anyway, the Dark Prince had a mind tae marry the Princess of Land-Under-Waves. The princess dinnae find the plan so palatable, so she reached out tae the Feans. The Dark Prince rode his water horse tae the shores of the isle of the Feans, demanding they refuse the princess's request. Oscar stepped forward and informed the Dark Prince the Feans were obligated tae aid the princess dae tae the fact that she saved one of their own once when he slipped under the waves during a storm."

He smiled to himself as Sloane leaned forward, already enthralled with his story. He cut the motor on the skiff and allowed them to drift.

"The Dark Prince spurred his great foaming water horse ontae the shore, intent on drowning the Feans who cowered back away from him. All but Oscar. Brandishing his great claymore that some say measured ten feet long—"

She blinked. "Ten feet?"

Davy nodded. "He stepped forward to slay the Dark Prince's horse. Timing his thrust perfectly, he plunged the blade deep intae the beast's blue-green chest as it roiled and reared above his head. The great crashing saltwater waves of the beast's mane, the flashing silver hooves kicking at the air, the seafoam spewing from its mouth to land on the sand at Oscar's feet signaled the monster's death throes. Then the waters receded, leaving the Dark Prince tae howl in frustration on the shores before he vanished in a cloud of white vapor."

Davy couldn't help but grin at the enthralled way Sloane looked at him.

"Was the horse a kel—"

Leaning forward, he covered her mouth with his hand before she could finish the word. "Donnae say that aloud while we sit exposed in this tiny boat, lass."

Both of them looked around at the placid water lapping at the boat and the shore. Davy expelled a relieved breath that Sloane hadn't managed to summon a kelpie. With a rueful smile, he continued his tale.

"Even after the Feans relieved the Princess of Land-Under-Waves of the threat of a disadvantageous marriage, the lass fell ill. Now it was up tae Jeermit, son of Aengus the Ever Young tae help her. But first, he had tae secure three portions of special red moss. In order tae find this red moss, he had tae travel intae the heart of the territory guarded by three fierce giants. By day, their lands were guarded by a fire-breathing dragon, one not even Saint George could have slain. Which meant Jeermit would have to cross the plains guarded by the giants in the dead of night when they were out and about. Jeermit thought and thought about how tae cross the plain tae reach the moss when an idea struck him."

Sloane's expression told him how eagerly she gobbled up his story. Sort of in the same way she was reaching into the satchel Hamish had packed and eating all the snacks. He chuckled and she shrugged. Her mouth full of crackers and cheese, she gestured with her free hand for him to go on.

"Jeermit lit a lamp but covered it with a black cloth. Since he was fleet of foot while the giants were slow and lumbering, he raced around the plain all night. First, he'd shine his light on the western side, then in the seeming blink of an eye, his light flickered in the east or the south or the north. Knowing the light came from an invader, the giants chased it all night. So intent were they on catching the light, they forgot tae pay attention tae the pink glow of morning until it was tae late. A shaft of sunlight broke the horizon, turning the giants intae stone.

"Jeermit wisely positioned himself at the edge of the plain in anticipation of morning and the rise of the dragon. He spent the daylight hours slumbering in safety on the opposite shore of the stream bordering the plain. The next night, he made his way tae the beds of moss, gathered his three portions, and was nearly tae the shores of the sea before daybreak, leaving the snorting dragon and stony giants far behind.

"Over the course of three days, he administered the moss tae the princess. On the last day, he revealed tae her that the moss was actually three life drops of her heart."

"So the Dark Prince's courtship of the princess broke her heart? Why?"

"The Princess of Land-Under-Waves was devoted tae her people. Marrying the Dark Prince meant she would have tae leave her home ferever, so she would never be of service tae them again. 'Twas a fate she couldn't bear."

A large swell buoyed the boat, telling Davy the tide was starting to come in, or it was the first salvo of the goddess. Surreptitiously glancing over the side of the skiff for the telltale roil of a kelpie, he satisfied himself that for the moment at least, they were safe. Still, he repositioned himself to fire up the motor and steer the skiff back to the harbor.

"Altruism is a hallmark of druids, despite what one Rio Sheridan sometimes likes tae believe."

Sloane sat back on her hands. "Is that why he went after you so hard in the training room?"

"Partly."

He marveled at the delicacy of her features as she quirked one raven-colored brow and awaited the rest of his answer.

"Mostly, he doesn't like it that I train as hard and in the same way as a warrior. Scathach even included me as she trained Alaisdair and the Sheridans last Samhain as we prepared fer Morgan's attack on Rio." He couldn't help the note of pride that crept into his voice as he told her about Scathach.

"You've met the warrior trainer who trained all the great heroes from Cuchulain to King Arthur? Really?"

Probably, he liked impressing this woman a bit too much, but he couldn't help his grin as he nodded.

"Wow. That explains a lot."

Before he could ask what she meant, a breeze skittered over the water, a sure sign they needed to return to the dock.

"Time tae go back."

Sloane glanced up at the clouds gathering over *An Teallach* in the distance and shivered. The breeze hadn't started to cool the air, which meant something else had come over her. Just when he knew he'd been making progress with her too. Again, he scanned the water and sky for the goddess.

Powering up the motor, he kept a sharp eye out for any of Macha's minions—those that wheeled through the skies and those that snorted and pranced their way through the waves—as he steered the skiff back to the safety of Ullapool. Only later as they unloaded the satchels from the skiff and walked them to the van did he remember they'd gathered protections in the melilot in the satchel. Or perhaps the goddess wasn't ready yet to show her hand.

CHAPTER NINETEEN

"WHY ARE YOU in such a state, Maeve? Have I not done exactly as I promised, confining my mischief to the isles, allowing you and Morgan your fun in North America?"

Maeve stomped more than paced the stone floor of Macha's Irish stronghold. "You took the wrong warrior at Lughnasadh. I wanted Seamus Lochlann's death."

Macha exchanged a look with Taranis, the impossibly beautiful thunder god, and idly contemplated a tryst later. His bored expression contradicted his presence in her stronghold near Tara in County Meath, Ireland. She had yet to discover why he had accompanied her sister goddesses Maeve and the Morrigan to this meeting. Returning her attention to Maeve's tantrum gave Macha a pain. Judging from the storm swirling in Taranis's silver eyes, he experienced a similar response.

With a practiced flick of her wrist she said, "Seamus Lochlann never left the enchanted fortress of the house that once belonged to Afton Sinclair, one of the most powerful druids Brighid ever trained." Macha leaned against the smooth racks of stag antlers comprising the back of her throne and motioned to an attendant rogue warrior to refill her cup of ambrosia. "You should be happy I took a warrior at all." Slanting her fellow goddess a look over the rim of her cup, she said, "After all, this little war the two of you have waged against the Sheridans and their friends all these centuries does not concern me. I was content with the slaughter on the battlefield a thousand years ago when you bested Findlay Sheridan."

Maeve stopped in front of her. "You do not understand, Macha."

"That whining tone does not work with me, Maeve. It is well you remember that." Turning from Maeve, she stared meaning-fully at Morgan who sat forward in the wooden chair flanking Macha's throne, looking like she wanted to interject. Macha pre-empted her. "I am Queen of Ireland. Not either of the two of you. Not Danu. I, Macha, am queen here and across the sea in Scotland. As such, I will do as *I* see fit, not as the two of you want me to do for your own petty entertainments."

Taranis, who had affected a languid pose leaning his shoulder against the hewn stone wall on the side of the dais, arms folded over his massive chest, unfolded himself to give a slow clap. "Well done, Macha." Glaring at the other two goddesses from beneath his brows, he sneered, "At least there is one deity you cannot bully into doing what she does not wish to do."

Morgan returned his glare before sitting back in her chair and addressing Macha. "As part of the triple goddess, you are exactly like us. You love battle, death"—she gave the rogue war-rior attending them a lecherous glance then shifted her attention back to Macha—"the pleasures of sex. In that particular regard, you are as voracious as we are."

"Yes, but I do not always require death in order to take my pleasure," Macha snapped.

With a tip of her chin, she sent the rogue out of her receiving chamber. At the moment, she rather liked this one, and not only was she not ready yet to expend him on a battlefield somewhere, she also did not want to share him with her sisters who would force him to pleasure them until he died. Knowing herself to be as capricious as the other two goddesses, she still prided herself on a sense of fairness. Not only was she one-third of the triple goddess of war, but she also presided over fertility. It was up to her to see to it that warriors continued to beget warriors, which meant some of the best ones had to live.

In America, she'd taken Gavin Scanlon, a promising warrior, one, it turned out, who had been fated to bond with a seer. As the patroness of seers, Macha had regretted Sloane MacIntosh's sacrifice. Yet until she'd taken the warrior, Macha had had no idea she'd asked a sacrifice from one of her own. Danu and the Dagda's insistence that the other deities in the pantheon remain ignorant of the skills of the talismans in the mortal world irritated her endlessly—an irritation she'd taken out on Sloane.

An evil smile stretched her mouth as she thought about the ways she'd intimidated the seer into doubting herself.

"What are you thinking, Macha?" Maeve asked.

"I was remembering the look of devastation on the talisman's face when I told her I demanded a sacrifice."

"That is an expression I would dearly love to see on Sian Sheridan's face." Morgan's words came out in a snarl.

"And Alyssa Sheridan's face, and Ceri Sheridan's face, and Lynnette Sheridan's face," Taranis added in a bored tone. Though he'd returned to his nonchalant pose, his body visibly vibrated with energy.

Yes, Macha thought, she would rather enjoy some private time in her bed with the mercurial god of weather. Perhaps their shared tiredness of Maeve and Morgan's machinations would encourage a tryst—purely to improve their attitudes.

"This time is not about the Sheridans!" Maeve stomped her foot. A snarl emanating from Morgan changed Maeve's tune.

"At least not entirely. If Seamus Lochlann succeeds in marrying Fallon Graham, the talisman's bardic powers to change the stories of mortals increase exponentially." Her arms akimbo as she stood before the dais, she stared down her fellow deities. "That is reason enough for *you* to help me take Seamus Lochlann."

"Really, Maeve? Is that what this is?" Taranis drawled. "Or is it that you want the warrior to remember you, to see you when he closes his eyes rather than the talisman who rivals your beauty." He laughed. "Face it, darling. Brighid won the last round when she wiped Seamus Lochlann's memory clear of his time in your bed after his talisman rescued him from you."

Macha watched in fascination as Maeve's anger seemed almost to light her on fire from within.

"You could have prevented that if you had kept that meddling golden-girl busy as Morgan asked," Maeve fumed.

The sound of thunder right outside the walls of her stronghold told Macha the grievances between the other deities ran hot. Time to discover what her sisters wanted of her before she ended up with a celestial civil war in her throne room.

Putting up a hand to stop the squabbling, she said, "It seems that for all their talk of peace, mortals—civilians and warriors alike—enjoy battle as much as we do. For example, the warrior I delivered to you at Lughnasadh"—she inclined her head to Morgan—"had been warned by his mate not to engage the rogues I brought with me. Yet he was incapable of withstanding the call to fight." With a manufactured sigh, she busied herself with fluffing out the folds of her long red dress.

"Your ability to mimic Scathach only works on those who have not trained directly with her," Morgan said with a huff. "You will not have such success with any of the Sheridans or their friends in whom she takes a personal and very hands-on interest. We will have to think of something else."

Macha stood and stretched before taking a little tour of her favorite room. The walls of her throne room were covered with paintings of battle, slaughter, and carnage reddening the once verdant lands of Ireland and Scotland. She never tired of looking at them, the faces of men contorted in pain and defeat, the bodies ravaged long ago with arrows and blades graduating to masses of men mangled in the aftermath of automatic weapons, cannons, and bombs. The scenes simultaneously soothed and revitalized her. Gliding her fingers over a particularly gruesome scene from the days of Brian Boru, she asked, "What is it you want this time?"

"After the clever way Fianna Conlan bargained her way into favor among those in our pantheon, it would be inviting a wasted millennium in hell to attack her manor house," Taranis reminded the goddesses.

"Calling up Formorians against Seamus Lochlann last summer drained me to the point I could not demand even a civilian sacrifice on Lughnasadh," Morgan said with a sneer at Maeve. "Which means I will not be calling them again."

"The Sheridans have defeated every zombie champion you have raised against them," Taranis said with what Macha could only interpret as ill-disguised glee.

Both Morgan and Maeve seemed to glow red at Taranis's comment, which elicited a dazzling grin from the god while the thunder crashing outside the castle walls receded into the distance.

Maeve sucked in a long breath. "Obviously, we will have to lure them away from Conlan Manor and its grounds before the wedding rites on the autumnal equinox."

"Your stronghold on the Black Isle might be a suitable venue, Morgan." Macha made her way back to the dais and seated herself on her throne. "The enchantments there would allow for a lovely battle obscured from curious civilians."

"But whom would we call against the Sheridans?" Seeming not to notice its lack of comfort, Morgan slumped back into her ornately carved chair. "Unfortunately, Taranis is correct. The

Sheridans have been uncommonly successful against my zombie champions. Against all odds or even good reason, they brought down Ysbaddaden and the Morhaus together in one night when I used them to attack Rio."

Macha smiled, and a welcome chill descended on the room. "Then we will not call your zombies this time. Nor will we launch our attack against the Sheridans."

Morgan shot up, her face contorted in rage.

Macha placidly continued on. "Nor will we attack your pet target Seamus Lochlann," she said, addressing Maeve who raised her hands as though to throttle Macha, who ignored her threat. "We will attack the heart of Conlan Manor—Hamish Buchanan."

Morgan narrowed her eyes. "How?"

Taranis pushed away from the wall and stalked over to the dais. "Be careful, Morgan," he warned. "That old druid has paid homage to you—and to me—every Samhain for nearly the last hundred years. I will not be inclined to harm him."

"Except for last year," she said through gritted teeth.

He stared at her from hooded eyes. "I was entertained quite satisfactorily at the manor last Samhain."

"I do not propose to attack Hamish directly."

Taranis pushed his hands into the pockets of his immaculately fitted trousers, and once again, Macha admired the perfection of the god in his human form.

"For the past little while, I have been amusing myself by toying with Hamish's protégé Davy Sutherland," Macha began.

"Why would the Sheridans concern themselves with a *druid?*" Maeve asked with a sniff. Apparently, she still harbored a great deal of animus against the patron goddess of druids.

"Because he has spent most of the last year training with Rio Sheridan—and Scathach. For a druid, he has uncommon skills as a warrior."

Morgan sat on the edge of her chair. Maeve climbed the dais

and took her place in the opposite wooden chair flanking Macha's throne. Neither said anything, a sure sign Macha had their undivided attention.

"If we put Davy Sutherland in mortal danger, Hamish Buchanan will demand the Sheridans go to his aid. After all, Davy was the one to rescue Ceri and Lynnette Sheridan from your rogue warriors last Samhain."

Morgan glared at her. "You knew what we attempted at Conlan Manor last year and you remained here in Ireland and did nothing?"

"You did not ask for my help."

Morgan bared her teeth and remained silent.

"As I was saying—after the way Davy came to the aid of the Sheridans and the Conlans, the two clans will be honor-bound to help him. When they do, we can indulge in orgasmic ecstasy at the expense of all your warrior nemeses—Alaisdair Graham who eluded you for nearly fourteen years, Duncan MacManus who defied you by marrying a druid while retaining his talisman, Seamus Lochlann who cannot remember his time in your bed." She couldn't help the smirk she directed in Maeve's direction. "The Sheridans—Owen who escaped your clutches at the last hour when he discovered Sian literally a stroke before midnight on his twenty-eighth birthday, Riley who managed to bond with Lynnette before you could steal the enchantments surrounding her, Rowan who, upon discovering his bond with Alyssa, reversed your curse on warriors, and Rio whose bond with Ceri Ross extends protections to any warrior associated with her clan for the next ten generations." She turned her smirk to Morgan. "We can bring down all of your enemies."

"How?" Maeve and Morgan asked simultaneously.

Taranis had resumed his bored stance against the stone wall. "Yes, how? I'm quite curious about your plan."

"We'll lure the druid to the Green Isle."

Chapter Twenty

LOANE TOOK TWO steps toward the back door of the manor when Davy's hand on her upper arm halted her progress.

"No' that way, lass."

She quirked a brow.

"We need tae bring the protection plants intae the house in the formal way."

He led her around the manor through the ivy-covered archway guarding the entrance to the kitchen garden. The leaves of the ivy had started to turn, and privately, Sloane lamented not being in residence when they came into their full autumn glory. In silence, they walked along the stone path until they came to where it converged with the cement sidewalk in front of the house and led to the wide stone steps of the veranda. Davy jogged up the steps ahead of her and opened the door for her. As before, she heard him muttering something under his breath and understood he chanted protection spells as they entered the house.

Instead of leading her down to the kitchens as she'd expected, he tugged her through the doors of the salon. With a snick of the catch on the lock, he closed the doors behind them. He glanced around them before he slipped his hand beneath the strap of the satchel she'd slung over her shoulder and let it drop to the floor to land simultaneously with his. Then he pulled her into his arms.

His mesmerizing amber eyes searched hers for interminable seconds desire apparent in those beautiful irises of his before he lowered his head and brushed his lips over hers. When their mouths met, the dull throbbing of her thigh, which she'd studiously ignored all morning, erupted into electric pulses that pleasured her deep in her core. Instinctively, she pushed herself into him, sliding her hands up his arms from his elbows to the tops of his biceps. As she tightened her hands on him, he slid his hands over the globes of her ass, roughly tugging her into the cradle of his hips. There was no mistaking the hardness she discovered there, an answering response to the sensations rippling through her.

He deepened the kiss, his tongue dancing so erotically with hers she couldn't stop the moan rising from her throat. Flexing her fingers, she clung to his arms, and the pressure seemed to ignite something inside him as he began moving rhythmically against her. The friction of his thighs along the tops of hers lit an answering fire inside her, a raging conflagration that had her wrapping her arms around his neck and trying to climb him like a tree.

Tearing his lips from hers, he trailed open-mouthed kisses along the edge of her jaw until he reached her earlobe. Taking it between his teeth, he bit down gently and tugged. At his touch, a ragged sigh escaped her. He nosed her hair from behind her ear, baring the sensitive skin, his lips and tongue teasing and tasting her until she couldn't suppress the moan building inside her.

His hands had slipped under the hem of her sweater, their destination obvious as he palmed his way up the skin of her belly, when the handle of the doors to the salon jiggled loudly behind them. For a second, they both froze before a soft chuckle escaped Davy's mouth.

Resting his forehead on hers, he sucked in a breath.

"Hey, someone locked the salon," Rio called from the foyer.

"Damn," Davy whispered. "I've been dying tae dae that all morning."

"Yet you waited until we returned to the house where we were certain not to be disturbed," Sloane said with a grin. "Unlike when we were completely alone together on the side of a mountain or all by ourselves in your skiff in the middle of the lake."

"Tae be fair, lass, juniper bushes donnae offer much in the way of privacy, and the skiff is none tae stable fer certain activities."

He waggled his brows, and Sloane cracked up.

The mood broken, they gathered their satchels from the floor, and he rested his forefinger on his lips. When she questioned him with a tilt of her head, he motioned for her to follow him. He led her over to the far side of the salon to a wall flanking the fireplace. A mischievous grin crossed his face before he turned away from her. She couldn't see past his satchel and the broad shoulders from which it hung, but she heard a loud click, like tumblers rolling inside a lock. Davy took a step to his right and pushed on the oak paneling of the wall.

The wall came alive as it grumbled and moved. The paneling slid away, and like something out of a Harry Potter movie she watched when she was a kid, Davy led her through the opening into a dark hallway. Reaching around her, he touched something on the wall, and the panel slid back into place leaving them in cave-like darkness.

"Davy?"

A hand brushed over her thigh. "I should have thought of this place earlier."

Sounds of conversation coming from the other side of the panel made her bat his hand away.

His soft laughter teased her ear. "Guess it's time tae go."

Glowing light suddenly illuminated the space in which they stood. A narrow hallway big enough to walk single file opened in front of them. She followed Davy as they made their way through the hall, turning a sharp left, and after forty or fifty steps—she'd lost count—they took another sharp left before coming to a staircase. When they reached the bottom, Davy turned to her and motioned again for her to remain quiet. He cracked open the door and peeked around it. Apparently finding the coast clear, he opened the door all the way into the kitchens.

"Clever," she said as she walked over to the battered table.

"It is, isn't it? All the houses built back in the day have these ingenious features. They came in handy when ye needed tae hide contraband," he said casually as he unloaded the juniper berries from his satchel into a bowl he'd placed on the table. "Or people."

Sloane blinked. "What kind of contraband?" Visions of pirates and treasure flitted through her head. Somehow, she thought, Davy would have fit right in.

"This close tae the sea, it wouldn't be uncommon tae appropriate most anything from a shipwreck or a passing vessel. Silks, whisky, spices." He grabbed her satchel and carefully began to remove the melilot from it, laying the flowers on the scarred surface of the table.

Fascinated, she sat on the bench and stared up at his face as he continued his task. "Did the Conlan family participate in piracy?"

"No' tae my knowledge. The hidden passages in Conlan Manor were mainly used by servants moving unseen through the house." He started twisting stems of the melilot to create small bundles. "And the occasional warrior trying tae avoid the Morrigan if he chanced tae reach his twenty-eighth birthday without discovering his talisman."

He caught her eye, and his hands stopped moving midtwist.

The playful mood of the morning's adventures, including their near discovery in the salon and the trip through the hidden passage, evaporated. As attracted as she was to the hot druid, her experiences at Lughnasadh had taught her a powerful lesson about loss. Macha's constant reminders made sure she didn't forget it.

"Ye're no' meant tae live yer life alone, Sloane MacIntosh," Davy said quietly. "A woman who has as much life and passion inside her as ye dae is meant fer love."

She squeezed her eyes shut against the need—and something deeper, something that must remain unnamed—that she couldn't miss in his expressive amber eyes.

"You don't understand, Davy. Macha—"

Hamish's booming laughter at the top of the stairs interrupted her. Seconds later, the spry old druid fairly danced down the stairs into the room. "There the twa o' ye are. I thought I saw ye arrive quite some time ago. Must have been a trick o' the light." The twinkle in his eye should have warned her. "Would ye have any idea how the salon came tae be locked, lad?"

With his concentration seemingly focused on his task with the flowers on the table, Davy shrugged. The speed of his recovery from their interrupted conversation stunned her. How could he be so nonchalant? Then she noticed the tick of his jaw and figured out maybe their conversation wasn't quite finished.

Davy cleared his throat. "Couldn't tell ye, auld man, since Sloane and I spent the morning fetching and gathering fer the likes of ye."

Hamish chortled at Davy and sent a wink in Sloane's direction. But he let them off the hook. "How did ye dae?" He picked up and set down several bundles of flowers before he gathered a handful of juniper berries and rolled them over his palm with his fingers. "Nice and fat. Fully ripe. These are perfect, lad." Returning his attention to the yellow blossoms with their long green stems littering the table, he added, "I cannae believe ye found melilot still in bloom this time o' year. Must be a good omen."

Davy gave a noncommittal grunt as he finished bundling the last of the flowers.

"If ye donnae mind, could ye take the melilot tae the ballroom fer me? The juniper berries can go tae my apartment. Ye know the proper place fer 'em."

"I can take the flowers upstairs. I need to go to my room to freshen up, and the ballroom is on my way."

"Sloane."

There was a command in Davy's tone she decided not to hear.

Apparently, Hamish didn't hear it either. "That's kind o' ye, lass. Thank ye." As he refilled the satchel with flowers, he said, "Donnae take tae much time on yer toilet though, lass. Lunch is ready, and ye know how the Sheridans can eat."

Hamish's admonishment drew her attention to the rich aroma of roasting meat. How had she missed that during all their time in the kitchen? Then she caught Davy trying to bore a hole through her with his eyes—or more like willing her to open her shield to him—and she remembered why she hadn't noticed anything else in the room, not even the mouth-watering fragrance of cooking food.

Needing to escape what she feared to be building between Davy and her, she stood and grabbed the satchel from Hamish. "Shall I leave this in the ballroom as is, or should I unload it?"

"Ye should find a basket o' rowan branches on the dais. Leave the satchel on top o' them. That'll be fine. Thank ye, lass."

As she nodded at Hamish, from the corner of her eye, she saw Davy open his mouth to speak. In a rush, she said, "Thanks for letting me tag along this morning, Davy. It was—fun."

On that lame description, she hustled up the stairs. Whatever he'd wanted to say, whatever he'd wanted to start, she couldn't let him go there. In the maze, she'd allowed herself to give in to her attraction, to her need to be close to someone, which had been a mistake. In the salon, she'd learned that after giving in to him once, she didn't have the willpower to push him away again. Wanting and needing him to remain safe from the goddess gave her no choice but to stay away from him.

After their tryst, he kept saying they were destined to be together, but she knew better. The gods had destined her for one man, and Macha had taken him from her as a sacrifice. The constant presence of Macha's minions cawing at her warned her the goddess intended to take another sacrifice from her. Having experienced Davy Sutherland so completely, she knew she could never bear it if Macha took him as that sacrifice.

So she would do what was needed to stay away from him, to shut down her growing feelings for him. She couldn't give the goddess a reason to target Davy. Walking away from him was a loss she would bear. Knowing he lived somewhere in the world, that Macha hadn't given him to Morgan for their mutual orgasmic pleasure in Davy's death, would be her comfort during her lonely nights.

Only knowing her warrior for an hour, she hadn't had the chance to develop strong feelings for him beyond those his sign had immediately demanded from her, the trick the gods used to bond and mate warrior-talisman pairs. Davy Sutherland was different. When she closed her eyes, she could picture with perfect detail his strong build, feel the callouses of his fingers on her skin, hear his resonating Scots burr encouraging her to take her pleasure. She could see the sparkle in his amber-colored eyes as he told her stories of giants or shared the properties of plants or explained the powers of the maze. Every time he flashed his dimples at her, her core tightened, and her body heated in response. It wasn't difficult for her to wish the gods had had another idea in mind for her, to wish that Davy was right about their shared destiny. But wishing didn't change anything.

As she set the satchel of melilot bundles on top of the rowan branches in the basket in the ballroom, a weird sensation of warmth stole over her. The room glowed with an otherworldly golden light. Turning in a circle, she saw the glow haloed her, like some sort of protective shield.

"Brighid?" she asked in a small voice.

She had to squint as the light intensified.

Brighid is Fallon's patron goddess. Why is she shielding me?

The only answer to her question was a compulsion to pull a melilot bundle from the satchel. With the flowers in her hand, she exited the ballroom, the golden glow receding behind her. Yet the sensation of warmth remained with her, easing the ache of past and future loss.

CHAPTER TWENTY-ONE

USING FAR MORE force than the task required, Davy ground a handful of juniper berries through the special sieve. It was either that or grinding his back teeth to powder, a distinct possibility under the circumstances.

"I'll need some pulp if ye could leave some behind, lad."

Davy almost growled at the amusement he heard in Hamish's voice. As usual, the old man was up to something. Normally, Davy didn't care. But then normally, Hamish's machinations didn't directly involve him. At least not as the recipient of them. However, the way the old man had all but encouraged Sloane's hasty exit from the kitchen when it was clear Davy wasn't finished with her told him his teacher had set his sights on Davy.

Glaring at the fragments of berry skins in the bottom of the sieve, he shoved the sieve and the bowlful of berry juice beneath it at Hamish with enough force he nearly spilled the fruits of his labors on the prep table in Hamish's quarters. Muttering obscenities both in English and in Gaelic, he moved down the table to the mortar and pestle and went to work grinding shelled hazelnuts to paste. Usually, the preparation of the foundations of Hamish's dishes, the ones the old druid specifically concocted to produce particular responses in those who ate them, entertained him. Hamish's subtle yet effective method of manipulating others to bring out their best traits was one lesson Davy had truly wanted to master. But today's events with Sloane soured his mood.

Something changed when Hamish interrupted them. He nearly forced the heavy stone mortar through the marble pestle as his conscience corrected him. Hamish hadn't ruined the lovely mood he'd worked all morning to create with Sloane. He'd done that all by himself the second he'd mentioned hiding warriors gone to ground inside the manor. Mentioning that part of the history of the manor had become mundane, almost like a fairy story in the year since Rowan and Alyssa Sheridan had lifted the curse on warriors. Yet lifting the curse didn't leave them any less vulnerable to attacks from the unholy trio, as Sloane was well aware. He wanted to kick himself for his insensitivity. Instead, he took out his frustration on the inanimate objects at his mercy.

Even as certain as he was the two of them were meant to be together, something their time in the maze only crystallized in his mind, Sloane's actions told him she wasn't on board with the program. Yeah, she responded to his advances with her whole physical self, yet when he pressed for intimacy, she ran away.

"Give the lass time, lad. She's only been home a few days."

"I donnae have time, Hamish. If I donnae convince her she belongs tae me before her friends marry, she'll go back tae the States, and I'll never see her again." He set his tools carefully aside, his shoulders slumped in defeat. Hamish's words echoed in his mind. A thought jerked his head up as he stared down his mentor. "Ye said home. 'She's only been home a few days.' Sloane is American, so what did ye mean by 'home?'"

Hamish placidly continued mixing juniper berry juice with chicory and honeysuckle. "The lass is home. She just hasnae figured it out yet. But have nae doubt, she will. Hand me that hazelnut paste."

Davy passed the pestle over to him, and Hamish chuckled. "Nearly ground it intae syrup, lad. Perhaps ye should take yerself off tae the cottage, shower off the mornin' and yer attitude."

Though delivered in Hamish's usual amiable tone, Davy knew a command when he heard one. With a nod, he untied his leather apron and hung it on its appropriate peg beside the door leading to the tunnel and the cottage. Inserting his key into the lock, he gave his wrist the requisite twist to engage the key properly, and turned the handle. As he made his way to the cottage, undressed, and stood beneath the hot spray in his matchbox of a shower, Hamish's words ricocheted in his head. Sloane was home. Somehow, he had to make her see she belonged here in Scotland—with him.

For the rest of the day, the wedding conspired to keep Sloane from him. With the autumnal equinox only five days away, the preparations suddenly moved into high gear. Though he'd had the idea he'd sit next to her during lunch, perhaps whisper in her ear they needed to talk in private afterward, maybe sneak in a kiss to make the point, Sloane had something else in mind. Namely, avoiding him. When he'd carried up the last of the platters of food Hamish had cooked, he discovered to his chagrin that she'd managed to seat herself between Fallon and Keela. Short of being rude, and abundantly obvious, he'd had no choice but to take the open seat down the bench on the opposite side of the table. Seated as he was beside Alaisdair, he spent the meal sharing stories about Hamish and the goings-on at the manor with his old friend.

Later, when he'd finished helping Hamish and Rio with cleanup, he'd returned to the main floor to find Sloane ensconced in the salon with the rest of the women. Whatever they were doing involved a great deal of feminine laughter a sane man would do well not to interrupt. As he stood in the middle of the foyer staring at the closed doors to the salon, he blew out a frustrated sigh.

"I hear you, buddy," Rio said as he jogged up the stairs. "After watching what my brothers and Alaisdair went through with all their wedding craziness, I'm pretty damn glad I talked Ceri into eloping. Bet Seamus is rethinking his big idea to marry on a major feast day." His chuckle sounded a bit smug, but Davy couldn't blame him. Women in wedding mode were truly terrifying.

"What do you mean?" Seamus asked as he sauntered down the stairs from the second floor.

With his thumb, Rio gestured at the sound of giggling coming from behind the closed doors to the salon. Somehow, it sounded like the ladies were sharing inside jokes at the men's expense. Or maybe his charitable feelings had decided to take a vacation. Either way, the wedding had preempted his opportunity for a heart-to-heart with Sloane, which left him with a sour taste in his mouth.

"I think I'll do some time in the weight room. Anyone up for spotting me?" Davy asked.

After Rio took up residence in the manor, he'd convinced the Conlan family trust to invest in an impressive array of free weights and some renovations to one of the bedrooms on the third floor. Davy had enthusiastically approved of this American obsession with working out, especially when it was made clear the space and the gear were for the use of anyone staying in the residence.

"I could use some work," Seamus said.

"Yeah? Me too."

The way Rio said it sounded like a challenge more than an acceptance of Davy's invitation. Accustomed to Rio's attitude, he wouldn't have paid him much attention, except he noticed the warrior staring down Seamus. There was some history there, something Davy thought would focus Rio's more competitive nature at Seamus rather than at him for once.

"I'll grab a pair of shorts and trainers and meet you there in fifteen," Davy said as he headed down the stairs to Hamish's quarters and the entrance to the tunnel. A smile ghosted over his face. Jogging to the cottage and back to the manor gave him a warm-up the others wouldn't have. Which meant in all likelihood, he would lift better than the warriors. A feral sound issuing from his throat echoed in the tunnel. Rio wasn't the only competitor among them.

When he arrived in the weight room, he found not only Rio and Seamus warming up with sets of dumbbells, but also Rowan and Riley already engaged in some heavy lifting. Riley spotted for Rowan who had racked an impressive number of plates on the bar he was benching in front of the rows of neatly stacked weights awaiting their workout. Beside them, Seamus and Rio stood in front of the floor-to-ceiling mirrors attached to the wall beside the door while sunlight streamed in from the windows facing the garden. When Davy worked out by himself, he often liked to look out of those windows at the world he sought to protect with both his druidic and warrior training rather than watch his form in the mirrors.

Nodding at the others, he walked over to the rows of weights, picked up a pair of fifty-pound dumbbells, and, standing slightly apart from the others, started his warm-up. Out of the corner of his eye, he kept watch on Rio and Seamus. From the way each of them aggressively curled their weights, the two of them had apparently already engaged in their competition. A smile threatened to erupt on his face, but wisely, he stifled it. It wouldn't do to have the whole warrior band turn on him, something he could anticipate more from their familial ties than from the difference in their ethnicity within the community.

"Should have guessed this is where the lot of ye got off tae when ye disappeared after lunch," Alaisdair said as he walked into the room.

"It's the best way to avoid getting roped into any kind of wedding nonsense," Rio said, the look on his face daring Seamus.

"That's because you know those skinny legs of yours won't look nearly as good in a kilt as these manly specimens," Seamus said, striking a pose for emphasis.

Davy's lips twitched, but he kept his rhythm.

"Is that right?" Rio drawled. "Then maybe you can explain to me why all the local ladies were swooning last year when I entered the ballroom in a kilt for the king stag ritual at Samhain."

"We entered the ballroom together, bro. I think all that feminine appreciation was about me," Riley said as he switched places with Rowan on the bench.

Rio glared at his brother in the mirror, and the smirk on Rowan's lips broke out in laughter. "You're both wrong. As the oldest—and handsomest Sheridan brother—all the ladies were checking me out."

"Och, lads. Nae need tae squabble among yerselves when ye have the manly man among ye." Alaisdair tossed back his mane of auburn hair and flexed his biceps.

Davy nearly dropped his weights as a loud guffaw escaped him.

"What? Ye donnae think I'm a manly man, lad?" The pout on Alaisdair's face was at odds with the twinkle in his eyes. "I believe I've landed ye on yer arse a time or twa in the trainin' room over the years."

"Because I'm only a minute more than half yer age, auld man." Grinning at Alaisdair in the mirror, Davy resumed his rhythm.

"Good timing, Alaisdair," Rowan said as he helped Riley position the weighted bar to begin his set.

Davy stared at him, and Rowan shrugged. "You need a spotter, and now everyone has a partner."

"Of course," Davy dragged out the phrase as he returned his weights to their cradles. "I think I'll dae some squats tae start. Since lookin' good in a kilt is important tae this lot," he said to Alaisdair who grinned back at him.

"Or is that more fer a certain lassie who's part of the weddin' party?" Alaisdair asked with an air of practiced nonchalance as he grabbed a couple of fifty-pound plates and headed over to the bar resting on a pair of stanchions near the windows.

"See, Seamus? There's a prime example of what happens even when you don't tempt fate—but especially if you do," Rio said as he stalked over to the rows of plates, grabbed a couple of fifty-pounders, and stomped over to the bar racked above the bench opposite Riley and Rowan.

"What happened to Sloane's warrior had everything to do with Macha demanding a sacrifice and nothing to do with the man tempting fate." Seamus carried two plates over to Rio, and together they slid their weights onto the bar and secured them before going back for additional plates. "Sloane tried to warn him it was a trap, and he was too arrogant to listen to her. Not the same thing as you've accused me of at all." He gestured to Rio to take the first turn.

With a sneer, Rio positioned himself on the bench. "You were too cavalier about finding your talisman, and you know it."

Seamus helped him with the bar and counted out the set. Meanwhile, Davy finished his first set and traded places with Alaisdair. It was all he could do to keep his focus on spotting for his friend when he really wanted to listen to Seamus and Rio's conversation across the room.

"Give it a rest, Rio. It's ancient history," Rowan interrupted. "We three are all bonded and married. Seamus is about to be married. We've taken on the more vindictive pair of the unholy trio and bested them—repeatedly. I'd say we're doing well enough to enjoy ourselves. So maybe you could jack down a bit."

Rio's response was to rack his bar with a bang, not giving Seamus any warning let alone a chance to help him. Typical Rio in Davy's experience. He rolled his eyes at Alaisdair, who nodded back in agreement. No doubt Rio Sheridan was the quintessential warrior of the age, something he'd shown on multiple occasions on his home continent and his adopted one. He was also making progress in his attitude most of the time. But there were times when, damn, the man could be a diva.

After he sat up on his bench, Rio rolled his shoulders and neck before resting his hands on his knees, head down. Seeming to come to a decision, he blew out a breath and stood facing the rest of the men. "You're right, Rowan. My prejudices have everything to do with the loss of Dad's brother, something the unholy trio engineered, not a warrior"—he glanced at Seamus—"or a druid." He nodded in Davy's direction. "I'm working on it, all right?"

Seamus clapped him on the shoulder before extending his hand. "Thank you for letting us disrupt your life so Fallon and I have a chance together."

They clasped elbows in the age-old way of warrior brothers before Rio pulled Seamus in for a one-armed hug.

A broad grin spread over Rowan's face as he slow-clapped for the truce playing out in front of them. "About damn time, little brother."

Rio pulled away, and Davy watched in amazement as a red tinge climbed the other man's cheeks. "There's something else," he began. Flicking his eyes to the ceiling, he muttered an obscenity under his breath before glancing around at the other warriors. "Ceri wanted to wait until after the wedding, but I have an announcement."

As one unit, the men stepped over to Rio. Davy crossed his arms and awaited the fireworks. Being a druid among warriors sometimes had its advantages.

Rio blinked. "Since Ceri descends from one of the most powerful druids in the history of Scotland, and since we managed to achieve our little feat inside the walls of this house, there's a better than even chance she's carrying a druid."

Silence rang through the room.

"Well? Is someone going to say something?" Rio demanded.

Seamus let out a whoop before he jerked Rio off the ground and swung him around. When Seamus let him go, Rio's sputtering protest was drowned in the shouts and cheers of his brothers and Alaisdair. After all the back-slapping and hand-shaking congratulations started to die down, Davy shot him a wry grin.

"Was wondering when ye were going tae tell yer family the happy news."

"You knew?" Rio's voice hiked an octave from the first to the second word. "Did Ceri tell you?"

The fire in Rio's eyes told him that even though the man was making progress, he still had some prejudice where Davy was concerned.

"My forte might be storytelling, but I'm still a healer, which makes me sensitive tae the people around me. Ceri's been showing signs fer a while now if one knows what he's looking at."

Satisfied, Rio nodded.

"Looking at what?" Owen Sheridan asked as he strolled into the room, followed by Duncan MacManus and Griffin Walsh.

"You," Riley said with a smirk at Rio.

"Yeah, for someone who's about to become a granddad, you don't have nearly enough gray hair." Rio's eyes danced.

Owen stared down each of his sons. "Which one?"

Rio stepped toward his dad. "The best-looking one, of course."

"Be damned," Owen swore. "Your mom and I kind of expected it to be Riley." He pulled Rio into a tight embrace. "Congratulations, son. That's the best news."

Davy could have sworn he saw a sheen of moisture cloud over

Owen's eyes as he held his son. Watching the two of them together reminded Davy that for all Rio's strength, skill, and courage as a warrior, he was still mortal. And he mattered a great deal to his clan. Because druids tended to be more reserved, he missed the kind of camaraderie and shared emotion warriors often engaged in when they were together. He caught Griffin's eye, and the other druid nodded, like he could see that deep inside, Davy wished he'd been born a warrior.

The newcomers offered a fresh round of best wishes that left everyone smiling and laughing, the mood considerably different from when Davy had suggested letting off some steam in the weight room. "Looks like we're finished workin' out fer now," he said. "Since the ladies have commandeered the salon and its stash of fine uisge-beatha, might I suggest toastin' the happy news in the kitchens?"

Alaisdair raised a brow to which he responded, "Ye're no' the only one who knows where Hamish keeps his extra whisky. And I might have procured a key tae the hidden cupboard in the pantry."

"Ye're a sly one, Davy Sutherland."

He shrugged. "What can I say? The auld man willnae share his recipe with me, which forces me tae make other 'arrangements,' if ye will." His fingers curled around the word.

The assembly of warriors and druids laughed both at Davy's antics and at Rio's good news. Their laughter and congratulations echoed down three flights as they descended the stairs to the kitchen together.

CHAPTER TWENTY-TWO

SLOANE LOVED THE grand salon with its huge windows looking out on the gardens, the artfully placed groupings of furniture, the crackling fireplace. The antique chairs and sofas had been reupholstered using modern padding and fabrics with floral and tartan patterns, rendering them both beautiful and comfortable. The carved oak occasional tables, side and coffee tables gleamed with the reflected light from the lamps resting on their surfaces or from the wall sconces positioned at intervals on the narrow walls between the windows. The massive grand piano anchoring the room opposite the doors made her think of long-ago musicales. Normally not given to such flights of fancy, the room took her out of herself in a way she rather enjoyed. Like a vacation. Though the salon took up nearly one entire side of the manor, experience told her the room wasn't big enough for her to hide from Davy there.

At the moment, she wasn't vacationing in the salon. Instead, she'd seated herself on the plush salmon-colored cushion in the bay window in the library. From her vantage point, she could catch the waning pinks, purples, and oranges of another spectacular Scots sunset painting the sky. So absorbed was she in the natural goings-on happening in the ether she didn't notice she was no longer alone. The scent of cold outdoors, citrus, and spice teased her nose, alerting her to Davy's presence.

On a gasp, she said, "What are you doing here? Weren't you in the kitchens a minute ago?"

"Keeping tabs on me, are ye, lass?"

Her face heated at what she'd revealed, and she remained silent.

"Alas, we druids cannae bend time and space tae be able tae move like warriors." He sat on the edge of the cushion and faced her. "Ye want tae explain tae me why ye've been avoiding me since we returned tae the manor this morning?"

"I—" She swallowed, started over. "I wasn't avoiding you." Her eyes darted back to the sunset. "As Fallon's maid of honor, I have obligations to her." Involuntarily, she fisted her hands. "To do wedding things." She glanced back at him. "After all, Fallon's wedding is the whole reason why I'm even here in Scotland."

"Did it occur tae ye maybe Fallon's weddin' is the excuse the fates used tae bring ye here? Tae me?"

"Davy," she said, her tone a warning. "You know I was fated for a warrior. You also know Macha trampled all over the fates when she took him from me." She hugged her knees to her chest. "Since then, she's made sure I understand that my destiny is to remain alone."

"Pardon me, Sloane, but that's bollocks."

She blinked at the vehemence in his voice.

"Total shite. Ye're nae more destined tae be alone than any talisman in this house. All of whom are paired up, even Keela Walsh." The way he looked at her made her think he wanted to see into her very soul. "Especially Keela Walsh, a talisman who lost her warrior before they could bond and who then married a druid."

"Y-you know about that?"

"We druids aren't confined merely tae sharin' recipes fer

potions and salves and such. There might be other things tae talk about." He hitched himself farther onto the cushion, crowding her. "Griffin told me all about how he and Keela came taegether."

"But Keela didn't have Macha following her every move. Torturing her with crows interrupting her peace. Reminding her what she'd lost." Sloane's voice dropped to an agitated whisper. "Keela never met her warrior, Davy. Griffin told her about him after Morgan led him across her evil river of blood into death."

He stared at her hand where she gripped his forearm. Until that moment, she didn't know she'd reached out to him. Still, she had to convince him, make him see the danger he faced if he continued to pursue her. "I've already lost one man, a brave and selfless warrior who raced into danger to help a civilian kidnapped by a band of rogues. My conscience struggles enough with that to last me my whole life. I can't risk another loss like that," she finished, her throat burning with unshed tears.

His voice was low, soothing. "No' the same at all, lass."

Slipping his arm beneath her legs, he pulled them over his lap then slid his other arm around her waist, pulling her close to him. Her good sense screamed at her to resist him, but her body had never paid attention to her good sense. Dropping her head on his shoulder, she savored the solidness of his body where he held her against him and let his words wash over her.

"We're connected, we two." His forefinger traced her upper thigh. "We connected the moment we met, Sloane. I saw the flair of recognition in the beautiful violets of yer eyes. Ye know it as much as I dae."

Sensations spiraled through her, his words, his touch pushing her ever closer to the edge.

"Every casual conversation, every shared look, every soft kiss was leading tae the two of us coming taegether in the maze."

A shiver of delight puckered her nipples beneath the layers of her clothes, and she squeezed her knees together at Davy's reminder.

"Ye haven't stopped thinkin' about it either, have ye, lass."

It wasn't a question.

She sucked in a breath and willed the tattoo on her thigh to stop throbbing. Davy squeezed her thigh like he knew exactly what lay hidden beneath the denim of her jeans.

"Davy."

"It's nae use fighting it, Sloane. The fates have their plan, and we have nae choice but tae follow it."

"How can you be so certain?"

"Because we're always aware of where the other is." He winked at her. "Even when one of us is trying tae hide herself away."

She tried to shift away from him.

"Nae need tae feel embarrassed." His dimples were killing her—slowly. "I know ye think ye're protecting me from the goddess, but that's no' yer place."

"But Davy—"

He covered her mouth with his finger. "Shh, lass. If ye deny our connection, then ye're lettin' the auld girl win."

His fingers returned to tracing a pattern over her thigh, the special pattern reserved for her warrior alone. The special pattern she'd had tattooed there after she'd lost Gavin. How could Davy know? Had he seen it when they'd made love in the maze? Lazily, he traced the pattern again, and she gasped. Involuntarily, she arched into him, the throbbing deep in her core making her desperate to be filled with him again.

"Davy, I have to know," she said, panting. "Did you *see* me when we were in the maze?"

"More than anything, I wanted tae, but it was dark." He searched her eyes. "It doesn't matter. You sneaked in under my skin and sizzled through my blood before ye burrowed yer way intae the marrow of my bones. Ye're a part of me now." He gave her some respite when he moved his hand from the top of her thigh to push a strand of hair from her cheek. His forefinger trailing over her bare skin had her dropping her head back, opening herself to him. "Exactly like the fates intended," he whispered.

His lips descended on the sensitive skin of her neck, brushing, kissing, nibbling their way to her jawbone. She turned to him, but he changed direction, teasing her with his tongue and teeth, licking and nipping her earlobe and the secret spot behind her ear. The books lining the walls of the library absorbed the sound of the moan that escaped her as his hand slipped down to cup and knead her breast.

Tangling her fingers in his hair, she coaxed him to her mouth. He grinned against her lips and whispered, "Ye see, lass, we're two halves of one whole. Ye need me every bit as much as I need you."

Sloane didn't argue. Argument required thought, something she discovered herself wholly incapable of. Instead, she welded her mouth to his. Holding this man, kissing this man had become more important to her than thinking, more important even than breathing. Their tongues sallied and retreated, one chasing the other, one giving while the other took, trading roles back and forth, chase and retreat, give and take.

Though chest to chest, Sloane wanted to be closer, needed to be closer to him. Deep in the recesses of her heart, she apprehended the difference between the possibility of her relationship with her warrior and the reality of what had taken root and grown like a magical thing between Davy and her. She ground herself against him, her groans matching his, her heart beating in rhythm with his.

This man.

By all the gods, this man.

Sliding her hand between them, she found and cupped him, stroking the hard length she discovered behind the zipper of his trousers. The way he thrust up into her palm told her he was as close to losing control as she.

At last, they tore away from each other's mouths. Foreheads

touching, arms clasped tightly around each other, they gasped for air, the sound loud in the silence of the library. Sloane sensed more than saw Davy's grin, before he said, "Are ye convinced about us yet? 'Cause if ye're no', I'll be happy tae keep working on it." He laughed. "I'm happy tae keep working on it regardless."

"And if I am?" she teased.

"I'll be happy tae keep reminding ye of our connection."

He stole a kiss from the corner of her mouth, and she couldn't stop the giggle that escaped her.

Pulling back enough to look her in the face, he sobered. "Dae ye have any idea how incredibly beautiful ye are when ye're happy? I could listen tae ye laugh like that all day every day."

Sloane blinked.

Happy.

She couldn't remember the last time she'd truly felt happy. As she stared into the arresting amber of Davy's eyes, her heart hammered behind her ribs. What she felt with Davy was so much more than happy.

"There you are," Siobhan said as she breezed into the room. "I've been looking all over for you."

Hastily, Sloane tried to disentangle herself from Davy who was disinclined to let her go. "What does Fallon need?" She swatted at Davy's hands, but he dialed up his dimples to full sexy and held her tight.

"I was looking for Davy. We're supposed to be in the ballroom creating the spells over the protection wreaths." With her arms crossed over her chest and her weight on her back foot, she was meant to look stern, but the sparkle in her eyes and the twitch of her lips ruined the effect. "Guess you were distracted and forgot?"

He pulled Sloane closer. "Sloane is many things, but a distraction isnae one of them. Tell Hamish I'll be up in a few minutes."

Siobhan winked and turned on her heel to exit the room, humming some sort of melody as she walked away.

"Damn." Davy blew out a breath. "It's like the auld man times it."

"You should probably go. The protection spells are especially important for this particular wedding, what with Seamus and Fallon's union increasing her ability to change people's stories even after they've already been told."

"Ye're right, my gorgeous lass. Ye're no' the only one with duties tae perform fer this wedding. But just so ye know, there are other things I'd *much* rather be doing right now than weaving spells and protection wreaths." He punctuated his words with another pass of his fingers over her tattooed thigh and a kiss that branded her as his and his alone.

Gently, he disentangled them before he pushed himself up to stand in front of her. "Donnae try tae hide from me anymore, Sloane. There's nae point."

His expression was more serious than anything she'd ever seen, and his tone brooked no rebuttal.

With a satisfied nod at what he must have interpreted in her lack of response, he walked to the door of the library. With one hand on the jamb, he said over his shoulder, "This little episode will be continued later. Count on it."

For several long minutes, she stared at the space in the door where Davy had stood, her body tingling with his promise. Then a familiar unwelcome noise popped the iridescent bubble of desire he'd conjured over her. When she glanced out the window, her heart leaped into her throat. In full-throated cacophonous cawing, a murder of crows flew up into the air in an ever-widening spiral. The kind of pain that forced her to double over on herself shot through her from her thigh to her chest.

Happy, Davy had said.

Not at all.

More like terrified.

CHAPTER TWENTY-THREE

"DAVY?"

The sleep-roughened timbre of her voice aroused him as much as seeing her body limned in the glow of a small lamp on the night-stand. Though her white sleep shirt hit her at midthigh and didn't expose any skin above that point, he could still make out the lines of her body through it. A black-haired woman wearing white was some kind of classical expression of beauty, wasn't it?

"Is something wrong? What time is it?"

"The only thing wrong is that I'm still standing at yer door in the middle of the night. May I come in?"

She pulled the door open wider and stepped aside to let him in. Gently, he took the door from her and closed it behind himself.

"Davy?"

"We were interrupted in the middle of something important. Something we need tae finish." He pulled her into his arms, lowered his lips to hers, and kissed her softly, giving her a chance to join him. With their bodies touching, he could relax for the first time since the two of them had returned to the manor late the previous morning. His woman belonged in his arms—in his bed—or he in hers where he intended to spend what was left of the night.

Dropping kisses on her face, he continued. "We finished casting protection spells"—he kissed her cheek—"a few minutes ago." He kissed her eyelids. "Hamish wanted tae take care of the plants"—he kissed her jaw—"while they were still fresh." He found his way to the sweet spot behind her ear and added his tongue to his barrage of kisses.

Sloane moaned and wrapped her arms tighter around his neck.

"We were rudely interrupted earlier by all these druidic duties. But I would never dream of leaving ye unsatisfied fer the whole night, lass."

"I was asleep before you knocked on my door, druid."

She maybe thought she sounded stern, but as she spoke, he transferred his attentions to the column of her neck, and her words ended on a breathy sigh. His lips stretched into a smile on her skin before he continued his explorations to the edge of her over-sized long-sleeved T-shirt.

"Dreamin' of me, I bet. Dreamin' of this." Sliding his hands over her, he squeezed the firm globes of her ass as he slowly and deliberately thrust himself against the front of her, leaving her no doubt about where he wanted this to go.

"Davy." His name escaped her on a sigh.

"Ye want me as much as I want ye, Sloane. Admit it."

"Yes."

He grinned. "That is one of the sweetest words in the Eng-lish language."

Deliberately, he walked her backward to the queen-sized bed with its rumpled sheets and blankets. In the glow of the lamp, he watched the violets of her eyes turn to black, and he knew his teasing words held the truth. Her dreams included him. For a brief moment, he let her go, long enough for him to toe off his shoes and shed his trousers, boxers, and socks. As he pulled his sweater up over his head, he sensed Sloane shifting before the light went out.

"Lass," he warned.

"Please, Davy?"

He found her easily in the dark, his hands on the thin cotton of her shirt. Grasping the hem, he pulled it up over her head and dropped it somewhere on the floor behind him. "Ye leave me nae choice, lass, but tae see ye by touch." With his hands squeezing her hips, he warned her before he skimmed them slowly up the sides of her torso. "I cannae be held responsible if any of the others pound on the door tae shush ye when ye're screamin' my name after I've wound ye up with my hands." Finding and holding her heavy breasts, he couldn't stop the groan escaping his own lips when he thumbed her gorgeously hard nipples.

Her answering moan and her hands on his biceps had him pushing her back onto the bed where he lowered himself on top of her.

"This is crazy," she whispered as he dragged his lips down her throat and over her chest.

"It's right."

Giving her no chance to argue, he pulled a ripe nipple into his mouth, savoring its firmness with his tongue before sucking her hard. Nothing in the world tasted as sweet as the raspberries of his Sloane's skin. Nothing in the world felt as good as giving her pleasure. She rewarded him by plowing her fingers into his hair and holding him to her as she chanted his name. Beneath him, she squirmed and bucked, one foot sliding up the back of his leg to his hip as she opened herself to him.

Taking his time, he gave her other breast equal attention while she panted and arched her body into him, silently begging him to fill her. Instead, he danced his fingertips along her belly and down until he found her center. He palmed her while he teased her clit with the pad of his thumb. Finding patience he had no idea he possessed, he ratcheted up her pleasure with his hands and his mouth, even as his body throbbed and begged for release.

Meandering kisses down her taut belly, he continued to tease her. When he gave in to her moans and incoherent pleas and tongued the tight bud between her legs, she fisted the sheets on either side of her hips, arched into him, and screamed. He allowed himself a tiny smile of satisfaction before he slid two fingers into her slick channel and worked her while he continued to kiss and suck her, her taste and her responses to him the most incredible aphrodisiacs he'd ever encountered. Nothing in druidic lore could reproduce the salty-sweet flavor of Sloane's body or the way her sighs and moans and inability to remain still beneath him fired his desire.

"Davy! Davy! Davy! *Davy!*" rang in his ears as she arched one last time, her body going taut with her climax. Only then did he give her a reprieve. Long enough for him to climb up her body and settle between her legs.

"Any minute now, we're going tae hear a knock at the door, Sloane." With his eyes adjusted to the dark, he caught the flash of alarm in hers, and he chuckled. "Ye cannae say I didn't warn ye."

"Davy," she hissed, but there was no heat in it.

He centered himself at her entrance. "Donnae worry, lass. I promised ye I'd satisfy ye, and I always keep my promises."

With a prolonged thrust into her tight, wet heat, he joined them together. As he held himself inside her, sweat beaded on his forehead and gathered at the base of his spine. It was his turn to hiss in a breath before he groaned her name into the stillness of the night.

"Ahh, Sloane. There is nae one in the world like ye. Ye were made fer me."

She wrapped her arms and legs around him, pulling him even deeper inside her. When her hand slipped to his upper arm, unerringly finding the swirling tattoo there, her touch gave him no choice but to thrust into her. The ink on his arm pulsed along the swirls, radiating a sensation of power and strength like he could conquer the world. Their bodies in perfect rhythm, they moved together, their need matching and building in each other. Never in his life had he imagined experiencing a connection like the one he shared with Sloane. Lightning crackled through him, making him feel like a superhero, like he could command the universe. This woman took him to places he had no idea could even exist.

He covered her thigh with his hand, and she surged up, lifting them both off the bed. Her body vised around him as she came, his name tearing harshly from the back of her throat. Two thrusts later, he joined her, violet stars flashing behind his eyes as he shouted his release. For an eternity, he held himself above her, his fingers finding their own way over the smooth skin of her thigh, his other hand fisted in the sheets beside her shoulder as the aftershocks rolled over and through them. Violet eyes like jewels glittered up at him as she labored to control her breathing, her hands gliding up and down his torso.

He hated pulling out of her, but his arm and shoulder needed a break. As he started to move, she wrapped her legs around him, holding him inside her. "Not yet, Davy. Please."

"Sloane, I—"

"I can take your weight. Please." Something in her tone tugged at him. "I'm not ready to let you go."

"I'll never be ready tae let ye go, lass."

She blinked her beautiful eyes several times, but in the darkness, he couldn't be sure of the tears he thought he saw in them.

Gathering her in his arms, he carefully maintained their connection as he rolled them so she lay on top of him. In the aftermath of their lovemaking, silence echoed in the room. Then the first tear sizzled the skin in the crook of his neck.

"Lass, what is it?"

"I don't want to lose you, Davy Sutherland."

He'd been smoothing his hands up and down her spine, but the sadness in her tone, perhaps because he could hear it even more clearly as they communicated telepathically, reverberated through him. Wrapping her tightly in his arms, he said, "I'm no' going anywhere, Sloane. That's a promise. Ye know how I always keep my promises." To emphasize his point, he pushed up into her, reminding her.

A tiny puff of air and the sensation of her smile on his skin told him his ploy had worked.

"We're a fine pair, we two. Ye know that, lass."

She nodded, but that was all. Her response told him he still had work to do.

⁊

Sloane awoke to something tickling her face. When she batted at it, she discovered a big hand teasing her with her hair. Slowly, she blinked her eyes open to weak daylight inching its way into the sky outside her windows and a fully dressed Davy Sutherland seated beside her on her bed.

"Good morning, sleeping beauty."

"What time is it?" Her morning voice sounded scratchier than normal. Images of the night before flashed through her mind, and she smiled.

"Tae late fer another round of lovin', I'm afraid." If anything, the expression on his face was even poutier than the tone of his voice.

"It is?" Then she noticed the dampness of his hair. "You showered? In my bathroom?"

"That a problem, lass?"

She shook her head. "How did I sleep through that? The old pipes in that bathroom protest exercise rather loudly when they're put to use."

Davy chuckled. "That's a fact. But ye may have had a reason

fer sleeping so soundly." He waggled his eyebrows as he leered at her like a villain in a melodrama.

"Proud of yourself, are you?" She smacked him with a pillow.

Laughing, he jerked it out of her hands and tossed it onto the end of the bed. Caging her in with his hands on either side of her shoulders, he took up her personal space and stared at her with so much naked desire in his eyes, she thought she might combust from the fires he lit inside her with that look. "There's nae place in this world I'd rather be right now than lying naked beside ye in this bed."

With a tilt of her head, she peeked up at him from beneath her lashes. In her best imitation of a coquette, she said, "Then why aren't you lying naked beside me in this bed?"

He blew out a long-suffering breath. "In the botanical world, the timing of a harvest matters. I have tae meet the other druids tae gather plants from the gardens tae brew some healing potions Hamish believes we should have on hand. In case any unwanted visitors decide tae crash the wedding."

It wasn't necessary for him to name names. She knew exactly who he meant. His oblique reference to the unholy trio doused the sparks of her desire as effectively as if he'd splashed a bucket of icy water over her.

"All will be well, lass. Ye have tae believe that." Glancing around the room, he said, "This house is a fortress against the scheming attacks of the deities who wish us harm. Fianna Conlan created powerful enchantments that every generation reiterates. Everyone who lives in the manor sees tae that."

She nodded, but she must not have looked convinced because he continued.

"Yer friends are being married in the safest place they could ever choose." He traced one calloused finger over the contours of her face before he palmed her cheek. "Ye won't lose any of them. No' this time."

Reaching up, she held his wrist, securing his hand to her face before turning to place a kiss on his palm. Her friends weren't the only people she worried about. Though she'd arrived at Conlan Manor with no expectations, in a few short days Davy had walked through a door in her heart she'd thought had closed forever when the goddess stood before her in all her black glory and told her that her warrior had crossed the ford. Now, she wanted a little time with this unexpected man.

"It's only the garden, Sloane, no' the moon." He turned his dimples loose. "But I like it that ye want tae keep me in yer bed. Ye can keep entertaining those thoughts fer as long as ye like."

With both hands, she pushed at his chest, budging him not at all. "You're unbelievable."

"Ye Yanks use interesting terms of endearment." He leaned down and gifted her with a smacking kiss on her mouth before he stood and walked to the door. "It's still early, lass. Ye can go back tae sleep fer a bit and still catch breakfast. I'll see ye in the dining room in a couple of hours."

He slipped through the door, closing it behind him with a soft snick.

If not for the slight soreness between her legs, she might have thought the events of the darkest hours of the morning had been another erotic dream. She'd been dreaming of him since they met, dreams that had resulted in twisted wet sheets, much like those in which she now found herself. With a sigh, she reached down to grab the pillow at the bottom of the bed, the one Davy had slept on for the few minutes they'd actually slept after he knocked on her door. Rolling onto her side, she hugged the pillow to her chest and filled her head with his scent. "Oh, Davy. It will never do to become attached to you. Except I'm scared it's too late."

Crushing the pillow to her body, she breathed in his smell as deeply as she could. If only she could hold him this tightly, fill herself this fully with him, maybe she wouldn't lose him too.

Chapter Twenty-Four

LAISDAIR BLEW IN through the back door to the kitchen, his wife Shanley following close behind him. "Has anyone seen Hamish?"

Sloane, Fallon, and Ceri looked up from where they were enjoying a cup of afternoon tea and a lovely cake Ceri had picked up from the bakery in Ullapool. She'd made a trip to the village before lunch the day before when Sloane and Davy were gathering flowers and berries and "accidentally" found herself in the bakery as she ran errands. Spicy, moist, and delicious, the bite of cake Sloane had taken seconds before turned to ash in her mouth as she observed the disarray of the newcomers' hair and clothes. If she weren't mistaken, they'd encountered something—or someone—who'd sent them on a dead run back to the manor.

"What is it?" Standing up in a rush, Ceri nearly knocked over the bench on which she sat.

"We were out walking," Shanley began when Alaisdair, placing a gentle hand on his wife's forearm, interrupted.

"Let's gather the whole clan and tell 'em all at once, eh lass?"

Shanley nodded. "Good idea. I really don't want to have to say this more than once."

"Hamish and the other druids are working on something in Hamish's apartment," Sloane said. "I'll get them." She stood from the bench and headed out of the kitchen. Behind her, she heard Ceri say the warriors were in the billiards room and she thought Alyssa, Sian, Keela, and Lynnette were in the library.

With a sharp rap of her knuckles on the heavy oak door to Hamish's apartment, Sloane announced herself before she turned the handle. When she entered the room, she discovered Hamish staring at her, his usual jovial expression replaced by one of determination. Davy, Siobhan, and Griff flanked him, looking equally driven.

"I take it you're aware that Alaisdair and Shanley have news," she said. Though her eyes lingered on Davy longer than the others, she nodded at each of them in turn. "And I take it you have a clue what that news is."

"Been waitin' fer the auld girl tae make her move," Hamish said as he stepped toward her. "Ever since she gave ye that warnin' out in the woods yer first week here, I knew she wasnae goin' tae let our festivities go on without a visit."

In silence, Sloane stepped aside to let Hamish pass and followed him back to the kitchen.

It was selfish of me to come here. After everything Macha has put me through already, I should have heeded her warnings and stayed home. Now I've put my friends in danger, churned through her mind.

Davy snagged the back of her sweater and pulled her into his chest, stopping her before she could join the others gathered in the kitchen. "This is no' about you," he hissed in her ear.

Turning to stare at him, she gifted him with an incredulous lift of her brow and would have confronted him about breeching her shield if he hadn't preempted her. "I didn't have tae sneak a peek intae yer head tae know what ye're thinking, lass. But this is bigger than ye alone."

Crossing her arms over her chest, she jacked up the wattage of her glare. "Really? Is that why she sent me an omen the second you stepped out of the library last night?"

Davy's eyes nearly bugged out of his head as he grasped her by the shoulders. "Why didn't ye say something? Jesus, Sloane. If we're tae have any chance at all of being a team, ye have tae tell me these things."

"Maybe the twa o' ye could have yer lovers' spat later," Hamish said from behind her. "Right now, we need tae hear what Alaisdair and Shanley have tae say. I suggest we take ourselves up tae the salon tae meet with the rest o' the clan."

Davy squeezed her shoulders and pulled her close. For her ears only, he whispered, "We are a team, Sloane MacIntosh. Which means ye donnae have tae face the auld girl alone anymore." He emphasized his words with a brush of his lips over the corner of her jaw before he turned her to precede him up the stairs.

Alaisdair and Shanley stood hand in hand in front of the fireplace facing the assembled party of warriors, talismans, and druids arranged on sofas and settees or standing behind said sofas or near the sideboard. Though Sloane had separated herself from Davy by wedging herself into the corner of the sofa beside Fallon, she felt his solid presence directly behind her where he stood. The hurt in his eyes when she'd revealed the omen the goddess sent the day before only confirmed for her what she had to do—sacrifice her happiness for his life. There could be no other way.

Alaisdair's deep Scots burr interrupted her morose thoughts. "If no' fer the heavy enchantments over the garden, I think Macha might have been tempted tae take another sacrifice." He gave Sloane a look of sympathy. "Even if it meant the White Lady did the honors of leadin' one of us intae the mists and denying Macha and her sisters their terrible pleasure."

"Why didn't you come back in through the front door since she was so close?" Ceri demanded from where she stood wrapped in Rio's arms. "How could you take a chance with Aunt Shanley in her condition?"

"After she said what she came to say, Macha disappeared," Shanley said, but no one could miss the protective way she covered her distended belly with her hand.

"We dinnae want tae risk weakening the spells over the threshold intae the manor since that's the door Taranis and Morgan use every year when Hamish invites them tae Samhain," Alaisdair said. "Besides, as Shanley said, the witch had already disappeared in a cloud of purple mist, so I think we were safe enough."

"We donnae have time tae argue about what's done," Hamish said with an impatience in his tone Sloane had never heard before. "What we need tae know is what the auld girl had tae say." He fixed Alaisdair with a look from beneath his unruly white eyebrows.

"She knows about the babies, both the obvious one," he looked at his wife with so much love as he covered her hand on her belly with his that Sloane had to grit her teeth to keep from crying out. As if he sensed her distress, Davy squeezed her shoulders then left his hands on her. Oblivious to the drama playing out in front of him, Alaisdair continued. "And the no'-so-obvious one." He smiled at Ceri and Rio. "Of course, the entire Celtic pantheon is aware of the significance of the wedding we came here tae celebrate." He shifted a glance to Fallon and Seamus seated beside Sloane on the sofa. "That in itself would likely be enough tae set the auld girls on a tear. The promise of the wee babes is adding insult tae injury by their lights."

"Is that what Macha told you?" Hamish asked.

"That's where she started. But her real focus was you." Shanley turned her attention to Sloane.

Sloane swallowed and wrapped her arms tightly around herself. The news didn't surprise her—after all, the goddess had sent enough omens over the last couple of months—but having her fears confirmed only intensified them.

"Don't even say it," Fallon insisted as she turned to face Sloane.

"You know it's true, Fallon."

Fallon vigorously shook her head in the negative.

"But it is," Sloane insisted.

"I would never marry without my oldest and dearest friend standing beside me, supporting me," Fallon said. "*None* of this is your fault. Not what the goddess did at Lughnasadh and not what she threatens here."

Alaisdair cleared his throat. After throwing her one last stern look, Fallon gave him her attention while Sloane stared unseeingly at the carpet on the floor in front of her.

"The goddess does threaten Sloane, I'm afraid."

Though she tried to hold back, a gasp escaped her.

"And someone protected by Conlan Manor."

Everyone started talking at once, a cacophony that sounded to Sloane's ears like the cawing of crows, and she closed into herself even more tightly.

Those the manor protected were all connected to it by clan membership or marriage or both. In that sense, nearly everyone in the room was a target, including the venerable Hamish Buchanan who drew himself up to his full five feet eight inches as his voice boomed over every other in the room. "If ye're finished speculatin', perhaps we can start havin' a more productive conversation. What exactly did the goddess threaten?"

"She said a talisman with Sloane's particular skill will always be a problem for the goddesses of war. If they can't take her outright"—Shanley's expression of sympathy nearly undid her—

"then they will exact another sacrifice from her to remind her of her place as a 'mere mortal.'"

Sloane slowly faced Fallon. "You see. I never should have come here. You're far too important to the entire warrior community to be put in any jeopardy let alone threatened directly by the goddess."

Seamus's expression was so fierce it made Sloane ache for the loss of her warrior and the protections their union would have given each of them. Yet he directed his words to her. "For the last time, Sloane, you're not to blame for any of this. Don't you dare let the goddesses win."

Owen stepped away from where he'd been leaning against the sideboard and walked up to join Alaisdair and Shanley in front of the fireplace. "The goddesses have been focused on our family for centuries. That means our friends become targets as well." Nodding at the Walshes and MacManuses seated on the sofa opposite Sloane, he huffed out a self-deprecating laugh. "It's a wonder we have any friends at all."

"Overdramatic, much?" Duncan asked sardonically. "After the way the Sheridans have bested the unholy trio over the years, especially in recent years, the entire warrior community wants to be friends with you guys."

"Thank you, Duncan." The sincerity of gratitude rang in Owen's voice. "But it doesn't change the fact that Morgan and her nasty sisters target our family more than others and by extension, they drag our friends into the messes they create." He squatted down beside the sofa where Sloane sat. "You are not to blame, here, young lady. Macha is targeting you for her own purposes, and once we discover them, we can best her. Just like we did when Morgan tried to keep Alyssa and Rowan apart so she could maintain her evil curse on warriors. And when she targeted Ceri and Rio to stop the Conlan family prophecy from its rightful manifestation."

Siobhan leaned forward from her place across from Sloane. "Or when Maeve tried to steal Seamus from Fallon to stop a bard from assuming her full powers."

Shanley slipped her arm around Alaisdair. "Or when Morgan sent her zombies and a rogue to kill Alaisdair out of pure selfish frustration that this house and the people in it"—she smiled at Davy and Hamish—"kept him safe until he could fulfill his destiny."

Owen stood but remained beside her. "You see, Sloane, even when they've deliberately targeted us and our friends, we've prevailed against them." The stern expression on his face underscored his words. "We'll prevail this time too. Seamus and Fallon will reach their wedding day safely, and you'll be standing in your appointed place to serve your best friend."

"Ye could reassure yerself, lass, if ye used yer special skill," Hamish said.

Though his tone had been gentle, his words terrorized her.

"It appears we need to make another trip to the training room," Owen announced. "Do we have urgent wedding preparations today, or can we spare the afternoon to do some work?"

Seamus and Fallon exchanged a look before Seamus said, "Training is far more important than setting up tables and organizing catering lists. But it worries me to ask Shanley and Ceri to train right now."

"Set your mind at ease, little brother. Talismans carrying children have gone to battle since the beginning of our race," Siobhan said. "You, on the other hand, could use all the training, spells, enchantments, and stories available to keep you safe."

Beside her, Sloane sensed Fallon's sudden tension. Though Brighid, goddess of stories, had wiped Seamus's memory clean of his experience in Maeve's bed the previous summer, everyone else who had helped to free him remembered his anguish all too well.

"Owen and Siobhan have a point. We should spend the afternoon in the training room. Wedding planning will be pointless if I don't have a groom," Fallon said.

"Or if I don't have a bride." Seamus tugged Fallon under his arm, and Sloane sensed the increasing of her friend's tension.

"Right. That's settled." Hamish rubbed his hands together. "I'll need help puttin' taegether the snacks fer the afternoon, and we should partake in a bit o' lunch before we head up tae *An Teallach*. Griff, Siobhan? Join me?"

The party exited the salon in pairs. Fallon and Seamus waited out the others while Sloane remained where she was. Fallon squeezed her knee before giving in and pulling her into a tight embrace. "You're the sister I never had. Next to Seamus, you're the most important person in the world to me. I won't lose you." She pulled back and stared deeply into Sloane's eyes, the worlds swirling in Fallon's changeable hazel eyes nearly mesmerizing her. "And you're not losing me. Ever." She emphasized her words by giving Sloane a tiny shake. "Even without a warrior, you were able to help Uncle Griff and Aunt Keela and the others when they rescued Seamus and me. You are powerful in your own right. You have to remember that."

Sloane nodded, but the way Fallon shook her head told her she wasn't convincing.

Seamus stood and pulled Fallon to her feet. "Sloane, you did your very best to help your warrior. No one could have anticipated an attack within an hour of the two of you meeting. Even with everything riding on Rowan and Alyssa's pairing—both for the immortals and for us—the two of them had days to bond before Morgan made her first half-hearted sally. You have to stop blaming yourself and rejoin the living." A smile crossed his face as he winked at the man still standing behind her. "I think you know a guy who could help you with that."

With a smile, Fallon joined Seamus. Hand in hand, the two of them walked out of the salon, leaving her alone with Davy.

He vaulted over the sofa to land in the place Fallon had recently vacated. Sliding an arm along the back of the cushion and placing his other hand on the arm of the sofa, he penned her in. His face was so close to hers, she could count the gold flecks in his amber eyes or melt into the dark chocolate ringing their irises.

"Ye going tae tell me what yer skill is? Seems only right that I know, especially considering I'm the only one in the house who isn't in on the secret."

Closing her eyes against the concern and the deep affection she saw in his, Sloane dragged in a breath and nodded. "I'm a seer." Opening her eyes, she stared at his mouth. "It's why I used to enjoy taking risks."

"Because you already knew the outcome?"

"Because the outcome is never completely certain, so I could test it, test my skill. But yes, I have an advantage when I calculate risks."

"Except fer one time when ye took a risk, but ye didn't have time tae change the odds."

"I didn't take the risk," she said quietly. "He did. And I couldn't tell him without taking a risk with even worse odds."

The warmth of his hand holding her jaw was more than she could resist. She rubbed her cheek against his calloused palm and tried to slow down the speeding of her heart.

"It's true Macha changed yer world that night, but if ye give us a chance, take a risk on me being right about our shared destiny"—she watched him as he caressed the outline of her lips with his thumb—"ye still might find yer happiness."

As though he couldn't help himself, Davy leaned in and kissed her. The press of his lips on hers, an assurance rather than a demand, devastated her resolve.

When he pulled back from her enough to speak, he wrecked her. "I already knew ye were a seer, Sloane."

"How? I—"

"From the moment ye walked intae this room that first day, I couldn't take my eyes from ye. So I noticed how careful ye are never tae touch another person's hands. On the few occasions when I reached fer ye, ye very deftly managed tae keep yer hands from touching mine. I've studied my histories of the skills of warriors and talismans, so I had a clue what that meant." He pushed a stray strand of her hair from the side of her face, his hand lingering on her neck.

"You never said anything."

"Wasnae my place. When ye were ready, ye would tell me."

This time she leaned in to kiss him. For a long moment, she pressed her lips to his, drawing on his quiet strength, savoring his touch, his breath, his very essence. When she pulled away, she said, "Thank you."

"Fer what?"

"Not giving up."

The smile he gave her was pure mischief. No doubt flashing those dimples had always resulted in a win for him. Yet she couldn't help but smile back as he pushed her down into the couch cushions and kissed the breath right out of her.

CHAPTER TWENTY-FIVE

OUD THROAT-CLEARING INTERRUPTED the rather pleasurable way Davy had been deliberately composing a new story for Sloane. When he poked his head up over the top of the cushions of the sofa, he spied Alaisdair standing in the space between the doors into the salon.

"Hate tae bother ye, Davy," he said, the grin on his face belying his words. "But ye might want tae have some lunch before we head off tae the training room."

"Definitely. We were just discussing that, weren't we, lass?" He glanced down at the woman lying beneath him, her inky hair spread over the arm of the sofa, her sweater in delightful disarray.

"Best get on it, then"—Alaisdair chuckled at his own joke—"before there's naething left fer ye." He sketched an insolent bow and walked away, leaving the doors to the salon wide open.

Beneath him, Sloane blew out a breath. "That's the second time we've been caught making out in the salon, Davy."

He grinned at her, and she rolled her eyes. But he saw an answering grin twitching at the side of her mouth. Because he couldn't seem to help himself where Sloane was concerned, he dipped his head and kissed that budding grin before pushing himself up off the sofa. When he reached for her, she studiously grasped his forearm rather than his hand, and he couldn't decide if he was disappointed or relieved. Being crazy about a seer, he was coming to understand, came with a certain set of complications.

She straightened her sweater and tried to smooth her hair. "How do I look?"

"Like ye've been kissed within an inch o' yer life. Which ye have, lucky lass."

"You're unbelievable," she hissed with a smack of the back of her hand against his biceps.

Laughing, he said, "Ye didn't find me so unbelievable a few minutes ago."

"Grrrr." But she was laughing too.

Linking arms with her, he led her out of the salon and across the foyer to the dining room, the smile on his face feeling very much like a permanent fixture.

When they entered the room, they found the others seated at the long table in deep discussion. Guiding Sloane to the sideboard, they saw what was left of cold roast beef, homemade bread, cheese, lettuce, and sliced tomatoes and onions. The platters on which the sandwich ingredients had been arrayed were nearly bare. Apparently, Alaisdair had waited a bit long before fetching them to lunch.

Davy noted the look of disappointment on Sloane's face and whispered, "Donnae worry, lass. We have other options."

He winked at the skepticism she conveyed with her raised brow and tugged her out of the dining room. As they made their way down the stairs to the kitchen, he said, "I happen tae know where Hamish has hidden a lovely meat pie in the pantry."

"I have to hand it to you. You're quite resourceful, Davy Sutherland," she said, a hint of admiration in her tone that morphed into a full smile when he walked out of the pantry a minute later with a large pastry in his hands.

"Stick with me, lass. I know all the secrets."

"Now you're just showing off." She laughed before she busied herself pulling two plates from the cupboard beside the sink and setting them on the counter.

"Whatever it takes tae put that smile on yer face, lass," he said with a wry grin as he sliced and plated each of them a generous piece of meat pie. "This is tasty as is, or ye can heat it up."

"When in Scotland—"

She carried her lunch to the table then returned to the cupboard for utensils and napkins, gathering place settings for each of them. A year ago, the easy domesticity of their movements probably would have made him itch. With this woman, they felt natural and right. Like something he wanted to repeat as often as possible.

They'd barely tucked into their meal when the horde descended the stairs from the dining room. "WTF? Where did you find that?" Rio demanded as he led the others into the kitchen.

"One of the perks of practically growing up in this auld pile is knowing all the hidey-holes. If ye give yerself enough time, Rio, ye tae will figure them out. But no' taeday." Knowing he antagonized the warrior, he forked a big bite of savory pie into his mouth and smirked around it before chewing and swallowing.

"They left most of it on the counter, Rio," Alaisdair said as he opened the industrial-sized dishwasher to deposit his plate and utensils.

"I'll add it tae the hamper tae take tae the trainin' room," Hamish said as he followed the others down the stairs and entered the room. He nodded at Davy. "Ye're tryin' my patience, lad."

"No' at all, auld man." He wiped his mouth with his napkin. "Tryin' yer patience would mean in addition tae enjoying this delicious pie, we'd also be enjoying a wee dram of yer best uisge-beatha." Gesturing expansively at the table, he said, "Ye'll notice, there's no' a dram in sight."

Hamish shook his head with exasperation, but Davy heard him chortle under his breath and knew the old druid was only bluffing.

"I hate to wreck the mood, but after Macha made her threats this morning, it's a safe bet Scathach knows about it. I wouldn't be surprised to find her pacing impatiently in the training room awaiting our arrival," Owen said as he joined Alaisdair with more dinnerware to load into the dishwasher.

Hamish nodded at the clan leader before taking over the kitchen. "Keela, Siobhan, if ye donnae mind, I could use yer help gatherin' up snacks fer this lot."

The women nodded at him.

"We can worry about cleaning up the rest o' lunch when we return."

Ceri called down the stairs. "We've pretty much taken care of that, Hamish." She walked down the stairs with her sisters-in-law, carrying the platters with the remnants of lunch.

"That's grand, lass. Well, then, I imagine ye warriors need tae gather yer leathers and claymores and such before we make our journey. As Owen said, 'tis very likely Scathach will be trainin' ye taeday. Better no' keep her waitin'."

The reminder of the rough training the warrior goddess was wont to employ when her charges annoyed her was enough to send warriors and talismans scurrying to grab their gear. Though the goddess wasn't averse to training Davy alongside her warriors, she didn't harbor warrior expectations of him. After watching her train the Sheridans, especially Rio, he discovered one advantage to being a druid. No less exacting in her demands of her charges, nonetheless, when he trained with his patron goddess, Brighid never dropped him hard on his arse when he didn't perform a spell or tell a story exactly as she wanted. The same couldn't be said for Scathach who seemed to delight in doing that very thing to her warriors—in front of a crowd no less.

Davy shot a look across the table at Sloane and finished his lunch at his leisure. By the time they carried their empty plates to the dishwasher, Hamish, Keela, and Siobhan had the gathering of snacks well under control. By silent agreement, he and Sloane finished the cleanup from lunch, which gave him multiple opportunities to brush her arm or to lean into her body as they worked. Her shivers of awareness gratified him. It was good to know she wasn't trying to pull away from him. At least not at the moment.

"It's looking a mite gloomy outside, Sloane. Ye'll want tae grab yer coat before we go," Davy said.

With a barely perceptible smile, she inclined her head and headed to the stairs. Unabashedly, Davy stared after her, admiring the view of sexy hips swaying above long legs walking up the stairs.

"The twa o' ye have come tae an understandin' then, have ye?" Hamish asked from behind him.

Facing his druid master, Davy answered with a smirk. "What can I say? I chased her until she caught me, lucky lass."

Keela hid a grin while Siobhan burst out laughing. When she sobered, she reached out and rubbed Davy's shoulder. "I'm glad you're persistent. After what Macha put her through at Lughnasadh, Sloane deserves some happiness."

Two hours after arriving at the training room in the heart of *An Teallach*, Davy's T-shirt clung to his skin and sweat dripped off his forehead to splat on the floor. For some unfathomable reason, Scathach had decided to focus on him, which dumbfounded him. He was a druid not a warrior for crying-in-yer-beer.

"Again." The goddess's command brooked no argument.

Davy assumed his battle stance opposite Rowan Sheridan,

two hands on his claymore poised in front of him, his weight on the balls of his feet. At Scathach's signal, they thrust and parried, flashed and danced, pirouetted and thrust again. Because he kept himself in shape, he didn't lack Rowan in fitness. However, the three-inch difference in their heights was giving Davy loads of trouble, from Rowan's longer reach to his superior angles. To compensate, Davy moved faster, but since he was a druid, he couldn't bend time and space to change positions or to outmaneuver his opponent. As a result, he'd found himself on his arse more than once. The circumstance jarred him physically every time but didn't hurt nearly as much as knowing Sloane saw his every failure at besting his opponent.

"You are an exceptional fighter, David Sutherland," Scathach said as she lent him a hand up from yet another unceremonial landing. His tenth or one hundredth of the afternoon.

Before he could bask in her praise, she added, "But you will have to be much better." She stood before him, petite and fierce, hands planted on her hips in the blood-red glow of her strength. "My sisters do not battle with druids. They use the zombie versions of legendary monsters and villains they badger Arawn to release from the Underworld and the rogue warriors they have suborned with false promises of paradise." Turning from him, she paced before the rest of the assembled party. "I had thought Macha was not interested in Morgan's relentless war with the Sheridan clan, but the stunt she pulled at Lughnasadh tells me either she has acquired an interest or Morgan has harassed her into having one. Either way, stealing Gavin Scanlon on her low feast day sent a message, one I have received loud and clear.

"After Macha revealed herself to you today," she glanced at Alaisdair, "I have no doubt the terrible trio plans an attack before the autumnal equinox. Everyone in this party will be called into battle. Count on it."

Around the room, the other warriors and their talismans had

been practicing together. However, after Scathach had set them on their tasks, she'd zeroed in on training Davy. As he panted for breath, she returned her focus to him. "You may rest for a few moments."

"Thank ye, milady."

He bowed deeply to her before dragging himself over to the table near the entrance where Hamish had set up snacks and drinks. Barely acknowledging the three druids gathered there, he grabbed a bottle of icy water and poured half of it down his throat before dumping the other half over his head. Only then did he catch their expressions.

"'Tis obvious ye've learned a great deal from yer sparrin' sessions with Rio, Davy."

Siobhan stared at him with undisguised admiration.

"You're equal to any of the warriors in this lot when they don't resort to bending time and space," Griffin said, as he handed Davy an herbal concoction. "I would have never believed a druid capable of fighting like that if I hadn't seen it with my own eyes. Well done."

Davy sniffed at the contents of the opaque glass tumbler, his keen sense of smell picking up apples, rosehips, hazelnut, white oak, and honey. With a nod to Griff, he quaffed half of it, licking the residual honey from his lips as he tried to hand the tumbler back.

Griff pushed his hand back toward him. "You're going to want to drain that. In case the goddess isn't finished with you yet."

Glancing at Scathach and back at Griff again, Davy pleaded, "Please donnae say that aloud." But he heeded Griff's advice and downed the rest of the brew.

A towel appeared over his shoulder, and he reached for it without thinking. Sloane snatched her hand away so fast, the towel nearly dropped to the floor. Reflexively, Davy grabbed it and turned to her.

"I thought you might need that."

"Thanks, lass."

He ran the cloth over his head, neck, and torso and glanced up at the woman who'd considered his comfort. Really looked at her. Fear swirled in Sloane's eyes even as she attempted a ghost of a smile.

Grabbing her by the elbow, he pulled her over to the wall away from the others. Keeping his voice down, he demanded, "What is it? Tell me what's wrong, Sloane."

"I don't understand why Scathach is so interested in you. She must know something. After all, she is a goddess."

Davy ran his hand up and down her back, soothing her—and himself. "Ye heard her, lass. She's training all of us hard fer the battle we all know is coming." He rested his forehead against hers. "More than any of the rest of us, ye've sensed this battle coming."

Sloane pulled away from him on a gasp. "H-How did you know?"

"Like I told ye before. I can't keep my eyes off ye, and ye can't keep from looking around, watching fer signs. The fear clouding the beautiful violets in yer eyes tells me ye've seen something."

"As we climbed the mountain this afternoon, I saw... " She swallowed and tried again. "I saw an island covered in foliage so green it hurt to look at it. In the center of the island, rose a mountain, the top obscured by thunderous clouds. The flashing lightning was made more terrible because of its beautiful irides-cent colors." Tears brimmed in her eyes as she sucked a deep breath in through her nose, trying to control herself. "You were dragging your skiff onto the shale of the shoreline." She cleared her throat. "Macha, wearing her dreadful cape of raven's feathers, awaited you with a smug expression on her face."

Placing his forefinger beneath her chin, he lifted her face to look into her eyes. "I didn't notice ye touched my hand."

"It was merely a brush as we neared the entrance to the training room. Rio called out to you, and when you turned to answer him, the backs of our hands accidentally came into contact for a second."

He nodded. "Dae ye have any idea when the auld girl plans tae launch her attack?"

Sloane shook her head. "The Sight is an inexact gift. But considering her visitation at the manor this morning, I'd guess she's on a short clock." She hugged herself, looking like she was trying not to throw up.

Davy pulled her into his arms, his lips brushing a kiss across her temple before he pressed her face into the crook of his neck. "I told ye before. I'm in yer life, and I'm no' going anywhere." He tried to convey his conviction with his touch as he held her close, molding their bodies together from shoulders to knees.

"Davy, your rest is over. I want you to watch as Rio executes this move. It is one you can do even without the ability to bend time and space."

After the way she'd been working him all afternoon, Davy knew better than to keep the goddess waiting. Even though at the moment, the only thing he wanted to learn was how to reassure Sloane that he was never leaving her.

CHAPTER TWENTY-SIX

"YOU'RE LOOKING RATHER pleased with yourself, Macha. What have you done now?" Taranis asked as he stared at her reflection in the window rather than at the cloudless cerulean skies outside Macha's stronghold.

Strolling over to join him, she said, "Morgan may be the supreme goddess of our deadly trio"—she cleared her throat of the words that tried to stick there—"but sleeping with the Dagda a millennium ago did not gain her additional powers beyond waging war." She stood a touch straighter. "On the other hand, I, as the goddess of seers as well as of war, have certain powers I can use to manipulate the seers among the mortals."

Taranis turned from the window to face her. As usual, the storm god stole her breath with his unbelievable beauty. Only a god could inhabit the perfection of human form that was Taranis from his mid-night black hair to the sculpted breadth of his shoulders, arms, and chest tapering to his trim waist and powerful legs. However, as much as she appreciated his male form, it was his stormy silver-gray eyes that always arrested her. At the moment, the tempests in those eyes seemed at rest even as he crossed his arms over his chest and waited.

"I've given a vision to the seer traveling with the bard and the Sheridan clan, a vision I plan to make real momentarily. It should be enough to draw the Sheridans away from their enchanted fortress and the safety of their training room." She ran a long black fingernail along the contours of Taranis's bicep to his elbow before tracing a path across his forearm to his wrist. "I rather hoped you would be a part of the festivities."

Tilting his head with a nonchalance at odds with the storms building in his eyes, he asked, "In what way?"

"I would like you to unleash a spectacular thunderstorm over the mountaintop on the Green Isle." In her enthusiasm, she grasped his wrist. "One of those wondrous events you do sometimes where the lightning crackles in a rainbow of colors, the contrast so deliciously terrifying to mortals."

"Is that all? A small lightning storm?"

"Your skepticism is not worthy of you," she said with a sniff as she spun away from him, the black feathers of her cape swirling and catching the light like a conspiracy of ravens lifting angrily into the air. A thought occurred to her, and she narrowed her eyes at him. "Have the other two been using you in their ongoing war?"

Taranis huffed out a mirthless laugh. "Of course they have. You are all the same, always summoning me away from whatever pleasures I have devised, always wanting me to give you an advantage over mortals whom you should be able to best using nothing more than your little fingers." Turning back to the window, he leaned against the sill and stared out. "It is time to introduce fall to these northern climes, roil them up with a strong wind chasing clouds fat with cold rain. Instead, I am relegated to keeping the peace between sea and sky because you think it will contrast so well with whatever machinations you are devising. Quite frankly, I am growing increasingly tired of the three of you using me as you do."

"You have not gone unrewarded, Taranis." Macha sidled back over to him. "As I understand it, you have spent considerable time in Maeve's bed as well as an arranged tryst with Brighid, something you have not enjoyed very often over the last several centuries."

"What about you, Macha? What are you willing to give me in exchange for my help?"

"What would you like?"

Taranis blinked at her, the storms in his eyes disappearing like a raindrop in the sunshine. "I have a choice in my reward? That is a first." Furrowing his brow, he leaned back against the sill and crossed his arms again. "There is a catch."

"You have the wrong war goddess, my friend." She traced the textured frame of a painted battle scene, considered, and turned back to him. "As much as I enjoy battle and slaughter, unlike my sisters, I always play fair. That includes with you."

"Hmmm. You call using a storm to interfere with the mortals in the battle you plan to wage playing fair?"

"Your storm will be part of a test. You see, I do not target a warrior this time but a druid." Macha seated herself on a nearby chair, taking care to arrange her feathered cape to show herself to her best advantage. "Scathach has a particular interest in a druid who lives with the Sheridans. While I do not share my sisters' singular interest in that clan, I do have an interest in the goings-on in the isles. The warrior trainer working with a druid does not bode well for us."

"I know what Morgan feared, and her fears became reality." A smile ghosted over his face. "The Sheridans lifted her curses and gave mortals more time before their choices are limited to those benefiting Morgan. What has Scathach working with a druid have to do with us?"

His emphasis on that last word told her she had to tread carefully if she were to be successful at convincing him to give her what she wanted.

"There has not been a warrior druid since the days of Brian Boru. He used his skills to trick Morgan, avoid Maeve, and deny me my due in the battles we waged against him. If not for his abilities as a prophet as well as a warrior, we could have had our way." Leaning back in her chair, she lifted and crossed her leg slowly, drawing his attention to its shapeliness—and to the fact that she wore nothing beneath her cape. "I've had my eye on Davy Sutherland for some time because he strikes me as the same sort of threat."

"All you want from me is a lightning storm over the Green Isle, correct?"

"That is all."

"In return, you will give me whatever I ask for."

"Within my purview."

"Ah, so there is the catch." Taranis paced toward her. "In return for my services"—he stretched out the word—"I want a fortnight, in celestial time, with you and your sisters taking care of my every carnal desire. Then I want to be left to my own whims for at least a year."

"In celestial time? An entire generation of mortals will come and go from the earth while you are off doing your own thing, as the mortals like to call it."

"No, for a year in mortal time."

She hoped he didn't hear the tiny sigh of relief that escaped her at his clarification.

"Done."

A world of skepticism manifested itself in a single raised eyebrow. "You are certain you can convince Morgan and Maeve to come to my terms?"

"Morgan and Maeve adore you in their beds every bit as much as I do. Plus, it has been eons since the three of us have enjoyed a man—mortal or god—together. I am quite certain they will come to your terms."

She didn't need to tell him how his interference with the weather would benefit her sisters in their never-waning pursuit of wreaking revenge on the Sheridans whose long-ago ancestor had denied Maeve her desire for his entertainment in her bed. Based on their previous conversations, Macha had an idea about Taranis's attitude toward helping her sisters against the Sheridans. The other two had tested Taranis's patience as far as he would willingly allow. From her perspective, her sisters owed him the small, and quite pleasurable, favor he asked of them.

"Perhaps you would enjoy a preview of your reward, Taranis? After all, as a guest in my demesne, you should be accorded every entertainment."

Glancing toward the window, he said, "You are nearly as transparent as this pane of glass." He smiled as he stalked toward her. "I will direct my thunderous climax at the top of the mountain per your request." Placing his hands on the arms of her chair, he caged her in. "However, I will cease the storm in one beat of a mortal's heart if I do not have what I want from all three of you."

Electricity crackled off the storm god, desire building a tempest in his eyes. Macha shivered in delicious anticipation of the coupling to come and nodded her assent to his terms.

Standing to his full height, he reached a hand to her. "Shall we?"

Macha couldn't help the triumphant smile stretching her lips as she placed her hand in his and led him through the great hall and up the stairs to her private chambers.

⌑

"Milady," Hamish said from somewhere in the circle of warriors, druids, and talismans surrounding Davy, Rio, and Scathach as she instructed the two men on battle tactics. "It draws close tae sundown."

"Stop!" the goddess commanded.

She didn't have to ask Davy twice. Rio must have been of a like mind. From the corner of his eye, Davy noticed the warrior resting his forehead on top of his hands crossed over the hilt of his claymore. Rio's was an exact copy of Davy's pose as both of them gasped for breath.

"As usual, I doubt we are ready for whatever the vengeful and unscrupulous of the pantheon are planning," the goddess said from where she stood beside Rio.

A collective groan came from those assembled around them. Davy didn't have the breath for even that much.

"Yet I am more confident this time than I was a year ago at Samhain. At least this time, we know each talisman's skill and have been able to practice for the scenarios my wretched sisters have used in the past." Davy turned his head to see her staring down Fallon, Seamus, and Siobhan who stood together. "Including the use of a Fomorian."

Scathach paced the inside of the circle of warriors. "Perhaps we will enjoy some luck and discover Morgan and Maeve to be otherwise occupied on the feast day of the autumnal equinox."

Alaisdair cleared his throat. "Riskin' yer ire, milady, it's no' Morgan and Maeve worryin' us this time."

Scathach's aura glowed red and gold, but she remained quiet as she awaited his explanation.

"We've had several visitations from Macha." With a shrug, he said, "Rather, Sloane has had several visitations from Macha. Shanley and I have only experienced the one that prompted us tae return tae this room taeday."

"I am aware." Scathach crossed her arms, an expression of concern crossing her face. "Since the troubles pretty much ended in Ireland, she has been rather bored, I think. Yet she has not shown any interest in the ongoing feud between my favorite warrior family and those other two witches." Zeroing in on Sloane, she added, "Until now. What have you seen, Sloane?"

Helplessly, Davy watched Sloane's throat work and knew what it cost her to speak. Taking a chance on the goddess's displeasure, he sheathed his claymore and walked over to stand in front of Sloane, shielding her from the goddess's penetrating stare. Placing his hands on her shoulders, he gave her a reassuring squeeze. "'Tis going tae be all right, lass. How many times have I told ye I'm no' leaving ye?" he whispered for her ears only.

Sloane covered her face, pushing the heels of her hands into her eyes. Davy knew no matter how much she might wish for a different skill, possessing the Sight was her lot in life. He took her by the wrists and dragged her hands from her face. Staring deeply into the troubled depths of her beautiful violet eyes, he said, "Ye have nae choice, lass. The goddess needs tae know what we might be up against."

"But she's already worked you so hard today. And you heard Hamish," Sloane whispered.

"Sloane."

Sucking in a deep breath, she nodded. Stepping forward into the circle, she addressed Scathach. "I try very hard not to touch people's hands. Druids, talismans, warriors—civilians—I don't want to have a say in the course of people's lives."

"Admirable. A seer with a set of ethics. It shows your character."

The goddess's compliment almost brought a tiny smile to Sloane's lips. Then she looked back at Davy, and her expression sobered. "Today, I accidentally brushed the back of Davy's hand, and I saw." She swallowed and tried again. "I saw him on an island so green it hurt to look at it even in my mind."

Hamish and Griff exchanged a charged look, but Davy didn't have to penetrate their shields to know what that conversation was about. The Green Isle existed in legend, the beautiful location of the Fountain of Youth, the Celtic version of Shangri-la. Like its Asian counterpart, one could live there forever, but he gave up his life in the temporal world. He gave up his life, but not his memories. It seemed to Davy a rather torturous price to pay for eternal youth.

Sloane interrupted his thoughts. "Dressed in her raven-feather cloak, Macha awaited him on the shore. Behind her, an iridescent lightning storm of terrifying beauty crackled high up on a mountain. Davy unsheathed his claymore, and she smiled at him like the Cheshire cat."

Davy wanted to spirit Sloane away, kiss the bleak shadows from her eyes. Scathach had other plans.

"What else did you see?" the goddess demanded.

"Nothing. We were entering the training room when I brushed against him, and once I stepped over the threshold, the vision dissipated."

Scathach paced back and forth. "This is most curious. She does not wish to sacrifice Davy to Morgan to take across the ford, but she also seeks to deny the White Lady her rightful place delivering him peacefully into the mists."

"It is a singular torture to live forever with memories of loved ones you can never see again, even after leaving this earth for the land beyond the mists either with Morgan or with the White Lady," Griffin said. Again, he exchanged a look with Hamish, and Davy wondered what the two older druids discussed in the privacy of their minds.

"As you are all keenly aware, the three war goddesses enjoy slaughter and blood. Their pleasures depend on it. Yet since Macha was once Queen of Ireland, she alone has developed a sense of fairness. Perhaps she seeks to test Davy, to give him a chance to prove himself."

The look of speculation on the goddess's face as she considered his fate reinforced Davy's belief in himself. When he told Sloane he would never leave her, he'd meant his words from the depths of his soul.

"If the auld girl takes our boy tae the Green Isle, even if he returns, most o' us will be dust. Perhaps the lass will live yet." Hamish glanced at Sloane. "But she'll be an ancient lady."

"There are four powerful druids in this room. Certainly between you, you can devise a spell or an enchantment over Davy to maintain the temporal passage of time should Sloane's vision come to pass," Scathach said, tapping her impatience with Hamish with the toe of her boot on the stone floor. "It would give him an advantage in his sense of urgency to leave the isle."

Owen Sheridan, who had been standing beside Hamish, slipped his arm across the druid's shoulder. "That right there, my friend, is the true advantage of having gained the warrior trainer's favor."

Hamish cocked a brow.

"She never ever wants to lose one of her protégés. Even a druid."

Siobhan said, "After the chaos I nearly caused when Morgan attacked Alyssa in another training room in another country, I believe we will have to do our work elsewhere."

"Well done, Siobhan. It is good to see you learn from your mistakes," Scathach said, but something in her tone made her words sound less than complimentary.

The way Siobhan colored confirmed Davy's observation. At some point, he wanted to learn the story prompting their exchange if for no other reason than to avoid Scathach's displeasure. He'd had enough of that as a sparring partner for Rio Sheridan over the past year.

"Right. You druids shall visualize yourselves back to the manor and set to work. The rest of you are safe enough to return the conventional way, I believe." Having made her pronouncement, Scathach disappeared, leaving nothing behind except a cloud of red and gold drops suspended in the air where she'd stood.

CHAPTER TWENTY-SEVEN

FROM HER SEAT in the box bay window in the library, Sloane stared unseeing through the glass. Resolutely, she worked to blank her mind and keep it that way. Some might call what she did meditation. If you asked her, she would have called it desperation. Any time she let down her guard, even for a second, she could see the kelpie rising up and bearing Davy away across the loch while she looked on helplessly from the dock.

Staring at the empty seat in her Mustang where Gavin had been before he visualized himself to his death caused her pain so intense it left her numb. She'd thought that pain was the worst she could ever experience. She was wrong. Losing Davy would be the kind of heart-stabbing agony that would render her lifeless no matter how long her lungs actually drew breath. With Gavin, she hadn't had time to fall in love. The same couldn't be said about Davy.

Even without the benefit of a sign telling her she belonged to him, Sloane had been drawn to Davy from the moment they locked eyes across the salon on her first day in Scotland. The sound of his voice worked its way inside her.

His quickness to tease, his mastery of the well-told tale, his willingness to put everyone else ahead of himself showed him to be a man of exceptional character. His competitive nature spoke to her own. Most of all, the easy way he let her be herself no matter what told her how well he knew her already and showed her how much he valued her. After the way she'd grown up with parents who were never satisfied with her as she was, Davy's acceptance of her, indeed his unadulterated delight in her as she was, gave her a freedom she'd craved her whole life. That in itself was enough to make her love him.

Toss in his insanely hot body and what he could do to her with it plus those dimples that melted her resolve every single time, and she knew she could never want anyone but Davy Sutherland.

As though thinking of him conjured him up, Davy strolled into the library. "Thought I might find ye here since ye weren't in yer favorite chair in the salon."

"Are you finished with your spell-casting and enchantments?"

Upon returning from the training room, the four druids had ensconced themselves in Hamish's apartments all the previous evening and night and all of the morning. Around lunchtime, Sloane had given in and hung out in the kitchens in the hopes of seeing Davy even for a minute. After an hour of loitering over a sandwich and a cold cup of tea with no sign of him, she'd retreated to the library.

"Between Griffin and me, we know all the auld stories. Methodically, we worked through them as Siobhan and Hamish devised spells and enchantments tae alter those pertaining tae the Green Isle." He stood in front of her, his hand sliding up and down her shin. "Of course, it would be rather convenient if Macha held off until after the wedding when yer friend Fallon's bardic powers increase."

The familiar way Davy touched her, like he had a right to as her lover, played havoc with her resolve. After everything that had happened at Lughnasadh and the ceaseless omens visited on her since then, she knew she was the key to keeping him safe—by letting him go.

"No' going tae happen, lass. Like I keep tellin' ye, I'm no' going anywhere. At least no' without ye."

"What are you doing in my head? I know I had my shield up." She pulled her knees up tight to her chest and wrapped her arms around her shins, breaking free of his mesmerizing touch.

"We're connected, we two. I'll keep reminding ye of that as many times as it takes fer ye tae hop on board with the facts," he said, the patience in his tone mirrored in the amber depths of his eyes. "As far as shields go, ye're welcome tae breach mine whenever ye have an interest. Of course, if ye dae, ye'll find I have pretty much one track where ye're concerned." The grin on his face emphasized his point.

Proving his words, he slipped one arm beneath her legs and the other around her back. He picked her up as though she weighed nothing and carried her across the room to a set of book shelves. Though he set her back on her feet, he kept one arm possessively around her while he reached up and gave a book at the end of a row a hard shove and tugged Sloane to the side of the shelves. With a soft whoosh, the section of shelves turned on an invisible axis, reminding her of an old Indiana Jones movie she and Fallon watched once where the hero escaped the villains via a hidden passageway behind the books.

"After ye, milady."

She jacked up a brow. "How many secret passages does this place have?"

"Ye'd be surprised." He gestured to the darkness beyond the books. "Please."

As Sloane stepped into the passageway, Davy slipped in behind her. A light flickered on overhead before he pushed down a lever on the wall beside her. With another soft whoosh, the shelves of books returned to their rightful place, leaving the two of them alone in a deafeningly quiet hallway.

Clearing her throat, she whispered, "One could commit all kinds of mayhem between the walls of this house, and no one would ever know."

"Donnae think that hasn't happened a time or two," he said with a chuckle.

A shiver overtook her, and he smiled in that way he had of reassuring her while simultaneously revving up her motor.

"Where are we going?"

"Somewhere we can be comfortably alone. Follow me."

He led her along the passageway, down a short flight of stairs, through another passageway, and down another flight of stairs ending at a door he didn't hesitate to open fully. When she stepped in behind him, she discovered they were standing in a broom closet. Above them dangled a string, which Davy pulled, spilling light into the closet from a bare bulb. He reached behind her and flipped the light switch at the bottom of the stairs, plunging the passageway from which they'd come back into darkness. When he closed the door, the closet closed in on her.

Davy smiled into her eyes. "This next part will be tricky. We have to be very, very quiet." He put a finger to his lips. "Shhh."

Since she wasn't the one talking, she gave him "the look." Mirth danced in his eyes, and he compressed his lips to keep from laughing. When he had himself back under control, he doused the light and cracked open the door. For several seconds, he remained still. She detected the strong scent of herbs and burning incense and guessed where they were. Satisfied the room beyond the door was empty, Davy opened it wider and stepped through. Sloane followed close enough behind him that she nearly gave him a flat tire.

Of course there would be a secret passage into Hamish's apartment. How could there not be? She almost laughed at herself. But the old druid's rooms were not their destination. Davy walked over to a door at the back of the living room opposite the door she knew led to a hallway and the manor kitchen. Extracting a key from his pocket, he inserted it into the heavy oak door, gave the key a little wiggle, and turned the handle.

"Another secret passage?"

"This one isn't very secret, which is why the door has a lock on it. Come on."

When she stepped past him through the door, she discovered a tunnel hewn out of solid slate. The air inside it was chilly, and though she wore her favorite cashmere sweater, she wrapped her arms around herself to stave off the cold. Along the floor, soft blue lights illuminated as if by magic, but as she continued to walk forward, she realized they were triggered by motion sensors. After they walked for what seemed an age, they reached another door, which Davy unlocked with the same odd motion he used on the one in Hamish's apartment.

Again, he motioned for her to precede him into a beautifully appointed living room in a completely different house.

"Where are we?"

"My cottage."

She wandered farther into the room to stand before the fireplace where a stunning oil painting of the manor held pride of place above the mantel.

"That explains it."

She sensed Davy's heat behind her. "Explains what, lass?"

"How you're always around for breakfast, but I've never seen you climb the stairs to the upper floors to the bedrooms in the manor."

He wrapped his arms around her waist and pulled her against his chest. "I could live in the manor, but it feels a mite crowded."

Sloane half turned in his arms. "Only Hamish and Ceri and Rio live there, don't they?"

"Aye."

As she turned back to admire the painting, she chuckled. "I met the man for the first time when we arrived at the manor, but you're right. Rio does tend to take up a lot of room."

Davy gave her a little squeeze and buried his face in the crook of her neck. "Alaisdair lived here before he moved with Shanley tae the States. Hamish didn't want the place tae fall intae disrepair, so he invited me tae use it." He nuzzled her behind her ear. "It's nice and private." The sexy burr of his voice told her exactly what was on his mind without her even attempting to penetrate his shield.

Butterflies took flight in her belly, and her skin tightened everywhere in anticipation of Davy's intentions. Placing his hands on her hips, he turned her to face him. She blinked at the desire she'd heard in his voice amplified in his eyes, the amber rings barely containing his pupils. Unlike their previous encounters, his dimples hid in the determined expression he wore. Whatever was about to happen between them, Davy was dead serious.

"If ye donnae believe in me, now is the time tae say it, lass."

"Davy."

"I *know* we have a connection. Something so strong even the gods cannae break it." A calloused finger traced the contours of her cheek. "But ye can," he whispered.

His words thumped her square in the chest.

Air was hard to come by, but still, she managed to speak. "The Sight is mostly accurate. But sometimes people do things no one can predict, probably not even the fates." She spread her hands over the heavy muscles of his chest. "For instance, you, Davy Sutherland, have been completely unexpected."

His brow shot up, but he said nothing.

"I think you even surprise Scathach."

He waited.

Staring at the base of his neck where the opened top button

of his Henley bared his skin, she leaned in and kissed him there. The vibrations of his heartbeat beneath her lips gave her strength. Pulling back enough to gaze into his eyes, she said, "It's always been in my nature to take risks. But you, Davy, are a risk on a whole different scale."

He tightened his arms around her like he feared she was about to take flight.

"Yet I can't resist taking this risk."

He didn't relax his hold of her.

"Because I feel our connection too."

For a long heartbeat, he stared at her. Then his dimples appeared, and that was it. Sloane met him in a kiss that went from zero to inferno in a nanosecond. Her body zinged and sparked everywhere it came into contact with his. The inside of her bra chafed her nipples while her sex pulsed a happy dance in anticipation of the promise of that kiss.

Plowing his hands into her hair, he held her still while he plundered her mouth. Plunging and stroking, teasing and sucking, he drove her wild with his lips and tongue. Then he slid a hand down her body to palm and plump her breast, his thumb stroking her sensitive tip through clothes that were suddenly too constraining.

She writhed and squirmed against him, begging him with her body. When her leg decided to take a tour of the back of his thigh and hip, he tore his mouth from hers with a pop that echoed in the room.

"All right, lass. That's it."

Her head spinning from his kiss, she blinked up at him. "Wh-what?"

In one smooth motion, he whisked her up high in his arms and strode purposefully down the short hall to a large bedroom at the end of it. Without bothering to close the door, he carried her to the bed and tossed her onto the middle of it. "Hey!" she cried out.

A muffled chuckle came from somewhere near his knees as he bent over to unlace his boots before he toed them off. Then he went to work on her boots, unlacing and pulling them off and tossing them over his shoulder to thud on the carpet somewhere behind him. Climbing up the bed, he straddled her, the glint in his eye telling her what came next. He slipped his hands beneath the hem of her sweater, catching it on his forearms as he skimmed his fingertips along her sides to the band of her bra where he stopped.

"Dilemmas, dilemmas."

"What do you mean?"

"Do I want tae tease ye through yer bra, or dae I want tae please ye in all yer beautiful naked glory?"

While he debated, he rubbed the callouses of his fingertips along her skin, driving her absolutely wild. Though she tried to swallow it, a moan escaped her as she arched up into his hands, begging him to touch more of her.

"Naked it is."

She sucked in a breath as he slipped his fingers beneath the cups of her bra and pushed her underwear up and off her simultaneously with her sweater, tossing the whole works over his shoulder to land the gods-knew-where.

When he saw her bared torso beneath him, all the playfulness leached out of him. She moved to cover herself, but Davy stayed her with his hands on her wrists, holding her hands at her sides. He drank her in from the top of her head to her hips before his eyes bore into hers.

"When we were taegether before, it was mostly dark, so I could only imagine ye from what I could see with my lips and hands. I dinnae have a clue how incredible ye are." Letting go of her wrist, he traced a line from her chin, to the hollow of her throat, between her breasts, down to her navel. "Jesus, Sloane, nothing in the world is as beautiful as ye." The reverence in his voice sounded like a prayer.

Nodding at his Henley, she said, "Your turn."

He reached behind his head to grab two handfuls of his sweater before he dragged it over his head in the effortless way guys do and tossed it to the side. That's when Sloane caught sight of the ink on his upper arm, and her whole world telescoped down to the swirl tattooed on his biceps. Without thinking, she reached up to trace the mark, and Davy hissed in a breath. Though she stopped moving her fingers, she didn't break contact with him. She couldn't.

Davy rubbed his crotch against the fly of her jeans like he couldn't help himself. She knew the feeling, the ink on her thigh throbbing in rhythm with his thrusts.

"How long have you had this?"

"Since last summer." He panted. "I had it done on summer solstice."

She traced it again, and he groaned. "Every time ye touch me there, clothes or nae clothes, it gives me an instant hard-on." His jaw worked like he was trying to maintain his control. "In case ye were wonderin'."

"Get up," she commanded.

"Huh?" The dazed expression on his face in another time and place might have made her laugh. But there was nothing funny about what she needed to show him.

"Get off me for a second."

Shaking his head like he was trying to clear it, he pushed himself off her only to sit beside her, his back leaning against the pillows stacked at the head of the bed.

She undid her fly and shimmied out of her jeans. Then she sat up and turned to show him her thigh.

He sat bolt upright, shifting his gaze back and forth between her ink and her eyes. Fascinated, she watched his Adam's apple bob as he swallowed hard. Tentatively, he reached out and touched her tattoo that perfectly matched his. "What is this, lass?"

"The sign my warrior traced on me when he discovered me," she whispered.

His eyes saucered, but he didn't stop tracing his finger over the pattern on her skin.

"Every time you touch me there, you set my whole body on fire."

"When?" He swallowed. "When did ye get this?"

Because she couldn't seem to help herself, she reached up to trace the pattern on his arm, mimicking the pace and pressure of his touch on her thigh. Staring deep into his eyes, her voice barely audible to her own ears, she said, "After Lughnasadh. After Gavin crossed the ford."

For a long minute, he stared at his finger moving over her skin. He sucked in a breath like he'd come to a decision and looked into her eyes. "Ye have tae believe me when I tell ye I'm sorry the goddess took yer warrior, Sloane. But this"—he gestured between them at the ink on their skin—"this proves we two were meant tae be. I donnae pretend tae understand it, but I know it tae be true." He cupped her cheek with his other hand. "So dae ye. Especially now."

She nodded solemnly. "I-I think you're right, Davy."

With his hand still on her face, he coaxed her toward him. After everything they'd just discovered about each other, and after what led up to that discovery, she expected a ravishing mating of lips, teeth, and tongues. Instead, he took her mouth slowly, sweetly, almost reverently. Then he kissed her eyes, her forehead, her cheeks, and along her jaw before he returned to her mouth. All the time he was kissing her, his fingers traced her tattoo.

Sloane whimpered and rhythmically bobbed on her knees, clinging to his shoulder with one hand while she ran her fingers over his tat with the other. Never in her life had she felt so alive, so excited, so needy.

"Davy." Her voice sounded harsh, desperate.

He tore himself away from her and stood beside the bed. Not taking his eyes from hers, he shed his jeans and boxers, his impressive erection springing free of his clothes. For a long moment, he let her drink him in with her eyes before he rejoined her on the bed, returning to his seated position reclined against the pillows.

"Come here, lass."

He didn't need to say it twice. She straddled him, sheathing him inside her as he surged up when she seated herself on his lap. Simultaneously, they put their hands on each other's ink while their lips met in a breath-stealing kiss. As they moved together, Sloane lost herself in Davy and the sensations he made her feel. Before he spirited her away to his cottage, she hadn't believed in paradise. Now she discovered it existed in Davy Sutherland's bed where the two of them together were more beautiful and perfect than anything she'd ever imagined.

Together, they set their rhythm, their bodies moving as one, each giving and taking completely. Being so in sync with another human being stole all her coherent thought. Every nerve in her body sparkled, and when she opened her eyes as she came up once for air, she swore she saw a golden glow pulsing around them. He shifted beneath her, slightly changing his angle, and sent her into the stratosphere. She lost all contact with reality as her body pulsed and convulsed around his, her inner muscles firing beyond her control.

Davy thrust deep inside her again. Her name tore from his throat and reverberated around the room. Both of them went utterly rigid, their eyes locked in wonder. Then Sloane slumped onto his chest as he sank back against the pillows, his right hand idly tracing her tattoo while his left hand smoothed up and down the length of her spine.

When at last he had breath enough to speak, Davy said quietly, "On Lughnasadh, a searing pain ripped around the spiral on my arm, followed almost immediately by a pleasure so intense, I feared I might be hard fer days. Later, I learned ye lost yer warrior on that day."

He said the words gently, and she discovered for the first time since meeting Davy, mention of her warrior didn't hurt. Hugging him closer to her, she reassured him with her touch.

"Our first time when we were in the maze and ye put yer hand on my shoulder, that's when I knew we were meant tae be."

Lifting her head from his chest, she asked the question with her eyes.

"Nae other's touch gave me the sensations I felt when ye covered my ink with yer hand even though a layer of clothes separated our skin." She rested her head again. "Ye're no' the only one who's been receiving signs and omens, lass. I knew ye were on yer way tae me long before ye arrived."

With a gasp, she bolted upright. "How could you know that? We had no idea of each other's existence."

"Maybe I didn't know it was ye personally, but I sensed the one the fates determined fer me was near."

Furrowing her brow, she said, "I didn't know that happened for druids."

Davy tangled his fingers in her hair then smoothed them through it. Shifting her closer to him, he said, "It's no' like warriors trying their signs on talismans tae find their fated mates. Druids can marry where we choose within our race." He pulled back to catch her eye. "Or outside it when circumstances work that way." Settling her back on his chest, he continued. "In my case, something beyond my ken compelled me tae acquire my tat. Later, the omens started coming—a murder of crows outside the cottage all times of the day and night, the sensations in my ink on Lughnasadh and afterward at the same time it turns out ye were en route tae Scotland, and the way my spiral often pulses when ye're nearby."

She turned her face into his pecs and smiled.

"Of course, the omen that even grabbed Hamish's attention was the attack of the kelpie when I was on the loch on Lughnasadh."

Sloane's body went rigid. "What did you say?"

He continued as though she hadn't spoken. "So I'm no' quite convinced ye saw what ye think ye saw yesterday afternoon at the training room. Perhaps, ye saw a vision of what might have happened in the past if I hadn't heeded the warning radiating from my arm."

The happy glow of the afternoon dissipated in the stark reality of Davy's words. Sitting up, she stared into the intoxicating amber and chocolate of his eyes and willed him to understand. "The Sight always shows a version of the *future*, Davy. Always."

Palming her thigh, he said, "I think this afternoon, we altered the future, lass." He shifted onto his side facing her. "But I'm up fer more of altering the future"—he gazed down as he bumped his erect cock against her lower belly—"if ye've a mind tae."

Sloane didn't know whether to laugh or slam her fist into his shoulder. Macha had been torturing him too? They needed to talk about this.

Davy's eyes trailed his knuckles as they traveled over her shoulder, across her chest, and down to her breasts where he lightly teased a turgid nipple. Sloane grasped his wrist. "Davy." She meant to be stern, but his name came out on a sigh.

In the end, they went for another round of trying to alter the future.

CHAPTER TWENTY-EIGHT

S SHE AND Davy dressed to return to the manor, Sloane said, "Tell me about that amulet you wear around your neck."

"This?" He fingered a sapphire-blue crystal the size and shape of a robin's egg delicately nested in strands of gold suspended from his neck by a heavy gold chain. "'Tis a *glam-nan-Druidhe*—a Druid's crystal. Some people call it a Druid's egg or a Druid's glass."

She stood in front of him and inspected it more closely. "What's the story behind it?"

The radiance of his smile nearly blinded her. "Ye see? Ye're already talking like a druid's woman."

His dancing eyes demanded a response. Sloane planted her hands on her hips, hiked a brow and said, "Yeah? So, what's the story?"

Grinning, he finished doing up the fly of his jeans, grabbed his socks and boots, and sat on the chair in the corner of the room opposite the bed. Pulling on his socks, he said, "An egg is a powerful symbol of regeneration, no' only among us Celts, but in many cultures. A Druid's egg works as a protection amulet as well as a means fer making predictions." With his boots laced, he stood and went in search of his shirt. "We were in a bit of a hurry this afternoon, weren't we, lass?" He chuckled as he lifted the quilt on the bed to find his shirt lying halfway underneath it.

After retrieving his Henley, he faced her again, holding the amulet in front of his face as though he was seeing a vision through it. "I received this from Hamish after I completed the ritual fer my first *Tairbhfheis*."

"Your what?"

"Bull sleep. Though we donnae crown warriors as kings anymore, we still dae the ritual tae make predictions fer certain warriors when circumstances warrant."

Even though she was fully dressed, she experienced a pang of longing as she watched him push his arms through the sleeves of his shirt and pull it over his head, covering up their conversation piece and all those glorious muscles and smooth golden skin.

"I never noticed it before. Do you wear it all the time?"

"Never take it off."

He gestured toward the door, and Sloane preceded him through it.

How did I miss that?

"Other, more interestin' things tae look at."

Without turning around, she knew he was grinning. "Is breaching my shield going to become a habit with you?"

"We spent the entire afternoon makin' love and still ye have tae ask?" Grabbing her hips, he pulled her up short, fitting her back to his front. "I will always want tae know what ye're thinking, *mo ghràdh*." Nuzzling her hair away from her neck, he kissed the skin he bared and squeezed her hips. "Now stop distracting me with yer lascivious thoughts, woman. We're due at the manor fer dinner."

Cupping his hands on her ass, he gave her a gentle push

toward the living room. She laughed as she crossed the room to the door leading to the tunnel. Even though she watched closely, she still couldn't quite figure out the way he flipped his wrist as he unlocked the door.

"Why do you do that?"

"As Hamish is fond of saying—layers, lass. Layers. I'll teach ye another time."

He pulled the door open and ushered her into the tunnel ahead of him so he could lock up behind them. Apparently, the afternoon's activities had warmed her because she didn't notice the cold of the tunnel as much on the return trip to the manor. Thoughts of their afternoon together brought a tiny smile to her face.

Behind her, Davy chuckled. "I truly dae like the places yer mind wanders."

Looking back over her shoulder, she gifted him with a saucy smile and put a little extra sway in her hips as she preceded him up the illuminated passageway back to the manor.

∽

Hamish's booming voice greeted them as they rounded the corner into the kitchen. "Ye're right on time, ye twa. Put this tureen in the dumbwaiter fer me, would ye, lad?"

An expression of pure bliss covered Davy's face as he lifted the lid on the tureen and sniffed the steam wafting up from its contents. "Ye cooked us hotchpotch, Hamish. All Brighid's blessings on ye."

From up on her toes, Sloane peeked over his shoulder. "Hotchpotch?"

"It's minced meat and barley soup, and one o' the best dishes Hamish cooks."

Davy snagged the tasting spoon resting on a trivet beside the stove and spooned up a bite for her, first blowing on it to cool it a touch before lifting it to her lips. Leaning toward him, she closed her mouth around the spoon and its contents and blinked at the desire dilating Davy's eyes as he watched her. Piquant flavors of onion, rosemary, parsley, and lamb exploded in her mouth, and she closed her eyes to savor them.

"Delicious, yeah?"

"Mmm. This is one of the best soups I've ever tasted."

"It's meant tae be served pipin' hot, lad," Hamish groused. "And I need tae open the oven fer the bread, so if ye donnae mind—" He glared at Davy from beneath unruly white brows before he caught Sloane's eye and winked.

"Could ye open the dumbwaiter fer me, please, lass?" Davy asked as he returned the lid to the tureen and lifted the heavy pot off the AGA, the term she'd heard both Hamish and Davy call the stove.

She hustled over and pushed the button to open the doors to the dumbwaiter cleverly set into the wall to the right of the stairs. Davy slid the tureen inside and sent it up to the dining room.

"What else needs to go upstairs?" she asked.

"Ye can take this basket o' bread, lass." Hamish handed her a basket requiring both of her hands to carry. "Ye can take this up with ye, lad." He plopped a bowl big enough for bathing a small child into Davy's waiting arms. An enormous salad all but spilled out of it, and Sloane wondered how anyone would eat all the food Hamish had prepared.

Loud laughter echoed down the stairs from the dining room, answering her silent question.

"They're all up there waitin'," Hamish said. "I imagine they'll have somethin' tae say." The grin spreading over the old druid's face was pure mischief.

Sloane faltered on the stairs.

"Tae late now, lass. Davy already sent the soup up. Thanks tae someone not mindin' his own business"—he shot Davy a pointed glare—"Rio discovered my stash o' pies in the pantry."

"Like ripping off a plaster." He grinned back at Hamish. "After the initial sting, it's all over." Davy gave her shoulder a playful bump as he joined her on the steps. "Come on, mo ghràdh."

He waggled his eyebrows toward the dining room. Sloane sucked in a long breath and huffed out a long sigh.

"That's the spirit, lass," Hamish said as he danced past them and up the stairs. "Such enthusiasm will dae wonders fer Davy's reputation."

He was still chuckling at his own joke when he disappeared into the dining room.

"Davy, I know how this bunch acts when a warrior finds his talisman." She stared down at the marble of the stairs. "I've already experienced it. Even though I don't embarrass easily, it was a little—awkward having everyone know exactly what was going on."

Leaning down, he caught her eye. "It's part of the ritual the gods decreed fer warriors and talismans, lass. When a warrior discovers his mate, the whole community celebrates." Deliberately, he brushed his thigh against hers, radiating a wave of electric shocks through her. "We definitely have somethin' tae celebrate, Sloane." He brushed a kiss over her lips. "Come on, my love. They're waiting fer us."

Sloane blinked at the endearment.

"I've been callin' ye that all day, mo ghràdh. Tae late tae object now."

The gentle smile on his face disarmed her even more than his Gaelic reference to her.

They climbed the rest of the stairs in silence and walked through the doors to dinner. As they entered the dining room side by side, loud applause broke out, which told Sloane the meal was going to last for an eternity.

❧

The next morning as she worked with Fallon to weave cloth garlands out of Graham family tartan, she admired their handiwork. "The teal green, periwinkle, and black plaid of your family complements the light green and heather plaid of the Ross tartans already accenting this room."

"They do, don't they? An added bonus to holding our wedding here," Fallon said, fingering the cloth with a smile.

Sloane kept her eyes on her work, deliberately trying to deny her best friend an opening. Like that was going to work.

"Sooo, you didn't spend the night in the manor last night."

"Aren't you too busy with your own life right now to be spying on mine?"

Fallon let go of the laugh that had been twitching the corners of her lips since the two of them had met up in the ballroom. "Oh, sugar, you have no idea how happy I am about you and Davy." She dropped her end of the cloth to come around the table to wrap her arms around Sloane.

For a moment, she allowed herself to absorb her friend's love.

"There's something I have to tell you."

At her tone, Fallon sobered and slowly moved back around the table to sit gingerly in her chair.

"Gavin's sign was a spiral he traced over my left thigh."

Fallon visibly relaxed. "Seamus traced a trinity knot on the inside of my right wrist. A problem for him the first time he tried it while I was wearing this." Smirking, she held up her arm to draw attention to the thick cuff bracelet Sloane knew Fallon rarely removed since Griff and Keela had given it to her on her twenty-first birthday.

Sloane gifted her with a weak smile. "After he passed into the mists, I had Gavin's sign tattooed onto my thigh."

Wide-eyed, Fallon gasped. "You did? But I've never seen it."

"I've been careful to keep it hidden. I meant it to be something I had of Gavin to carry me through the rest of my lonely life."

Her friend shook her head in warning, and Sloane halted her with her palm. "Turns out, Davy has the same design inked on his right bicep." Swallowing, she gathered herself. "When we touch each other where we've decorated our skin"—she blew out a breath—"hypererotic is a tame way to describe the sensations that spark through us."

Rapt, Fallon leaned across the table. "It sounds like bonding with a warrior, Sloane."

"It's weird. The moment we met, we both noticed a throbbing where our tats are. Davy recognized our connection right away. I-I think I did too, but after everything that happened last summer, I didn't want to believe it."

Her friend reached across the table to cover her wrist with a reassuring grip. "And now?"

Tipping her head back, she closed her eyes against the pain stabbing her every time she let her mind wander. "After the vision I had of Davy, I'm so afraid, Fallon." Sitting up straight, she added, "Losing him will be so much worse than losing Gavin. I barely knew Gavin."

"But you love Davy," Fallon quietly finished for her.

Sloane nodded. "I love Davy."

"Then we have to do everything we can to keep both of you safe. That will actually be easier since Davy doesn't have to go into battle whenever those nasty witches decide they want an orgasm—or a hundred."

"But Ceri said Davy fought off the rogues trying to steal Lynnette and her last year on Samhain." Though she tried, she couldn't keep the fear from her voice. Not that she would have fooled her best friend anyway. "Somehow, I can't shake the idea that if given the choice, Davy would have been a warrior. After witnessing how she trains him, if Scathach calls Davy to battle, I have no doubt he will go."

"Siobhan and Uncle Griff say Davy is an accomplished druid. The spells and enchantments they worked on after you shared your vision give him a fighting chance to outwit and overcome the terrible trio should they try to take him. You have to trust them—and him."

"I know." She swallowed. "But if Macha takes him too…"

"We won't give her the chance."

The conviction in her friend's voice mollified her. They finished weaving one garland and had picked up the cloth for a second when Davy strolled into the room.

"I'd wondered where you'd gone off tae, mo ghràdh." Those dimples were all for her. Then he turned them on Fallon. "Dae ye mind if I steal yer maid of honor for a bit?"

"You can have her all day if you want," Fallon said with a smirk.

Fallon was sounding more and more like her fiancé Seamus with every passing day.

Not that Davy noticed or cared. The wattage of his smile could have lit a small country. "Right. Come on, lass. I want tae show ye something."

With a helpless what-can-you-do shrug and a tiny grin, Sloane stood and followed him from the room. Visions of their trip into the maze filled her head only to be chased out by visions of the two of them in his cottage when he'd given her the grand tour the night before. The bathroom was far too small for the kind of shenanigans he'd wanted to get up to, but there was plenty of room on the heavy oak table in the kitchen and on the buttery soft cushions of the leather sofa in the living room. Not to mention in the middle of his king-sized bed.

Studiously, she kept the other visions, the ones conjured

by her conversation with Fallon, on the far-flung fringes of her consciousness.

Davy slipped his arm through hers, and together they descended the stairs from the third story to the foyer. "We've completed our enchantments of the house. Four druids chanting makes short work of it, but I need some air. Thought the two of us could go fer a walk."

His tone was light, playful even. But she detected a roiling going on underneath, giving him an edginess at odds with his usual easygoing manner. She couldn't figure out if he feared or anticipated something. When she tried to breach his shield, to her great frustration, she discovered he had it firmly in place. She noticed he quite deliberately walked on her left, which meant he could brush against her mark at will, their connection sparking hot between them. Yet whatever was going on with him, he didn't want her to know.

Times like these tested her resolve never to touch another person's hand unless she needed to see what that person's future held.

Davy interrupted her darkening thoughts. "Have I told ye about *Tomnahurich*?" he asked as he let them out the front door of the manor.

"No."

Somehow, she knew he meant to distract her, but she loved to listen to his Scots burr as he wove a story. It seemed he always lowered the timbre of his voice when he told a tale. Academically, she knew he intended this tactic to mesmerize his listener. Emotionally, it never failed to draw her in.

"Tomnahurich is a fairy hill on the edge o' Inversneckie."

"Inversneckie? Do you mean Inverness?"

They walked into the garden before Davy guided her to her right toward the area where the croquet game still remained from her first day at Conlan Manor. "Yeah."

"That's an odd nickname for such a beautiful city."

He laughed. "Scots humor. Anyway, the fairy hill has a long and rather treacherous history. In olden times, the fairies were known tae hold some rowdy events there. One time, two fiddlers crossed the bridge over the River Ness on a frigid Christmas Eve. They were talking about how much they'd like tae have somewhere warm tae play and perhaps earn enough coin tae cover their supper."

They walked along a path paralleling the manor on a trajectory toward the back of the property. Glancing around her, Sloane appreciated another perfect late-summer day. Though the temperature demanded a sweater, something she'd been told was true of Scotland year 'round, the deep cerulean blue of the cloudless skies and the calmness of the air relaxed her. Or maybe it was the company.

"Did they have success?"

"In a manner of speakin'. A fellow curiously dressed in a shimmery green suit predating the men by a hundred years appeared before them and told them they could earn one hundred gold pieces each fer a night of fiddle playing. That was enough blunt tae set them up fer life, so of course the two of them jumped on the opportunity without asking any questions."

"There was a catch."

"A rather big one as it turns out. The oddly dressed fellow led them along a circuitous path until they reached a wooden door set in the side of the hill at Tomnahurich. He produced a key from his pocket and let the two fiddlers inside.

"The men blinked in awe at the massive chamber lit up like sunshine in front of them. People were drinking and eating, telling stories and laughing. A buffet piled nearly tae the ceiling provided fer the throngs of people in the room."

She stared at him, rapt with attention.

"The little fellow led the two fiddlers tae a dais opposite the buffet and told them tae set up their instruments," he continued.

"Before long, the two had the whole crowd on their feet. They played fer hours, and when they asked the fellow dressed in green if they could take a break, he shook his head, but he handed them each a tankard of ale, and the two played on.

"They played all night. At last, when morning arrived, they were exhausted. They'd played every tune they knew—and some they didn't," he said with a sly wink.

Sloane grinned back at him.

They'd left the open grassy area behind the manor and were now skirting the woods where she'd gone to retrieve her croquet ball and the crow cawed its warning. This day was so beautiful, she almost couldn't remember the trepidation she'd felt the first time she'd gone near these woods.

"Were they paid their hundred gold pieces?"

"Of course. During their evening, they'd been introduced tae the queen of the fairies herself who was well pleased with their entertainment. She gave the little green man the pouches containing the gold her very self. Trouble is, fairy gold turns tae dust when it encounters sunlight. Turns out, so did the two fiddlers when the little green man ushered them through the doorway and back intae the world."

Sloane stopped walking midstride. "The fiddlers turned to dust? Why?"

"Because one night underground with the fairies translates intae two hundred years on this side of the dirt. The sunlight beamed down on the men, and naething was left save their fiddles resting on a pile of old clothes."

"So you're saying it's wise to avoid the fairy hill at Tomnahurich?" She stumbled over the pronunciation of the Gaelic word but received a warm smile for her efforts.

"Most residents of Inverness want tae avoid going tae Tomnahurich until they absolutely can't avoid it," Davy said with a chuckle as the two of them ambled along.

"Why can't they avoid it?"

Vaguely, Sloane registered the tumble and rush of a creek nearby.

"Because Tomnahurich is an auld esker, a hill composed of sand and gravel. Perfect fer burying the dead."

Sloane gasped, and Davy grinned.

"The top of the hill houses the final resting places of the ancient dead. Around the bottom is where ye'll find the more modern cemetery. People pay tae tour it."

She bumped his shoulder hard. "That was a terrible story."

"Admit it, lass. Ye were totally intae it even tae the end."

She adored the sound of his laughter, even if it was at her expense.

The gurgling and splashing sound of the stream was louder now. "I didn't know a creek flowed through the manor grounds."

"It's a deceptively pretty little brook here, but over behind the cottage, it drops similar tae the Corrieshalloch Gorge ye checked out on yer drive tae manor." He led her along the path to the edge of the water. "The ravine this innocuous little brook has carved over the millennia nearly stole Rio's life last Samhain." The playfulness went out of his tone as he stared down at the water tumbling over the rocks where they stood on the bank of the stream.

"In the story I heard from the Sheridans, Morgan was to blame."

Davy nodded as he stared at the water. Then he shifted, shoving her hard behind him. Before she could ask what he was about, a massive snarling beast arose from the shallow creek. At first, Sloane couldn't understand what she saw. Then it shook its head, its flowing mane of green kelp sending droplets flying. When it reared up, its hooves flashed iridescently in the sunlight slanting through the trees.

"Run! Run, Sloane!"

She screamed instead as the giant animal's hoof slashed out, tripping Davy before the beast lowered its head and flipped him onto its back. Overhead, a crow irritated the world with its cacophonous caw while the kelpie spirited Davy down the stream and away from her. Sloane stood on the bank and flexed her hand where his touch lingered, an image of him taking on the goddess's champion swimming in front of her eyes.

Chapter Twenty-Nine

"ONE MORE TIME, if ye please, lass," Hamish said. "I know 'tis painful, but we need every last detail."

Sloane glanced around the salon at the friends encircling her like a fortress. As grateful as she was for their concern, didn't they understand the need for action? Davy's life in this world was at stake—unless he decided he'd rather remain immortal. Pain seared through her at the thought.

"Love transcends time and space, lass," Hamish said quietly, patting her knee from his place beside her on the sofa.

With the heel of her hand, she brushed an errant tear from her cheek, pulled much-needed air into her lungs, and started over. "From the time we left the manor, Davy acted like he anticipated something, like he was expecting or even daring the goddess to strike." She gripped her hands tightly in her lap. "On the surface, he was his usual teasing, easygoing self, but he had an edge. When I tried to sneak into his head, I discovered his shield firmly in place. Thinking back on it, it seems like he deliberately guided us to the stream. My first vision happened on the loch, but kelpies can use any body of water, can't they?"

"That they can, lass."

"He'd just finished telling me a story about the fairy hill in Inverness, the one that's a graveyard today." She choked back a sob. "The story about the fiddlers who thought they'd spent one night with the fairies only to discover two hundred years had passed while they were underground. Do you think he was trying to warn me? Tell me he was leaving us—leaving me—forever?"

"Likely, he told ye the story tae distract ye." Hamish glanced up at Alaisdair.

"Hate tae say it, but I think ye have the right of it, Sloane. The part where ye said Davy was daring the goddess. That's certainly in his wheelhouse," Alaisdair said.

"It would explain why he's spent the last year training like a warrior," Rio added, staring down at her from where he stood behind his wife seated on the opposite sofa.

"He's always trained like a warrior. Started begging me when he was a strip of a lad," Alaisdair said. "Since I had limited options, I agreed tae work with him." He glanced at Rio. "Seein' his progress after sparring with ye fer a year makes me wonder if he's a druid at all."

"From what I saw in the training room, Scathach appeared to have a concentrated interest in him," Griffin said from beside Sloane on the sofa. "Perhaps we should return to the training room and call upon our patron goddesses for a little help and guidance."

"We can't call up spells and enchantments in the training room," Siobhan reminded him.

Hamish leaned forward to see around Griff. "No' tae worry, Siobhan. The Great Goddess is a water deity. The Green Isle hovers over water. It stands tae reason we'll need tae be on or at least near a large body o' water in order tae bring Davy back tae us," he said. "That should take o' yer concern."

"After the dirty tricks Morgan and Maeve played with Seamus and Fallon last summer, I think we should consider being near the training room at least," Rowan said from where he stood between Rio and Seamus. "We know Morgan will stop at nothing to take any or all of us if she has the chance. I mean, the witch attacked us with *Fomorians* last time." The exasperation in his tone would have been almost comical if the circumstances hadn't been so dire.

When Rowan winked at her, Sloane knew what he did and appreciated it, but his attempt at humor didn't do anything for her peace of mind. The keen loss she'd experienced when Macha took Gavin was like a pinprick compared to the gaping hole the goddess drilled into her when she sent her water horse to spirit Davy away. Knowing Davy still lived gave her scant peace. If he was forced to remain on the Green Isle—or if he chose that fate—Sloane would never know. It was even more of a torture than knowing he'd crossed into the mists. From the moment the kelpie tossed Davy onto its back, Sloane knew she would spend the rest of her life waiting for him to return to her. There would never be anyone else.

Hamish and Griff encircled her between them, but they were careful not to touch her hands as they clasped each other's elbows across her lap. "Ye have the man's heart, lass. Davy will come back tae ye if he can. It's up tae ye—with a little help from yer friends—tae guide him back home."

Siobhan knelt in front of her, inserting herself into the circle, and a bone-warming calm settled over Sloane.

An intense exchange silently passed between Siobhan and Griff before Siobhan said, "We'll start the protection spells here. When we're on the shores of Loch Broom"—she glanced over her shoulder at Rowan—"near the training room, we're going to have to take your hands."

Sloane startled and instinctively tucked her hands beneath her thighs.

"Ye were the last one tae touch Davy, lass. Even if ye donnae believe it, ye know where he is. We need that information if we're tae be successful."

This close, she noticed Hamish's dark brown eyes swirled with worlds and worlds in them. Exactly like her best friend's did when Fallon was in the throes of changing someone's story.

From the sofa across from her, Fallon caught her attention, and Sloane saw the worlds swirling in the depths of her friend's hazel eyes as well. Fallon stood and walked around behind Sloane, completing the circle of storytellers—three druids and a bard. The warmth she'd experienced earlier intensified, and yet she could have sworn it radiated out from her rather than poured in as she'd initially thought.

"That's it, Sloane. You're already showing Davy the way back. Don't think about what you have to lose. Surrender yourself to what you want more than anything."

She blinked at Griff.

"Surrender yourself to him. It's the only way he can return to you."

"Be his light in the darkness, Sloane. Be the beacon in the lighthouse for whichever sea the Green Isle is hovering over," Siobhan said, a gentle smile on her lips.

Fallon whispered in her ear. "We can help you bring him back, but only if you let go and open yourself to hope instead of loss."

Sloane closed her eyes and pulled her hands from beneath her thighs to rest on top of them, allowing the druids to have what they wanted.

"No' here, lass. No' yet."

Hamish broke the circle to stand before the assembled clan. "If I know anythin' about Macha, she's like her sister goddesses. She'll dae whatever it takes tae have what she wants." He stared down the warriors standing mostly across from him. "Ye lot will need tae be ready tae protect us as we chant over Sloane on the shores o' the loch." His expression turned thoughtful when his gaze fell on Ceri. "Lass, I believe ye and yer aunt should direct yer warriors from the safety o' the trainin' room. Considerin' the twa o' ye are carryin' the future o' the clan in yer bellies."

"Hamish." There was a warning in Ceri's voice.

"For once I agree with the old man," Rio growled. "Don't argue with him."

Sian Sheridan, who had been standing with her husband beside Shanley near the fireplace glared at her son before turning her attention to Ceri. "I'll join you there."

"Thank you, Mom," Rio said, but his attention was all on Ceri.

Sloane watched as he cupped Ceri's shoulders over the back of the sofa, and she nodded. Whatever passed between the two of them must have mollified Ceri. When Sloane glanced over at Alaisdair and Shanley, she saw that they too were in private, tele-pathic communication. In fact, it appeared every couple in the room was engaged in private conversation with each other, send-ing a pang of longing through her that left her gasping for breath.

Seemingly unaware of Sloane's turmoil, Hamish rubbed his hands together in a satisfied fashion. "I take it ye're all set, then." He smiled at each person in turn.

"I'll join Ceri, Shanley, and Sian in the training room," Alyssa said.

"Me too," Lynnette said from somewhere behind her.

"I don't like it, Fallon," Seamus said, his expression dark. "Not this close to our wedding day when you come into your full power. Perhaps this whole thing with Davy is a trap, a way for the goddesses to take you into the mists before you have the chance to fight them with the power of your stories."

"Or it's my first opportunity to do what I'm meant to do."

Seamus's expression said he had no intention of back-ing down.

"Mercifully, Brighid wiped part of your memory, brother. But I saw how your talisman did her job for you when she hadn't had any training at all," Siobhan said as she stood and faced Seamus. "Griff and I have been working Fallon hard since summer solstice, and she needs to do this. She needs to help her friend."

Knowing the way Siobhan had fought alongside Fallon for Seamus's life, Sloane could hardly believe the woman was now willing to risk his well-being for her. Seamus needed Fallon. If anything happened to him in the future, Fallon could retell his story, weave a version to save him.

"It's all right, Siobhan. Fallon can weave stories from the safety of the training room, I'm sure," Sloane said.

"I'm afraid she can't. Not yet anyway," Griff said.

"See?" That single word sounded like a plea on Seamus's lips.

"I'll be careful. As will you, Superman."

"I'll be watching out for you as well, Seamus," Keela said.

"Right. That's sorted. This undertakin' is best done in daylight, so we'll dispense with the niceties o' civilian transportation and visualize ourselves tae the dock at the foot o' the path tae the trainin' room." He eyed the warriors, his fellow druids, and Sloane and Fallon. "Ye talismans will visualize yerselves tae the trainin' room. I have nae doubt one or twa o' our favorite deities await us already."

Davy stood on the beach of an island in the middle of the ocean. A foaming froth of water swirling a few feet offshore was the last vestige of the ferocious water horse that had sped him from the grounds of Conlan Manor to what he suspected to be the mythical Green Isle itself. For most of his life, even as he wove stories about those who had landed on it, he'd wondered at its existence. Like Atlantis or Shangri-la, the Green Isle seemed more of a dream than a real place.

Staring at the endless expanse of water appearing to flow off the edge of the horizon in front of him wasn't going to help him escape his circumstances. He kicked at one of the jagged stones littering the beach and turned his attention toward the island on which he stood. If indeed he stood on the Green Isle, someone had some explaining to do. The shores of paradise ought to be endless white sand beaches over which soft on-shore breezes blew. Not this vast expanse of jagged slate and basalt, slick and sharp underfoot. The winds swirling around him alternately plastered his sweater to his chest then to his back. Zephyrs these winds most certainly were not.

On the cliffs above him rose a forest of trees so green they almost stole the light from the sun. He'd never imagined he'd have to squint to look at trees, but he found himself shielding his eyes with his hand as he gazed up at where he guessed he needed to go if he wanted to find any answers as to how he could escape this place.

As he picked his way across the rocks on the beach, he thought about Sloane's Sight and how she'd described his landing on this island. After his near-miss with the kelpie at Lughnasadh, he'd believed she'd had the right of it with the water horse rising from the loch to spirit him away in his skiff. As the two of them had walked along the path, he'd remembered too late that kelpies were known to frequent rivers and streams as well as the vast lochs and inland seas surrounding his home. Now he found himself without even driftwood from which to construct a raft let alone access to his skiff.

Surveying the rocky cliffs rising at least four stories above him, he looked for a break in the stone, something resembling a path to the top. Having no landmarks to guide him, he thought perhaps he'd wandered about a quarter of a mile from where the kelpie had dropped him on the shore when he noticed an opening. At the base of the cliff, he discovered a narrow path that seemed to have been carved into the rocks, a rather treacherous-looking climb. Seeing no alternative, he scrambled over a collection of boulders at the bottom of the trail and started climbing.

The route began as a narrow gravel track that evolved into an often slick collection of what some would call flagstones if they'd made up a walkway through a garden. More than once, Davy slipped and found himself on his knees or flat on his belly sliding backward down the rocks. After the third or fourth slip, he lay flat, catching his breath between curses. Hiking over trails among the munros surrounding Loch Broom hadn't given him much preparation for practically free-soloing a cliff on an island in the middle of nowhere. When he steeled himself to look up to gauge how much more climbing torture he had to endure, he discovered the end of the trail was only fifteen or twenty meters ahead of him. Slowly and carefully, he gathered his legs back beneath himself, and clinging to the wall with his left hand, he inched his way up the cliffside.

When he crested the top of the trail, he wanted to punch something. A wall of vegetation stretching as far as he could see in either direction impeded his progress forward. The idea of shimmying back down the treacherous track he'd just climbed held little appeal—as did trying to skirt the top of the cliff on a ledge no wider than the length of his foot. Yet instinctively, he knew the answer to his escape, to returning to Sloane, lay somewhere in the middle of the island.

For long minutes, he stared at the dense growth of bushes, vines, and trees in full green leaf. Endless green, the color of life, hope, energy—rebirth. Reaching into his druidic lore, he remembered in addition to her warmongering pursuits and delight in slaughter, Macha was also a fertility goddess. The color green would suit her. At the moment, it frustratingly impeded him. He could hear the sardonic tone of his own thoughts. *If only I'd thought to bring along my claymore as I took a stroll with my beautiful woman on a perfect afternoon.* That, of course, would have been ridiculous. Still, it would have been nice to have been a warrior who could summon his claymore at will since it looked like his only option was to force his way through the green wall in front of him.

A familiar weight settled over his back, and for a long minute, he couldn't be sure if his heart beat at all as air backed up in his lungs.

"Cannae be," he whispered to the empty air.

Gingerly, he reached behind his head to pat the space between his shoulder blades.

"By all the gods, how can—"

With both hands, he pulled his weapon from its sheath and blinked as it caught the sunlight when he held it in front of himself.

"Druids cannae summon our swords," he said, wonder warring with a nameless dread settling over him.

He glanced around, even daring to look back down toward the beach from the breath-stealing height of the cliffs. Seeing nothing to indicate he had any company other than his own, he sucked in air, let it out slowly, and stared once again at the greenery in front of him. "Donnae look a gift horse in the mouth, as the auld saying goes." Grabbing a vine with one hand, he hacked at it with the other, discovering to his consternation that at the whisper touch of the steel of his blade, the vine shriveled away.

"*Fuck!* Should have known the auld witch would send me tae an island in fairyland."

Hope those enchantments ye wove over me work like ye think they will, Hamish.

Touching his blade to the thick vegetation shrunk it out of his way, the leaves and vines curling and shriveling as though they'd been singed. As he walked forward, he saw where a trail of flagstones lay hidden beneath the undergrowth. With his claymore in front of him parting the shrubs and vines and his eyes on the ground, he discovered he could move quickly, though he could only guess at his destination.

The trees lining the track shivered as a breeze blew through their tops. Davy stopped and took stock of his surroundings. Behind him, he saw that like the living—or more likely enchanted—entities they were, the bushes and vines had closed back together, obscuring his back trail like he'd never walked it. In front of him, the vegetation thinned enough he no longer needed his claymore to cut his way along the track.

Meanwhile, the skies overhead darkened ominously, and the rumble of thunder in the distance caught his attention.

"That explains the winds on the beach," he said to the forest around him.

He knew he dared the gods by refusing to acknowledge their presence. Yet he declined to show fear. Whatever they had in store for him, he'd fight. As long as he still drew breath, he still had a chance to return home—to return to Sloane and how she looked at him through beautiful violet eyes.

A couple of short steps later, he broke through the forest to find himself facing a long walk over an uneven trail through a wasteland. *At least it's no' a bog.* He chuckled at his own joke before a sigh escaped him. In the center of the wasteland rose a huge black cone. He hoped the volcano was long dead because the lightning show taking place over the top of it was terrifying enough without the additional fireworks of bone-melting molten lava shooting into the air, possibly to land on him. Of course, traveling over open ground during a lightning storm didn't sound much like a picnic either.

Behind him lay the wall of forest and the endless ocean beyond it. His destination awaited him across the open expanse of land surrounding the black mountain in the distance. Sheathing his claymore, his eyes trained on the iridescent lightning bolts

Taranis threw like spears to split the sky, he stepped away from the shelter of the trees and set off down the path. If the stories were true, that black mountain was the heart of the island, and somewhere at its base a fountain of water splashed and danced up from the ground. A fountain of eternity if one chose to drink from it.

Chapter Thirty

CHILL BREEZE BLEW off the loch where the warriors and druids gathered at the base of *An Teallach*. Sloane hugged her arms around herself, fearing the circling crows cawing high above them far more than the threat of a storm. Standing steadfast beside her, Fallon rubbed her hand up and down Sloane's back.

Fallon glanced at the birds obscenely cavorting overhead and returned her attention to her friend. "Ignore her. It's going to be all right, Sloane. You have to believe that."

"She makes it hard to ignore her. Especially when she keeps taking the men the fates destined for me." With the back of her hand, Sloane swiped at a tear that escaped without her permission. "She sent Gavin into the mists. What if she's already sent Davy there as well?" She swallowed over the lump in her throat. "A murder of crows signaled her arrival with her terrible news the last time." Involuntarily, she glanced into the skies above them again.

"This is Davy's favorite sweater," Hamish said as he came to stand in front of the two women. "It's no' the same as touchin' his hand, I know, but perhaps if ye hold it close, it will trigger a vision or give ye a sign." He handed Sloane a wool sweater hand-knit of gold yarn shot through with a dark chocolate-colored, never-ending Celtic knotwork design over the chest and repeated on the biceps area of the sleeves.

The sweater reminded Sloane of Davy's eyes. Hugging it close to her chest, she inhaled the citrusy, musky scent of him, which flooded her mind with memories—in the garden, in the maze, in her room at the manor, in his cottage. The dimples in his smile, the way his pupils dilated to meet the chocolate rings of his eyes when he looked at her, the rich depth of his voice, especially when he told a story, all of it came to her in a rush. But those were pictures of the past, not the future.

A low growl coming from somewhere on the mountainside above them distracted her. From the corner of her eye, Sloane caught the protective way Seamus, who stood behind her friend, hugged Fallon to him, and a wave of sorrow washed over her. Not only had she lost Gavin and now Davy, but because of her, her friends were in danger too.

"Morgan appears to have run out of ideas," Rio said as he regarded the origin of the low growl.

Sloane turned around and followed his gaze up the side of the mountain. Her eyes saucered as she stared at the biggest man-like being she'd ever seen. From her vantage point, the giant's shoulders appeared to scrape the clouds in the sky. Its black hair stood straight up on its head and porcupined out from its back. Elf-like pointed ears the size of dinner plates stuck out from the sides of its head, and its gaping mouth revealed rows of teeth resembling the maw of a shark. In its massive hands, it wielded a wickedly knobby club Sloane feared could crack a skull wide open with one strategic swing.

"Wh-what do you mean?"

"*Gog Magog*? Really? It didn't take much for a regular Roman fighter to best him the first time way back in the day," Rowan replied, the derision in his voice telling her exactly how little he feared this monster.

The giant growled again and lumbered down the hill. His huge round eyes remained laser-focused on Fallon, and Seamus grimaced.

"Hamish are you sure Fallon needs to be here? Can't she do her job just as well from the safety of the training room?" he asked as he stepped in front of his fiancée, shielding her from the monster's view.

Hamish's tone personified patience. "Sloane must be near the water in order tae reach out tae Davy. Fallon must remain near Sloane in order tae change her story. It's simple as that, lad. Now stop fussin'. Ye have a job tae dae tae."

Seamus and the Sheridan brothers—Rio, Rowan, and Riley—formed a human wall between the zombie giant and the talismans they were there to protect. Behind Gog Magog, they could see a red and black shimmer in the air, a sure sign Morgan hovered nearby. Farther down the dock, Duncan MacManus balanced on the balls of his feet with his claymore in front of him ready to fight as he guarded his wife Siobhan and Griffin Walsh who were casting spells to draw the Green Isle to Loch Broom from wherever in the world the goddesses had concealed it.

With a roar like something out of a nightmare, Gog Magog ran down the mountainside toward the group of warriors and talismans on the dock. Instinctively, Sloane reached for Fallon, and a scream ripped from her throat as she saw a vision of a hoof flashing out from a rearing kelpie to take Fallon down.

Fallon slanted her a look, her hazel eyes seeming to swirl like the pinwheels she and Sloane had made in elementary school a lifetime ago. Then she very deliberately plastered herself against Seamus's back while Rowan and Riley spun around to protect them from threats in the water. From out of the depths of the loch, the kelpie reared with an otherworldly shriek simultaneously with the giant descending on them, its club driving downward with deadly intent. As though they were a single entity, the warriors moved, leaving nothing but air where the whole group had stood a nanosecond earlier.

Sloane stared as the monsters collided, the scene seeming to unfold in slow motion before her terrified eyes. Hooves flashed and sparks flew as they caught the descending club, the momentum pulling the giant over the edge of the dock to land on the snarling water horse. As the monsters sank beneath the surface of the loch, it foamed and hissed around them, a cauldron of sulfurous bubbles rising to the top before popping their foul odor into the atmosphere. Beside her, Hamish chanted a protection spell, and she sucked in a breath of fresh air.

Several long minutes later, she looked around at her friends, zeroing in on Fallon. "What just happened? I saw the kelpie take you." To her own ears, her voice sounded like sandpaper.

"I breached your shield, saw your vision, and changed the story," Fallon said matter-of-factly.

"H-how did you do that?"

"Breach your shield? I think that's the reason Hamish insisted I remain near you. Somehow he knew how tuned in to each other we are."

"Not that. My visions are nearly one hundred percent accurate. How did you change it?"

Fallon gifted her an enigmatic smile.

"What did you see, Sloane?" Seamus demanded.

Fallon spared her. "She saw the kelpie take me. I changed the story so we could take down Gog Magog together and the kelpie as a bonus." She smiled at Hamish. "I know the stories of the great warriors and some of the lesser-known ones as well. Like an obscure Roman who lured this particular giant to his death by falling off a cliff."

"Well done, lass. Ye've passed yer first test with flyin' colors."

Rio interrupted. "Before you all congratulate yourselves like you've saved the world, you might want to consider what Morgan has on deck for round two."

Sloane gasped as a massive troll barreled down the mountainside toward them. "What *is* that thing?"

"That, lass, is a *buggane*. 'Tis native tae the Isle o' Man, but from the looks o' this one, the zombie version can be called tae appear anywhere the Morrigan chooses."

"A troll? Aren't they supposed to be susceptible to light?" she asked.

"Usually, lass. Unless the Morrigan has called on Arawn tae bring one up from the dead. Then all bets are off."

"How does it die, then?"

All tufts of hair and knuckle-dragging gait, the massive beast lumbered down the mountainside. Though its movements appeared clumsy and slow, it was closing down on their little group rather too rapidly for Sloane's comfort.

"We take it out," Rio said as he stepped forward. "You care to join me on this one, Rowan?"

"On it. Seamus and Riley, take care of the talismans."

Riley stepped in front of her, reaching his left arm back and around her while he guarded them both with his claymore in his right hand. "Move when I move, Sloane," he commanded.

She nodded.

"Words, Sloane."

"Move with you, Riley."

He grunted a response, his eyes trained on the action coming at them.

Beside them, Seamus similarly held on to Fallon. An ache gnawed at Sloane at the reminder she would never experience the oneness Fallon shared with Seamus. Riley held her impersonally, like taking care of an important package, not in the way Fallon and Seamus were so obviously one unit.

A terrible stench of wet earth and rotting flesh fell over them. Sloane gagged and coughed, but she didn't let go of Riley. Instead, she buried her nose between his shoulder blades and tried to keep her breaths shallow. Behind her, she could hear Hamish chanting furiously.

The sound of rocks crashing down the side of the mountain and loud chuffing of air sawing in and out of massive lungs told her the monster bore down on them, but she didn't lift her face away from where she'd buried her nose in Riley's back. Watching the troll's progress changed nothing anyway. Riley's arm tightened around her as he held their ground. Sounds of grunting and swords shearing off talons sent shivers through her, and she tightened her hold on the warrior protecting her. A scream terrible enough to tear the sky in two dragged an answering one from her. A few seconds later, Riley loosened his hold. Sloane looked over his shoulder to see Duncan MacManus standing above the inert form of the zombie troll sprawled on the earth at Rio and Rowan's feet.

"Thanks, Duncan," Rowan said. "Now what do we do with it?"

"Leave that tae me, lad," Hamish said as he tossed herbs and chanted over the newly dead undead.

To Sloane's astonishment, within a couple of minutes, the zombie started melting into the dirt, a fine mist spiraling up out the middle of it. She stared at Hamish and back at the troll, stunned to watch as the monster disappeared into the earth.

"Your power is a bit terrifying, Hamish."

"No' more so than yers, lass. When ye come intae yer full potential."

She wrapped her arms around herself. Understanding that Hamish didn't mean to be cruel didn't lessen the ache of being the living half of a pair that would never exist. Then she caught sight of Davy's sweater where she'd apparently dropped it on the dock as they were set upon by the troll. Snatching it up, she decided the only way to keep it safe was to wear it. When she pulled it on and settled it over herself, the hem of it brushed the top of her thigh. She cried out as a searing pain shot through her tattoo. Yet before her friends could come to her aid, calming warmth she could feel in the marrow of her bones spread through her.

Fallon held her as tears ran unchecked down her face.

"He's alive. The witch hasn't taken him yet." She saw the concern on her friend's face. "I haven't lost him," she whispered.

Exasperation colored Hamish's tone. "O' course he's alive, lass. Yer vision in the trainin' room the other day told ye as much."

"Ye might give this one a break, Hamish," Alaisdair said as he strolled down the trail to the dock. "After what Macha has already put her through, 'tis understandable she's feeling her losses."

Rio glared at him. "Aren't you supposed to be helping Dad guard the training room—and the valuable people inside it?"

"Our resident prophetesses wanted me tae relay a message. They've experienced another shared prophecy like the two of them went through last year at Samhain."

Rio paled.

If they lived through this, Sloane was going to have to ask about a story that could so frighten a warrior with Rio Sheridan's prowess and courage.

Alaisdair ignored him. "All of ye need tae be on yer guard when the Green Isle makes its appearance. We donnae want tae lose anyone tae the temptation of eternal life when we're trying tae save our friend."

"Thank ye, Alaisdair. Ye gave us the missin' piece."

The warrior nodded, glared at Rio, and headed back up the trail to his assigned job.

"What missing piece, Hamish?" Sloane asked.

"I've been trying tae figure out how we'll spirit Davy off the island. 'Tis no' a place ye can visualize yerself intae or out of." He rubbed his hands together. "Now we can build an enchanted bridge, one he can cross tae return tae us."

"The trick will be to maintain a one-way gate on this side of it, so that none of us can open it no matter how hard we try," Griff added as he joined them. He turned to Hamish. "Siobhan and I have finished casting the protection spells."

Hamish beamed at him. "That's grand, Griffin. Perhaps ye can begin weavin' those spells over this lot"—he waved a hand in the direction of the assembled warriors and talismans—"while Siobhan and I take a look at that special book o' notes she copied from Alyssa's grandmother."

Griff nodded, and Hamish ambled over to where Siobhan and Duncan stood in quiet conversation. A minute later, Duncan joined them while Griff circled them and began his chant.

"May the four winds embrace you,

"May the earth await you,

"May the sun always warm you,

"May your hearts forever beat strong.

"May the rains give life to you,

"May your days lengthen before you,

"May the gardens provide for you,

"May you know love.

"May you not resist when at last the darkness falls."

A collective shiver rippled over the group, and Griff inclined his head, a satisfied expression on his face.

The winds shifted, lifting off into the skies where they worried the clouds enough to part them and allow beams of sunlight through. The murder of crows circling overhead shrieked one long ear-splitting note before winging away toward the open sea beyond the estuary where fresh water met salt. Sloane watched until they disappeared into the horizon. When she returned her attention to the friends gathered around her, she discovered all eyes on her.

"It's time, sugar," Fallon said gently. "Time for you to match wits with a goddess—and win."

CHAPTER THIRTY-ONE

WHEN DAVY CALCULATED it from the shelter of the trees, the trek across the wasteland to the base of the black mountain hadn't seemed all that far. Yet after walking for what his body told him had been hours, he didn't seem any closer to his destination. The booming thunder overhead had long ago faded to background noise. The lightning crackling across the sky morphed from terrifying to entertaining, a show put on solely for him. Being so exposed probably should have disturbed him more. Instead, he experienced an odd sense of security. Unless a threat materialized out of thin air, he'd see it coming for days across the wide-open expanse surrounding him.

Of course, a threat absolutely could materialize from thin air. He'd seen the goddesses in action often enough to know that. Still, he believed his test awaited him at the black mountain. It appeared time didn't pass as he walked along the trail. The light, obscured by Taranis's cloud cover, didn't change. No slant of sun lengthened his shadow keeping pace almost directly beneath his feet. A thought occurred to him. *The auld girl thinks to tire me, weaken me, steal my will tae fight.* He stopped walking and squatted in the middle of the track to rest.

With his eyes closed, his thoughts turned to Sloane as they frequently had on his solitary journey through a deserted land. As he'd been doing for the duration of his lonely walk, he told himself a story about her. This time, her smile appeared in his mind: Sloane smiling her secret smile when she thought he wasn't looking. Sloane smiling openly at a joke she shared with Fallon. Sloane smiling up at him slow and sexy as he took his time with her, joining them inch by breath-stealing pleasurable inch. When they first met, she'd hoarded her smiles, like giving them away might mean she could still feel happiness after the loss she'd suffered. Before the kelpie appeared during the afternoon as they'd walked along the path at the manor, she'd gifted him over and over with tiny smiles and open smiles and so-sexy-he-had-to-kiss-her smiles. Somewhere in the fortnight they'd known each other, she'd surrendered herself to him, leaving him no choice but to find his way back to her... if he could figure out how to escape his current predicament.

His eyes popped open when a new sound penetrated the pounding and crashing of Taranis's tantrum playing out overhead. Carefully, he pushed himself back to standing and took stock of his surroundings. Seeing nothing coming at him on the trail in front of him or on his back trail, he scanned the endless sea of browned grasses on either side of the path. Again, he saw nothing as far as the horizon met the sky. But as he returned his focus to the mountain, he saw that somehow during his rest, either the path had continued moving forward, or the weird sound pulling him from his thoughts belonged to a mountain with legs. Whichever way it had happened, he discovered himself closing in on his destination.

Hunger gnawed at his insides, and his mouth begged for a drink of water. Too bad the goddess hadn't given him a little advance warning. He would have packed himself a snack and a flask. Shaking his head, he laughed at his silly notions, like his whole situation was nothing more than a lark.

At that moment, the monster struck. With a snarl, it bowled Davy over from behind. Pushing himself onto his hands and knees, Davy spit out a mouthful of dirt stained with his blood. The coppery taste filled his mouth, and he spit another stream of blood into the dust before he was able to take stock of his injuries. He'd bitten his tongue hard enough to explain all the blood, his left wrist throbbed, and his knees stung. With the exception of the dirt, he felt pretty much the same as when he sparred with Rio in the training room at *An Teallach*. He shook his head and rolled back up to his feet.

In front of him, the monster stared him down with close-set, red-rimmed, piggy eyes. Huge tusks like a boar's stuck out from either side of the ogre's jaws. It had covered its scaly body with animal skins, which only added to its general ugliness. As Davy's eyes roamed over his enemy, he saw that the thing in front of him—some sort of part boar, part human—carried no weapon. Instead, it flexed its huge club-like hands at its sides, its weight balanced on its hoof-like feet as though it was preparing for another run at him.

The razor-sharp tusks grabbed his attention far more urgently than the monster's club-like hands. If the ogre's initial attack was a hello, Davy had no doubt its get-to-know-you shot would involve spilling more than a mouthful of his blood. Raising both hands behind him, he unsheathed his claymore and awaited the beast's next move.

Lightning bolts reflected in the polished surface of his blade forced his attacker to shield its eyes. Davy debated using his momentary advantage, but in that second, the ogre rallied and launched itself at him. On all fours, the boar-like creature bore down on him like an out-of-control freight train. Without quite knowing what he did, Davy visualized himself into the next minute, jumping through space and time to land behind the monster, slashing its hamstrings with one smooth arc of his sword. A scream, wicked and raw enough to wake the ancient dead, rent the air as the beast went down.

Davy blinked.

What the hell?

Before he had a chance to contemplate how he'd executed a maneuver reserved for warriors alone, the beast shook itself and stood up once again. Its massive head swung back and forth as it stared at him. A garbled sound rumbled from its throat, and to his surprise, Davy understood the ogre's words.

"Druid. You don't play fair."

"Running me down from behind was fair, then, was it?"

"A druid should not be able to bend time and space."

From his peripheral vision, Davy saw the blood drying on the back of the beast's legs. "As distraction tactics go, ye need tae work on yers."

Taking advantage of his new powers, he bent time and space again to land a blow to the middle of the ogre's chest as he vaulted it and alighted on the path behind it. Before it could follow his movements, Davy stabbed it again between the shoulder blades, dropping it to its knees. Kneeling in the path, the ogre muttered curses, most of which were aimed at a particular goddess. Definitely not dead even after Davy executed the tricky move he'd watched Scathach employ to wear out Rio until he'd perfected it.

What. The. Hell?

"You're on the Green Isle, Davy Sutherland, where immortality is not reserved solely for humans. Although, you may want to play a bit more nicely with *Searbhàn* if you're going to be staying with us here for eternity," Macha said as she casually strolled up to them from wherever she'd materialized.

His voice cracked. "You sicced Surly on me?" Turning to the ogre, he said, "Sorry. I dinnae recognize you. In my defense, I dinnae expect tae experience a being from ancient stories attacking me."

Macha dragged a talon-like fingernail, as glossy black as the feathers making up her cape, down the length of his arm. "Besting Searbhàn as you did has already gone down in the annals of the exploits of the great heroes."

Dread snaked through his bowels. "What are you saying, Macha?" His voice was low, dangerous.

"The storytellers of your race even now are regaling their friends with the tale of how you bested Searbhàn when you met him on the road as you journeyed through the Trossachs on a mission to save your clan." She trailed her hand over his shoulders as she circled him. "You, Davy Sutherland, are known far and wide as one of the greatest heroes of all time. In fact, your exploits in Scotland rank as high as those of Brian Boru in Ireland."

He detected a bit of a choking sound as she uttered that name. Then she stole his thoughts when she drew her fingers down his right bicep, stroking the tattoo inked on his skin. "You are a great warrior, indeed. One who could even tempt a goddess."

For a second, his thoughts scattered before coming back together, focused on shutting down the desire hardening his cock to rival the steel of his blade. If the goddess took him to her bed, unlike Seamus Lochlann, there would be no help for him. Here, he was on his own with no expectation of aid from his friends.

"I am a druid. I tell stories. I do no' star in them."

Macha crossed her arms, giving his libido a reprieve as she regarded him skeptically. "Do not lie to me. You have always wanted to be the hero of the story, Davy."

He worked to control his response. Hearing his secret wish stated so baldly left him exposed, like all his inner covetousness and selfishness were on display. Suddenly, the attack Surly executed on him didn't seem so random. The ogre embodied Davy's lifelong inner turmoil perfectly. Celtic culture revered the boar as the ultimate symbol of power and strength while the snake remained a thief in the grass, an animal never to be trusted, whose story was always a lie.

He feigned bravado. "How long have I been here?"

"That depends."

"On what?"

"You." Macha spared a glance at the ogre hovering nearby, hoping for another go at the man. "If you want to realize your lifelong dream of being a warrior-hero, you have been here for an age." The stare she gave him chilled him to the marrow. "And you will remain here."

"If I want tae return tae my mortal life?"

"You will always be on the sidelines of battle, telling the story, not being the story. In other words, you will never achieve your greatest desire." The pure malice flashing in her smile told him she knew his heart.

How could that be? He'd never revealed his deepest wish, not to Alaisdair, not to Hamish, certainly not to Rio. Yet he never missed a chance to spar with warriors, never missed an opportunity for Scathach's training, even when, as a druid, he was relegated to watching from the edge of the sparring circle. That was how he'd learned the move that had sidelined Surly earlier even though he'd never had a chance to try it before. All the goddess had to do was observe him to know what stories he longed in his heart to tell. Stories of cunning and celebrated deeds, strength and terrifying skill besting the monsters the goddesses sent against—him. He wanted to be the hero the bards and druids lauded when they told the stories to remind warriors of the possibilities, to encourage their bloodlust against their enemies, to inspire them to be as great a hero as he.

"I have a choice."

"You have a choice," she said. "In theory."

He slid his hand into the sleeve of his sweater and passed the wool along the blade of his sword, cleaning the vestiges of Surly's blood from it. "What does that mean, in theory?"

"Can you deny your beloved dream, the story you've been weaving in the recesses of your heart for your entire life?" With a nearly imperceptible nod, she summoned a raven from the air to land in a whir of feathers on her shoulder. "You have always wanted to be a warrior, David Sutherland. Here in this place, you can realize that dream and live it until the end of time." Instead of watching him, she focused on the bird blending in with the feathers on her cape, smoothing her hands over its inky wings, producing a morsel of meat from the air, and feeding it.

Insight flashed in his mind. Like the bird, the goddess drew him in, fed him his preferred food, expected something in return.

"What dae ye want, Macha?"

"To give you your heart's desire." Perhaps the smile stretching her red lips was meant to seduce, but it left him cold.

"At what price?"

"You remain here in a warrior's paradise, fighting gods and monsters, becoming a legendary hero sung and praised down through the ages." Again, the smile.

"You haven't answered the question."

Waving a dismissive hand, she said, "She will be an old woman by now. Is she still worth it? When you can remain here, couple with goddesses and live forever as the greatest warrior who ever was?"

"I give up Sloane. The price is Sloane."

"Of course. It is expected that heroes make sacrifices." She went back to stroking the big black bird who stared down at him with its soulless eyes.

"Yer promise of eternity is temptin', I cannae lie. Yet I can see how well living without love has worked out fer ye."

As the skies overhead darkened to deep charcoal, her eyes flashed a warning.

Davy plowed on. "I'll take my chances with mortality. Thank ye all the same fer yer offer."

A silver and black aura sparkling around her gave the goddess the illusion of increasing stature. Still, Davy held his ground, his sword arm tensing, anticipating action.

"You will give up an eternity of living your deepest desire for a woman who even now is old enough to be your grandmother?" Her voice rose nearly to a shriek.

"Somehow, I think ye're no' telling the whole truth. But it doesn't matter. I will spend whatever time I have left with her loving her with everything I have tae give."

The goddess flew into a rage, the raven on her shoulder flapping into the air with an ominous croak. "You cannot possibly make that choice," she roared.

Davy quirked a brow at the goddess's anger.

A large group of immortals descended upon them then.

The first to speak was a rather grandfatherly-looking gentleman. "Are you sure this is what you want, Davy Sutherland? For if you make this choice, you shall never again be offered immortality."

"Thank you, Anind. Someone needs to talk sense into this ungrateful human," Macha said with a snarl.

"No' meanin' tae offend, but dae ye know ye look like the Father Time cliché?" Davy said to the god of immortality.

Anind chuckled. "You mean you humans modeled your Father Time after my likeness, do you not?"

A point for the god. Davy grinned.

The most handsome being Davy had ever seen stepped forward. "Though you planned your temptation well, Macha, this one will not be turned. His love for the woman runs too deep." The god smiled at him. "After all, he descends from my people, the Feans. For us, love will always win."

"I should have known you would not keep yourself out

of this, Aengus the Ever-Young. You have impeded my plans throughout time," Macha raged.

"There is something else, Davy."

At the sound of his patron goddess's voice, he turned to face her. "What is that, milady?"

"Your wish for immortality," Brighid began.

"That I have already offered to grant," Macha fumed.

Ignoring her fellow goddess as though she hadn't interrupted, Brighid said, "It is something for which every mortal aspires. You believe the only way to have it is by being a hero whose exploits the bards repeat down through time."

"We dae remember the heroes, milady," Davy said, his tone dangerously close to chiding.

"The bards too."

He questioned her with a cocked brow.

"The Greeks had Homer, the Irish had Fergus mac Ròich, your own Scots have Ossian. In modern times, the English had Shakespeare—storytellers all whose fame often transcends that of the heroes whose stories they told," Brighid said. "That you forgot disappoints me."

Davy inclined his head. "Ye're right. Donnae know what got intae me."

"Rowan and Rio Sheridan, whom you count among your friends, are the greatest heroes of your community, the Lancelot and Gawaine of the modern age. If you are not there to tell their stories, who will tell them?" Brighid asked, her golden aura intensifying around her. "Certainly not druids like Siobhan MacManus or Griffin Walsh. They are healers."

"Hamish—"

"Hamish Buchanan is a teacher. Yes, he can tell a tale and heal any wound, but his job is to teach other druids those skills."

She touched his claymore, sending an almost uncomfortable heat through the hilt. He took the hint and sheathed it. After all, his sword would do him little good among immortals anyway. Hadn't his recent bout with Surly proved that?

"It is up to you to tell the Sheridans' story, a saga that in your capable hands will resonate down through the generations. Like the exploits of the Round Table Knights, Cuchulain, and Brian Boru, their story will educate warriors, talismans—and bards for centuries. But only if it is told by the storyteller who was there, the one who knows every detail and can tell it with truth and power." Brighid stepped away, allowing him space to make up his mind.

Macha drew his attention from his patroness. "Behold, Davy Sutherland. You have reached the base of the mountain where the waters of immortality bubble and dance freely. One taste, and your greatest wish will be reality from now until time ends." Seemingly from the air, she produced a silver goblet, its rim inlaid with onyx and diamonds, and extended it to him.

Taking his place beside her, Anind said, "Remember, Davy Sutherland. If you turn down this offer, it will never be extended to you again." The god crossed his massive arms over his chest, trapping his flowing white beard beneath them—a study in contrasts, young and old. "Consider your decision carefully. No matter what happens in the future, you can never return here if you choose now to leave us."

Aengus flanked Davy opposite Anind and Macha. "Love is eternal too, Davy. Your love for Sloane—and hers for you—will transcend time. But only if together you let it grow."

Brighid joined Aengus. "Your choice is a weighty one, druid. Be wise in making it."

Davy's gaze traveled from goddess to god, god to goddess, to the silver chalice within his grasp. And his chest ached with the sensation of his soul being torn in two.

CHAPTER THIRTY-TWO

LOANE STARED AT the breathtaking silver chalice, the multifaceted onyx and diamond gems along the rim winking in the sunlight. Fresh, sweet water overflowed the cup, a never-ending cascade of life-giving elixir. Mesmerized, she reached out to grasp the goblet when a sensation of fire singed her wrist. With a hiss, she snatched her hand back.

Her eyes watered with pain—from both the blistering heat on her skin and the loss of the beautiful vision she'd wanted to watch forever.

"You can't give her what she wants so easily, Sloane," Fallon said.

The two of them sat side by side on a stone bench above the dock. Sloane stared at the red welt stinging on her wrist and back to her friend. "Did you do this?"

"It was the only way to stop you from turning your vision into reality."

"Donnae worry, lass. I have a salve fer yer hurt. But I'm afraid it will dae naethin' fer yer heart if ye allow the goddess tae win," Hamish said as he walked away from the other druids to stand in front of them. "Siobhan and Griff are daein' all they can to conjure the Green Isle intae the loch, but it willnae matter if ye've already helped Macha win her prize."

"You should have seen it, Fallon. It was the most beautiful silver chalice. I wanted to hold it so much, feel its healing water flow over my hands." She stared at the angry red wound on her wrist. "Wait. How did you know?"

"We're in this together." She wrapped her arm around Sloane. "When you suddenly dropped into a trance, I breached your shield."

Sloane sensed her eyebrows scraping her hairline.

"It's fairly easy for me to do when you're lost in the Sight," Fallon said matter-of-factly.

Turning to Hamish, Sloane asked, "Did you see my vision too?"

"Afraid no', but no' fer lack o' tryin'." He chuckled. "It seems only yer friend here can overcome yer defenses when ye disappear intae the Sight. So it's lucky fer Davy—and fer ye—that she's here tae help."

"Macha tempts him with immortality," Sloane said. "How can he resist immortality? It's the gift all humans wish to have." She didn't try to hide how forlorn and lost the thought left her.

"Immortality can come in many forms, lass."

She cocked her head and raised her brow at him.

"Think about it." Hamish squatted down in front of her. "Ye know who King Arthur is, dae ye no'?"

"Yes," she said, drawing out the word.

"Because ye know who he is and what his exploits were, he lives on. He lives on in story and imagination. That auld king has been a part o' the collective memory o' Celtic peoples fer over a millennium. If that's no' immortality, I donnae know what is." He patted her on the knee and stood up. "Our Davy's a storyteller, a giver o' immortality."

Sloane slumped against the back of the bench. "It's not the same as actually being immortal, Hamish."

"There's something else that's immortal, Sloane," Fallon said quietly.

She waited.

"Love transcends every obstacle put in front of it—if you let it." Fallon turned on the bench to face her. "You have to believe in it, though. You have to believe with everything you have inside you that your love is stronger than any temptation, any theft—any loss."

The compassion in Fallon's expression nearly undid her.

"If you want Davy to return to you, you have to surrender to your love." She cleared her throat. "Even if that means he makes a choice that breaks your heart."

By the time Fallon finished speaking, the warriors and druids were gathered around them, each looking at her with expressions ranging from empathy and concern to expectation. The time had come to act. It was up to her to decide how big of a risk taker she truly was.

Addressing Siobhan and Griff, she said, "I take it you've lured the Green Isle to the loch."

Griff tipped his head toward the neck of the loch where its waters mingled with the sea beyond. "We should see it momentarily. Unlike the floating funhouse in which Maeve imprisoned Fallon and Seamus last summer, the Green Isle is not a mirage. But it will not remain near us for long. The time has come, Sloane."

Locking eyes first with Fallon then with each member of their party encircling her, Sloane knew she had no choice. As mesmerizingly tempting as the chalice of immortality had been in her vision, living forever without Davy's love would be the same as not living at all. She at least had to try to convince him he needed her love as much.

"What do I have to do?" she asked Griff.

Hamish answered for him. "Ye have to take yer place on that promontory there." He pointed to a rocky point about fifty yards from the dock. "The warriors and our talisman here will make sure the Morrigan and Maeve can no' attack ye successfully from the land."

"But if a kelpie or a selkie or some other creature comes for me from the water, I'm on my own?"

"We'll protect ye as best we can with enchantments."

She nodded.

"We have a secret weapon, Sloane," Griff said and glanced with affection at his niece. "We have a bard among us, one who loves you like a sister."

With a watery smile, Fallon squeezed Sloane's forearm.

✦

"I feel so exposed standing out here like this."

"Just keep your shield open. Make sure I can see your entire vision."

Sloane knew her best friend was near, even though Fallon, like the rest of their party, had concealed herself somewhere among the rocks and scrub bushes lining the beach. Still, the memory of the massive, rearing, snarling kelpie rising out of the tiny creek lingered in her mind. If one arrived on the promontory at the speed of the one she saw in her vision—or worse, the one she saw up close and personal in all its terrifying physical form— she doubted her friends could move fast enough to save her.

Then a sight arrived, replacing all her personal worries with marrow-freezing fear for Davy. An island glided over the loch in front of her, covering all the water except for the tiny waves lapping at the promontory below her feet. Treacherous rocks lined the shores leading back to sheer cliffs on the isle. Skimming her view up the sheer rock face, she could see a dense forest clinging to the edges of the cliffs. Over the center of the island, thunder boomed from clouds black enough to rival night. When the first purple and pink lightning strikes flashed through the clouds, she couldn't contain the scream that ripped from her throat.

"Davy!"

A whoosh of wind carried away her cries.

She no longer stood on the lonely promontory of a Scots lake. She sat before the fireplace in the grand salon of Conlan Manor, her hair the silver-white of an ancient lady. The open book in her lap told of the exploits of a warrior who battled gods and monsters and won. This warrior was the greatest Celtic hero since Tristan of the Round Table knights. His stories were Sloane's favorites. She closed her eyes, and a smile turned up the corners of her mouth as she fingered the ink time hadn't erased from the skin on the top of her left thigh.

When she opened her eyes, the famed warrior knelt in front of her. Young and virile and impossibly handsome, those dimples that had been her undoing so long ago deepened as he smiled at her.

"Hello Sloane."

"You're here."

With a shaky hand, she stroked the cheek of the only man she had ever loved. He turned his face and kissed her palm, his eyes never leaving hers. A lone tear slid down a groove time and sadness had worn in her face. The fire of his touch now burned a low ember, a heat she could never match again.

"You realized your dream. You're one of the greatest warriors of all time," she rasped out of a tear-clogged throat. "The stories of your valor, strength, and cunning were all that kept me warm through the long nights all these years."

"It was only a day, Sloane." The tears in his voice broke her heart. "I was only gone for one day."

"Time means nothing to the immortals, Davy. You know that."

"I'm here now. And I will never leave you again."

Too tired to be able to hold up her hand to his handsome face, she dropped it back to the book in her lap. "I believe you. It is I who will be leaving you, I'm afraid. Unlike Macha, the White Lady does not allow return trips from the land beyond the mists."

Davy sat beside her on the sofa and gathered her frail body into his arms. "What happened to us? How could this happen to us?"

"Don't give in to her, Sloane. Let me give you a different vision."

Shaking her head at the sound of Fallon's voice in her thoughts, Sloane blinked her eyes. She grabbed a handful of her hair, inspecting the black strands like she'd never seen them before. When she looked up, the Green Isle still hovered before her.

"I love you, Davy. The ink on our bodies, the omens the goddess Danu sent each of us, the way we bonded—all of it proves we belong together. It doesn't matter you're a druid and I'm a talisman," she called out over the sound of the winds swirling over loch and land.

A vision of Gavin Scanlon materialized in front of her. He smiled at her, pointed at her thigh, and nodded. Then he blew her a kiss through time and space before he faded from her view. The last she saw of him was the love shining out from his eyes. She had her warrior's blessing. A feeling of utter calm settled over her.

She and Davy were together walking hand in hand along the shores of Loch Broom. The sun glittered off the water as Davy regaled her with stories of giants building a causeway between Scotland and Ireland and mermaids trying to seduce Feans to join them in the Land Under the Waves because the Feans were so handsome. His dimples let loose as he reminded her that he descended from those very same Feans. Her laughter rang out over the water before he picked her up, swung her around, and kissed the breath right out of her.

A cawing scream rent the air, jerking her from the lovely story taking shape in her mind. Thunder broke the sound barrier. Winds from every direction buffeted her until she thought she might be dragged into the furious skies above her or tossed into the waves roiling below her. Putting a hand up to shield her face, she stared determinedly at the island floating barely beyond her reach.

"I'm here, Davy."

A sensation of turmoil buffeted her like sound waves. Like David setting up to send a powerful rock at Goliath, Sloane worked her feet into the gravel, tightened her muscles in preparation for a fight, and held on to wait.

"I will always be here for you. Always."

Another series of sensations pulsed over her, and she put her hands out in front of her against the forces trying to break her will. Still, she held her ground.

"Your story is my story. Tell our story, Davy."

A crackle of iridescent lightning spider-webbed the skies, followed by a low rumbling thunder that crescendoed to an ear-popping crash directly above her. The Green Isle started shaking like an earthquake had bucked through it. Rocks tumbled down the cliffside, trees swayed in a macabre dance along the top of the ridge, and the winds swirled like a tornado. Sloane watched in horrified fascination as a kelpie reared up out of the water onto the shoreline of the island, its hooves flashing in the lightning strikes. As if by magic, a man appeared on the beach, walked confidently over to the fearsome water horse, and climbed up onto its back.

She blinked, and Davy stepped off the back of the monster. At least she thought it was Davy. The man striding up the promontory toward her appeared bigger, stronger, his gait more powerful than the man with whom she'd been strolling the grounds of Conlan Manor earlier in the day. Had it only been that morning? His smile broke over his face, the dimples deepening as he came closer to her, and her heart split wide open.

With a joyful cry, she ran to him, launching herself into his arms. "You're here! Oh, Davy, you're here!"

"Ye brought me back, Sloane. Yer love was tae powerful fer the goddess." His gaze bored into hers. "I felt it all the way intae eternity."

"I do love you, Davy. I love you so much." She buried her face in his neck and hugged him close to her, clinging to him like she'd never let him go.

For long minutes, they held each other before Davy pulled away enough to set his lips on hers. The kiss began as a hello, soft and gentle. But it wasn't enough. Sloane increased the pressure, and Davy slid his tongue along the seam of her lips, a request she answered eagerly. In half a heartbeat, their mouths fused together, their tongues gliding over each other, dancing and tasting, probing and pumping, the beautiful prelude to another kind of joining.

At last, Davy tore his mouth away and rested his forehead against hers while they caught their breaths. "Sloane," he panted. "I think I fell in love with ye the day we met. Something in yer beautiful violet eyes called tae me, and I couldn't walk away, even when ye tried tae make me."

"I sensed something between us too, which is why I tried to avoid you." Squeezing her eyes shut, she pulled a long breath. "Somehow, I knew if Macha took you from me too, it would be so much worse than when she stole my warrior." Staring deep into the amber depths of his eyes she added, "I was right. When the kelpie took you, Davy—" The lump in her throat threatened to choke her. Swallowing over it, she continued. "When I couldn't stop another loss from happening again, I died a little inside. Because this time, I know you. I know your laughter and your smile and the way your voice deepens and fills when you tell a story and how amazingly fearless you are. Losing you would have wrecked me for the rest of my life."

Davy's arms tightened around her as he peppered kisses over her hair, her temple, her eyes, her cheek, and along her jaw. "It's time fer a new story. Our story. Taeday, we started it, and we're going tae add chapters tae it fer the next fifty or sixty years." His mouth descended on hers again, his passion feeding hers until her legs joined her arms and vined around him as he held her flush against his body.

A sound broke their kiss. The rumble started low and surged into a tearing screech. Like a hurricane, the winds buffeted them. Davy held his ground and Sloane against the onslaught while she buried her face in his chest and hung on. The wind screamed, a sound of defiance and anger before it abruptly stopped. When they looked up, the Green Isle had vanished, leaving a quiet loch behind. The sun parted the clouds, its warmth enveloping them where they stood on the promontory. A smile lit up Davy's face, and Sloane couldn't contain the laughter bursting from her chest. He picked her up and swung her around and around.

Their smiles preceded them as they joined the others at the base of *An Teallach*.

"We did it, Fallon," Sloane exclaimed, her happiness bubbling out of her like a fountain. "We saved him from Macha."

Fallon grinned back at her. "You saved him, Sloane." She glanced around at the rest of their friends. "We were just backup."

"You might want to save the congrats for a few more minutes," Rio said, a scowl on his handsome face.

Sloane's heart leaped into her throat. "Why?"

Rio nodded down the beach toward the dock. "Looks like the terrible trio isn't finished."

Turning her head, she caught sight of what appeared to be an army of rogue warriors climbing out of an armada of skiffs lined up along the edge of the water. Instinctively, she tightened her arm around Davy's waist.

"That's got Morgan written all over it," Rowan said with a growl. "Her fascination with us sincerely tries my patience."

"You're starting to sound like Dad, old man," Riley teased. Then he sobered. "But you have a point."

"Clue in your talismans, lads. Time to rid the world of another one of Morgan's armies of rogues," Rio said. Like magic, his claymore appeared in his hands, the expression on his face pure determination.

Sloane blinked as Davy stepped away from her, claymore in hand. "Davy?"

"I'll explain later. After we've kicked some rogue ass." Turning to the warriors, he said, "Shall we, lads?"

Like Davy leading the warriors was nothing out of the ordinary, they nodded and fell in behind Rio and him in a vee formation. The rogues swarming over the beach toward them didn't give Sloane time to question. Fallon grabbed her and pulled her into the safety of the circle of remaining druids who chanted protection spells while the eerie laughter of the goddess haunted the air.

CHAPTER THIRTY-THREE

"*SLOANE, I NEED ye tae put that seer skill of yers tae work. Preferably about three minutes ago, but now works tae.*"

He could feel her surprise washing over him, but they didn't have time for that. Not with the horde of rogue warriors bearing down on them.

"*Ye were born tae perform a special job, lass. It's time tae go tae work. What dae ye see?*"

"*I-I see you besting the five rogues coming down from where they climbed the hillside to your left. You—*" She stopped. Right when he nearly slipped into exasperation at her slowness at catching on, she said, "*You use the tricky maneuver Scathach taught Rio. The one where you stick the first rogue, flip over him to take out the next two, and spin to finish off the rest.*"

"*Excellent. Thanks, love.*"

Having a talisman who could see the future in split-second time was going to come in quite handy, he thought as he took on the brute of a warrior leading the traitorous quints on his left. If his brothers-in-arms were surprised at his ability to bend time and space in the same way they could, no one had time to comment. As soon as Davy dispatched the rogues coming at him from the mountainside, another group seemed to materialize on the beach. Behind him, Duncan and Seamus grunted and swore as they took on half a score of men who had jettisoned their ethics long ago. Beside him, the three Sheridan brothers busily cut, thrust, and parried another score of Morgan's army, and still more came. The rogues stepped over or on their fallen comrades, eager to advance on the small party of Scathach's warriors.

Above the fray, a blood-red mist shimmered in the air, followed by a purple-black one and a silver-black one. From the corner of his eye, Davy saw the goddesses resolve into their human forms, standing on the side of *An Teallach* where they could enjoy the view of the battle raging on the shores of Loch Broom. Determined not to let them win, he redoubled his efforts, fighting for the love he wanted time to share with Sloane.

"Scathach is proud of you, Davy. She shows it by urging you to step into the fight going on behind you. Duncan is in trouble, and you save him with the timing of your blow, cutting the rogue across his middle. He and his companions slip on his gore and fall. You deal them quick deaths, dispatching them with single thrusts to their throats or the backs of their necks."

Davy didn't question Sloane. His woman was a seer after all. Turning from the battle directly in front of him, he timed his swing perfectly, taking out the rogue sneaking up on Duncan from the waterside.

"Thanks, man. I didn't see that one," Duncan said. Then, "Duck!"

Davy dropped, and Duncan returned the favor, neatly stabbing the rogue who appeared behind Davy's back.

"That was close. Sloane must no' have seen that one."

"Stop gossiping, ladies. There's another boatload of these jerks headed up the beach," Rio said from behind them.

"Fan out, my warriors. Take them head-on."

Davy had been so focused on Sloane's sight and its aftermath he missed when the warriors' patron goddess joined the party. He didn't have time to marvel at being included in her instructions before another goddess stood beside her. Brighid's warm glow settled over him as he heard her words in his head.

"Though you are in the thick of this battle, do not lose sight of it. For you must compose the story of it and teach it to future warriors. You are always a druid, Davy."

The sting of a blade caressing his forearm pulled him abruptly from further conversation with his patroness.

"You don't have any business fighting in this battle, druid. Let me show you how a real warrior fights."

The rogue's sword flashed in the sunlight, but the blade didn't meet Davy's. Instead, the rogue leaped over him, headed straight for the group of druids guarding the talismans—his talisman. An evil oath escaped Davy's lips as he broke rank and chased after the rogue. He heard Rio swear and Scathach shout, but they didn't matter. Not when Sloane was in danger.

"We've got them, lad. Get back tae yer place," Hamish yelled.

"Sloane!"

"Save her by daein' yer job, lad. Go back tae the line."

"She's mine! I willnae let a rogue hurt her," Davy declared.

Siobhan stepped forward, the spells falling off her lips building a wall around the talismans.

"We've got them, Davy. Fer the love o' Aengus, go back tae the line."

Long ago, he'd seen that look on Hamish's face when the old man was training him on a powerful protection spell he could only use against the Morrigan. The memory triggered his druidic training. Gritting his teeth on the thought of leaving Sloane exposed, he returned to his place beside the warriors. By rote, he began chanting, the blows of his sword on the blades of his enemy forcing power into his words.

"May the four winds carry ye back tae Tara,

"May the light of the sun expose yer darkness

"May the rain wash yer evil away

"May the earth spring forth flowers in yer wake."

His chant rang in a rhythm with the clang of his claymore on his enemies' swords.

"You dare too much, druid. I will have my way here!" Morgan screamed.

He glanced up to see the goddess tearing at her hair. Maeve stared with undisguised lust at Seamus, while Macha pulled her magnificent plumage around herself and nodded to him. A great roaring filled the air as a whirlwind spun around his friends and him. It disturbed not one hair on his head, nor did it touch his brothers-in-arms. But when it blew itself out over the water, not a single rogue, alive or dead, remained. On the mountainside above them, there was no trace of the triple goddess of war.

Davy sheathed his claymore, and eyes closed, hands resting on his hips, he walked in a tight circle, his breath sawing in and out of his lungs. When he blinked his eyes open, he discovered himself to be the center of attention. Even Brighid and Scathach watched him with undisguised curiosity.

Hamish broke the silence. "What happened on that island, lad?"

"I donnae rightly know, auld man. I thought Macha was only trying tae tempt me tae remain on the Green Isle with her promise tae make me a warrior."

"But that's not what ended the battle, Davy," Sloane said softly as she approached him.

"I heard ye in my head, lass. Directing me like a talisman is supposed tae direct her warrior."

"I know. But you're still a druid." She reached out and covered his wrist with her hand. "Your chanting is what sent Morgan away, taking her rogue army with her. My Sight didn't reveal that."

Sloane lifted a tentative hand to stroke his shoulder, and his worn-out body came alive in a pleasurable way. The gentle smile on her lips told him they needed private time together to process the changes upending both of their lives.

"I've read about hybrids like you, Davy," Griff said. "But they're born with both traits. Macha giving you powers she allowed you to keep—" He shook his head. "I don't know what to make of it."

"Perhaps it has to do with Sloane," Fallon said, a thoughtful expression on her face. "After what Macha has put her through"—she reached out and brushed her hand over Sloane's forearm—"and the way Sloane's handled it, maybe the goddess wanted to reward her."

"Macha? She loves battle and slaughter every bit as much as her sisters," Rio scoffed.

"She's also the goddess o' fertility. She can give, and she can take away," Hamish said, his tone speculative.

"Whatever our sister goddess has done for whatever reason she has done it, you now belong to me as well as to your patroness Brighid." Scathach nodded to Brighid who inclined her head in return. "Which means you will train with each of us."

An involuntary groan escaped Davy's lips.

"None of that, warrior," Scathach scolded.

"Can we hold off until after the equinox at least? Maybe let me enjoy my new friends' wedding celebration?" he asked, hopefully.

Brighid's smile warmed him, energized him.

"I've sent the talismans who battled from the training room to the manor ahead of us," Owen said as he and Alaisdair strolled up to join them. "It appears we've been given a reprieve to hold a wedding."

Seamus pulled Fallon into his arms, his eyes never leaving hers as he said, "Can't think of anything I want to do more than marry this woman."

A similar thought rolled through Davy's head as he covered Sloane's hand with his. She gasped at the contact, and he whispered in her ear, "We're headed tae the cottage, lass. But I think ye knew that already."

"We will guard your journey back to the manor. Though I believe the war goddesses have returned to Macha's stronghold on Tara to lick their wounds once again"—Scathach didn't bother to hide her delight in her tone—"it never hurts to be cautious."

When nobody moved, she gave them the shooing gesture. "Go on. Off with you."

The Sheridan brothers chuckled while Hamish and Griff headed up the beach to where the skiffs were tethered to the dock. Davy didn't wait for the goddess to change her mind. He pulled Sloane close to his side and said, "The cottage, lass."

In two heartbeats, they were alone together in the middle of the living room of his home. The unhappiness in Sloane's expression didn't bode well for his plans for the rest of the day.

"Lass."

"Davy. You can't take my hand like that. You just can't." If possible, her mouth turned down even farther.

"I've been thinking about that, love. I've developed a cream ye can smooth on yer hands so ye can touch others without fear of seeing their future."

Her breath caught. "You have? Why?"

"Because I want tae hold yer hand sometimes." He grinned. "I want tae hold yer hand often, as a matter of fact."

She stepped into him, her arms wrapping around his middle while she buried her face in his neck. "I love you, Davy Sutherland."

"I know. When I was on the Green Isle, I heard ye say it."

Leaning back, she looked into his eyes. "I wanted to tell you in person."

With his lips on hers, he said, "Yer love saved me, Sloane MacIntosh. I love ye."

He wrapped his arms tightly around her and smashed his mouth to hers. There was no finesse, just fiery passion. She met him with equal eagerness, her mouth grinding on his before she opened for him. The mating dance of their tongues tasting and chasing told him how much she needed him. Pleasure pulsed through his body, his shoulder sending an unmistakable message to his cock while Sloane rubbed her thigh against him.

Tearing his mouth from hers, he leaned his forehead on hers and gulped air. "Lass, I have a great idea."

"Let's go to bed."

"Aye, that's the one." He chuckled.

Lifting her high in his arms, he carried her down the narrow hallway to the bedroom, not stopping until he laid her on the pillowy mattress. Her hooded eyes watched him as he divested her of shoes, jeans, and lacy pink panties. On another day, he might have stopped to admire the frothy confection of her knickers hugging her beautiful body so perfectly, but after the day he'd had, he needed her too much for that. His eyes caught on the swirling tattoo on her thigh and stayed there except for the split second it took to pull his sweater over his head. His jeans and boxers joined the rest of his clothes on the floor before he climbed up on the bed.

For several seconds, he traced the ink on her skin. She moaned and reached for him, but he stayed her with a look. Sliding his hands behind her knees, he pushed them up and apart. Only then did he stop to admire her gorgeous pink pussy in all its glistening glory. "Sloane, lass. Ye're the most perfect woman in the world."

"Davy."

He grinned up at her before he buried his face in her salty sweetness, teasing her clit with the tip of his tongue before kissing her deeply. The way she moaned and thrashed on the bed egged him on. When she lifted her hips to his eager mouth, he slid his hand over her thigh, tracing the swirls there, and Sloane rewarded him, going off like fireworks on *Hogmany*.

Giving her no quarter, he pushed her sweater and bra up off her body as he climbed up over her and covered her. With a slow, deep thrust, he joined them together. His body nearly locked up at the intense pleasure radiating through him. Sloane played her fingers over the swirling tattoo on his shoulder, and he lost all control. He wouldn't have been able to stop moving inside her if the goddess herself stepped into the room.

"Sloane, Sloane, Sloane," he chanted like a love song.

Her smile lit up his heart before the most powerful orgasm of his life overtook every last vestige of his reason. Lightning radiated from the base of his spine outward, while violet-colored stars danced in his vision. Unable to stop, he kept pumping into her. Hearing his name torn from her lips as she clamped down on him sent a new kind of fire through him. His whole body stiffened and pleasure like he'd never experienced before curled his toes and stole his breath.

When his arms refused to hold him anymore, he collapsed on top of her. Her hands roaming up and down his spine sent goosebumps skittering over his body. With every breath he panted in, he drew in her vanilla and sugar scent, drew her essence deep inside him. Everything in his life had led to this one moment with this one woman. No matter what awaited them in the future, Sloane MacIntosh was his whole life.

At last, he rolled over, taking her with him and settling her on his chest. "You're everything in the world tae me, love. A fortnight ago, I thought my purpose in life was tae serve Conlan Manor as its resident druid when Hamish passed on." He tangled his hand in her hair and tugged to draw her eyes to his. "Then a raven-haired beauty with the most arresting violet-colored eyes walked intae the salon in the manor, and I knew I'd never be the same again. Ye've changed me in all the best ways, lass. Fer as long as I live, I will love ye with everything I have. Heart, body, and soul. Ye're mine, Sloane MacIntosh."

"And you belong to me, Davy Sutherland." She smiled, an expression he would never tire of seeing.

"Then ye willnae mind a short courtship."

One raven-black brow lifted.

"I'll court ye fer the rest of my life, lass. I promise. But I'm no' wasting time marrying ye."

The argument he anticipated didn't materialize. Instead, she snuggled closer to him and sighed. "You're the biggest and the best risk I've ever taken. You already know the answer, druid, but you're still going to have to ask the question."

He barked out a laugh. Up until Sloane arrived, his life had gone rather predictably. He was reasonably sure that wouldn't be the case from now on. Oh, how he was looking forward to that.

CHAPTER THIRTY-FOUR

THE AUTUMNAL EQUINOX dawned clear, crisp, and bright. The skies were so blue they brought tears to her eyes as Sloane stepped off the veranda to lead Fallon, escorted by her Uncle Griff, along the path to the center of the garden where her groom awaited her. When they arrived, Sloane stepped to the side as Hamish, Siobhan, and Davy surrounded Fallon, chanting the marriage ritual in Gaelic as they showered her in herbs—rosemary, lavender, and coriander. Joined by Griff, they formed a living barrier around her, one Seamus had to "fight" his way through to much laughter and ribald teasing from those in attendance, especially from the Sheridan brothers.

At last, they were allowed to join hands as Hamish, together with his acolyte Davy, chanted the prayers and offered the chalice of honey mead Hamish had brewed especially for the occasion. When Davy held the mistletoe above them, Sloane's eyes filled with tears as she watched Seamus tenderly kiss his bride.

Afterward, they convened in the salon where Hamish offered a toast with his special whisky. "Tae Fallon and Seamus Lochlann. May ye live ferever in each other's hearts. May yer union bring honor tae ye and strength tae our community."

A chorus of "Hear! Hear!" "Congratulations!" "Love you guys!" and "Oh, yeah!" followed Hamish's words as family and friends toasted the happy couple.

Then Davy cleared his throat, and with a pointed look at the druid master said, "Hamish, isn't it about time ye shared yer recipe fer yer uisge-beatha with me?"

Hamish chortled. "Thought ye might bring that up taeday, lad." The old druid slipped his arm through Sloane's and smiled at his protégé. "I've been waitin' fer ye tae find the lady strong enough tae take ye on. Now that ye've done that, she can help ye avoid the temptations that come with knowin' how tae brew such a powerful version o' the water o' life."

"About time," Davy grumbled before he shot her a tiny private grin.

He pulled her into his arms, kissed her on the side of her head, and turned to the others. "Sloane and I have an announcement, but we wanted tae wait until the two of ye were good and married before we made it," he said, addressing Fallon and Seamus.

Her heart hammered in her chest. The two of them hadn't spent much of the previous night sleeping between bonding and making plans for their future. They'd agreed to tell their friends about those plans following the ceremony. Now that the time had come, worry fluttered in her chest.

"Sloane and I have decided she is moving tae Scotland tae live here with me."

His arms tightened around her, reassuring her of the rightness of their—of her decision.

"Sounds like a damn fine plan to me," Rio said.

"I'm not surprised, Sloane. But I'm going to miss you," Fallon said. "So much."

The hitch in her best friend's voice put a lump in her throat. She swallowed over it, and said, "I'm going to miss you too. But you of all people knew this was coming."

Fallon gifted her a watery smile. "I did. I'm happy for you, my friend. Very happy for you. If anyone deserves some happiness, it's you."

"Thank you. It means so much to me that you understand and approve." She pulled Fallon into her arms, both of them sniffing back happy, melancholy tears.

"As you're well aware, we have a big house, so you can visit Sloane and Davy—and Rio and me, any time you want," Ceri chimed in from where she stood in the circle of her husband's arms.

Fallon smiled at Ceri through her tears and nodded.

"Don't worry, Fireworks. I'll keep you so busy you won't have much time for missing Sloane," Seamus said. A wicked grin stretched over his face as he reclaimed his wife.

"Come tae think of it, I wouldn't mind seeing the States. After we're married, of course," Davy said as he pulled Sloane back into his side.

"Ooh, when are you getting married?" Ceri asked, her tone giddy. "As you'll see at the reception upstairs, I'm an excellent wedding planner."

"Donnae think ye'll have much time tae plan, Ceri," Davy said.

Sloane caught him winking at Rio who returned it with a nearly imperceptible nod.

Huh.

"When are you guys getting married?" Fallon asked, and Sloane knew that tone.

Davy didn't care. "Soon," was all he answered. Then he whispered in Sloane's ear. "Listen. Dae ye hear it?"

She gazed at him, a question in her eyes.

"I hear the maze calling us, lass. Come on."

His fingers brushed over hers as he took her whisky glass and set it on a nearby table with his. The contact sent shivers through her, but she didn't see anything of his future. She smiled to herself. Of all the gifts she'd ever received, Davy Sutherland was the very best one.

"You two going somewhere?" Rowan asked, his voice deepening with suspicion as he exchanged a glance with Rio.

"Thought I'd take Sloane on a wee wander about the grounds before the big party starts in the ballroom."

Fallon gasped.

"Donnae worry, Fallon. I wasn't planning on going anywhere near water. In fact, I promise we won't leave the enchanted part of the gardens." He tilted his head. "Good?"

"As long as you're not planning something ridiculous." Fallon glared at him. "Like eloping with my best friend on my wedding day."

"Wouldn't dream of it."

Rio choked back a laugh, and Fallon narrowed her eyes at Davy who gazed back at her with the most innocent expression Sloane had ever seen on a guilty man. Promptly, he grabbed her hand and led her out of the salon and through the front door. Behind her, she could hear the cacophony of their friends' speculation and more than one warrior trying to restrain his talisman from following them.

"Why did you tease them like that?" she asked as they rounded the side of the manor and followed the stone path to the maze.

"Because it's fun," he said like she should know the answer. "After all we've been through over the past fortnight, I deserved tae have a little fun taking the mickey out of yer friends."

"Our friends," she corrected him.

He grinned at her. "Our friends." Stopping at the entrance to the maze, he said, "After ye, love."

Davy was apparently in a bit of a hurry since he didn't let her wander. Whenever she was about to take a wrong turn, he corrected her until at last, she said, "Why don't you lead?"

"Because the view is better from back here."

Turning her head, she caught his smirk as he hastily lifted his eyes from her ass.

"You're unbelievable," she huffed, but she couldn't help her laugh.

His eyes danced. "Ye've said that before, lass. I have tae admit, I like it when ye compliment me."

"Argggh!" She threw up her hands. "This way?" she asked, pointing toward an avenue opening up to her right.

"Aye, take that one." With an exaggerated motion of his head and shoulders and waggling eyebrows, he angled his body for another look at her backside.

She stuck her tongue out at him, turned, and ran down the path. At the end of it, she saw if she made another right, she'd enter the heart of the maze. But before she could hop the steps down into the garden, Davy caught her around the waist and hauled her up against him.

"Cheeky, lass. Very cheeky."

"Oh, I do like it when you compliment me," she said, turning her head enough so he could see her batting her lashes at him.

His laughter echoed around the space as he carried her to the bench under the tree. In daylight, the garden revealed all its glory. The vibrancy of the roses contrasted beautifully with the leaves turning to fall on the apple tree. In this protected place, the grass pretended high summer, its green shoots creating the perfect backdrop for the deep red roses edging the path to the center of the labyrinth.

When he sat on the bench, Davy held her close on his lap. His laughter dried up as he gazed into her eyes with the most serious expression she'd ever seen on his face. "It was in this sacred space where we were truly honest with each other, Sloane."

Holding her breath, she nodded.

"We need that same honesty now."

For the first time in her life, she wished she could touch his hand and see the future, see where this conversation was headed because his grave tone scared her.

"Yesterday, we both suffered a fair amount of trauma."

"Yes," she said and hated how small her voice sounded.

"Last night, we soothed ourselves by getting lost in each other."

Her skin heated at the memory, but she said nothing.

"We made promises tae each other, promises we shared with our friends a few minutes ago. But as much as I want ye, as much as I need ye Sloane, asking ye tae leave everything ye know, everything ye love tae move here with me is asking a lot." He smoothed a finger along her hairline before tangling his hand in the inky skeins falling over her shoulder. "If ye need time tae think about it—"

She put a finger to his lips. "I know druids and warriors are trained differently, so maybe you didn't learn much about bonding. But what happened between us last night?"

His eyes heated at the memory her words conjured, and an answering heat bubbled in her veins.

"What happened between us is what we're told will happen between a warrior and his talisman," she said. "I don't know what Macha did to change you, but she did change you. In changing you, she made you mine—forever. So wherever you are, that's where I am." She palmed the face she knew she'd see in her dreams for her whole life. "While you were on the island, Gavin appeared to me." Beneath her legs, she felt Davy stiffen, and she rushed on. "He gave me—us—his blessing." Leaning in, she pressed a soft kiss to his mouth. "You were right from the beginning. You and I were meant to be."

"I'm still a druid. I will always be a druid."

"A special one who can fight with his sword, but whose true powers lie in his words." She trailed her finger over his bicep. "It's a very sexy trait."

"Well then." He grinned. "How dae ye feel about a small wedding?"

"How small?"

"The two of us, a druid, perhaps a witness..."

"Elope?"

He shrugged. "It seemed tae work out rather well fer Ceri and Rio."

A slow smile spread over her lips. "It did, didn't it?"

Davy let his dimples out to play, and Sloane's laughter rippled through the garden. Later when the shadows lengthened over the grass, they dressed and walked hand in hand back through the maze. As they stepped onto the stone path leading to the manor, a lone raven feather floated down from the sky. Sloane grabbed it and held it up in the waning light before carefully securing it to her hair. Davy nodded his approval.

From that day on, Sloane always wore a raven feather in her hair, a homage to the goddess who took a life from her and rewarded her surrender with another. Davy told the story until the end of their days.

Epilogue

"WE'RE A BIT late fer breakfast, lad," Hamish said from his seat at the scarred table in the kitchen.

"No' tae worried about it taeday, auld man," Davy said with a grin in Sloane's direction as he grabbed two tea mugs from the cupboard. "I suppose I could have bent time and space and arrived ahead of ye, but then I would have had tae brew the tea."

Hamish chuckled. "Ye rather like yer warrior skills, dae ye, Davy?"

"Aye." He set a mug in front of Sloane and sat on the bench beside her. "But I like bein' the center of attention when I'm telling a story more." He slid a sly grin at Sloane. "And I cannae seem tae help myself around plants. At all."

The self-satisfied smirk on Hamish's face confirmed Davy's suspicions.

Sloane smiled at Ceri who sat across the table from her. "Thank you again for holding Fallon's wedding in your amazing home. If not for your generous invitation—"

The women's hands brushed as they simultaneously reached for the teapot. For several long seconds, Sloane stared at her hand. Then tears started trickling down her face.

Davy wrapped his arms around her and held her close until her body relaxed into him. "Ye forgot tae put on yer cream this morning, didn't ye?"

She nodded.

"It's tae late now, lass." He smoothed his hand over the silken skeins of her ink-dark hair. "What did ye see?"

Across the table, Ceri's wide, frightened eyes never left Sloane's face.

The happy sound of whistling preceded Rio as he jogged down the stairs. "Hey, love, I was wondering—" The tableau at the table cut him off. "What's wrong?"

"We was havin' a spot o' tea when the lasses accidentally brushed their fingers taegether," Hamish said. "We're waitin' tae hear what Sloane saw."

The serene expression on Hamish's face should have mollified them, but Davy didn't miss the way Sloane tensed at the sound of the old druid's voice.

He nuzzled his face into Sloane's neck and whispered for her ears only, "It'll be fine, lass. Ye'll see."

She swallowed hard and trained her focus on Ceri. "I saw your baby."

Ceri gasped, and Rio placed his hands protectively on his wife's shoulders.

"She's a perfect little girl, a druid"—she glanced up at Rio—"you'll name Fianna Ross Sheridan."

"Huh," was all Rio said.

"She's the next Conlan druid."

"That's incredible," Ceri said, a smile spreading across her face. Then her smile disappeared in a blink. "So why are you crying?"

"Because there can only be one druid at a time fer the manor."

Hamish trained his eyes on Sloane. "Dae I have any time at all with the wee lass?"

Sloane nodded. "A little." She swallowed. "Not enough."

"Hamish, no!" Ceri pushed back against Rio and tried to stand. Rio held firm, and she remained seated on the bench.

Hamish put up his hand. "'Tis all right, Ceri. 'Tis the natural way o' things." He reached over the table and placed his hand over hers. "I've been anticipatin' this situation since ye stepped intae the manor, lass. 'Tis time. I've been potterin' around this auld pile fer a long time waiting fer my successor."

"But, who will train her?" Ceri asked in a small voice that tore at Davy's heart.

Beside him, Sloane deflated.

"The most powerful druid I know," Hamish said with a nod in Davy's direction. "Rather fittin' tae, considerin' his skills and those o' young Fianna's da."

He winked at Rio, and Davy almost grinned. He had to hand it to the old man—he knew exactly how to work that warrior. Then Hamish turned his attention on Davy.

"Guess ye'll be needin' tae learn the secret tae distillin' proper uisge-beatha, lad. We'll work on it as the others ready the manor fer the comin' o' the wee lassie."

Sloane swiped at her eyes and stared at Hamish. "How can you be so calm about this?"

"Dae ye know, even on the days we donnae eat in the dinin' room, I spend a bit o' time in there with Fianna? Perhaps ye'll see fit tae add another portrait tae those hangin' in there, Ceri."

Reaching across the scarred table, she squeezed the old man's hand and nodded.

"There have been twa druids fer this manor. Now a third is comin'. As long as she lives, Fianna lives." He glanced around at them. "I live. 'Tis the way o' things." He turned his attention to Sloane. "Ye said I have a little time with the wee lass? Did ye happen tae see how much?"

Sloane swallowed and shook her head. Davy held her tighter to his side, trying to absorb her pain.

"However long it is will be enough. Love is like that. We're selfish creatures, always wantin' more time with those we love, but they never leave us." A tiny fire burned in his kindly eyes as he turned them to Sloane. "Dae they, lass?"

After a beat, Sloane gifted Hamish with a watery smile. "No, Hamish. They never leave us. Thank you."

Hamish clapped his hands together. "Right. Well, this is the time o' year fer makin' the proper mash fer the water o' life. We'll start workin' on a new batch taeday. Davy's goin' tae need yer help, Sloane. This will be a special one in honor o' the wee lassie, the best I've ever distilled, I expect."

"But—"

"Nae doubt ye'll savor every last drop when ye serve it fer the first time on young Fianna's twenty-first birthday, Davy. And when ye raise that first dram tae her, remember, ye'll also be raisin' it tae her namesake—and tae me." A secret smile hovered in the grooves lining his mouth. "I'm sure we'll all enjoy it very much."

ACKNOWLEDGEMENTS

When I started this writing journey, I didn't intend to write a series. But I'm so grateful to Coleene Brookshier Torgerson and Dodo Rosling for their early encouragement that led to all these characters and stories. Developing the Talisman Series has been a blast. The fact that you, my reader, have loved the characters as much as I do has made all the difference.

A little backstory on Davy Sutherland. He first appears in *Warrior*, and I intended for him to be an infiltrator, emphasis on traitor, to the Conlan and Sheridan clans. But he absolutely refused to play along. He wanted to be on the side of the good guys rather than a pawn for the goddesses. (I can't blame him there. =)) So when it came time to write the fifth book, he was the natural choice for the main character. When I gave the manuscript to my editor, Nikki's response was, "I'm so glad you decided to write Davy's story." She'd fallen in love with him in *Warrior*. I did too, perhaps because of the fact that he wouldn't give in to my initial plans for him. I've adored all of my characters, but I think I like Davy and Sloane best. Their relationship opened the door for so many possibilities to share Scotland, and Celtic legends, and a lasting, loving relationship. I loved writing their story. I hope you've enjoyed reading it too.

Special thanks to Bri Brasher Weigel who gave this one a last minute read even though she was teaching college summer courses and making final plans for her wedding. Thank you for reaching out and volunteering to help me. As always, your insights help me produce a better book.

Your encouragement and checking in to see how things are going are always welcome and necessary, Sue Ellen Turnbull. Thank you.

Angela Forester, you are my role model and so much help with all things marketing and tech related. Thank you for lighting the way for my indie publishing career.

I am so lucky to have connected with my incredibly skilled editor, Nikki Busch. Your insights, gentle nudges in the better direction, and genuine enthusiasm for my writing give me confidence. You make my words shine, and I'm ever grateful to you.

Throughout the series, I've worked with two fantastic designers. Maria Kusel at Steamy Designs (*https://www.steamydesigns.net*) is the genius behind the stunning covers for the Talisman Series. Chrissy H. at Damonza (*https://www.damonza.com*) created the beautiful interior design and formatting. Seeing my words as rendered with your visual artistry gives me all the feels. Thank you both.

Levi Meyer at Wyosites *(https://wyosites.com)* is the web master behind my gorgeous website. Thank you for making me look good (and competent) out in the world.

The magic wouldn't happen without the love and support of the man who has believed in me from the beginning. Grady, I love you with all my heart. Thank you for all the adventures.

I thought when I finished the epilogue to this book that I was finished with the series. However, reader response and readers' kickass ideas make me wonder if I'm truly finished with these characters. I'm not making any promises, but as you're already aware, *Talisman* was supposed to be a stand-alone book... I'm not saying it's over yet, but I do have something completely different in the works that I hope readers will love as much as the Talisman Series. More ideas of what you want are welcome too. Join my newsletter (the link is on my website), and tell me where you want these characters to go or what stories you'd like me to add to the series.

Reviews help authors connect with new readers. If you would kindly leave a review wherever you enjoy doing so, I'd truly appreciate it. You can find me on Amazon, Barnes & Noble, BookBub, and GoodReads. You can also connect with me on Instagram @tamstales32, on Facebook at Tam DeRudder Jackson, on my website at *www.tamderudderjackson.com*, and on my blog: Try Thirty New Things (*https://www.trythirtynewthings.blog/wordpress*). Let's grow together.

ABOUT THE AUTHOR

Tam DeRudder Jackson is the author of the Talisman Series. In her previous career, Tam was an award-winning high school English teacher. Today, she's living her dream of writing novels. When she's not writing, she's reading all the books or carving turns on the ski runs in the mountains near her home in northwest Wyoming or traveling to places on her ever-expanding bucket list. Her two grown sons are the joys of her life, and she likes supporting her husband's old car habit. If you ever see her holding a map, do her a favor and point her in the right direction. Navigation has never been her strong suit.